SILENT CREEK

SILENT CREEK

JEAN M. GRANT

Dedication

To five a.m. champions —
parents, artists, dreamers, goal-achievers...
And especially to the #5amwritersclub.
Thanks for helping me not give up on this book.

1

JOSIE

Freedom teased my bloodstream as I perched on the front porch, watching the breeze flutter early spring leaves on the red maple tree. Silence swayed in my new reality. The wrens and robins were too quiet. Did they leave the nest to forage today? Where was the garbage truck? Even my neighbor Branson wasn't out with his new puppy this morning for their daily training walk.

No awakening birdsong. No playful yipping. No clunk of trash cans.

Quiet.

Was the universe telling me to not leave?

Signs or not, I would disappear.

Clenching a hand at my side, I rose, stepped out onto the mown lawn, and wiggled my toes to experience the sensation of the dew-kissed grass. I inhaled, committing the scent to memory. Glittery stars blinked at me from small seas of teal on my toenails.

The sight of my toes reminded me of foot rubs. Some days, I missed the Tate from before. Before he ruined my life.

I peered into the imposing maples down the road. The inconspicuous red sedan appeared yesterday. Donovan's guy. His presence here, shadowing my escape, eased my stomach's roiling.

After my departure, Donovan's hired guy would rifle through the trash and search for me online, testing what I'd learned from my lessons. Six months of preparation brought me to this day. Although I told myself I would be okay, the last stubborn rumbles of disquiet remained.

My lawyer had updated me this week, cementing my decision to move. The state had set another parole hearing for Tate in a few months. Of course, my cunning, manipulative ex-husband would get out early. The time to leave was yesterday.

It's not like Tate ever physically hurt me. No, instead he suckered me repeatedly and emptied my bank accounts. Would he return to exact revenge for me standing up against him, resulting in his arrest and imprisonment? Or for me filing for divorce? Would he lure me in with another ploy, begging forgiveness?

Tate didn't beg. He blamed, even during the criminal charges and prosecution.

I grunted defiantly. I wiped the dew off my feet and slid on socks and sneakers. Though not a necessity, I'd packed the bottles of nail polish into shipping boxes last week. A woman needed some luxuries in the backwoods of New Hampshire. There, I would let my vibrancy shine, even if nobody else saw it. I licked dry lips as I tied my shoelaces.

Today, I would follow a lesser-used trail five miles into town. Then I would catch a paid ride to the bus station in Boston. One more bus to Concord, New Hampshire, then another to Silent Creek. My weary soul would find a new home nestled in the White Mountains. Away from everything.

Today's silence felt ominous though. I wasn't sure what would happen when I got to the cabin.

Would Silent Creek live up to its name?

Did I want it to?

I stretched my hamstrings, then checked the rest of the condo. The door to the cupboard creaked as I shut it, slicing through the silence. Eloise Peterson's wind chimes sung in the light wind.

I reviewed my checklist.

Back door: unlocked for Hannah.

Letter to Hannah: in my hand to be mailed. Shame bubbled to the surface. When my life had fallen apart, Hannah was the only one besides my brother, Kyle, who stood by me. She deserved a goodbye and an apology in place of a letter.

I blinked wet eyes and came back to reviewing my list.

Lawyer info: included in Hannah's letter, and another copy rested on the barren kitchen island. For whoever found it.

Meeting with the second lawyer nobody knew about, the one handling my uncle's estate: scheduled for next week, after my arrival.

Keys: left on the counter.

Grass: mowed. Flowers: watered. Blinds: closed. Bills: paid. Bank account: emptied and closed. Rent: paid until the lease's termination in ninety days.

Bleak emptiness stared back at me during a final cursory check upstairs, then downstairs. My footsteps echoed off bare walls, and floorboards moaned. I rolled up the blanket to deposit it in the donation bin at the gas station. My furniture had already found new homes.

Eloise only inquired once about the trucks coming to the condo. I told her I was donating items and waiting for the delivery of new furniture. The lies came easier now.

"Good for you, Josie," my busybody neighbor had said. "Embrace the new, let go of the old. Sometimes we need a fresh start."

Yesterday, I shipped a dozen boxes of the essential items to the cabin, including the deed and tax information from Uncle Morgan. Memories—the ones I chose to remember—fit into one large box. Just because I could, I filled half of a box with three dozen Oh Henry! chocolate bars.

If I was moving to a neglected backwoods cabin—at least that's how I remembered it from childhood visits—I needed a treat. Painted toenails, chocolate bars, and daily coffee were my trio of indulgences, and they would get me through what lay ahead. Tate and I once made a game of trying to find Oh Henry! bars when we visited obscure places, as my favorite candy slowly disappeared off the grocery shelves over the years. They existed. They were out there. One just had to look.

I packed a few of the tokens from my students, too—a mug, handwritten notes, ornaments, crafts, and a magnet for the fridge. I rubbed my nose, stifling the sniffle. Despite being let go by the school district, I missed the kids and their bright eyes as we mastered speech, language, and auditory challenges through games and puzzles. Like the whiteboard in my classroom, today I wiped the slate clean.

Munching on a crunchy, gooey peanut-buttery chocolate bar—the breakfast of champions—I ducked into the empty garage. A basketball-sized grease spot stained the floor where Tate's gas-guzzling truck used to sit before I sold it.

After zipping my jacket, I clipped on a slim backpack, light with its contents of a protein bar, lip balm, cash, Massachusetts driver's license, birth certificate, Social Security card, pepper spray, and burner phone. I grabbed my water bottle.

For the first time in a year, no ripples of anxiety constricted my throat, nor did heart palpitations seize me.

I wasn't crazy.

Crazy people always said that, right?

I held the power now. Paranoia joined the rubbish on the curb. Hope paved a new path for me.

I stepped outside for my last day in Massachusetts, the door clicking behind me.

In her blue slippers and matching fuzzy bathrobe, Eloise shuffled from her front door to the community mailbox and deposited a few outgoing envelopes. She gave me a wave and a nod. Okay, so the universe wasn't out of whack this morning. It wasn't giving me a sign through its silence. I released a breath at my ridiculous thinking earlier. Don's guy waited at the end of the driveway to watch me leave. All was set.

"G'morning, Josie. Good to see you out." Pink blushed Eloise's cheeks and she turned away, silently conveying a gesture of understanding.

Responding with a half-smile, I deposited Hannah's letter in the mailbox, too, and tucked the candy bar wrapper and checklist into my backpack.

Ready or not, silence and solitude and freedom awaited me.

With jelly legs, I stepped onto the path and walked off the grid.

2

—·—

Everett

Lark wanted a homemade unicorn cake.

For her fifth birthday, she insisted on a four-layer, loaded confection of artificial flavor and colors, iced with star sprinkles, and topped with a freaking horn. *That* kind of unicorn cake.

My wallet thanked her. My lack of culinary skills did not. Making a unicorn cake, or any cake, was beyond my knowledge. Baking required pans, and ingredients, and me turning on the oven for something beyond re-heating left-overs or cooking a frozen pizza or chicken nuggets.

As we drove past the new bakery on Main Street, a pang thwacked me in the gut. I missed the cannoli, bacon, and maple donuts, Boston crème pie, and sticky buns of the North End. Easy, delicious, and not *here*. A time before my life took a turn for the worse. "When life was simple," as Gram would say.

I sighed. "You sure you don't want me to order one?" I asked Lark again, cringing at my offer. Since returning home to Silent Creek, I'd walked into the new bakery once and quickly turned around. Overpriced was an understate-ment.

"No! We're gonna bake it." She waved the magazine page at me. "You said you're on a bun-jet."

"Budget, yes." I blew another sigh, and she mimicked me from the back seat.

"It's going to be so pretty, Daddy!" she said, bouncing. "A horn, sparkly eyes, a pink nose, and a bubblegum taste!"

"Bubblegum?"

"Mm-hmm." She nodded.

"How about strawberry?"

She tapped a finger on her chin. "Maybe."

My truck idled, while we waited for a parking spot in front of the grocery store. I sucked on a cinnamon breath mint, trying to abate, or at least distract myself from, a headache and my non-excitement over this cake. But this was Lark.

I owed her. Big-time.

I inched forward, then stopped. Main Street still rumbled beneath my tires the same way it did years ago, except now I drove slower. I tapped the steering wheel with a finger, reminding myself patience was a virtue, while the driver of a Buick took their sweet time to parallel park.

Along with the bakery, a hippy-dippy rock and crystal shop called Michelle's Mystic, the Just Like New upscale consignment shop, an art gallery, and a few other new stores flanked Main Street. I wondered if they would find the right market in this sleepy town.

Other things remained the same though. The large ornamental pear trees offered a familiar sense of greenery on the sidewalks, along with window boxes overflowing with early mums and late asters. The feed and hardware store, the grocery store, and Deanna's Cafe, known to locals as The Daily Donut, churned with good business, the same as they had a decade ago.

Thankfully, the grocery store's owner, who was new, didn't know the young punk me who stole ten-cent gum from the store.

Nostalgia and remorse snatched my brain energy today.

I crunched on the mint, enjoying the sunshine and view of the mountains encircling the small town. It was postcard perfect.

"Daddy!" Lark said, covering her ears. "Yuck!"

I stopped crunching and sucked on the remnants.

My gaze snagged on the roots of the trees displacing sidewalk slabs, and it got me thinking of other things while I waited on Old Man Whoever to get his rust bucket parked. Silent Creek needed some TLC to go along with the snazzy storefronts. I might suggest that Penny put in a quote to the town board to fix the trees or enhance the town square. I'd love the chance to be more than a hired hand in the business my sister-in-law managed until Jake came home. I could help her gain new clients and grow the company. I had ideas. This town had untapped potential and details were my thing. Just wished she'd trust me with it.

Could my attention to detail transfer to this darn cake?

Lark flapped her photo, still talking nonstop, and I only half-listened. "—and silver balls, and food colors, and a blue mane..."

The old man finally finished his eternal adjustments to his parking job. I parked in the space in front of him. That Lark's picture was from one of the old baking magazines in Gram's pile made me think the unicorn phase had come and gone like the mystical creature itself. I didn't know about cake trends. After three years away, I struggled to catch up.

We made a beeline for the baking aisle. I contemplated what to get while the dollar amounts stacked in my brain.

"Here, Daddy!" Lark shoved the shopping basket at me.

Choices. Too many. Red velvet, butter, gluten-free, triple chocolate, carrot. Triple chocolate? Weren't there only two kinds of chocolate, milk and dark? White chocolate didn't count.

My stomach growled. I tossed a wrapped whoopie pie into the shopping basket. Then two more for Penny's boys.

I released Lark's hand for a milli-moment and tunneled calloused fingers through my shaggy hair. Disappear from life for 912 days and you forget the small tasks. Regardless, I didn't have to check the hair care aisle to know a $3 gel bottle was cheaper than a clipper.

"How do I make a horn?"

Lark's small voice trickled up from beside me. "Use a cone, Daddy! An ice cream cone. De pointy sugar kind."

I squeezed her hand. So smart. Genes inherited from Grandma Nora. "Did Nana tell you this?" Since moving back here six months ago, we'd been visiting Gram a lot at Lupine Meadows, a prestigious retirement community. Thank God for her. I tried to not grimace at the reminder that I dumped Lark with my eighty-three-year-young grandmother a few days a week. Hypocrite. I was no better than my ex, Fran. But Penny warned me about bringing Lark on site where she could get hurt. If my BFF Carolyn at the Division for Children, Youth, and Families found out, I would be screwed. Lark needed to be in school, but her birthday fell after the kindergarten cutoff date this year. For a moment, I imagined her, twenty-two, in a cap and gown, finishing college, succeeding where I had failed.

Unicorn cake it was.

Lark nodded, the traces of what she nibbled on in the car stuck to the corners of her lips. Chocolate oat cookies were half healthy, right?

"Mm-hmm. We can cover it wif fondant, and use buttercream frosting, and..." Her rattled-off words and phrases flew over me like a jet. Give me computers, give me code, and lately, give me hydrangeas and stone pavers, but Lord, don't give me cakes.

"What's fondant?"

"It's like Play-doh."

"You eat Play-doh?" I teased.

Lark giggled, wiping her runny nose.

Allergy medicine. Add that to the list, too. Ragweed gave her the sniffles.

"No. It's marshies and sugar!"

"Not going to make fondant, Birdie."

"What if we make it out of chocolate like de fancy guy on dose shows?"

"Let's stick to cake and pre-made frosting, okay? Help Dad figure out cakes. Oh, these have rainbow chips."

She perked up when I pointed to the box.

My head hurt. I wanted an aspirin or eight.

As I grabbed two containers of vanilla frosting, she pointed to another shelf. "Use colors for de rainbows."

"Don't tell me I melt crayons into it?"

More giggles. At least she liked my sense of humor. Fran never laughed. Our one-night stand had turned into a forever deal with Lark's birth nine months later. Quick marriage. Quicker divorce. Followed by a lengthy probate court to decide shared custody. *Shared, my ass.* Then, I effed that all up when Lark was a baby.

Keep it together, O'Reagan.

I handed Lark a tissue from my pocket.

She wiped her nose. "No. *Food* coloring. You squirt it in." She wiggled from my grip and grabbed a box from the shelf.

"See? Cooks on de shows I watch wif Nana use dese." She imitated a pretend squirt bottle. "Drip, drop, drup."

"They're small. Toss 'em in, Birdie." I assessed the basket. "Do we really need four boxes of cake mix?"

I cringed as I found myself relying on my child to teach me crucial adult skills. Where was that aspirin?

Lark threw more things into the basket.

"Hold up." I pulled out my wallet and thumbed through the handful of twenties to sustain me until payday. I returned two cake boxes to the shelf and kept two in the basket. "Not making a wedding cake."

Lark grabbed my arm. "Daddy, we need pans."

My shoulders slumped and the knot from the pulled muscle in my upper back twitched. *No, not now.* I needed to stay in shape to keep working. The phone app with the grocery list stared back at me. "Can't we use Aunt Penny's pans?"

"No! It has to be round. Den you cut it to look like a unicorn's head."

I grabbed one pan. This trip was taking an eternity.

She insisted, "We need two."

"We can re-use the one. I'm sure they do that on the baking shows?" I quirked an eyebrow at her.

She wiggled from foot to foot. "I guess."

Or, more likely, if Penny didn't have pans, we'd borrow some from Gram.

We hit the personal care aisle next. I added antihistamine, a cold remedy, aspirin, and hair gel into our basket. I twisted open the aspirin and crunched on two pills, the hit bitter and chalky.

"Ruth makes cool cakes if you want to order one," Mitch's son—I forgot his name—said at the register as he scanned our purchases.

I nodded. "Mm-hmm. I forgot oil. Be right back. Lark, come." I hurried to the aisle and stared at the array of bottles. "Which one?"

Lark frowned. "I can't read dem, Daddy. Veggie." She tapped one.

Olives were vegetables. I grabbed the olive oil, and we returned to the checkout. The clock above the register ticked as Mitch's kid—Sam? Seth? Smartass?—scanned at a turtle's pace. I tapped a foot.

He blew and popped a bubble. "I need ID for this."

The cold remedy? I eyed him. "This doesn't have ephedrine."

He blinked like I spoke in an alien language. Did he not recognize me? I thought by now, after six months of living here, I'd be accepted, known. Besides, I came here weekly. Word also got around in small towns though. So maybe he *did* know who I was. Well, the town could take a hike. I was here. For good. Gram was here. Jake's kids and Penny were here.

I slapped the ID down to appease the pimpled punk.

"You related to Grady O'Reagan?"

To hear my grandfather's name sent prickles of goose-flesh rising on my skin. He'd been a prominent police officer in town, then high sheriff for the county. A plaque on the common commemorated his service. If Granddad knew what I'd done with my life, he'd be rolling in his grave.

I bagged and paid.

We stopped at the public bulletin board by the exit. I skimmed the listings for jobs first. Pathetic. Then on to rentals. Nothing good. Nothing cheap.

I bit my tongue in frustration and returned to the cashier. "Any other places that are renting? Apartments or a small house?"

"Did you check the board?"

"Yeah. Just wondering...word of mouth?"

The kid stared at me. Was he a stoner or just dense?

"Never mind." I went back to the bulletin board, Lark humming a tune beside me about unicorns and rainbows. I had orders from Carolyn and DCYF: find housing, secure a job more stable than seasonal work for my sister-in-law (or get unemployment, which I refused), and set up health insurance, pediatrician, dentist, and daycare, and don't miss one weekly recovery program meeting. If I did, she'd find out. My case was so close to being shut, but one screwup...

Penny's bungalow didn't crawl with cockroaches. I cleaned on weekends and repaired anything falling apart. However, they needed space for the baby and Lark bunked in her cousins' room. A new place for me and Lark would benefit everyone. Living with my boss wasn't exactly awesome either.

A man brushed by me, smelling of butterscotch. "Oh, sorry, kiddo."

"No prob."

He eyed me through caterpillar eyebrows as he turned a candy around in his mouth. "You lookin' for a place?"

Ah, he was the parking snail with the Buick.

"Maybe. Know a place?" I pointed to the board.

"Pickings are slim. Doubt Nancy has any good offerings, either. Market's been dry."

Who the hell was Nancy?

He continued, "If you don't mind the drive to Clemens Ridge, Jo Sawyer has an extra cabin. It's old but has character. It's a thirty-minute drive, and winter can be tricky, but it's not too far from town by bird. The sticks, we like to call it. Used to be Morgan Caldwell's place."

Was I supposed to know who these people were? "Nothing closer?"

He shrugged and lifted a shaky, liver-spotted hand, seeking a thumbtack. I found one and handed it to him. He centered a paper that advertised the cabin with a job as a groundskeeper.

"He's looking for a hired hand, too?" Hmm. Price was doable, especially with work along with a home.

"The place is old, needs some extra love." He scratched his balding head as if trying to remember. "Jobs like animal care, gardens, groundwork, mechanical things, all the fancy off-the-grid circuit thingies. Keep the ship running tight."

I whipped out my cell and plugged in the address for J. Sawyer's rental as listed on the ad. "No phone number?"

"Stop by to inquire." He handed me another paper—an application—then tacked a few of them beneath the ad.

"This Joe is a nice person?" *Willing to give someone like me a chance?*

He nodded. "The best kind. Heart of gold. I live in the other cabin. We could be neighbors. We'd love company in our neck of the woods." He turned toward Lark. "This your girl?"

"Yes," I responded. "Thanks. I'll do that. Let me give you my phone number, too, and you can pass it on to Joe?" I grabbed the pen hanging from a string on the pegboard. He waited for me to scribble on the receipt. "Please, have him call or text me. I'm flexible. I can move in as early as next week and I have lots of labor experience."

Not lots, but enough.

"Jo doesn't text," he said as he folded the receipt.

Okay, another old-timer like this man. Made sense they needed to hire a groundskeeper. "I'll swing by, then. But have him call me if he wants."

The man nodded, tucking the receipt into his shirt pocket. "Enjoy your day, young man."

"You, too."

Lark beamed at me. "A cabin, Daddy?"

"Maybe." Hope visited fleetingly, but when it did, it felt good. "Let's go, Birdie."

As we walked to the door, a brawny guy pushed past me, and his shoulder bump sent me into a bunch of shopping carts.

My senses fired first in irritation, then in dread as I registered who he was. Brian Dumont. The uniform remained mostly unchanged from twenty years ago. Decked in his taupe top, brown tie, stiff hat, and holster at the waist of his striped trousers, the county sheriff kept walking without so much as an apology.

Though the sheriff's office was thirty minutes west, he sure spent a lot of time in Silent Creek. Ten years my senior, Dumont had been a rookie police officer in my heyday. Nice to see he moved up in ranks to torment me.

Perhaps he didn't recognize me. I tried to remain as inconspicuous as possible around town. Swell coincidence, either way.

Lark turned to see why I stopped. "You okay, Daddy?"

I snapped out of my stupor. *Get a grip, O'Reagan.* It was like all my skills to remain chill, not react, had flown out the window lately. "Yeah, Birdie. Coming."

Dumont spun around, shined shoes squeaking on the floor. "Shouldn't she be in school this week?"

Pretending I hadn't heard him, I ushered Lark through the swinging door, my paper bag handle threatening to tear.

I felt eyes on me and hurried to the truck while Lark lingered on the sidewalk to examine a weed in a crack in the concrete.

"Come, Birdie. Interested in going for a drive to see a cabin in the woods?"

3

— · —

Josie

The ancient grandfather clock in the living room chimed
ten. I pulled on a jacket and snaked around pipes and tools
spread out on the kitchen floor. There was no delaying my
monthly trip into town, especially now. Back to the drawing
board on fixing this sink upon my return.

I sighed. None of this off-the-grid stuff was simple.

A shiver rippled down my back at the cooler-than-nor-
mal end-of-August day greeting me, and I dreaded starting
Uncle Morgan's old truck. Would it seize and gag or light
up like a Christmas tree? The deadline for obtaining a new
vehicle had passed, so I was stuck with it.

I was able to lug more groceries home if I took the junker
with its extended cab and long bed rather than the older
sedan sitting in the barn. I was tempted to sell both vehicles
and snag a decent deal on a used truck. Silent Creek had a
used car dealer with a flashy red *Cash for Cars* sign. A new
vehicle meant a paper trail of registration and insurance,
though.

Hence why I procrastinated.

Either way, the junker was my ride today. My long list of
errands included grabbing two bags of manure along with

a handful of veggie seeds to grow over winter in my kitchen window with a heating mat, while getting more sink parts at the hardware store. I never did much yard work at my former condo aside from potted flowers. Unfortunately, this place wasn't the watertight submarine the lawyer claimed. He wanted to be done with the legal paperwork and get his cut, so he'd exaggerated the cabin in the woods as a great windfall. Ha! And I, naïve and exhausted by the Tate mess, didn't question it for a minute.

Off-the-grid technology glitches, leaks, repairs, defunct gardens, and electrical snafus had welcomed me in May. Even with Don's training, I couldn't transform into an engineer overnight. His lessons were about disappearing, covering tracks, and creating a new, safer home. Not Homesteading 101.

The gardens were winding down from their paltry summer and entering their fall dearth with brown, shriveled leaves and vines. Pros made this stuff look and sound easier than it was. I bought seeds, planted, and followed the instructions of the gardening books, only for rodents, inadequate watering, pests, and plagues to befall my crops. Even the proclaimed trouble-free veggies died under my care.

Mother Nature had been kind to the apple trees and raspberry bushes, at least. What a surprise the raspberries were—everbearing, the type that fruited in the fall. The berries had just begun ripening on the vines.

I had no shortage of glass jars to make jam and applesauce. Uncle Morgan's doomsday bunker-meets-root cellar had held...oddities. This summer, I tossed the questionable stuff, ate the palatable foods, and saved the jars. How many pickles could a person eat? Apparently, a lot. Canned beets, too. Last week I unleashed my creativity with Amish beet-pickled eggs, beets hidden in "red velvet" cookies I tested on Hank, and even a beet hummus. To stay on budget and avoid the remaining beets, I needed to up my game this winter.

I was halfway to the truck when the landline inside rang. Hank's car wasn't here. Was there an issue with his trip into town?

During my first week here, his doctor came for a home visit after Hank burned his wrist on the stove. The stubborn old man concealed the injury, citing my busyness with house setup. My keen dog, Chip, sensed trouble, and we found my tenant in his cabin, icing the nasty burn with a bag of frozen corn. The lawyer, in telling me about Uncle Morgan's package deal, was remiss in mentioning me being caregiver to the octogenarian living on the property...so it had been, uh, a transition. There was also the goat, chickens, and cat to contend with.

However, Hank was a gem in the rough. Although his ability to help around the property was limited, he was a morale booster and pleasant company.

I rubbed my hands together as I hurried up the creaking steps of the porch to grab the phone. Was it Rafe calling to cancel this week's dog-training session? In my rush, as I had no answering machine, I forgot about the one testy plank at the top step. A crunch, crack, and split alerted me to my mistake.

"Oomph!" My leg dropped through it, calf deep. A curse rolled off my tongue.

Chip barked from inside. Holly parroted him with a meow of...something. I still hadn't deciphered the meaning of all her sounds.

I caught myself on the solid railing before plummeting farther. Pain soared from ankle to shin as I righted myself.

Please don't be more than a sprain. What had I whacked it against beneath the boards? A boulder?

Three rings.

Ankle throbbing, I limped inside, still hoping it wasn't Hank on the other end.

Chip paced, alert and ready, sniffing the air to assess my mood. I swear he had a sixth sense. "Not well, buddy," I mumbled. I caught the phone on ring six. "Hello?"

"Hi, Jo. Mitch here."

"Hi, Mitch." The tightness in my throat loosened.

Chip bobbed around me, tail rapping against my thigh, as I babied my left foot. I tapped his head to let him know I was okay.

Mitch continued, "Your delivery's been waiting. You come the third Tuesday?"

Today was Thursday. Oops. "The truck's been acting up."

"Want me to deliver? I have a trip to the ridge sched-uled—"

"No, I'll be there soon. Thanks for holding it. Was plan-ning on coming to town today, anyway. Just fell behind schedule."

"Found a new puzzle for you. One Hank may appreciate."

I smiled. "Fabulous."

We disconnected. I hobbled to the sofa and sat. Chip nuzzled my knee, vigilant whisky-brown eyes measuring me.

"I'm fine. Thanks for worrying." I rubbed his dense ma-hogany coat dappled with dark spots, hence his moniker of Chocolate Chip. His Belgian Malinois signature black mask matched the spots. I scratched him behind a lean shoulder blade. The shepherd in him—either German or Dutch, Rafe wasn't a hundred percent sure—pepped up, alert with one quick warning bark. Ears rigid, he hurried to the window, where he barked once again.

My sweet dog was new at this protection gig and required visits to review his training commands by the former marine. His trainer, Rafe, rocked. Didn't ask questions. Without complaint, he ate my first-ever batch of homemade zucchini bread—made before the zucchinis got a yellow end rot and died. He liked to remind me that the sessions were more for me, though. Chip and I were in our dating phase.

Dating aside, I knew what one bark meant. Stranger.

My stomach twisted. Tires spun on the gravel at the bottom of the long, steep driveway.

I was in no shape to go outside until I treated my ankle. Regardless, I staggered across the room and joined Chip at the window. I didn't need to hold his collar.

Holly meowed from the kitchen, not moving from her spot. She did a better job of catching mice than protecting the cabin. I shushed her needlessly.

Chip released a low growl. "Wait." I pointed my finger up. He remained in place.

I squinted through the window. At the end of the driveway, a faded blue pickup idled behind the monster-sized rhododendron and azalea plants partially concealing the driver. I grabbed my binoculars, but shrubbery obscured the plate, too. I found it peculiar for Uncle Morgan, a bachelor to the end, to have appreciated flowers. I bet Hank's wife, Tillie, planted the flowers before she died, so it was better if I ran the idea of pruning them by him first.

I moved to the other window and got a better view. Hard to tell, but the driver looked like a guy. No passengers in front.

Was he watching me? The house?

I counted to five, inhaled deeply, and then released the breath. Chip waited beside me, not barking.

Was the driver turning around to get something from the back seat? Was it a crew size or double cab? I adjusted my focus. Double. Toyota? The truck seemed familiar, but I didn't know who owned it. Was he speaking to somebody behind him?

One, two, three, four, five. Breathe in. Out.

Observe, Josie. If I could do something, control something, it calmed me.

He turned to the steering wheel, empty-handed.

Chin-length sandy-brown hair. Blue shirt. Broad shoulders. Tate had Nordic-blond hair and a slimmer build. I let my head fall back.

Tate had more important tasks after he was released from prison, instead of searching for me. Or so I hoped.

My fluttering pulse didn't agree with that line of thinking. I'd watched far too many movies to think he would be cool with his ex-wife leaving the state like a ghost. I didn't know if he'd been released yet.

Was this man a lost traveler? On a road only leading to a few properties north, a handful of hiking trails, and national forest land? Six hundred acres of woodland surrounded my homestead to the north and west, and the lake flanked the eastern border. Perhaps he was a hiker? Silent Creek was in the White Mountains and both Franconia Notch and Mount Washington were quick day trips away.

"Look at the sign, buddy. Private property. No trespassing. No hunting. No bugging me," I whispered. Hank called our place a compound. I preferred "homestead" because of the homeyness, even if it was rustic. Hank Buchanan didn't get many visitors, and he went to Silent Creek on Thursdays to hang with his donut crew. He attended church on

Sundays, followed by his grocery shopping trip and another visit to the Jolly Jellies. Donuts twice a week—what a life.

The blue truck wasn't here to see my tenant.

A quick and painful scurry to the kitchen brought me to my notebook. I flipped through it to the "vehicles" section as the person drove off.

"Okay, Chip." I patted him. His lean, tense body released into a settled waiting position with his head and nose lowered to his front paws, belly on the ground. "Good." I handed him a dog treat. He licked my palm and returned to his spot beside the sofa.

I logged this person into the notebook.

Under *Vehicles—Trucks* I had:

William Smart—red Dodge pickup, wife Sandra (school principal), (Will) works construction

Nadia Cash—rusty orange Ford truck, retired, deceased husband

John and Jim Elliot (brothers)—Elliot Maple Farm, two trucks, one new black Ford, and an old brown Ford, family logo on sides of both

Mitch DeMarks—grocer, dark gray Toyota pickup, dent in rear bumper, grocery deliveries by Jonah and Sam (sons), Mondays and Wednesdays

I skimmed the rest of it, a list compiled over the past few months. Names, physical descriptions, cars, marital status, jobs, hobbies, and any red flags of several hundred residents. I admit it was neurotic, but it went with Don's training, so I complied. Charting came naturally to me, anyway.

It would take a while to log everyone from town, given the population of three thousand. The list had no other blue pickups. I tucked the book away.

Avoiding a stumble over the pipes, rags, and tools in the middle of my kitchen floor, I grabbed a hand-sewn rice pack from the freezer and plopped onto the sofa, elevating my foot.

I prodded my ankle with a wince. No health insurance meant only emergency trips to the doctor. Morgan had bequeathed me a respectable amount of money, but it needed to last if I wasn't working yet.

Could I live off his savings for decades? Off the land?

Tate and the lawyers had emptied my measly retirement accounts.

I sat. I stewed.

The broken sink and porch board sullied my optimism. What rot hid under the porch? What grossness hid in my pipes? And how much would they cost me? Everything seemed to be about money. After the rice pack cooled, I staggered to the shed, each step eliciting a flavorful curse. I spun the combination lock and entered the code, then opened the door.

Dust motes and sawdust floated in the dim light as I rummaged through decades of junk: rusty metal scraps, old bags of God-knows-what, broken terra-cotta pots, rakes, shovels, the mower, snowblower, gasoline, and animal traps. I kept the suitable tools and toolbox in the house for quick access. No spare wood here.

Now what?

Rot implied a bigger issue. And plumbing? Not even my books were helping me. YouTube tutorials were a thing of my past.

Should I hire someone?

No. Nobody else was coming to my sanctuary. I'd get another home improvement book. Thursdays were the quietest days at the tiny Silent Creek Library. The morning preschool hour had ended by now. I'd buy enough wood to fix the steps and talk to George in the hardware store about the sink.

I tested my ankle with light steps along the garden path back to the house. Twenty minutes later, with less throbbing and a clearer mental state, I started the junker and was off to run errands.

After pickups at the grocery and hardware stores, I walked along Oak Avenue to the cafe, flinching. Stupid ankle.

Scrimp as I may, coffee was a luxury I allowed. Deanna promised me a good bargain if I bought beans in bulk. Besides, as much as I liked the weekly dinners I had with Hank, I needed connection to humans. Isolation and I weren't compatible. The goat he got me as a housewarming present—seriously, a goat was a lot of work—and the hens, rooster, and cat I inherited were okay company, but they were animals. Not humans. How could I fulfill that part of me while also avoiding unwanted attention? The thoughts were ping-pong balls in my brain. Initially, I gave vague responses to store clerks' hellos. Eventually, I chatted a little. Barely enough to keep loneliness at bay.

My pleasure at smelling the heavenly delight of spice and hazelnut plummeted as I walked into the cafe. The sheriff sat at a table by the window, sipping coffee, conversing with two men in suits.

Not the interaction I wanted. *Thanks, Universe. Forget I asked, okay?*

Sheriff Dumont's gaze met mine, and he approached with his usual swagger, intercepting my path to the counter. *Son of a...*

He adjusted the knot in his uniform's tie. In suburban Massachusetts, our sheriff wore a suit for public appearances. Things here were...*different.* And something about his presence, his uniform, his *something* always sent the hairs on my neck rising.

"Hi, Josie. Had a feeling you'd be in town today."

Did he? How? Did the universe send him a text message?

Deanna gave me a limp smile. She faced the woman at the register. "Your latte, Shanae."

"Thanks, Dee. See you tomorrow." The woman strolled past me and gave Sheriff Dumont a nod on her way out. She wore a deputy's uniform.

How convenient was it that on my two recent ventures to town, I ran into the sheriff?

Too convenient, in my opinion.

Thankfully, he hadn't called me out on the truck's expired tags yet. Playing nice was how I would do it. "Morning, Sheriff," I finally said.

"How many times have I told you to call me Brian?"

Too many for my comfort. "You're an elected official."

He stepped closer, biting down on a sunflower seed. He discreetly removed and cupped the shell in his palm. "You might want to chat with your tenant. Hank was hanging flyers again in Mitch's store."

What? I bit my lip. Hank needed to stop meddling. I didn't want another renter. Nothing burned my bacon more than somebody who was trying to "help" me. Where was help during three years of hell with Tate? Family, friends, and coworkers disappeared one by one. I could count on two fingers the people who hadn't abandoned me: my friend Hannah, and my brother, Kyle.

Forget help. Never had it. Didn't want it now. Not Hank's and not this bozo's.

"Don't worry, I removed the flyers." He winked at me from beneath his bushy brown eyebrows.

"No need." I awkwardly chuckled. My peopling skills were getting rustier than my shed and Hank's truck.

He gestured to the *Friends of the Sheriff's Office* binder on the table and an open laptop. "Want to sit and join us? I would love a new resident's opinion on my campaign slogan." The two suits sipped their drinks, then nodded, though I got the vibe of "move along" from them.

"Perhaps another time." I made my way to Deanna.

"Hi, Josie. Tyler, can you get the case on the rack by the oven?"

The young man in an apron nodded and then disappeared to the back after cleaning the espresso machine's nozzle. Deanna inquired about the possibility of setting up an auto payment for recurring large orders. She shifted paperwork across the counter.

"No need."

"Just need a credit card. I deliver." Her cheerfulness twinkled in blue eyes behind matching framed glasses.

"Cash is fine," I said, laying down a small sum of twenties.

Tyler brought out the heavy parcel. After pocketing the change, I lifted the box.

"Let me help." Brian approached, plopping his hat on his thick but receding hairline.

"No need. I've got it. You must have work to do."

His shadow blocked the doorway. Extra weight padded his middle, but he appeared decently fit. Try as he did to mask it with his sunflower seed substitute, he smelled of cigarettes. Musky aftershave and his well-groomed mustache and beard just added to his intimidating presence.

"Not a bother. Your truck at the curb?" He took the box from my arms.

He knew my truck. He knew me.

Wasn't his office located somewhere else? What did this man *do*, anyway? Didn't he have policies, budgets, and complaints to manage? Meetings to attend? He frequented town more than I thought he would be expected to.

He tipped his hat to me after holding the door open with his hip.

I launched myself through, which said a lot with my bum ankle.

He slid the box into the passenger seat of the cab.

"Thanks."

He stood smiling on the sidewalk while I walked away. "Never a bother, Josie."

My stomach lurched with the way he said my name as he bookended every conversation with it.

One more stop in town—the library—then on to my primary mailbox, a three-hour round-trip to Montpelier, Vermont. I should have prioritized going there, but Mitch mixed cold packs with the perishables and I already delayed him.

I yawned, wishing I had grabbed a takeout cup of coffee to pull me through this day.

4

Everett

After we deposited the groceries at Penny's place and then checked out the rental off in no-man's-land, Lark reminded me she didn't have the decorating instructions for the cake. I didn't possess the prowess for winging it. At least the cake box had the baking recipe.

Would this mythical matter just end?

I didn't need a shrink to tell me I overcompensated for Fran's absence. Lark didn't like any of the images or instructions I had found online. So, to the library we went. She insisted on books. Lark tugged me along, pointing to the modest building, its century-old brick façade obscured by unkempt hedges and vines running amok.

I rubbed the back of my neck, willing the ache to not creep north. Asking for more pain relievers from the doctor wasn't wise. Heaven forbid if Carolyn got wind of it, and she would, since no records were off-limits with DCYF.

My phone pinged with her usual meeting reminder text. Did this woman have cosmic telepathic rays? Had her reach stretched into my subconscious? I typed a quick response. We had our monthly meeting next week.

I would not lose Lark to the foster care system. Or to Spencer and Ann-Marie and their posh oceanfront home in Portsmouth. Screw them for putting me in this predicament. *Their* daughter, Francesca—not me—was the shitty parent who ran out on her daughter. Fran might be lying in a ditch, possibly dead from an overdose right now. Her parents were the reason I was dealing with DCYF. I couldn't ignore the backwardness of this at all.

We entered through the breezeway of the library, my head roaring, my pulse soaring. I reread an email from ProspNet to distract me from my woes. They requested pen-testing, which was above the bar stuff. The company offered legit, white hat cybersecurity work. I had promised myself I wouldn't touch another keyboard for anything but shopping and emails... But bug hunting was lucrative and easy. Landscaping was not as profitable and temporary. How temporary, that was another question.

ProspNet requested simple tasks: find vulnerable points in their system's infrastructure, then submit the data so the company could patch it. Stuff I could do in my sleep.

I swiped the email closed. If my sigh were any louder, I'd get yelled at by the librarian.

The *other* email loomed in my *other* inbox, the one with better security. That message was a dangling carrot. The job was quick. Not legal. More...gray. Gray was soupy muck, and if you gave a mouse a cookie...

To slide from legit to shady was a slippery slope.

I'd missed three birthdays with Lark. Fran never brought her to visit me in prison, and it provided more fuel for the Rossis' bullshit allegations about me not being a fit parent. I would not mess up this birthday.

Why was I even considering door number two? I closed the email.

"'X'cuse meeeee, ma'am, where are cake books?" Lark peered over the high counter of the circulation desk at the middle-aged librarian checking in books.

Looking up from her pile of books, she asked, "You mean the *Cathy Cake* series?"

Lark rolled her eyes. "No. Dose are baby books. I'm making a cake wif my daddy."

"Whoa, Birdie. Watch the tone." She had Fran's dark brown eyes, and when she made that exact face, my frustration flared because she got the expression from her mother.

Lark tried again. "Please, could you tell me where to find cake books? For baking?"

I whispered, "Much better."

"I can show you," the librarian said. "What kind of cake are you making?"

"A unicorn cake!" Lark bounced and tugged on her rainbow beanie cap Gram knitted her as her curly dark hair—another thing she inherited from Fran—searched for a way out beneath the brim. My daughter wore the cap all day, even at bedtime, any season. Penny bought a second one for Lark's birthday, so I hoped she'd like it when she opened the present this weekend. Lark liked to hold on to things. Made me wonder if Fran had ever given her anything to call her own. I shut the memory of the day I'd found Lark at Fran's apartment out of my mind.

The librarian led us to the Home & Garden section in the nonfiction stacks. "Here are the baking books."

Lark squatted on the carpeted floor and began pulling a few books out.

I requested, half joking, half not, "No fancy French cookbooks by gourmet chefs, please."

She looked at the covers. "I need baking books, not cook-books. Cakes. Pretty dings."

"Cooks and chefs aren't bakers?"

A woman perusing the Home Improvement section smiled as she pretended to not listen to our conversation.

"Nana says dere are chefs, cooks, and bakers. Different cat-gories," Lark said, absorbed in one book splayed on her crossed legs. I was glad I made her wear leggings under her rainbow skirt. "Susie chefs, pastry chefs, Communist chefs..."

I stared. What the hell was Gram teaching my daughter?

Chuckling, the red-haired woman beside us turned down the row with a pile of books in her arms.

I kneeled next to Lark and retrieved glasses from the pocket of my jacket. Too much reading on the inside—fad-ed pages, poor lighting, late nights—had led to massive headaches. First thing when I was out, the doc suggested reading glasses. Lord, I was thirty-eight, not fifty-eight. My headaches were manageable now, so I guessed they helped. "Let me see that book."

Lark pointed to the page.

"Ah, *sous* chef, *commis* chef." At least Gram wasn't talking about Communism to my kid. "Does the book have instruc-tions, Birdie?" I scanned the chapter headings. The book was way too fancy for my taste. "I need simple. *Beginner's Guide to Decorating. Baking for Dummies.*"

"But we're not dummies, Daddy."

I patted her head. "You're right. We have the recipe on the cake box. We only need assembly and decorating in-structions."

Pickings were slim. "Here. *Baking in Easy Steps.* Perfect. Let's get this. It has a rainbow cake on the cover. We can try other recipes like, uh, pancakes, waffles, French toast."

"Dose are breakfasts, not cakes." Lark stood, dancing on twinkle toes. "I like de pictures in de oder one."

I grabbed both.

We went to the circulation desk, behind the woman who found our conversation humorous or adorable—I wasn't sure which. Lark kept wiggling. "Almost done. We'll be back at Aunt Penny's soon."

"I gotta goooo. I can't wait dat long."

My gaze darted around.

The red-headed woman pointed to the youth area, mentioning the nearby bathroom. Her green eyes sparkled with...something. Not disdain like most. Not a question. Something genuine flickered in their depths. I wondered if she had a kid here, too.

She tucked a long, wavy lock behind her ear, and I quickly assessed her. The habit of reading people grew in prison. I had to watch eyes, nods, and subtle body movements to survive. One scuffle with the wrong person could turn your time served into a living hell. My quick assessment of this woman? She gave off the leave-me-alone vibe, yet she had a soft side for kids, clearly.

"Thanks. Be right back," I said to the librarian.

Leaving the books on the desk, I walked with Lark's hand in mine.

I waited outside the single bathroom, too aware of onlookers. When we were on the road or in stores, I preferred unisex or individual bathrooms. Pervs were everywhere. I couldn't go into the women's bathroom, and I wasn't bringing her into the men's.

I caught the not-so-discreet gaze of the redhead as she checked her books out. While pretending to review the preschool Sing Along sign-up sheet on the children's table a few paces away from the bathroom, I shot a brief look to the woman's stack of books. DIY—woodworking, food preservation, plumbing, green energy... Hmm. Well, we did live in the boonies.

Maybe she hadn't been laughing *at me* in the DIY section. Lark *was* adorable.

I drummed fingers on my thigh, waiting. Lark liked to take her time.

I knocked on the door. "Need help?"

"Daddy, it has one of dose monsters!"

I sighed. The high-speed, earsplitting "good for the environment" hand dryers. "Open and I'll help."

She did, but terror twisted her brow.

"Wash with soap." A sick kid at home meant no work.

Usually, she hummed and made bubbles. Not today. She sobbed. "I'll help. We have three options. Dry your hands on my jeans, I cover your ears while you use the hand dryer, or wave your hands outside to air dry."

"I need paper towels."

The towel dispenser was empty. She finished washing and cowered, hugging my thighs, getting wet handprints on my dirty jeans. She crept back to the faucet, re-washed, and stood in front of the dryer, bracing herself.

"Three, two, one." I hit the button with my elbow while covering her ears. My hands remained over them once she finished, and the dryer continued droning as we lumbered out of the bathroom. Lark's eyes remained tightly shut, and my eyes were on her and the floor below us. As a result, I nearly collided with someone. Looking up, face heating, I saw the red-haired bibliophile.

Lark squeaked. "Is it over?"

I finally removed my hands. "Now it is."

The woman—fine, the *hot* woman—smiled at Lark. Upon closer inspection, she had eyes of deep pond green, curves

I'd drive a hundred miles to see, and kindness in a creamy complexion dusted with light freckles. Her books weighed down a large canvas bag slung over her shoulder.

"I—I thought your daughter might like this book."

She squatted before Lark and handed her a children's baking book. Lark's dark eyes widened, and her fear evaporated. "Dank you!"

The woman hurried out of the library before I could thank her.

Hmm.

On the way to the car, Penny phoned me.

"Hey, Ev."

"What's up?"

I waited, cradling the phone between ear and shoulder as I buckled Lark into her booster seat.

"We need to talk. Will you be back soon?"

"You okay?"

Another slight pause on her end. "Yeah, I'm fine."

"Kids?" I asked.

"They're fine."

Penny's call without a plea meant one thing: Jake or me. I swallowed and then winked at Lark while closing her door. "Is Jake—?"

"He's fine."

Well, shit. This was about me. Dread sucker punched me as I prepared for impact.

5

— · —

Josie

My brain felt like the sludge scraped off the bottom of a forgotten coffee pot. I forgot how much errands took out of me.

Now I was alone, dusk falling around me, a stark contrast to the busy day. Mixed emotions arose on days like today, when I caught a glimpse of the world I abandoned by moving here. That father guiding his daughter in the library, people chatting at outdoor cafes, couples holding hands in the park, commuters bustling from work to home...

A sigh was acid in my lungs, bitterness in my spirit.

The speech and language pathologist in me would ask: was I meeting all my goals?

No. Not even close.

Lists and assessments had been my constant companions as an SLP, but the plan I'd written for my homestead adventure? That foolish idea got tossed on week one. I didn't have parents or a committee or school district to hold me accountable anymore.

The only person you can trust is yourself. Morgan instilled this advice upon me as a child. Here I was, back at my uncle's home—his hermit haven where he plunged into madness.

Nostalgia hit me as I shuffled around the kitchen, putting away items between dinged and scratched pots and pans dating from my childhood. My siblings and I had been free spirits here while Mom and Dad took a weekend away. Kyle hung out in his treehouse made from old planks, Phoebe swam in the lake with the townies, and I went fishing with Uncle Morgan. Then our Camelot stopped—no more visits. I never understood why. Morgan never returned my calls and letters.

I moved on with marriage and a career—the life I thought I was expected to have. Then all the Tate shit happened. In early spring, I received the news about Morgan's passing and the will bequeathing the estate to me. A door to escape opened. And here I was.

I pulled out the sugar container with the cracked lid I remembered super-gluing with Morgan and dumped in the contents of a fresh bag. As I moved a dozen pickle jars out of the highest cabinet to make room for new canned goods, a metal box near the back caught my eye.

Holly jumped onto the counter, silent and curious.

I stroked her soft fur, and she arched her back, her tail upright and quivering with happiness. "Hey, girl. Let's see what Morgan hid within his arsenal of pickles." I stood on a stepstool, reached in, and grabbed the round tea canister that looked like something from the 1960s with its simple red robin emblem. I ran a finger over the ancient canister, then twisted the rusted lid open.

In place of tea bags, inside of it sat a roll of twenties bound in a rubber band.

Huh.

This wasn't the first hidden stash I found in my cleaning. I plopped the money back in and closed the lid, saving it for a rainy day.

I never thought my uncle was crazy. Better words to describe him were eccentric, troubled. Something in his past turned him into a hyper-vigilant loner who hid money throughout his house. Had his tour in Vietnam shaped him into the old man I envisioned living here, with just Hank and Tillie for companionship? During my childhood, he would endlessly discuss the government, poisons, and secret treasures.

Excessive solitude could lead to emotional collapse. Even with Hank here, Morgan still succumbed to mania. Speaking of Hank—he wasn't back yet. He didn't drive well at night, especially through the mountain pass. It worried me, but I had work to do. He'd turn up. He always did. A thousand-piece puzzle for him sat on the butcher block dining table. Mitch was right. He'd love it. Old red wagons, pinwheels, dolls, dollhouses, lollipops, toy cars, teddy bears...1950s classic. Hank had been a toy and game designer.

I hauled in the rest of the groceries and hardware supplies on my sore ankle as twilight settled around me. Shorter days lay ahead. Darker days. Lonelier days. I shivered. Was I turning into my uncle? Was I ready for the test of winter?

I blinked the thought away.

The growl of a truck on the driveway, and not Hank's Buick, halted my meticulous cataloging of groceries. Who now?

Chip's single bark, a signal for a stranger, propelled him toward the door with eager claws on the hardwood. Holly screeched as I tripped over her in my rush to join him. "Oof! Sorry, kitty." She skittered away, her tail puffing.

I grabbed the pepper spray from the closest end table. "Stay."

The same blue truck from this morning pulled up in front of my cabin. The chronic tension in my muscles tightened like a wire on a spool. Don did not prepare me for this. Rafe's visits for Chip's training—fine. The truck driver who came to empty the sewage tank—fine. The electrician I'd needed to call a few times—fine. Hank's online shopping deliveries—fine. My minimal trips and interactions in town—fine. That's it. I tried damn hard to limit the number of people coming *here*.

Why was this guy here? Again?

Go away!

I flung the door open.

The man from the library got out of his truck. Sans kid. This guy?

His brown eyes widened, and his forehead furrowed when he saw me. "Oh. Hi again," he said.

Really, Universe? Three times in one day. Longest day ever, by the way.

"Sorry to stop by so late. I'm looking for Mr. Sawyer."

"Mr. Sawyer isn't here." How did he know my name? My fingers went white-knuckled on Chip's collar in one hand and the pepper spray in the other. Firmly, I said to Chip, "Watch."

He assumed a hinged position, his triangle ears stiff, his nose lifted, every muscle in his body rigid but ready. I bet his heart raced in his chest, the same as mine.

The guy did a half-step back on one heel. Good.

He scratched his neck, his light brown hair catching glimmers of fading sunlight. "A Joe Sawyer?" he clarified with a lift of an eyebrow.

I eyed him, not responding. He eyed me in return, shifting in his position, his work boots crunching on the gravel. Erratic locks fell across his forehead, framing an edgy face. Prominent lines rippled his brow in question.

He didn't give off the creep vibe, but then again, charmers never did.

Don's training escaped my mushy mind. "Where's your daughter?"

"Oh, she's with my sister-in-law." He shielded his face from the last rays of sun glaring through the trees. "Apologies for interrupting, but I wanted to ensure someone would be present when I came by. The application lacked a phone number. Hope I didn't interrupt your dinner or something." He chewed on a thumbnail as if he realized his error in judgment. He glanced behind me, then reached into his jeans back pocket. "Can you give the application to Joe? A man at Mitch's Grocery mentioned this place to me. I'm interested in renting and learning about the job. Can you perhaps—" He flapped the folded papers.

I made no move to take them.

What job? Brian Dumont hadn't mentioned a job being on the flyers. I was going to wring Hank's neck. "Who told you this?" I snapped.

"The tenant. Uh, didn't catch his name. Older guy, wore brown tweed pants paired with a plain red t-shirt? Saw him today at the grocery store." He chuckled to himself. "He was eating butterscotch candies."

Yup. Hank. He needed to stop meddling. "It's not available." It could be, but I'd hardly spent five minutes checking the cabin out. Despite its seemingly sound condition, looks were deceiving. Like people.

This man had a mountaineer's appearance with a well-fitting blue flannel, one button open too many. He tunneled a hand through his hair and scratched the back of his neck. "Mr. Sawyer better tell the old man to stop hanging flyers. Look, uh—" He paused as if wondering what to call me. Ma'am? Miss? Lady?

I shoved icy fingers into my jeans pockets, tucking the pepper spray in, too.

"—I'm living with family in town, but it's temporary. My daughter and I need more space. I would love to talk with Joe about the opportunity here." His gaze took in my property. All of it, slowly, deliberately. The cabins, withering gardens, overgrown and weedy yard, wildflower meadow, rusty equipment I'd yet to find a place—or dump—for, sugar maples, chicken coop and goat pen, solar panels, and the battery shed. His eyes lingered, deep in thought. That shed scared me senselessly. I did the bare minimum with the batteries. And gosh, don't get me started on the monster-sized wind turbines farther back on the property that were due for maintenance soon, according to Hank. Morgan may have been looney—one level shy of crazy—but he had been ready for the apocalypse.

But without a manual for his successor. Me.

Gilda bleated.

Oh yes, I didn't forget you. A gift which needed milking twice daily. Some gift. But goat's milk wasn't half bad, and my cheese recipe was coming along. Baking and growing vegetables might remain an elusive skill, but I managed cooking just fine.

He cleared his throat, snapping us both back to his reason for being here. "I'm a landscaper with an eye for detail." He smiled, revealing two handsome dimples. "I took courses during vo-tech on woodworking, engineering. I see you have an independent energy grid. My knowledge is simple, but I'm a quick learner. I work with contractors through P&J Landscaping, so I'm familiar with many home needs. The ad requested an, uh, someone to take care of the property. I have references—"

"You came by this morning. Why?"

I maintained my position at the top of the steps. The man stood below the busted upper step. The jagged chasm in the boards didn't escape his notice either.

"Huh?" He took a step closer.

I flinched. Chip shifted forward, lifting his rear off the porch in his crouch.

"Oh, that. I wanted to visit the property and check the commute to Silent Creek. Get my daughter's opinion on it. She asked if you have fairies on the land."

A tiny smile tugged at my lips, but I clamped them down like Fort Knox.

"Thirty minutes is a stretch, but pickings are slim in town. I'll leave you to your dinner." He stepped back a hair. "I filled everything out. My number's on the application. I can pay the deposit and rent immediately. Please let Joe know about my interest. I'm Everett, by the way. Everett O'Reagan." His gaze slid to the broken boards and back again. "And a skilled laborer, like I said."

Heat flushed up my neck as those dimples popped out again. Man, he was sure selling himself well.

He approached, avoiding the bum step, and offered his hand. I allowed him to draw closer, even if my heart was pounding and my palms grew slick. Yes, irrationally. But, hey, it's how I rolled over the past few years. Paranoia champed at the bit. Despite being called crazy, I had been right about Tate.

Each footfall of his ascent matched a drumming in my chest. *Everything's fine. Everything's fine.* Chip waited. "Heel," I said. Rational Josie won in the moment and shut down Crazy Jo. *Everything's fine.*

This guy seemed desperate. Who was I to know if this man was sketchy or not? I mean, I had married a liar and succumbed to his deception. Thanks to him, I doubted everyone and everything. I ignored the man's extended hand as Crazy Jo attempted to regain control.

"Does Joe Sawyer live here or not?"

"Yes." Josephine Sawyer did.

"Good. Please, give this to him." He practically pushed the paperwork into my hand.

I took it, unable to produce a rebuttal.

I thumbed through the pages. The application showed my address and information about the cabin, listed a modest rent, and detailed a job for a groundskeeper. *Good gravy, Hank!*

"I appreciate it," he added, then hopped down the steps and returned to his truck. "I could come back—"

"No need."

He froze mid-slide into his seat. "Okay. Then have him call me, please?" His pleading eyes melted my resolve by a smidge.

He was gone before I could say no again, his truck circumnavigating the few big ruts in the driveway's bend with care.

Everett O'Reagan was both the last and first thing I needed on my property.

What if he were a drug dealer in need of a hideout, or a father fleeing with a kidnapped child? I'd read an entire book on the skill of deception. It only increased my paranoia. *Thanks, Don.*

More like thanks, Tate.

Bastard.

I returned to the cabin, weighing the pros and cons. Rent could help me cushion my budget. I had ideas about a greenhouse, and this property needed constant repairs. His kid was cute. He was, too. Okay, that fell under cons. No dating, no men, none of it. New Josie was done with trusting men. I wouldn't be fooled again. Gooseflesh prickled upon my arms.

Josie, he is not Tate, not the thief who stole your life.

By the time the signs had smacked me in the face, Tate was veering for the exit, our savings gambled away, my identity fractured with a million holes. If I hadn't been so preoccupied with building a career, I might've seen the writing on the wall.

I grabbed myself a few pretzels and munched. Pondered.

I should have dumped his rental application into the trash, but I suspected he would just come back. *If* I was going to rent the place and hire him, I would have to do so correctly. Could I hire him as a boarder? He could work for reduced rent.

Now and then, I contemplated homesteader employment options, but most relied on technology, setting up an online store, or more trips out. I needed a measure of security while I considered my future. The Josie Master Plan was due for a re-eval. If he was genuine, I could lease the place to him and his daughter for cash and lower his rent for his work on the property. No need for banking to be involved. The empty cabin was a hot mess, though. I'd need to make signs, explain how things around here worked—the solar and wind electricity, the lake water, ground source heat pumps, backup generator, wood stove, the compost toilet and the regular bathroom, our sewage tank—so many working parts that even I had yet to fully grasp. My polar opposite, Morgan had left zero instructions.

There would be rules. I pulled out a legal pad to jot a few down.

Oh, my. People. Near me. Here.

Was I really considering this?

6

JOSIE

Paranoid. Lonely. Obsessed. Weird. Creepy.

Those were the words my sister had used when she heard of Morgan's passing.

Words that tumbled in my head daily for the past few years...about myself. I saw Morgan in a different light than others. He was quirky, kind, mysterious.

After writing out my tentative plan for renting the cabin, I headed for the bedroom. I reached the closet, pushed clothes aside, and dug for the box of burner phones. Pre-paid everything was my new norm: phones, SIM cards, and credit cards. A portion of the money from the Morgan windfall kept me afloat, and the rest sat in an account with my "corporation." Keeping loads of cash on hand wasn't smart. I didn't keep any cash under the mattress. Fireproof lockbox was more like it. Crossing that banking bridge fast approached.

My phone stash was plentiful, as I hardly used them. I had Don's number memorized from our meetings before my disappearance. Don's Cardinal Rule Number One—leave no paper trail.

I positioned myself in the bathroom, the only room with reception bars.

Time to break Rule Number Two—no contact with the past. I hadn't once called Dad—he didn't care—nor Phoebe, who lived in Sydney and had become indifferent in recent years. Only my brother, Kyle, invested his time when my life hit the fan three years ago. But then one fateful patrol shift took him away. I wiped a tear from my cheek, forcing that memory to disappear.

Donovan Smythe fell into the past category, too. I could still feel the lingering desperation in my throat when I first entered his shop, which fronted as an IT firm in the North End of Boston. I expected his place to be seedy, not wedged within winding cobblestone streets, historic landmarks, and the delicious aromas of the best Italian food around.

A bell had chimed merrily above the door.

"Come in." His secretary waved.

A man, nothing like I imagined, greeted me in the waiting area with a firm handshake. Don was buff—more like ripped—mid-fifties, with dark, clipped hair and chiseled lines in a tawny beige complexion. Contrasting with his hard façade were his jeans and loose-fitting Bermuda shirt patterned with bubblegum-pink hibiscus flowers.

He watched me make my way into his office and then closed the opaque glass door behind us. I caught a whiff of spicy vanilla from his cologne as he moved around the desk.

The stock art on his walls matched the shirt. Fiji, Caymans, Puerto Rico. A framed photo of a cabin on an Alaskan inlet caught my attention. Should I go to Alaska? What about Idaho? The Caribbean? Farther afield?

"Mr. Smythe, I—"

"Don." He reclined in his chair. "If you could vanish, where would you go?"

I blinked at his bluntness. After tiptoeing around everyone for too long, I needed someone on my side. Someone to care about me. Someone who could be straight with me. Sure, my lawyer was an asset, but he took a hefty percent of my already diminished savings.

I fiddled with the disintegrating business card Kyle had given me—the one that made it through my washing machine, sat on my dryer for six months, and glared at me each time I did the laundry. Kyle's scribbled note was barely legible now.

He will help where I couldn't.

Don's thick black eyebrows moved up, then down, waiting for my answer. His dark brown eyes held a smooth luster like onyx. Eyes, brows, body movement...they said so much. Years of working with kids with speech and language disorders meant I read nonverbal cues well. Speech therapy was more than speaking though. It was conversation, interaction. A person's expression told a lot.

What did his face say?

Hope. Empathy. Certainty.

I plopped into the seat across from him. "Anywhere but here."

"That's a start."

We both laughed in that getting-to-know-someone way.

He said, "I'm thorough and systematic and will demand a lot from you. I only take on clients willing to put in two hundred percent. You in?"

"I'm in."

I'd already been a few months into my vanishing prep work when Morgan's windfall hit my doorstep. If that wasn't the universe cementing my decision...

Now, a year after that first meeting, with a gulp of courage, I dialed the former skip tracer turned "night mover," as he called himself. He picked up on the fourth ring. "Smythe here."

After a steadying breath, I said, using my nickname, "It's Hyacinth."

Don's even-keeled temperament was palpable through the phone. "How's Seattle?"

My hand trembled as I skimmed Everett O'Reagan's info on the basic rental questionnaire Hank must have downloaded at the library. First things first. I started with my customary opener, "The coffee makes up for the weather."

"I love a Peruvian brew in a French press."

This dance felt foolish. Who were we? Secret agents?

Reminded by the junker's struggle on the windy mountain road back to the cabin, I flipped through my notebook filled with Don's codewords, seeking the one for *driver's license*. Despite having a decent memory, I still had to write some things down, breaking rule one. "I need to hire an electrician." I was uncertain of his source for these codewords.

I heard a squeaky office chair and the thump of the door closing. Don trusted his secretary and longtime girlfriend, Libby, but he was always discreet. A passerby in the waiting area might mistake Don for an actual IT professional. I asked him once why he had never settled down and retired at one of his poster locations. Why carry on their three-decade relationship without making it official? Don had told me, "Marriage is for people who want to be found. More paper trails. Ways to get access to not one person, but two. It opens back doors and black doors."

"Lucky for me, I'm divorced, and the bastard is in jail."

"Lucky indeed," he'd said.

Now, he responded to my request with, "Callback?"

I recited the burner phone number. We disconnected. Then he called me back a moment later, likely on something untraceable on his end.

"I need a thorough search done on someone. The works."

"Thought you needed help with a driver's license? The *electrician*?"

"That, too." I tapped a finger on my thigh.

"Okay, one thing at a time. Are you following all the steps?"

"Yes. Everything. I need a better car and a state license. I'm not getting around by horseback or bicycle. And what if I get pulled over?"

"You can put the car purchase and registration under your corporation's name to keep it legal but off the radar. If you get pulled over, you're in state visiting. Or you're on vacation. Your out-of-state license has two years remaining."

The idea of lying to a police officer made me think of Kyle, and my stomach knotted. Every trip in Morgan's truck had me looking in my rearview mirror. Being such a rule-follower had hangups. "I want a license for New Hampshire. This is my residence now. It's a small town. I can't pass as a visitor anymore." *Hell, the sheriff knows me already. Way to go, Josie. I wish Morgan's cabin was in Wyoming or something.*

"A license puts you on the digital grid again, and I don't do fake IDs."

I swallowed. "I know."

"Okay. I'll check out the DMVs in your area. See which ones require the least amount of documentation. I have connections. If you prefer, we can arrange a car for you without insurance."

Crud, car insurance. "I want license, registration, and insurance. I will pay cash for the car." Ouch, that was going to hurt my budget big-time. And more paper trails. Dammit, this was hard.

"Got the private mail drops?"

"All four." I'd set them up at different mailbox stores, each a few hours away and across four states—in Montpelier, Manchester, Bethel, and Springfield. Don named them for their usage: main, burn, protected, and bluff. Montpelier was the main, so I checked it more frequently.

Besides his cardinal rules, Don's disappearing steps included: misinformation, deception, and rebirth. I was stuck on step two. He required an intense level of organization. Forget education plans; I created survival plans.

"Okay, next. The background check. Depending on what you want, it may take time. Weeks. Months."

Months? I cringed. Everett O'Reagan was surely going to come for another impromptu visit soon. I nibbled on the tip of a pen. "Okay."

"I'll need info. Got a pen?"

I pulled the notepad out of the burner phone box. "Yes."

Later, near nine p.m., while I sat with a cup of herbal tea and a novel from the library, Hank returned. Chip gave two barks. "Yes, buddy. He's home. Did he get lost?"

I would butter Hank up with the puzzle and then talk to him about his flyers. This had to stop.

Ten minutes later, I walked down the sloped driveway with Chip by my side. Hank's porch light flickered with my knock.

No response. Perhaps he was using the bathroom. I heard no Duke, Louis, or Ella blasting from Hank's record player, so he should have heard the knock. He wasn't an early-to-bed guy either, and he literally had just come home.

Chip began pawing at the door, claws scraping. He whimpered.

"Bud, I know you want treats," I mumbled. "Chill a minute."

He continued pawing. Rafe's training nudged my intuition. Chip was bothered. "Back," I ordered, my pulse shaky. The porch light flickered, snapped, and left us in darkness. Hadn't I just replaced that light bulb?

Chip barked three times.

Three times.

Crap. Crap! One: stranger, two: friend, three: danger.

"Down," I said again, my command wobbly.

Something wasn't right.

I threw open the never-locked door.

Hours later, I sat in the waiting room of the hospital several towns away, anticipating an update on Hank's status in the operating room.

The words from doctors clogged my brain like unfiltered coffee grounds.

Possible stroke. Hip fracture. It's fortunate you found him when you did.

What if I hadn't gone to ream Hank out for the ad he hung in Mitch's store? I shivered. Minutes tumbled into hours. My eyelids drifted shut, fatigue winning out. Nightmares captured me.

"No," I mumbled to Tate. He flicked his cigarette butt out the open car window as he drove away, and my heart broke even more. A familiar odor penetrated my nose.

My nightmares had become so vivid that now I could smell them.

A loud throat clearing jolted me from my sleep. Snapped upright from my slouched position in the uncomfortable waiting room chair, I opened my eyes.

The scent of cigarettes lingered. As did a dark shadow, a way-too-close one.

I pressed a hand to my racing heart.

"Sorry, saw you sleeping there. Didn't mean to bother you. Was on my way home from a late meeting when I saw Hank's Buick in the parking lot. Everything okay?"

I stared into the ashy-brown eyes of Sheriff Dumont—I still refused to call him Brian, out loud at least. Instead of his usual uniform, he wore a navy-blue suit, the knot of a tie loosened around the collar of an unbuttoned oxford shirt. Uh, he saw the car and came inside? At a hospital forty minutes away from Silent Creek? Was this even in his county still? He just moved himself up a level on my stalker scale. My stomach roiled. I answered with a numb nod.

"Need company?"

Heck no. I shook my head. So what if he was the sheriff? My sensors bleeped like a haywire robot around him. Sure, he had a campaign to run and voters to solicit, but seriously. I wasn't registered to vote, which would put me further on the grid.

"Coffee?" he offered, rubbing his nose. The scraping of fingertips across his salt-and-pepper mustache annoyed my sensitive ears.

"No, thanks." I hugged my handbag against me—one I bought from the local consignment boutique to feel normal when I ventured out. I covered a yawn. "I'll be fine, thanks."

A web of wrinkles circled tired eyes. He tipped his head, relenting. "Take care, Josie." His shoes squeaked on the bright white floor as he tossed a goodbye look to me. He jingled change in a pocket while he approached the nurses' station.

I felt cautious after his departure, unsure of potential watchers. How many people were looking at me?

Eyes. So many eyes.

I dropped my nose behind a magazine and pulled the hoodie over in-need-of-washing hair. Yawning for the umpteenth time an hour later, I grabbed coffee from the cafeteria.

By morning, after endless people in scrubs answered my worried questions, I felt reassured enough of Hank's condition to let myself go home. They would discharge him in a few days. Chip needed to be let out, and I needed to sleep in a safe bed.

As the days progressed slower than sloths climbing trees, a not-so-great discovery arose.

Turns out, Hank hadn't paid his Medicare premiums for some time now. Insert hours of phone calls with insurance and the hospital's billing department. Haggard from too much haggling on my now well-used landline, I parked at the hospital curb in his lower-to-the-ground Buick to pick up Hank on Wednesday.

A mountain of tasks lay ahead. Calls. Paperwork. Plans. A revolving door of therapists on my property. Morgan's will stipulated that Hank would take care of his own finances, but I was his healthcare proxy and some of the money was earmarked for his healthcare at my discretion. I never expected to touch that money for my own needs, but losing that cushion sent my pulse soaring. Numbers spiraled out of control in my head. Hank told me Tillie handled the money management. Hank really needed to schedule a financial advisor appointment.

On our drive home, I was the first to crack the silence. "Let's get you settled in, okay? Then we'll chat and go over the game plan."

He nodded. A quiet Hank wasn't a happy Hank. He stared out the window of the car, watching rain splatter against the glass, as we pulled into the driveway. "I screwed up your plan, Jo."

I lifted my raincoat hood over my head, got out, and hurried to his side. "We'll make a new plan," I said while my brain flew like a jet plane running low on fuel and searching for a runway. "Come. I've got your wood stove going, so it's warm and comfortable, and you have the new puzzle."

I pulled out the walker and rested it against the bottom step, then helped him out of the car.

"Not just this damn hip, but everything. Coming here. You didn't expect to have an old geezer—" he said, the fatigue straining his voice.

Rain and distance muffled Chip's two barks from inside my cabin, but my keen ears knew all the sounds here by now and registered them easily.

"Even Chip missed you. Let's get you comfortable. I'll write up notes and a plan. I'll use my fancy highlighter set you got me and one of the gazillion blank journals Morgan has on the bookshelf."

He grimaced with effort as we finally made it to the landing. "Oh! I bought you a birthday cake."

"I popped it in the freezer last week. We'll have it on Sunday at our dinner. The priority now is to get you inside, settled, rested. Nobody sleeps well in hospitals. Everything will be fine, Hank."

As I guided him inside, I tried to believe my lie. Nothing was ever fine.

7

Everett

A week passed with no call. Mr. Sawyer—whoever he was, the woman's husband, brother, or father—had either done a background check on me and said hells no or hadn't received my application at all because she tossed it in the trash. So much for my astute assessment of her when we met at the library. There she'd been...kind. On her doorstep, the opposite. Prickly outside, soft inside? What was her deal?

Radio silence didn't mean Sawyer found my criminal record, though. He'd require permission and a signature to run a CHRI check. Most landlords didn't ask for a criminal check without due cause. Plus, the state sealed my conviction record earlier this year so anyone looking for answers would find a clean slate. I presumed here in Silent Torture, property managers would run the usual credit check. My credit report was at least acceptable, despite a three-year gap.

After a long day building a walkway, I sat, nursing a soda, bobbing my knee, and rehearsing my spiel for my monthly visit with Carolyn. The walkway project was my last job, because oh yeah, that phone call from Penny the other week? Well, my sister-in-law laid me off.

It's been a blast living together since then. I could have used a steak knife to cut through the tension during Lark's birthday party.

Penny cried a lot. Apologized a lot. Even got defensive. That's when I knew she still harbored some animosity toward me over Jake's situation.

"It's temporary, Ev. It's not firing," she had said.

Was temporary my new middle name?

"I'm sor—"

I'd waved her sorry away.

She heaved the world's most tired sigh. This sucked for both of us. She appreciated my help while Jake wasn't here. But a part of me also felt like she blamed me for his mistakes.

She proclaimed, "I require someone available from eight to five daily, as I handle bookkeeping. I need someone else running the rest of the daily office work. Your help with that has been great, but I've moved Grylls into that role. To compensate him, I must let go of one landscaper."

Yeah, me. We both knew I was her lowest-earning employee, too. New guys always got cut first. *This bites.*

"Once Lark starts school next year, you'll have more time for this work. Next year, Ev. This is temporary." Her chin quivered and voice cracked. She rubbed her growing baby bump before saying, "Who knows? I may step away next year completely. Plus, Jake will be back."

She was screwing me over, big-time. "That project was a good one, Pen, providing me at least another eight weeks of cash flow. Besides, Lark enjoys hanging with Gram."

"You mentioned a cabin and a job. How is that going?" she asked.

"How can I afford rent with no job?" Never mind that Sawyer hadn't called me back.

"I'll put in a good word with Hollis and Meyers. But you mentioned the cabin included work. Two birds, one stone, right?"

"Hollis and Meyers are assholes. I've got nothing else. Do I go on the road again? Trucking? Better yet, track down Fran and put my daughter back in an unsafe situation?" *Do shady shit like your husband and get myself in trouble again?* I bit my tongue. Hard. I was only a few mouse clicks away from walking that dark path again.

"Stay here for as long as you need, Ev."

Fat chance. And DCYF wanted me to get a place of my own.

"I can recommend you to—"

"Don't worry about it." An idea sprang to my mind. "Do you really want to help?"

"Yes." She lifted her mug and blew on her tea, although it had been sitting there, getting cold for some time.

"Then I need you to provide a reference about my contracting company."

Her forehead crinkled as she swallowed. "Uh, you don't have one."

"I'll get the license."

"Saying you're already licensed is lying. The county and state have different requirements for landscaping and contracting. It's a good idea, but it takes time and money and proper steps. No fast-tracking."

"I'll get the business registration and liability insurance, the whole song and dance. Please, Pen."

"How about I get you info about licensure, insurance, and business registration, okay? Then we talk references." She hesitated.

"What?" I nibbled on a nail.

She fiddled with the amethyst birthstone necklace around her neck. "It takes money to start up. Equipment? Employees? Once you have everything lined up, yes, I will two hundred percent vouch for you."

A roll of antacids could not ease the tightness in my chest. Did she think I was a moron? I could type up contracts in my sleep. I assisted her in setting up her website, handling the programming and code work, and optimizing her spreadsheets and employee management database. I knew my stuff. And to boot, whenever the school called her to pick up one of her terrors, I filled in. I thought I was an asset around here.

Our conversation had ended on that high note last week.

Now, I waited for my check-in with Carolyn from DCYF, no closer to a rental agreement or long-term employment. Yesterday, I grabbed the local paper at Mitch's store and searched online. The classifieds were more pathetic than my résumé.

The doorbell rang. Carolyn, punctual as always.

She came inside and we went through our usual greetings. Yes, the weather is lovely for September. Yes, the town looks beautiful for fall.

I planted a hand on my knee to stop it from bobbing once I sat with her. I fought the urge to chew a nail.

She opened her bright red leather notebook. *The book of my sins.*

"Our primary concern is that you provide a safe and stable environment for Lark," she said, uncapping her pen.

"Penny's home is safe and stable. Lark's with family," I countered.

"Mr. O'Reagan, you know the stipulations. A home or rental of your own. You sleep on the couch while Lark shares a room with two older male cousins. Six months ago, you were driving across the country, and she was sleeping at truck stops with you. A child of Lark's background needs a stable home of her own."

I nodded, too eager to pass her tests.

I had spent most of the morning cleaning up. My gaze darted around spying toys and cups and a pile of laundry in a basket next to the couch. In the playroom beside us, Lark sneezed.

I played with the tab on the soda can.

"How's the job?" she asked.

"Good."

She lifted a brow over tired, unremarkable eyes and pushed her glasses up. The woman needed a better-fitting pair. "Elaborate."

She would check. I needed to be honest. I snapped the tab off the can. "Okay, well. It *was* good. I was laid off last week."

Her pen hovered.

What? No notes on me failing at yet another job?

I waved a defensive hand. "Cutting costs. The office work called for someone else. Nothing I did wrong. The newest guy gets cut first. You can ask Pen. She'll endorse me."

"We consider unemployment income. Have you applied?" Her eyes kept falling back on Lark, who colored in the unicorn book she got for her birthday.

"I've been looking into getting licensure for starting my own company. Was working on applications this morning." I refused to take a handout from the government. Not after what they'd given me for 912 days—deserved, but still. No way. I was on my own.

"Mr. O'Reagan, we've gone over this. If you choose not to collect unemployment, you need a full-time job. Or two part-time or seasonal jobs. I need proof of an exemplary work record. Setting up a business, while it sounds promising, takes an investment of time and money, doesn't it?"

My headache tiptoed toward the danger zone. I leaned into the couch, the leather crinkling as I rubbed my forehead with a sweaty hand. "I have a bunch of applications out. I'm following up on a rental this week, too."

I gave her the address of the cabin owned by the mysterious Joe Sawyer.

"Is there daycare nearby?"

"Yes."

A white lie. For now, Gram was suitable as daycare, and she enjoyed her time with Lark. If I moved to the cabin, it meant a longer commute to dropping Lark off daily. I'd figure it out. I always did.

Lark spilled her bin of crayons and whimpered, cupping her cheek. "Daddy, it hurts."

She came over to me and flopped into my lap like a wet noodle.

"What hurts, Lark?" Carolyn asked.

"My toof again."

Carolyn stopped writing. "Does she have a dental appointment?"

She would ask for the time and location, and Conscientious Carolyn would call.

I said, "Working on it."

"When is her next pediatrician appointment? How are her vaccinations?"

I rubbed Lark's back as she settled into my lap, fidgeting with my shirt collar. "Working on it."

Carolyn pulled out a leaflet on government health insurance and handed it to me. "Something to hold you over until your employer can cover it."

I thumbed through the pamphlet and nodded. Finding a job with insurance, full-time pay, and stability was like finding a white cat in a snowstorm. At least with government insurance, I could get Lark's healthcare covered for now.

Carolyn's mouth slackened. "School enrollment for next year?"

"Registration is in the spring." I needed to play up the positives. "The rental comes with a job." The cabin and property intrigued me, but the grounds needed massive TLC. Even if I had to refresh my brain on the mechanics of off-the-grid technology from my vocational school days, I could do it along with the manual labor. The job would provide a steady income while I set up the contracting biz. The cabin was my answer. If only this Sawyer would call me.

Her eyebrows wiggled like the caterpillar from Lark's book.

"Property groundskeeper," I said.

"Lark, could you give me and your daddy a few minutes alone, please?"

She shifted out of my hold.

"How about an ice pop, Birdie?" Did they help with toothaches? No. Dental visits did. I got her a pop from the freezer, anyway.

While Lark left the room, Carolyn adjusted her bargain-bin scarf for the hundredth time, then said, "Mr. O'Reagan, my job is to help you set up a safe home for your daughter, to assist in your recovery."

Recovery. That's what they called it. I gritted my teeth. One time! One awful mistake landed me here. Not my arrest and conviction for hacking. Something else, thanks to Fran's parents.

They could call it whatever they wanted. Fine. I'd recover like it was nobody's business if that's what it took to keep Lark.

"How are meetings going?" she asked.

"Good."

"You want this case closed, don't you?"

I rolled my eyes. Was I eight?

"You have a timeline. You need to show a safe environment for your daughter in all aspects. Job, home, healthcare, daycare. I need documented evidence for a year. You must show sobriety for a year."

Woman, I hardly take aspirin! I'm as sober as they come.

People saw what they wanted. Spencer and Ann-Marie Rossi had pulled the wool over DCYF's eyes.

"And schedule a dental appointment for your daughter's tooth."

No shit, Sherlock. I waved the health insurance pamphlet. "Consider it done."

After walking around the house, visiting with the two goblins known as Shawn and Liam, and chatting with Penny as she returned from grocery shopping, Carolyn saw herself out, tripping over Nerf guns and mock weapons the boys made of sticks.

"See you next month," she said to me. "Nice to see you again, Penny." She waved while stepping outside.

"Have a good evening, Carolyn," Penny said from the kitchen as she put food away in cabinets, her smile tight-lipped.

Penny gave me a remorseful look.

I flopped onto the sofa, and she handed me another can of soda. Soon, I'd need to see the dentist, too. I popped it open and gulped the fizzy, sugary goodness. Carolyn was only doing her job. I ran trembling hands through my hair, the shock of caffeine joining the unrest in my bloodstream.

Lark buzzed into the room, her arms overflowing with two hamsters. My daughter squealed in delight or terror as one rodent climbed up her chest, over her shoulder, and attempted to do a maneuver in her hair.

Penny pulled a box of mac and cheese out and set a pot to boil.

The house's rear was eerily silent. "I'll check on the boys."

"They need showers," Penny said.

"On it." I rounded up her devil children from the backyard, both covered in mud and God knows what else, and supervised showers while she assembled a meal for them.

Later, Lark whimpered beside me as I crashed on the couch. It wasn't even five p.m. but I covered another yawn.

"If we move, will I see Harry and Furry?" Little tears formed at the corners of her eyes.

"Your cousins will take good care of them."

Hardly. Wasn't it last week when Shawn tried to determine whether hamsters could swim? In the toilet? Liam was no better. He suggested they add soap and flush it to see if Furry or Harry would like a whirlpool bath.

Jake's return home was overdue. He had been released this spring and managed to knock up Penny before being sentenced again.

Lark rubbed my chin with a sticky hand. "Porcupine fur," she said.

I gave her shoulder a squeeze. "Go wash your hands for dinner."

After Lark made her way to the bathroom, Penny came over. "Ev, that wasn't too bad, right?"

I shrugged.

Her lip quivered again.

"It's fine, Pen." She had enough on her plate, so I cut her some slack. Being screwed over was my MO. I should be used to it by now.

My phone buzzed with a local number. Steeling myself and throwing some stock into the chance that somebody would call about one of the job applications, even on the weekend, I answered. "Everett here."

"Mr. O'Reagan?" a hoarse and familiar male voice said. "Does your daughter like cake?"

8

— · —

Josie

Body yearning for an early bedtime after the week from hell, I slogged up the steps to Hank's door, ignoring the overdue winterizing, overgrown lawn, and a pile of junk beside the shed. A clutter of paperwork waited for me back in my cabin. My usually type A self didn't give a damn at the moment.

The scent of pine and wax wafted out the open window. Tillie had loved candles, or so I was told. The Glenn Miller Orchestra blared from within the cabin. Hank's diminished hearing meant Miller was grooving outside, too.

Chip sniffed the air as we approached the door.

I set the dish on the porch table and rubbed him behind his ear. "I know, buddy. You smell Ruthie's cake, don't you? I'll save you a piece. Need to keep you fit." I needed a slice of buttery indulgence after this week.

I shook out my tired legs and knocked. "Hank..."

Come on, Hankster. Chip and I had just completed our long daily walk and my mood hinged on hangry. A Belgian Malinois needed lots of energy expenditure, so he kept me in shape, too, while I checked the fences, pumps, rain barrels, trails, wires, and anything begging attention. This afternoon we covered the eastern perimeter fencing of the six hundred acres I had come to know too well this summer. Property work distracted me from the Medicare disaster. The surgery, three days in a hospital, and the home visits were not cheap. It would quickly drain Hank's funds down to zero. The kicker? A daily influx of people on my property for his care over the next few months. Great.

After the half dozen conversations with hospital billing this week, and the arrangements for physical therapy, nurse visits, occupational therapy, and medications, I had a plan to use some of my money to help with Hank's needs once his share ran out. An ideal solution would be to sell a huge chunk of the land to developers, but my uncle's will prohibited the sale of the land. So here I was.

This situation just sucked. What happened to simplicity and solitude?

I knocked on his door again. The physical therapist said he should use his walker, so I waited.

I had needs and wishes aplenty. Money. A temporary ramp for Hank. A chauffeur for him for six to eight weeks. A fairy godmother to convince Hank that Lupine Meadows offered great care options. Affording it went back to number one on the list. Money.

I had to get my crap here together, too. What was the saying about getting your ducks in a row? Ha! My ducks were not remotely in a row and swam in the soon-to-freeze lake. The property would not winterize itself. Drafty windows, rotting wood, overgrown grounds, and the maintenance of pumps, batteries, and turbines all begged my attention.

My hanger morphed into frustration.

Chip's tail tapped the porch boards. His ears went upright in his waiting seated position. He always eagerly awaited a treat when left outside.

"How about pot roast instead of cake, my cookie boy? Better for your bod. Tillie's recipe, and one I can't mess up." Tate once laughed at my attempt at cookies that turned into scones. "How can a person screw up chocolate chip cookies?" he'd asked. Ass. At least I made a wicked lasagna, casserole, and now, pot roast. With Tillie's cookbooks that had become a staple to my kitchen, soon I would try applesauce, apple jam, pie filling, and raspberry jam. I hadn't killed the trees or fruit bushes, right? I counted every win I could.

Chip licked his jowls as if he knew my words.

I hollered again, "Hank!"

Impatiently, I picked up the roast pan. The pot roast with carrots and parsnips—something my gardens grew well—weighed a ton. While holding the pan with potholders, I juggled a jar of pickles under one arm, a notebook, and a half dozen eggs in a basket on the other. Despite the messy coop, the chickens I inherited were good at producing. I wasn't sure how old the six hens were, but hey, eggs. Another win. I found animal scat not far from the cabin, so reinforcement of the coop was also on my mile-long to-do list.

I knocked with an elbow one last time, my triceps getting wobbly. *Come on, Hank.* I considered setting the roast pan down again. Anger vanished when an icy draft circulated through my body at a thought. Had he fallen again? Had another stroke?

"Chip, speak."

He barked twice.

My courtship with Chip was messy, but he was doing well. Me, I gave myself a C minus.

"Yes, yes, coming," Hank's raspy voice called from within, loudly to be heard over Miller and his orchestra. He was likely in the kitchen, pretending to get ready for my visit and speaking with Tillie again.

I was no stranger to talking to ghosts. Or to myself. Being alone got lonely.

The record player stuck, skipping, before Hank turned it off. The dragging sound of a walker with tennis ball–covered wheels scratched on old wood.

He opened the door with a smile reaching his blue-gray eyes. "Jo! Happy Sunday."

Hank quickly adapted to the walker after overcoming the initial hurdle of day one. The nurses warned me that many people of his age deteriorated fast with a hip injury. Not Hank the Tank. "Happy Sunday," I greeted him as I stepped inside and moved through the open living-dining room area to the kitchen.

I plopped the roast pan on the stove, then wrangled the pickles from my armpit. I tactfully placed the jar in the fridge and the eggs in a ceramic bowl on the counter. I could dump a few more jars of beets into his pantry, too, and none would be the wiser.

Hank's record player resumed with Miller's "Pennsylvania 6-5000" and I found my feet doing the tiniest steps in place to the beat as I paused in the small hallway that connected the living area in front and bedroom in the rear. Some nights, when our brains grew tired with Scrabble, Hank entertained me with East Coast Swing lessons. The steps were easy enough to follow. He'd tell me joyful stories of his and Tillie's dancing days.

A gold-framed photo of her sitting on a rock wall hung in the hallway. In the candid shot, she endearingly scrunched a dainty, freckle-covered nose. Gray peppered her curly white hair, worn pinned high off her neck. A ruffled green blouse, strand of pearls, and flared navy skirt completed her look. She carried her petite stature with a larger-than-life personality. Her eyes laughed at her photographer—Hank, I presumed.

I peeked over my shoulder to find Hank standing at the front door, hand in pocket, hinged forward over the walker. Chip perched in front of him, eager for another treat.

"Hank, he needs to stay outside."

He waved a dismissive hand. He and Chip shared a moment. Hank laughed, gave him the treat, rubbed his head, and then guided him out front.

I glanced in the antique mirror across from Matilda Buchanan's portrait. Compared to Tillie, I looked...*horrendous*. I blew wisps of fading dark ginger hair from my face. I made funny faces as I inspected wrinkles and frown lines. My freckles seemed to be multiplying. Weren't women supposed to outgrow them? Bangs could hide my forehead, but they were more maintenance. I jabbed at gaunt cheeks.

Hank appeared beside me and poked my toned arm. "Ladies shouldn't be this thin. You have chicken wings for arms."

I jumped. "Do you have a stealth mode on that walker? I may need to put a bell on the handlebar," I teased.

He smiled. "Happy late birthday, doll. A stunning thirty-five," he whispered. "Come." He pointed to the kitchen bowl. "I refuse to let you give me more of your eggs." He paused halfway to take a breath on his way to the living room.

"There are plenty and they're your chickens, too. You took care of them before I got here." I untied the sweater around my waist and shrugged into it, then put the quilted vest back on top. Even with the residual warmth of the waning summer, a chill rested in my bones.

"Need me to put wood in the stove?" Hank asked.

"Let's save that cordwood for when we need it. You could turn the thermostat up though. We have plenty of power." I knocked on the kitchen doorframe in the hopes the heat pump would keep on working well.

"So proud of you, Jo. You're figuring it all out."

"Hardly. But I'm trying." Thank God for Morgan's ingenuity at least. If only he left instructions.

I shook my notebook as I left the hallway and settled at the dining room table. "I drew up our plan. No more moping. Time to dig in."

Hank eased himself into the chair closest to the oak sideboard to make drinks.

"Might you turn Mr. Miller down a little?" I could do it, but he needed the steps. "I've got a headache, and I want to review your care plan. No more putting this off, Hank. Let's meet with the financial advisor in town soon, okay?"

No response. I knew he heard me, though. He played up his impaired hearing when it was convenient.

At least we didn't have remiss power bills or anything. Everything on the property worked on an intricate grid that only cost money to repair and maintain. We had electricity from the solar panels and wind turbines, water from the pump system connected to the lake, and hot water made by solar power and ground source heat pump. Plus, we had wood stoves and a generator on standby. I had done gobs of reading on off-the-grid living after my arrival and had it mostly figured out.

So long as nothing else broke. My current sink repair was a bandage at best.

Money-wise, I covered the property taxes and sewage tank pumping and anything that needed inspected or repaired. Hank paid the phone bills. Replacing the truck, along with acquiring insurance, registration, and a state driver's license, now had to wait. I'd drive Hank's car into town when I could. I would have to press my luck on the expired tags of the truck for a few more months.

I opened the notebook and clicked a pen. "I was thinking about installing a temporary ramp."

He waved a hand. "Ramps are for old people. I want you to build that greenhouse you want instead."

I moved on to his busy schedule and speaking over Miller's blaring tunes. "Your nurse is coming on Fridays. How was she? I didn't have time to meet her."

"She poked my incision. Pricked my finger to run levels. Kept lecturing me about things I already know how to do."

"That was the initial check-in. She needs to adjust your blood thinners as needed."

"Great, pricks every week from the she-devil."

My inner educator persisted, knowing my instructions would reach him. "You take the warfarin at bedtime for four weeks. I'll make sure you remember."

"I can remember."

Not the last two nights. "We can put a note on your bathroom mirror."

He grunted. "I'm not a child."

"Adrienne is coming Mondays, Wednesdays, and Fridays for your physical therapy, but you must do the exercises *three* times a day. Would you like my help?"

He clinked ice.

"She talked about partial weight bearing for four weeks. You remember that?"

He hummed with an exaggerated clatter of bottles and jars.

"Hank..."

"Yes, I remember, sweet child. No, I don't need help with those stress-sizes. I put half my weight on the walker. Nurse Needles showed me with the scale she brought."

Tired of competing with Miller, I got up and turned the record player down. "The doctor at the hospital suggested you go to Lupine Meadows for rehab. Would you prefer that? I can drive you."

"That place is a death sentence."

Man, he was crusty. "You might change your mind if you visit?" I consulted the notebook filled with bullet points and charts. I'd laminate the schedule and hang it in several places for him. Laminating meant going to the library's resource center. After all the time spent in town and Plymouth this week, what harm was one more trip? Besides, laminating kind of made me giddy. Oh, the silly things I enjoyed.

"Your occupational therapist comes twice a week for the next month, Tuesdays and Thursdays." World War III had ensued when Victor came for his first visit. I left the room while Victor explained to Hank how to dress, shower, and exercise his upper body.

"Yes, yes, and the Lord Almighty himself is coming on Saturday?"

Bills, visitors, and a colossal headache burden me. Want to switch? I would never say that. Instead, I said, "No, *you* visit the Almighty on Sundays. I'll take you to church." Should I recruit some of his Jolly Jellies to help with that? That meant reaching out to more people. I'd just do it.

A part of me fought the idea, though. Peopling. People. Humans. Liars. People who stare at you like you're crazy. The tug-of-war was real. I missed human contact, but also knew socializing meant I was on the grid more.

Silence. Ice clinking.

Good gravy, these drinks took forever to make. I shifted in my seat. "How was your pain today? Did you need the oxy?"

His shoulders stiffened. "Don't need it. Took it the first few days, but I feel better today. The bottle is in the medicine cabinet, where it shall stay. What nature has made is good enough." He tapped the glass of what had to be an Old Fashioned, his signature drink.

"What are the four *no do* tasks?"

He groaned. "You are such a drag, Jo."

"You know I won't stop until—"

He flapped a hand at my persistence. "No tying shoes, no bends beyond ninety degrees, no pigeon toes, and no crossing legs," he snapped. "I'll wear slippers."

"Good."

The next page was *my* to-do list. I checked off the high-rise toilet, sturdy wingback chairs, slippers, wool socks, and schedule. What remained? Temporary ramp, bills, laminated schedules, daily check-ins, Hank's weekly laundry and groceries, driving him to appointments...

I flipped the page. Expenses. "Hank, we need to reinstate your Medicare coverage."

Louder humming, again. Hank was the slowest bartender ever.

I heaved a sigh and went to the kitchen to plate our meals.

Hank loved his routine. He paid his own bills (something that he'd gotten rusty at, apparently), took his two daily naps, and walked to the mailbox in the afternoons. Sundays, he went to church and got groceries. Twice a week he visited his friends at The Daily Donut.

Morgan wanted me to *care* for Hank, too, in whatever capacity it required. So, I gave him eggs, pickles, and goat milk. We played Scrabble on Sundays. I brought him at least one decent dinner a week, courtesy of Tillie's recipes. And much more.

His injury had been an earthquake to our sound routine, and I awaited the aftershock.

I returned to the living room with our dinners and laid the plates on the table, putting an extra empty plate in Tillie's spot, as was our custom. If Hank started asking me to pile food on her plate, we'd need to have a talk.

He shoved a drink in my hand. "A taste of sweet, a dash of bitter, and a long sip of vitality. May your birthday remind you of the sweet times, the hard moments, and the days when..." He took a hearty drag, and said, "...it calls for booze!"

Cherry, orange rind, dash of bitters, and ground-up sugar cubes completed the drink. Hank's metaphor did not escape my understanding. I sipped, inhaling the bitter with the sweet. His drinks were deadly. The bourbon burned.

"Hank, the Medicare..."

His smile slipped. "I will, Jo. I will."

I softened my tone. "I can help."

"Tomorrow, though. I—I'm tired."

I helped him readjust his posture, and we ate in mixed silence and chitchat.

"Top-notch, Jo." Hank scooped a bite of pot roast.

"I learned from the best."

He cast a look heavenward. "Yours may even be better, kiddo."

"You're too sweet, Hank." I yawned, despite the early hour.

"Did you have a pleasant walk today?" he asked.

I nodded. The wooded trails held a sense of peaceful silence.

"Find the bus yet?"

"*The Magic School Bus*?" I chuckled with a roll of my eyes, but suddenly felt a pang of nostalgia for my students.

"Morgan made it as a shelter for emergencies like anarchy, alien invasions, or Armageddon. You should keep looking."

One would think I'd have discovered the bus by the number of walks I took. If it existed. But my trails only covered the perimeter. I needed substantial debris clearance to extract the inner trails. Still, unless Morgan had a stockpile of money in the bus—with my luck it would be more beets—it was the least of my concerns. Speaking of money... "Hey, I found more hidden money. In an old tea canister in the kitchen."

Hank laughed. "Enough to pay our bills?"

"More like a grocery trip or two."

"Think we can have an electrician check out my stove? It's been acting funny."

Electrical wires and I didn't get along. One small zap had told me that. Pipes were going to be put in the category of No Dice, too.

Once we shifted from my checklist to enjoying dinner with stories, my anxiety loosened a bit. Hank had a way of distracting my jagged thoughts.

"While digging for his bunker, Morgan found these bones on the property, later identified as animal, not human. It gave me a great idea for a new game," he said, smiling widely.

Hank's deficient hearing missed Chip's bark as he recounted more details.

"...so as soon as my boss got wind of—"

Chip barked again, louder.

Once.

The fork slipped from my fingers and clinked on the fine wedding dish. I braved, "You expecting an eBay delivery?" Though Chip didn't bark at the delivery truck. Who would be here on a Sunday night?

He frowned. "Got it last week." He pointed to an un-opened shipping box, presumably holding the Legos he ordered, despite his fixed income, whenever he went to the library to use the internet. Had his late son, Theo, loved Legos?

Tires spinning in the rutted section of the driveway sounded in the clearing.

"One of your Jolly Jellies?" I asked, standing, heartbeat quickening as I shoved my hand into the vest pocket with the pepper spray.

"No."

Chip barked again. Once. Stranger.

What if it was someone I knew? Had Tate found me? Was he out? Would he...?

Why did Tate always come to mind first?

Hank's chair scraped the floor. I was halfway to the window by the time he stood and fumbled with his walker.

"Stay, Hank. I'll get it." I pulled the pepper spray from my vest's pocket.

9

— · —

HANK

Oh, Jo was not happy.

And I was about to change that, for I invited this visitor after all.

I firmly believed that serendipity was God's hand. Theo taught me that every chance in life is precious. When the Lord plops something in your lap, you take it. I blinked wet eyes and hustled my old bones to the door.

Showtime.

Everett and I had a friendly chat earlier this evening on the phone. He was perfect for the property. He had more labor experience than Jo and I combined. Tenfold. *If I'm being a bird on a branch, then fine, slap a label on my head and call me a meddler.* I'd dealt with worse. Somebody had to do something before Jo allowed this property to suck her under like it did to Morgan.

Jo whipped a thunderstruck expression at me. I braced for the impact.

"You invited him back here?" She drew the curtain closed.

Had she met him already? I scratched my head, trying to remember if she said so. "We're in a pickle, Jo. And not because of Morgan's stockpile of pickles. Winter is coming.

We could use this fella's help. We can get money from him paying rent. He has skills. Let's give him a chance."

She flung open the door but cooled her jets and planted on the formal Jo Sawyer façade. Heavens, she was good at faking it.

"Good evening?" Her words came out more like a question. She shifted to salty mode.

Chip blocked Everett and Lark's ascent to the porch, and they stood on the driveway beside his truck.

Jo said, "Chip, come," and he settled beside her, tail wagging.

"Hi, Everett. Good of you to come." I turned to the girl. She was adorable with her rainbow hat. Her mom seemed absent, as implied by Everett during our call. Poor thing. "And Lark, is it?"

She nodded.

Everett ran a hand through messy hair. At least he'd shaved since I last saw him at Mitch's. Smart kid. "Good evening, Hank. Thanks for the invite." He offered a small bouquet to Jo. "For you."

Even smarter. I winked at him, liking him more.

He cleared his throat. "I, uh, wanted to follow up on my application and Hank suggested we come by for cake to talk about it."

Jo met this with silence.

"About the rental and job?" he said, dark eyebrows lifting.

"This is Jo." I squeezed her shoulder. Though it sounded like these two had already met.

"Nice to meet you officially, Ms. Sawyer." He thrust out a hand, but his gesture went disregarded. Jo stood stock-still, her hands glued inside her vest pockets.

"Just Jo. She goes by Jo," I intervened. *Jesus, Mary, Joseph, and the wee donkey, Jo. Snap out of it!* Her nerves around strangers and computers stemmed from past experiences with her ex-husband. But this was now. She needed to stop living in the past.

"Josie is fine," she breathed.

"We can come later if now is inconvenient," he quickly corrected.

"I made a unicorn cake!" his daughter announced, brimming with a smile. Her high-pitched voice caused Chip's tail to tap a few times. He quivered in his waiting posture, wanting to lick her and play.

"Uh, what?" Pink bloomed on Jo's cheeks.

"For my birfday. It was last week. Dat book you suggested in de library was perfect! My nana baked it wif me. My daddy and I got de ingredients. We made four layers!"

A crinkle of a smile stretched across Everett's face. "Lark, we're here to discuss housing."

"And to have cake. How old are you, sweet lass?" I asked.

Delight puddled in her eyes. "Five! I go to school next year!" She nodded emphatically, her dark curls bobbing as they protruded from the hat.

"Well, I'll be. Got another birthday here last week, too, plus thirty." I nudged Jo, who was as statue-like as her dog protector. "We have cake inside. A lovely almond butter cake. Can you have nuts?"

"She doesn't have any allergies," Everett said. "We could come back another time..."

Don't wuss out, man. You're halfway in.

I squeezed Jo's shoulder in a gesture of *it's okay, they're okay.* Chip's tail tapped again.

"Do come in." I pivoted around in the walker to begin the trek to the table. "We were about to have the cake."

Lark eyed my ride. "Nana had wheels like yours. Wif pink tennis balls when she broke her bones."

"Is your grandmother a hipster, too?" I asked, the pun getting no response from the group. The crowd was rough tonight.

"She's my great-granny so we call her Nana!"

Jo rubbed Chip's head.

"Can I pet him?" Lark asked, approaching Chip.

"Yes," Jo said.

I said, "His name is Chocolate Chip."

Lark's eyes glowed. "Like de cookie!" She stroked his head.

I could see that the little girl's presence was softening Jo's hard edge. Children lowered your guard, melting you like chocolate left out in the summer sun.

Sweet harmony from Ella Fitzgerald filled the main cabin, slicing through a brittle awkwardness as we entered. Everett pulled up another chair at the round table to make four. He moved aside the pile of old Sunday newspapers after I gave him a nod of approval.

Jo disappeared into the kitchen and returned with the cake and knife.

"There are candles, too. Got teal ones. Your favorite color," I said. I coughed and sipped my diluted Old Fashioned. I should've been drinking warm tea. Eh, later.

"Don't need them," Jo said.

Lark said, "Everybody has to make a wish on deir birfday." At least the little girl was on my team.

Jo smiled tightly, rose, and grabbed the candles. Stuck a few into the cake.

Everett took the matches from her. "Bad luck to light your own birthday candles."

Earlier, I promised Jo I wouldn't sing, and so I made up a tradition on the spot. "We will let Jo close her eyes and make a wish. Ella will sing for us." And that she did, lovely and rich. A draft from the nearby window stirred the flames.

"Make a wish!" Lark said, wigging in her seat.

With a puff, the candles went out.

Jo needed to lighten up. Everett could be our saving grace. Letting her adjust to the idea, I made small talk about town, local work, and snow predictions, in between answering Everett's questions about the property and its history.

When we ran out of topics, I eyed Jo, who was dragging a fork through the frosting on her plate.

"Jo?" I coaxed. "Why don't we tell them about the cabin and the work we need done."

"I—I need to run a credit report before I decide."

I released a pent-up breath. That was a start. A weird one, but not for Jo I supposed.

Everett leaned forward. "Do you need more information from me? I can pay first month's rent and the security deposit now. The ad said cash." He reached into his shirt pocket and drew out a wad.

This was our kind of fella! Hiring him and forging a rental agreement wasn't on me, though.

Jo gaped at his offered handful of fifties but didn't take it. He hadn't even placed the money in an envelope. Is that what kids did now?

I gathered the dishes nearest to me. "Lark, my lady, would you like to help me? Then we can grab the Scrabble."

Lark picked up each plate and fork, stacking them into a neat pile in her small hands. "What's Scrabble?"

"Birdie, we can't stay for games." Everett pushed his chair out to stand.

"But, Daddy..." A fork fell off her dainty pile, and he bent to retrieve it.

"Help with the dishes, but we've got to get back to your aunt and cousins." He pulled on his jacket.

I patted Everett on the shoulder. "We'll handle the dishes. You two talk shop, okay?"

Chatty Lark made eavesdropping difficult. I caught snippets of their conversation from the kitchen sink.

Lark was a giggler, too, playing more than washing. And singing while she worked.

"Here, you wash, then put in the drying rack, okay?"

"Mm-hmm," she said, dipping forks into the water and twirling them around to get them soapy.

"I'll put the leftovers away." I inched—rolled was more like it—closer to the kitchen entrance, to listen.

"The cabin is equipped with a sofa, a table with chairs, shelves, appliances, two bedrooms with mattresses on frames, a few linens, and utensils. Utilities are free, but there is no Wi-Fi. You'll need to set up an account and pay for the landline."

Good, she was rambling. Way better than frozen-statue Jo.

"Did I see an outhouse?" Everett asked, a lightness in his tone.

I snorted, and Jo pierced me with a look. I ducked behind the wall.

"We use lake water and a sewage tank for indoor plumbing, but yes, each cabin has an outdoor compost toilet that you can use whenever you want," she said. She didn't hide the exasperation in her voice.

I snuck another look around the wall.

Everett's mouth tugged on a grin. "Did you like *Little House on the Prairie* as a kid?"

I chuckled, but a frown dropped the corners of Everett's lips in response to Jo's sourpuss expression. His banter didn't hit the mark.

I feel your pain, kid.

"I can give you information for the credit check. Whatever you need," he offered, as he sat across from her, his hands knotted together as if he were sitting for an interrogation or interview.

"Thank you."

I kept my thermostat low, but the frost from the living room was palpable. *Geesh, Jo.*

Chip barked from outside. He sensed Jo's anxiety.

I maneuvered to the sink. "When you're done, how about a pop?"

"An ice pop?"

I scratched my forehead, suddenly seeing stars. I should have taken another one of the pain pills today. "A lollipop? If your dad says it's okay, you can take one home." I wagged a finger toward the jar on the counter. "Tootsie filled. There are butterscotch candies in there, too."

Her brown eyes widened. "Yes, please! But I have a toofache."

"That's no good. No Tootsies, then. Just a plain one. Save it for tomorrow. We had a lot of sugar tonight." I inhaled, aching for a seat. Too much moving around with the stupid walker today. I made for the living room. Time to give Jo a push and provide moral support for Everett.

His posture straightened when he saw me, then he brushed a finger over his chin. Lark bounced to his side. "Can I use de bafroom?"

"That way." I pointed and Lark scurried down the hallway. I turned to Everett and Josie. "We'll need to get the place ready." Jo shot her ice my way. Lucky for her, I wore a sweater. "But that won't take long, right?"

She nodded. "Yes, that's if I decide—"

"How is October first?" I asked.

That would give Jo a few weeks to prepare...mostly mentally.

Everett stood and shoved hands in his jeans pockets. "How about next week? The credit check should be quick. I can pay for the partial month, too."

"I'll think about it," Jo said.

That was better than a no. My head felt heavy as a rush of sweat made my palms clammy. I needed to sit soon.

Determination gleamed in friendly brown eyes. "If you need urgent work around the property, we've got eight to twelve weeks left, depending on snow and ground freezing. The sooner I can get on, the better. Then, over winter, I'll handle anything inside which needs addressed. And the cabin...fixing that can wait. Really. Minimal is fine. Heat, power, water, bed, and I'm good. So, the work you need done...?"

Ah yes, the job. About time these two stumbling kids got to the heart of it. We needed a handyman, especially come wintertime. Morgan told me Jo only visited the cabin in the summers as a girl when our biggest adversary was mosquitoes.

Jo just chewed on her lip.

"What type of work needs to be done in particular? You have an extensive property—" He looked at me with the question since Jo had gone silent again.

I said, "We have six hundred acres. About a square mile. Nice, neat square in the middle of nowhere." I eased myself onto the sofa. I'd be damned if I sat in another uncomfortable hardback chair. The cushion was a hug around my bottom. I exhaled a soft moan.

Everett nodded. "That's a lot of property to maintain. Did you want to have coffee and review your job specifics? I can come by at your convenience or we can meet in town."

Come on, Jo, give him something! Say yes.

Everett tried again, spots of pink forming on his angled cheekbones. "Yard work, gardening, landscaping, pavers, woodwork, basic machinery upkeep, a bit with cars. You name it, I can do it. I'm a quick learner and have connections with electricians and contractors."

Everett's desperation was palpable. We'd had a good chat on the phone. He told me about his sister-in-law, the baby, and how important it was for him to settle somewhere with his daughter. "That greenhouse you want, too, Jo," I added, wiping my forehead with a handkerchief.

She looked up from her wringing hands. "That's only a wish, Hank. Not a priority," she said, her voice shaky. "But yes, we have a few overdue projects, daily maintenance, getting ready for winter, and I'm sure we may have troubleshooting. I don't know yet. Can you fix leaky sinks?"

His eyes danced. "You bet."

Jo nodded, her lips pressed thin.

Everett's eyebrows screwed into a dubious expression. "You haven't been here long?"

"Only since spring."

He turned to me.

"Oh, I've been here for decades. But my buddy Morgan was the one running the show. Ask Jo. I can hardly remember to feed the chickens. Why not schedule a day to chat? Jo is great with plans."

She tucked long hair behind her ear and gave me a *Will you stop sharing so much?* look.

Aww, shucks, everyone here knew about Morgan. Jo didn't like to talk about her past, but he was my past, too.

Lark bounced into the room, tucking the lollipop into her pocket.

Jo walked them outside. Setting up a time to meet, I hoped.

She returned, closing the front door behind her. Wide, mossy-green eyes stared at me. "Oh, Hank, why did you do that?"

"When will they move in?"

She grimaced and shifted her gaze away.

"Oh, Jo..."

Waving hands, she hurried away—likely to make me tea and avoid my pestering. "I told him I'll think about it and run that credit check," she said over her shoulder.

"What's there to think about?" I shifted my old bones into a better position, gathered the small pile of newspapers, and began tearing them into little pieces for compost.

She emerged a few minutes later with my tea. "You want me to say yes?"

"Does the sun shine?"

"But, Hank, he—"

"Is our answer. Now, be a dear and hand me the compost can."

10

EVERETT

Josie's phone call came when I was just about to give up.

The woman got right to the point. "Hi. You can have the place. Is a one-year lease okay with you?"

"Yes. Can I move in next week?" My pulse soared. Finally, some good news.

Silence. Had the call dropped?

"O-okay. See you then."

"W-wait. The job?"

Another pause. "I can offer you a steep reduction in rent for the work. Let's discuss work logistics when you arrive." She rattled off numbers. She was all business, but I liked the sound of her voice. Clear, pleasant, educated. Hmm. I'd be a boarder, so to speak, with no paycheck. Well, shit. If this was my next step on getting Lark back and closing my case, then so be it.

She must have sensed my disappointment.

"We can see how it goes and, after six months, evaluate, and then do an official hire on paper. Besides, you have that other job with P&J Landscaping."

Yeah, not exactly, but I wasn't going to correct her. With more enthusiasm, I said, "Okay."

I fiddled with the television remote control. Nerf darts flew over my head as Liam shot at Shawn. Penny screeched from the back of the house, probably finding some horrific mess.

"Great." She disconnected.

That was it.

I was taking a leap of faith here.

Fine, I was taking a gigantic leap. Would this be enough to get Carolyn off my back?

The cabin came furnished, so that helped. I'd pull money from my account to buy the essentials. Lark had it easy the past few months living here with Penny and the boys. Television, candy, company, toys. And here I was, moving her thirty minutes out of town where her closest companions would be an old guy in a walker and a woman who was a mystery.

I had trouble describing Josie Sawyer.

Those who isolated had something to hide...or run away from. She seemed capable and prickly, but I sensed a deeper tale. There always was.

With mixed feelings after the call, I emailed ProspNet about the pen-testing job. The contract work would pad my account. They issued 1099s, meaning proof of on-the-books pay. Once they saw my excellent work, they'd refer me to other cybersecurity jobs, or so I hoped. I could still proceed with the contractor licensure, too, over winter. Somehow, I would stitch these jobs into something to appease DCYF.

As for that *other* email...

I'd scooped it out of the trash email folder and kept re-reading it. They paid twice as much as ProspNet. The work was not the typical bug hunting and pen testing that ethical hacking involved.

It was...

A bit *more*. Gray was an understatement.

The idea of that job marinated in my brain ever since I got the email.

Locking the thought away, I got to packing.

I blew heat into my hands as I started my truck. It was moving day. It was kind of sad that all my belongings fit in the bed of my small pickup.

Carefully, I looked for light gloves while being mindful of the mums in the front seat. First impressions were crucial. I had been clumsy during my previous encounters with Josie. Now was the opportune moment to cement an amicable relationship with my landlady and employer.

My breath formed before me. This cold snap was early for mid-September. A light frost covered Penny's too-long front lawn and the rusty toy trucks, Nerf guns, a scattering of blue and neon orange darts, and broken this and that lodged in the weedy grass. I'd done my best to keep the place tidy when time allowed, more focused on keeping laundry and dishes clean than on the futile picking up of toys.

The truck's timing belt squealed. After I got us settled into the cabin, I'd fix the belt. The weather app showed a great forecast for the rest of the week, so I had to make the most of it. This drop in temps would fizzle out by tomorrow. Still, long, snowy winters lingered in the Whites. I mulled over getting a plow. People paid a decent penny for having their driveways snowplowed.

When the truck warmed up a decade later, I hollered for Lark. She dawdled. Always.

"But, Daddyyyy! I don't wanna say goodbye!" She pouted.

I gave her a hurry-up look.

She tiptoed to the truck, her eyes cast downward, and her pink consignment-store coat zipped to her chin. She buried her hands deep in the pockets and her chest seemed to be moving like the scene in *Alien* before the creature emerged from the person's abdomen.

"Lark..."

Something released a rapid succession of squeaks.

Penny hurried out of the house, her blonde hair a mop on her head, and peanut-butter splattered on her stretched-out, long sweater. Spawn One and Spawn Two had done something ungodly with peanut butter earlier. Deep circles lodged under tired eyes. "Hey, guys...another hug goodbye, sweetie pie?"

Penny would probably miss her niece more than me. I was just manual labor and another smelly male. I was also the one responsible for Jake's first incarceration. I persuaded him to do that job. My chest tightened. I was the sole male support for her and the boys until his return. Jake would be absent for the birth of his third kid. Penny's sister, Claire, was driving up from Nashua in six weeks to be on baby watch, at least.

Regardless of whether she was pissed at me about the first time or not, I held no blame for his return visit. That was all on Jake. Even so, guilt was my constant companion, a shadow to my every step.

"No hug, Lark?" Penny repeated.

Lark froze. She loved hugs. Especially baby-belly hugs.

"I think Furry"—I took a gamble on which hamster hid in her coat—"would appreciate staying home with Shawn and Liam." I wasn't bringing a rodent with me to the new place.

Lark handed the hamster over to Penny, then wrapped her arms around her as if Penny were a tree trunk. She rested a cheek on her aunt's expanding belly. "Aww! She kicked me. She knows I'm leaving, too?"

Penny swiped at her sweaty bangs. "She does. You'll be back. Your dad promised."

I gave a shaky laugh. "I'll check in on you, okay? And I'll be here to babysit the boys next week when you visit Jake."

More hugs, more tears, and off we went to a cabin in the peaceful woods.

JOSIE

I stood in front of my planters, hands on my hips, admiring the vibrant yellow and orange mums. I realized my mouth was gaping when a flying bug made a quick dive in and out. I quickly clamped it shut. The past few weeks had been an overload of the senses and the filled window boxes not only gave me a moment's pause, but they also floored me. Their simplicity, their beauty. Everett's act of kindness.

Then old Josie, the doubter, wondered why he was being over-the-top kind.

Here I was, suspecting a friendly gesture of being something Machiavellian instead of appreciating it. *Josie, he's a landscaper. He's trying to make a good first impression.* I let the non-cynical version of myself overrule the skeptic. As Hank would say, "Put some grease on those wheels."

Mums sat in all the planters, even at Hank's cabin. I hadn't been present for Everett's arrival, having gotten sidetracked on a walk with Chip to check out a recently broken piece in the fencing. Cataloging the chinks in the property was a daunting task. Now I had Everett to help.

My eyes passed over my lovely little porch project that was going nowhere. I hoped to limit the number of tasks I requested of him, so I had jumped headfirst into repairs this past week. Big mistake. Planks, hammer, nails, saw, sawhorses, and a colossal mess decorated the area in front of the porch. To top things off, I had a nasty splinter so deep it might stay there through winter. I gave the thumb another once-over, squinting at the little lodged-in bugger.

Chip stopped slopping up water in his bowl and barked twice.

I spun around, knowing who strolled up the driveway, boots crunching on the gravel rhythmically.

"Hi, Josie. Like the flowers? Got them discounted from work."

A flannel shirt with an open collar clung to broad shoulders, and his slimming jeans highlighted his muscular legs. Oh, yes, and the five o'clock shadow on a sharp chin was still there. Couldn't forget that. I halted my thoughts before I listed his other admirable physical attributes. He was here for work only.

Don't be frosty. Be nice. Hank's words echoed in my mind. I swallowed. "How much do I owe you?"

"How about coffee? Plus, we can talk about what you need done." He gave a subtle nod to the explosion of wood and nails before us. "You mentioned a sink?"

"Oh, yes. How is Lark settling in?"

"She claimed the bigger bedroom. The cabin is cozy. Looks nice. Thanks to you, I suspect?"

I gave a modest shrug.

"Have to sort out the wood stove. Chilly."

"I know it's weird how cold it is today, but there should be heat. I set the thermostat on the wall. Heat registers, uh, the vents. Are they open? The stove is more for the cold winter days." At least, according to Hank.

"I figured that. There's no reading on the thermostat. I felt heat from the vents earlier though. At first, I assumed it was on a timer, but the screen was blank when I checked it. Got any spare batteries? Might just be that."

"I put new ones in this week." I suppressed a groan. Everything had been working fine a few days ago, but Hank mentioned one incident of his power flickering and his stove was being temperamental. "Did you check the light switches? Power is on?"

He gave me a lopsided smile. There were his dimples again. One on each cheek.

Was that a yes or no?

"I hung laminated instructions beside the thermostat. It's more complicated than typical electrical setups, but you're familiar with these things. You mentioned vo-tech, right?"

"Yeah, my concentration was in electronics and computer programming, but I also took wood, auto, and metal shop classes. Anyway, didn't think to check the power, honestly. Thought it was just dead batteries. It's so sunny today that I didn't turn any lights on. I know a bit about battery banks, plumbing, and the basics of electrical circuits, but off-the-grid heating and water systems are not as familiar to me. I'm more focused on woodwork, landscaping, and building projects currently." He rubbed a hand on his beard scruff, a shade darker than his light brown hair. "But I'm eager to help with troubleshooting."

Electronics didn't excite me, but if he enjoyed it, I'd let him have it.

"Anyway, perhaps we can see what's what around here and I can familiarize myself with your system?" He tucked his thumbs into his pockets.

Goose bumps rose on my skin. I had not lost power at my place and my heat was fine. If Everett's power was down, it meant Hank's might be, too. Before the move, I purchased a dozen books on off-the-grid systems that covered everything from water to heat to power. Even gosh-darn compost toilets. I had taken a mental AP course on OTG living.

And I hated it.

My aversion to all things OTG brought back memories of a student, Nick, the most difficult kid to connect with during my speech and language sessions. The other kids enjoyed coming to my classroom. Not Nick. That bridge to open-mindedness with him was finally within reach...when my life fell apart and I got fired.

I rubbed my throat. Like my former student, no matter how many people—in my case, one, Hank—tried to coax me into enjoying this OTG-living crap, I wasn't having it. It was frustrating and often overwhelming.

I snapped out of my melancholy. "Okay, I'm going to throw you in the deep end. You ready?" I hadn't been and was still barely treading water.

His smile widened. "I'm a sponge. Bring it on."

"I'll grab my notebook. Once we figure out the power and heat, we can brew coffee to celebrate." Celebrate? *Good gravy, Josie.* I wanted to kick myself. Again. This summer, I learned *not* to kick the equipment.

I jumped over the porch pile of despair and ducked inside to grab the notebook I called Homestead Living 101 along with a few more batteries. Then we were off to his cabin. Dropping into educator mode, I said, "The property has communal utilities, each connected to the cabins so that we can set our own thermostats and manage water. I've determined the ideal thermostat temperature is seventy-eight degrees for summer, and what I read for winter is sixty-eight to seventy-two."

He nodded, keeping pace with me. "Would it be easier if we walked the grounds while you explain?"

"Tomorrow? Let's start with an overview and get your electricity and heat working."

"Okay. Then I will pop by later to look at your sink?"

"Thanks."

My brain was already on to the next tasks of the day. *Bring Hank dinner. Milk Gilda. Give Hank his meds. Finish Hank's laundry. Write out the first check for the hospital payment plan.* I disliked using the bank account, but there were unavoidable on-grid necessities. *Work on a grocery list. Make sure Everett and Lark have wood for their stove. Put an ax by his woodshed so he can do it himself. And...*

Ugh, my brain was waterlogged with tasks. I had no time or patience for my grid to be temperamental.

I must have been mumbling under my breath—an unfortunate new habit I formed with living alone—because Everett rested a hand on my forearm.

"Hey. Give me simple stuff, too. Anything. Assign me the work, and I'll get it done."

Can you pay our bills?

We entered his cabin, cold and dank despite the plug-in air fresheners I put in the outlets. They didn't work when the electricity went down. I tested a light switch. Nothing.

I pocketed the batteries. No point in trying them. "Give me the play-by-play of what happened."

"The heat kicked on at some point, as I heard the whoosh. I got distracted with unloading, and then Lark mentioned she was cold."

"Okay, so it *was* working, which means electricity was on at some point. Then something happened?" I plopped the notebook down and pointed to the laminated sheet on the counter. "The heat isn't electric. It's a ground source, but it requires electricity to work."

Looking in the fridge, I confirmed the power was truly out. I ran through my mental checklist when something wasn't working. "Perhaps it's corrosion on the battery connections. I haven't cleaned them in a while. In the fall, the electric system transitions from solar to wind. I had a technician come out once this summer to explain it to me. We still have a surplus of solar power from August, even on grayer days. If solar goes down, it would also affect the solar-heated hot water." I paused for a beat, surprised that I remembered it all. "Is that Greek to you?"

"No. I'm following. Fascinating. You use solar-heated water, not ground-source heated?"

"We use both. I think. My uncle covered his bases, that's for sure. Can you help me figure that all out?" I scrunched my face. "You really do like this stuff? Not just trying to impress me here?"

"Yes, ma'am. Glad you hired me?"

Relief filled my chest. "Oh my gosh, I'm not a ma'am. Josie is good. I'm not that old yet." I laughed at myself, but felt heat fill my cheeks.

"My brain and hands are yours."

Okay, he really needed to put those dimples away.

He tapped my diagrams in the notebook. "So, the solar panels and all that are fine, then."

"How is your water?"

He turned on the sink tap and ran a finger under the flow. "Warm. It might still be warm from the heated water in the tank."

"It comes from the lake. I have a submersible pump and tanks for storage."

"Glycol heats the pipes in winter?" he asked.

I shrugged, scratching my head. "Think so. I read something about that somewhere." I puffed out a sigh. "This stuff literally hurts my brain," I admitted, surprised at my candor around him. "Still want to live here?"

"Definitely. Sounds like you're doing okay. Nothing is ever hopeless." He tapped off fingers as he spoke. "Solar and wind components—check. Saw the panels on the roof. Where do you harness the wind?"

"Turbines. Farther back on the property, on a hill."

"Gotcha. Water—a non-issue. Now on to the electricity and heat components near the house."

I nodded.

"Tell me about the ground-source heat pump first." He leaned on his elbows, captivated by the notebook.

I traced a drawing with my finger. "There are loops of pipes in the ground filled with fluid. There's a bunch of moving parts, too many for me to remember. A whole slew of problems could be the cause." I turned a page and showed a checklist. "Thermostat, restricted air flow, filters, leaking ducts, refrigerant leak, power loss, closed registers, capacitor, reversing valve."

"Wow."

"Yeah, *wow* is an understatement. My uncle had been a game designer with Hank. I think he was a closet engineer.

The power going down suggests that this issue is not related to the heat pump. Thank goodness. Sounds electrical. The pump uses electricity to power the compressor, fan, and all that." I stretched a kink in my neck. "You can use the wood stove while I figure it out."

"We," he said.

"Huh?"

"We. Let's go check the battery bank first." He lifted a brow. "Remember, deep end. Drop me in and I'll swim." He added with a grin, "Or doggy-paddle."

He pointed to the book on the coffee table—*The Kilowatt Is Your Friend.* "Could you leave that here? It'll be a welcome refresher and help me help you."

Ah, that's where my book had run off to. I probably left it here while decorating the cabin.

He asked, "And your notebook, if you don't mind?"

I waved a hand. "Be my guest. The notebook and I need a short break."

We both smiled.

I heaved a breath. "Let's get the wood stove going so Lark doesn't get too cold, then check the battery bank."

Lark came bounding into the room, cocooned in a blanket. "Brr!"

She was too cute for her own good.

After setting up the stove, with about fifteen questions from her, we got the main room warm.

"Cell reception here is the pits," Everett said as we walked to the battery shed, Lark on our heels.

I would not commiserate. I was glad the surrounding mountains blocked most calls. "I left information on your table about the phone company so you can set up your landline. Internet in town is good."

Hank was on his porch, having just completed his journey to the mailbox at the end of the driveway. He was already moving a little faster in his walker. "My lady Lark!" His voice was loud and cheery, though he seemed out of breath. "Do you like Legos?"

She looked at Everett, hope spreading her chestnut-brown eyes wide.

"Sure, Birdie. Just for a little. We need to unpack."

She skipped to Hank's place.

Our steps crunched a path to a shed where the batteries lived. I unlocked it and stepped in. Even in the day, we needed flashlights. I handed him one from a small table just inside the entrance, then consulted the notebook. "My wish list includes an insulated box with a fan to remove hydrogen gas released during charging."

He shined the light around. "Do you have a wiring conduit that allows warm air from the house to be moved around the batteries during winter?" He approached the batteries and glanced at the terminals. "These may need cleaning."

I half shrugged, skimming notes. "No. Right now, I'm using heating pads. If we air seal it against drafts, it will work better. That may be our issue today. We've had colder nights already."

"I can check and get the insulation. You'll want this done before it gets too cold." He glanced at the thermometer. "This looks fine. Maybe it is the wind turbines if the system has already switched from solar to wind? We can check the blades, gearbox, and generator just to rule it out. If the solar is still active, can we inspect your roof panels?"

"In order to inspect the turbines, we'd need to hire somebody to come with a gin pole and tilt the tower down. And no way am I climbing on my roof to check my solar panels." I added, "Nor are you."

"Do the turbines need to be serviced? I can schedule that. Bet they'll inspect the solar panels, too. If not, I'll find out who can." He pulled out his phone and tapped in notes.

"Yes, thanks." Grateful, I wondered how much it would cost. I joined him by the batteries. "The batteries look okay, just a bit dirty. Next step is the inverter and controller. I think." I aimed the flashlight on the page of notes and pictures. Everett looked over my shoulder.

My throat felt warm under his scrutiny. I continued, pointing to my diagram, "One wire runs underground from the tower to the charge controller, then the inverter—where the solar power comes in and DC is converted to AC power, or something like that—then the conduit goes to the batteries." I glided my finger along the conduits going in and out. "Then the power continues to the cabins."

"Love it."

"At least one of us does."

"Let's try cleaning the batteries first before we check everything else. Sometimes the simplest solution is *the* solution."

I grabbed a rag, and we cleaned the terminals, then inspected the connections for corrosion. Nothing looked troublesome.

Chip's barks sounded from Hank's porch, followed by a whoop from Lark.

"The lights are on!" Hank hollered.

Everett smiled at me. "Guess that was it. But I sure appreciated the very thorough lesson. This place is fantastic."

"Coffee time?" I asked, relieved to be done with the tutorial. I was spent. How did people *like* this stuff?

Our proximity in the shed and his smile elicited heart palpitations that weren't entirely unpleasant. And I allowed myself one small smile as we strode to his cabin. *Let's see what this man can do.*

11

EVERETT

"Let dere be heat!" Lark rubbed her hands together and did a jig.

I adjusted the front intake on the wood stove with the heavy-duty gloves and then sank onto the couch. Dust motes flew into the air. I zipped my laptop case closed, then reviewed the task list on my phone.

"Achoo!" Lark sneezed with her signature exaggeration. The cuteness had worn off today though. "Daddy, I need a purple chewy again."

Antihistamine. "Let's see if fresh air helps. Those make you sleepy." A soft, swooshing hum came from the basement. "Let's not waste any more wood, even though it's been fun this week having fires." My back ached from chopping wood yesterday to keep the sheds stocked.

"Aww, but I wanna roast marshies dis time."

"Another time. We have the dentist today."

"I don't wanna see de dentist. My toof is fine." She winced even saying it.

"This wood made a mess. Let's vacuum and clean before leaving."

"Time to vroom de room?"

"Good one." I loved her rhyming series of books. Who needed kindergarten? Well, I did.

Today's plan involved errands. Josie and I discussed an extensive project list for me. I was psyched.

I'd spent many hours the past two days reading Josie's books to familiarize myself with the system. Made me regret not going to college. I crossed the ramp off her wish list after convincing Josie that we weren't equipped to set up the heavy-duty accessibility options Hank may need down the line. If his needs increased, he would benefit with a move to an assisted living facility, like Gram's, over outfitting the current cabin design. This place wasn't suitable for that setup. Gram broke her hip but recovered well due to the retirement home's accessibility.

With the sink already fixed, the list now included pruning and cleaning gardens, clearing paths, repairing the front porch, checking the turbines and scheduling a service for them along with the solar panels, insulating the battery bank, checking the propane tank (which I figured out was the fuel source for the glycol-heated water lines), cleaning the flues, servicing the generators, readying the sheds, adjusting the solar panels, chopping cord wood...and more. Plenty to keep me busy now and through winter. Josie said she'd help.

Hank mentioned Josie's dream list, which included a greenhouse, and as a landscaper, I was excited to tackle that project. I had a few friends who could use some cash.

I turned off the vacuum and moved on to wiping the counters.

Lark came out of hiding. She hated the vacuum. "Finish breakfast. We have lots to do." I needed to set up the landline, too. I could do my ProspNet work in town, but I preferred quiet hours at night at home.

Here in the sticks, I had several internet options, each with caveats: a satellite dish, a booster on the cell phone, fixed wireless broadband, or a turbo hub. Every solution had a *but*. I suspected a stipulation hid in the ten pages of the rental agreement about no building or additions, which meant a few of those options were off the table. Josie ran a tight ship, even if she had given me latitude to delve into the grid workings.

Going to the library or a cafe daily was another choice.

With Lark.

Peachy. How did single parents do this? How had Fran done this?

When I thought of Fran, my conscience tumbled down another path. Was I the reason she'd sought relief in drugs? Because she couldn't manage on her own with a baby while her ex-husband sat in prison? Was this all my fault? Sometimes I wanted to call my mom and ask her what to do. The last time I saw my parents was at my arraignment. Made me sad for Lark, Shawn, and Liam that my parents wanted nothing to do with any of us now.

I located the broom to clean my feelings away. What caused this spiral? Oh yeah, no internet.

I swept the main room of our one-story cabin. The décor followed a homey White Mountains theme: quilts, a bear lamp base, pine cones in a ceramic bowl at the table, and leaf-patterned hand towels.

The kitchen needed a better exhaust; it smelled of fried eggs and burned toast, evidence of my subpar cooking skills. Thank goodness Lark liked PB & J sandwiches. Josie had gifted us a jar of raspberry jam that I ate with a spoon. It was that good.

Bonus—no Nerf darts or toys to trip me. Or grumpy sister-in-law.

Our porch angled southeast, so the morning sun streamed in through the two windows flanking the front door. The comfort of my own place felt good.

I was thinking of buying a rainbow blanket or sheets or something for Lark's room. Her toys had fit into one box—three puzzles, a building set, a handful of books, a few small plush animals, Kitty doll, coloring books, Play-doh, a bin of kinetic sand Gram got her, and a box of broken crayons.

"I wanna see de chickens and goat." Lark pouted.

"Later."

After sweeping, I wriggled into my jacket. "Bundle up. It's cold today." A smudge of peanut butter traced the cuff of her beanie.

I adjusted the wood stove before we left.

A half hour later, we walked along Main Street of Silent Creek, Lark avoiding stepping on cracks. "Story hour is at two." She pointed to the large clock tower above the town hall as she collided with me. "Daddy! No cracks!"

"You can tell time?"

"Nana showed me."

"Dentist is first, Birdie. Library is after. Then Nana's and the hardware store and groceries."

After the dentist, Lark held my hand as we walked to the library. Thankfully, the dentist agreed to delay billing to give me time to sign up for the insurance. Lark gave me a crooked smile, one side of her face numbed. "I wuv story hour. Can we sthay de whole time?" she lisped, struggling with her tongue. "My voice is weird, Daddy."

"It will wear off. You did so well at the dentist. Proud of you, Birdie. We can stay longer. You okay with me working on the computer for a few hours?"

"Mm-hmm."

I deposited her at the story hour with the children's librarian, a thirty-something woman with apricot cheeks, stylish red glasses, a messy bun, and dangling silver hoops. She batted smiling eyes at me. "Welcome to story time." Her gaze was focused on me, not Lark.

I shifted. "Uh. Hi."

A screech emanated from the play kitchen in the corner. Then a yowl.

"I'll be over there," I told the librarian.

Her lips dropped into a frown. "You're not staying?"

"She's good on her own. I'll be in a cubicle."

I bent to Lark. She wiped her nose with the back of her hand. The fall allergens already sucked. If I could get her into the pediatrician—well, first I had to pick a pediatrician—they'd offer guidance. I felt bad giving her antihistamines all the time.

"Be right over there. 'K?" I pointed to the closest cubicle.

"'K."

Lark hung her beanie and jacket on a nearby clothing peg, then ran off to sit beside another girl on the worn-out braided rug. A dozen kids gathered around, some sniffling, some pulled away from toys by exhausted moms. A few parents sipped their lattes, faces glued to cell phones, and others were on the floor with their children, engaging them in a puzzle or something that would help them get into Harvard. Most of the children appeared preschool-aged. I bet the younger ones were home napping. Preschoolers did that, right? Nap?

I knew so little about parenting. Lark's life had passed at lightning speed even before I got sent away. Missed first words, first steps. Riding the high of hacking with Jake, I'd ignored Fran and my newborn daughter. I had a lot to make up for. I also worked hard to undo the damage Fran did, too.

Raising a kid alone is difficult, but single parents manage. Without drugs. The apartment had been a trash heap when I visited. I would never let Lark live like that again.

Druggie mom who neglected and abandoned her. Ex-con dad who got his thrills illegally. Gosh, was my daughter going to need therapy?

I smothered the question with a shiver.

With that, I sat in the closest cubicle and opened my laptop.

First, I spent thirty minutes searching for a pediatrician for Lark. They required insurance info. Of course. Then another hour on the state health insurance website, because the pamphlet Carolyn gave me only got me so far. As I clicked through menus, I kept hitting a wall with a slow and glitchy website. Time to call.

Miss Put-Together Librarian shushed me a few times, so I stepped outside after signaling to Lark I'd be right back. There, I played phone menu roulette until I found the option that let me speak to a human—an incompetent one—who explained where I could print the application. I sent it to the printer and paid at the circulation desk.

Two hours had come and gone. Story time was long over. Sleepy Lark came over and leaned against me, something I learned kids did. They were always hanging on you, an additional appendage.

"Can we go now?" she whined.

So much for job searches, researching contractor and landscaping business start-ups, and reading on possibilities for the cabin. I hadn't even started the ProspNet project yet. "Sorry, Birdie. Five more minutes, okay?"

She pouted.

In my online shopping cart, I put the components for a temporary fix to my cell phone and internet problem: indoor and outdoor antennas, coaxial cable, and the booster to give me better coverage. Satellite was the best choice for internet and meant no need for a landline. How to convince Josie to allow me to install a dish? I hesitated, my finger hovering over the touch pad, then hit "add" to the wireless turbo hub and batteries instead. The unit worked as a hotspot. I'd figure out service providers later. I could always return it.

A throat clearing above me snagged my attention.

The All-Superior Sheriff—aka ASS—stood near me and I deliberately moved my look slowly from what I was doing toward him, as I begged my racing heartbeat to slow down so my brain could do what it did best—read people and work an angle. I was rusty at coming up with my spiel on the spot. My conversations with Carolyn and even with Josie were perfect examples of my lack of practice. I'd grown soft while in prison. I was tired of manipulating to garner information. I closed that chapter of my life. The endgame was now Lark. And Lark only.

Even with leaving my social engineering and pre-texting skills behind, reading people was still my specialty. Ever since I saw this ASS at the grocery store, I'd kept my eye out for him on my town trips. Took mental notes. He walked the streets, drove his shiny new truck, or sat at tables in coffee shops and diners, schmoozing and observing his flock.

"Whatcha doing here, O'Reagan?" He clapped a hand on the cubicle divider.

I guess he remembered me. Peachy.

I closed the laptop. Prickles on my neck joined the party in my stomach. "Using the library. I'm here with my daughter."

His ashy-brown eyes locked with mine. "This is not a workplace."

Correction: it is not a place to campaign. I clamped my mouth shut. *People work here all the time, you ASS.* They came for meetings, schoolwork, printing, the whole she-bang. Public spaces and all that. I paid my taxes.

Chin down, quick answers, respect, I reminded myself. God, I really had grown soft, hadn't I? "Just finished enjoying story time."

The assistant librarian approached. "Uh, Sheriff Dumont, I..." She looked at me uneasily and lowered her voice. "Sloane saw Connor out back again. Thought you should know. He, uh..." She motioned her head to the side.

Dumont gave me one last glare, then guided the librarian with a firm hand on her back to the circulation desk as they spoke in hushed voices.

I shook out my hands, the clenching having left nail marks. Research about Brian Dumont moved to the top of my list. Gram knew his family, I believed. I didn't need enemies so soon upon returning, and it looked like this idiot had it out for me, though I'd done nothing wrong.

I grabbed Lark's beanie and jacket. "Come, Birdie. Quick trip to the grocery store and hardware store. We don't have time to see Nana today."

She moaned.

"We'll get marshmallows." Sure, bribe the kid. "And hot cocoa packets?"

Her eyes lit with giddiness, and she released a squeal.

With evening approaching and my car stocked with groceries and supplies to get started on Josie's projects, we drove up the driveway. "Chicken *ala* nugget tonight," I said in a French accent.

"Wif honey?"

"Always. Though mine will have ketchup."

As I navigated the bumpy turn, something didn't feel right. Chip was barking, running around Josie's house. Hank stood on his porch, craning his neck toward her cabin. He waved at me, his prominent forehead furrowed.

I parked and hurried over. "What's up, Hank?"

"I don't know. She started screaming and Chip's going crazy. Do check on them, will you? I'll be a moment."

I squinted. Josie paced near the chicken coop.

I turned to Lark. "Be a big helper and put the cold food away." I ran inside, toting the two bags of perishables, then flicked on the lights, not waiting for her acquiescence.

"Is Miss Josie okay?"

"Don't know, Birdie. Stay here, please. Cold stuff. Milk, butter, okay? You can have some cheesy crackers."

"'K."

I braced myself and scurried up the path to Josie's cabin. Chip kept barking in threes. *Woof-woof-woof.* Scratching paws, incessant pacing. *Woof-woof-woof.*

Josie kept saying, "Oh my God, oh my God, oh my God," her hands knotted, her face twisted and pale.

Long shadows of evening darkened the path beside her cabin. Instinct told me what happened before I saw it at the chicken coop. I stepped on a feather. Then another bloody one.

"You okay, Josie?" I approached with tender footsteps, glad I told Lark to stay back.

"Uh, um, no..." Josie whimpered, hugging herself.

Chip still barked like he was rabid. What was his order to be quiet?

Woof-woof-woof.

Yes, *buddy, we get it.* Danger. Three was danger. Josie had been quick to explain Chip's barks and behaviors to me this week.

The remaining chickens were squawking as if hell had rained down upon their decimated coop. "Oh, Christ," I said too loudly at the sight of the massacre. What creature did *that*? The chicken wire around the coop and run was intact, but I saw a clear hole dug where the wire met ground.

I counted four hens who were freaked the hell out, and two, no wait, three, uh, bloody heads stacked in a pile. Blood, entrails, feathers, a mess. Christ. Something had stacked the remains. I turned away briefly, steeling myself.

"Ronnie," she said, pointing a shaking finger to more brightly colored feathers and headless body in the corner.

Ronnie the rooster had put up a good fight for his flock. Poor bastard.

I covered my nose with the acrid scent in the air and stepped closer to her. "Josie, whatever did this is gone. Calm Chip down, please. He's going to wake the dead." Or have distant neighbors calling the cops.

"Quiet, Chip." She tapped her thigh. "H-h-heel."

The sound behind me made me jump out of my skin, and I whirled, my fists ready. "Oh, Hank." I blinked. He was fast with the walker.

"Weasel," he said, looking at the mess of a coop and run. "Or a family of them. They kill for fun. Sick little beasts hack them apart."

"And stack the heads?" I mumbled, "Little sickos."

Josie flinched and teetered. Was she going to faint?

Hank lowered his voice and patted her shoulder. "Sorry, Jo. Didn't mean to be so blunt."

From her other side, I put an arm around her to keep her upright.

She leaned into my hold. "Ch-Chip scared it away. I saw the weasel run into the woods."

Hank leaned one arm on the walker and lifted one to hug Josie. "We'll clean it up, Jo. You go inside."

She tucked hair behind her ears, unable to pull her gaze from the gory sight. "What about the other hens? They can't be safe now."

"We'll bring them inside tonight. Keep them in the bathroom or something, okay?" I suggested.

She nodded and stepped back from our embrace. "How is Gilda?"

"Who?"

Hank said, "The goat." He pointed to the other pen, where Gilda bleated, announcing her presence.

I drew a gaze over the goat's home. "That pen is separate. She should be okay, right?"

He bobbed his head. "Coyotes are our only concern for her safety, but Chip will keep them at bay. Also, some goats are escape artists, so we need to be careful with her fencing, to keep it high. Gilda has a nice pen. Guess the ladies are due for an upgrade now."

"I'll secure and reinforce it, and check Gilda's, too, in case. Hardware cloth or buried metal wire...whatever it needs. I'll read about it tonight." I asked Hank, "Can you help Josie inside, make her tea? I need to check on Lark, and then I'll clean this up and move the hens indoors. Chip will stand guard."

Josie nodded.

"Does the shed have shovels and such?"

Josie moved slowly away, her eyes still rapt on the massacre. "There's a lock. Combo is four-twenty-fifteen."

I didn't need the combination. The shed had no lock. After locating tools inside, I went about cleaning up the slaughter fest. It gave me qualms about ever eating chicken again.

Finished, I stretched my neck and returned to the shed. My phone, which was serving as my flashlight, slid from my hands near the door. As I picked it up, I stepped on the butt of a cigarette.

That was odd.

The butt looked recent. None of us smoked. Nicotine and tar left nasty residues and odors long term, and the cabins held no trace. This couldn't have been from Morgan, not if he'd been gone for a while now.

I dared to touch it. Not warm. Had one of Hank's therapists taken a quick smoke break? Though I tried to believe this simple explanation, I cast a look into the dark shadows of the forest and prayed the only predator here was the four-legged kind.

12

JOSIE

Someone or something had ripped—hacked—apart the poor hens and Ronnie.

Hack.

I hated that damn word. Sure, Hank had meant no harm with using it. I mean, the birds *had* been hacked to bits.

But that vile word went far deeper for me than for most. Weasels, computer hackers, stealing ex-husbands...they all sucked.

A few days after the Night of Death, I returned from my walk, replaying the gruesome scene, to the sound of a power saw in front of the cabin.

Everett bent over two sawhorses, slicing wood.

Chip ran right up to him, eager for whatever he had in his back pocket. Everett had already adopted Hank's treat habit, and my dog was such a sucker for it. Chip's shoulders were loose, and he licked his jowls, his tail flapping like a flag in a hurricane.

I fought the smile tugging at my lips. The sawdust scent, productive sounds, and warm late September day eased the sorrow of losing two hens and one cranky rooster.

Everett turned to me and wiped sawdust off his hands. He pushed up the protective goggles, leaving a pink indentation around his eyes and brows. Sweat dampened his shaggy locks.

He reached into his pocket. Chip assumed the position, tail tapping the ground.

"Just one," I said to Everett's unspoken question.

He gave Chip a treat.

On my way inside, I eyed the chipper. Hmm. The wood chips would be perfect to top off the cans used in the compost toilets.

I appreciated Everett's productivity—and after the weasel's satanic smorgasbord, his presence—but my anxiety still swelled. My quiet world was no longer, between therapists and new tenants.

Help always came with a catch. People. Here.

And something about Everett's smile—complete with two sexy dimples—propelled me back in time. There, in front of my home, stood a charming man who reminded me too much of my ex, the good parts. He blinded me. Like the early-years Tate.

Charming and sexy had fooled me once. Then I became careful. Fastidious. Scared.

Paranoid.

One fateful day, Tate had punctured the wall growing between us.

"You're paranoid, Josie," he'd said.

The incessant obsessing wheels in my head screeched to a grinding halt.

"What did you say?" I asked, as I grasped the meaning of his accusation.

"You're being paranoid, sweetheart." He adjusted his tie while looking in the hallway mirror, whistling in a way that grated on my nerves. When had I stopped liking his gestures and quirks?

"You think I'm making this up? That I'm crazy?"

He dropped the façade and paced our living room floor, dress shoes squeaking on the exposed wood, his fingers fidgeting. He itched for a smoke. Yet another filthy habit he picked up this year. I'd relegated him to the back porch for it.

Kissing him, something else that grew rarer by the day, lost its appeal entirely. Mints and mouthwash masked only so much. When did we last make love? Christmas? I couldn't remember. I didn't care. He'd become more reclusive, hiding away in his office late into the night, the door locked. I slept alone more than was healthy for our young marriage. Initially, I believed it was porn. Or an affair. Or depression. If only one of those things had taken my husband from me.

A deep line carved a ridge from Tate's blond hairline to his light brown eyebrows. "I never said that."

I rubbed a clenched fist against my temple. The migraine moved like a low-pressure front across a weather map, from the base of my skull to behind my right eye. There'd be no relief until bedtime. "You've implied it. Many times."

He approached, tension aging his sun-kissed face, lines encircling the hazel eyes I used to get lost in. Tate had checked out of our relationship months ago. In addition to my distant husband, someone had drained our bank accounts, my computer was infected with viruses and malware, and my boss was questioning me about the whereabouts of the fundraiser money.

How would I know? I deposited the cash and checks into the special account, as directed. Brianna, the PTA treasurer, came with me after we counted it together. She saw me deposit the money.

I swallowed an aching scratch.

Tate approached and rubbed hesitant hands on my shoulders, normally a placating gesture. The endearment twisted my stomach, and I wrenched myself out of his hold.

He snapped, "Fine, you're being paranoid, okay? You messed up somewhere with a password or something and a crook got hold of your info. It's not the end of the world."

Ice slid down my back. "You're blaming me? I caused this?"

"Sweetheart, you're not the best with tech." He shook his head as if chiding a child. "It's okay. I've got it under control."

"Tate, why won't you answer my questions?"

"I *have*. A million times." Red flushed across his cheeks as he fought for control. "Look, whatever the hacker did to you is messing with your head, making you doubt those who love you. Me." He heaved a sigh, swatting the air as he stepped back. "You should listen to Phoebe. She—"

"I haven't spoken to Pheebs."

"She sent you an email."

The fine hairs on my neck rose. "You read my emails?" My stomach grumbled. I woke each morning around four a.m. with a terrible case of the runs. Lost ten pounds in a few months. I was still disputing charges and restoring my credit from the initial wave of theft. I needed to run to the bathroom right now. Was I overreacting? What was I missing? "Why did you read my email?"

"I was concerned."

Phoebe was in Sydney, living the dream of marriage and job and contentment. She hadn't believed me when I told her I suspected someone close to me had screwed me over, that it wasn't a stranger or a bot.

I dropped onto the couch, uncertain my legs could support the rage or violation much longer. I played with the tea bag in my mug. The water was lukewarm now.

"You don't believe me," I said matter-of-factly.

He sat next to me, brittleness joining the condescending patience in his voice. "I want to believe you, sweetheart."

"I don't go online anymore because my computer is screwed up." *And I'm afraid to buy a new one.* "Somebody hacked my accounts, Tate. Stole my identity! These past few weeks have been hell. And now the fundraiser money is missing."

He didn't blink. Didn't even look shocked.

Who else knew about the fundraising account? The principal, the PTA, and Tate.

"I filed a police report, too."

He shot to his feet. "You what? Why? When?"

"Did you know a large percentage of identity scams and thefts are from people close to you?"

I watched his face for any hint of admission. I didn't need to be a math whiz to know one plus one equaled two.

Nothing.

He was as solid as a rock.

As a liar.

"Narcissists are good at lying. They are masters at gaslighting," Kyle had told me. "They make you question everything, and you doubt yourself. Josie, don't doubt. Trust your gut."

I had not screwed up online. Others played sports or knitted or made charcuterie boards for hobbies. Me? Organization. That was my hobby. I was meticulous. I was careful with passwords and accounts.

Tate grimaced. "We took care of it, Jo, sweetheart. Hired the fraud expert, filed reports with creditors, changed our accounts and information, did everything possible. We have my savings and retirement. We can rebuild your credit. Why bother with the police about the fundraiser money?"

Late at night I had done my own behind-closed-door digging. There was no Tate Safety Net. He remained mum about his emptied accounts—which were as barren as Death Valley. Where did *his* money go? Though we were married and had a joint account, we each had a personal savings account from our pre-married days. Last time I'd checked, which had been years ago, he had thousands in his savings and retirement accounts.

He lowered his eyes. "We moved everything to your maiden name. Josie Sullivan no longer exists. She is now Jo Sawyer."

Bitterness hung in the air.

Joe Sawyer was my dad, but yes, technicalities. I was Josephine Sawyer on my birth certificate. Josie Sullivan, the wife, soon would no longer exist, not on paper, not in person.

"You should go," I said, lifting the tea. The now cold drink numbed my words.

He grabbed his computer bag with an exaggerated sigh. "They need me in the office. Give it another weekend. Karen will extend your leave, but try returning to work. Somebody will fess up."

Karen had scheduled a meeting with me and the superintendent for this week. They could press criminal charges if I didn't figure out what the hell happened with the fundraising money and show evidence. They already interrogated Brianna. Now it was my turn. Usually, school employees didn't get involved with the PTA, but I was an SLP, and rules were different with my employment contract. Now I knew why there were rules.

I crushed the rock in my gut with an invisible sledgehammer, summoning the words, "No, I mean, *go.*"

His face showed he comprehended what I meant.

Kyle's words remained lodged in my memory. *Many thefts are friends, family.*

Spouses.

Tate's online gambling had caught up with him. My husband had taken my life and stood here, denying it. Gaslight me all he wanted, but I knew the truth.

The front door slammed, the sound reverberating within me.

Now, I swiped at tears as I stared out my kitchen window—over my now functional sink, thanks to Everett. Chip came to me, sensing my unease. I rubbed his head. "I'm okay, buddy."

Everett is not Tate. Not all men are liars.

Trust was a damn hard thing.

I poured two glasses of homemade iced tea. Chip curled up on his dog bed in the corner, let out a deep yawn, then rested his chin on his paws.

I steadied my mind and walked outside, the screen door swinging behind me. "Thirsty?"

Everett looked up from measuring a board and marking it with a pencil, giving me a way too handsome smile. Darn sexy. I ripped my mind from that kind of thought. I would not be a fool again.

Not Tate. Not Tate. Not. Tate.

He leaned against a sawhorse, removing his gloves. "Oh, good, you found gloves." Ice clinked as I handed him a glass.

"These were mine. Can't find yours. Are they buried in the wood pile?" He smiled.

I shrugged. I wouldn't be surprised if I lost my mind along with everything else I misplaced this week. My gloves, the lock on the shed...what else?

He released an audible sigh after downing the entire glass.

"Want more?"

"Yes, please."

A timer beeped from inside the cabin. "Ah, that's dinner in the oven. Why don't you come in and I'll pour you another?"

I popped inside to check on the baked ziti.

"Smells wicked good in here," he said, following me into the living room.

I blinked. Wicked good. Tate used to always say that, too.

Josie, many New Englanders use that phrase. I was looking for faults in him on purpose. *Not Tate. Not Tate.*

As the timer beeped, I hurried to the stove and peeked into the oven. Bubbling and delicious. With potholders, I pulled the dish out and laid it on the stove, steam and the waft of oregano hitting my nose.

I returned with a pitcher of tea. Everett stood at Morgan's bookshelf.

"These are..." He grabbed a journal.

"Empty, yes." My pulse flickered.

He eyed the color-coded spectrum of journals. Why had Morgan invested his time in making a bookshelf and filling it with empty notebooks?

"Planning to write the great American novel?" His voice bounced off the exposed ceiling beams that were more structural than aesthetic. I imagined heat would get trapped up there in winter.

"Perhaps he was. *Tabula rasa.*"

"He? Oh, your uncle?"

"Yeah." Oops. *Share nothing*, Don advised me. Don't trip up on bits about your past. I let the silence continue for a few beats. Hank had already mentioned Morgan to Everett. It's not like my uncle was a secret.

A muscle pulsed in his jawline as he held out his glass for me to refill. "Thank you. What's *tabula rasa*?"

I answered with a dismissive wave while filling his cup. "It's Latin, translates to 'blank slate.'"

To me, it meant starting anew, like a clean slate.

I swallowed, glancing at the rudimentary sketches and a price list for a greenhouse on the coffee table. After meeting with Everett for coffee and going over our ambitious master plan, a new sense of energy had taken hold of me. I daydreamed again, starting with the greenhouse.

Everett crouched in front of the lower shelf. Beneath the three rows of empty journals, my arsenal of off-the-grid-living books, bought before my move here, stood lined up—not in color order. I lined up by size. Novels for escape, and homestead books for survival. Yup, that was me.

Finally, he rose and turned to me. He held my look, expectant.

My conversation skills had gone the way of the dinosaurs.

He shuffled his feet. "Could I read a few of these? Almost done with the kilowatt one and your detailed journal." He gestured to my shelf. "How about *Off the Grid 101*?"

"That's a fabulous book if you have trouble falling asleep."

"No trouble with staying awake. Lark keeps me up a lot."

"Oh?"

He shrugged. "Nightmares." He tucked the book under his arm, then took a drag of tea. "Thanks again. I better keep working while there's daylight."

"See you later."

The meaning of those words stirred me...in both a positive and negative way.

Everett is not Tate. Not all men are liars. I repeated the phrases until my mind settled.

I repositioned two of the journals jutting out at the end. One slipped and fell. As I picked it up, two fifty-dollar bills fell out of the pages. Shaking my head, I tucked the journal, minus the cash back on the shelf. Those bills went right in my pocket. At this point, why not? I'd check the other journals later, but if they were similar to Uncle Morgan's caches, this would be the only journal with money inside.

13

— · —

LARK

The bins matched the Lego bricks. Red for red bricks. Blue for blue bricks. Mr. B even had a black bin for the black ones. All the colors mixed made black, so black was my favorite color. Daddy said white was the absence of colors, so that made it my least favorite. Who wouldn't want some color? Rainbows were the prettiest.

Mr. B's house had a hundred cobwebs, but I loved his basement. Bins and bins and bins of Legos. Since he wasn't allowed to go down the steps now because of his walker and new hip, he asked me to bring his bins up and put them on his table.

It took me four trips, but I got them all upstairs. On each trip, I explored a corner of the basement. Four trips, four corners! A square. So many boxes and bins! I also found a door the size of my backpack. The door was locked and hidden behind a big, rusty metal cabinet. Did it lead to a secret hiding place? Maybe Mr. B hid bones like the criminals did on the one show Daddy didn't know I watched one night on his computer when he was in the shower.

Daddy would say the secret door was for electricity stuff and to leave it alone. I would need a flashlight to explore and somebody strong to move the filing cabinet. Mr. B couldn't do that. Did he have a treasure chest hidden there? Was he a pirate? Where was his ship?

I came upstairs, and he made me chocolate milk.

"Brown moo juice," he said with a twinkle in his eyes. His eyes changed from gray to blue with the sunlight. Maybe that was a magical pirate thing?

"You like rainbows, don't you?" he asked as he took apart a Lego set, dropping each piece into the matching bins.

"How did you know?"

He pointed to my unicorn beanie.

"Oh."

Click. Snap. Click. Snap. Our job was to take them apart, but that made my fingers hurt, so he let me play with them, too. I built a rainbow tree. I enjoyed building more. Clack, clack, clack. I riffled through the red bin.

"Do you have a bin for see-frough parts?" I wanted to make a cloud.

He dragged another bin over from the edge of the table. "Right here, kiddo."

"My daddy calls me Birdie."

"What a special name. *La nana*," he said.

"No, Nana is my great-grammy."

He laughed. "*La nana* means bird or doll in French."

"What's French? Like fries?"

He chuckled and moved his jaw, making a weird sound. Old people had dentures, Nana said. Did Mr. B? The clicking hurt my ears. He breathed noisily, always grunting, huffing, or clearing his throat. Even with that, Mr. B didn't act like other old people. He didn't ask me about Mommy. He didn't ask me any questions. He also smelled like Nana. Not sweet like her hand lotion, but old. Like a basement. Most smells made my tummy flop.

"A lark is a bird, too," I added. "Nana showed me once in her magazines."

"Then a lovely name your father gave you. Does he like birds?"

I played with a set of wheels stuck to the other bricks, spinning the tiny tires. "He didn't give me my name. He was gone for a long time." I flicked the wheels harder. I didn't want to think about that time.

I didn't remember if it was Mommy, Daddy, or Nana who started calling me Birdie. Daddy said he lived with me as a baby, but I didn't remember that. Mommy said Daddy got in trouble and he wasn't coming back.

But he came back.

And then Mommy left.

Mr. B said nothing.

I stopped spinning wheels. "My great-grammy's real name is Nora. She calls me Birdie, too."

He cleared his throat. For a long time. It sounded like a spider was trying to climb out. He grabbed a cloth thingy from his pocket and sneezed into it. Then he waved it. "Gets dusty sometimes. I called my grandmother *seanmhair*, but that's a hard one to say and spell, so as a kid we called her Cookie. She always smelled of vanilla and butter and she snuck me cookies." He smiled big, yellow-stained teeth.

Right now, his eyes were the color of the grayish-blue Lego piece I thought of adding to my clouds. Sometimes rain filled the clouds. Rain was ugly. Mr. B's eyes were not. They matched his sweater today.

He shoved a small pile of bricks toward me. "How about gold at the end of your rainbow?"

"Gold!" I'd never seen gold Lego pieces. "Are dey special?"

"They are rare."

"What's dat mean?"

"Very few of them. Valuable. Worth more."

Valuable as Mommy would say. I fiddled with the pile in front of me, and when Mr. B looked back at his Legos, I slid five of the gold pieces into my pocket. They would be safe there. Nobody would sell them. It was important to hide and protect precious things.

After I finished the rainbow, I got bored. Mr. B talked more than Daddy and a lot more than Miss Josie. She walked all over the property with her cute doggie always by her side. I liked him. He licked my face. Mr. B showed me how to make Chip sit and how to give him doggie treats.

"I love cookies. Miss Josie named her dog Chocolate Chip. I wonder if she makes cookies, too."

He shifted in his chair, releasing a sigh like Nana made when she moved. His house creaked, too.

The lights flickered, and I yelped.

"No need to fret, just my Tillie saying hello."

A little pitter-patter danced in my chest. Oh my gosh! I hoped our cabin didn't have ghosts. The monster I heard out my window at night already scared me. Once I saw the monster's shadow. Should I tell Mr. B? Instead, I asked, "You have a ghost?"

Big wrinkles crinkled his face. "No, not really. But the lights get wonky now and then. It stops. I tell myself it's my Tillie talking to me." He looked up at the dining room light, which flickered twice more, then stopped. "See?"

Mr. B's name was hard to say. Mr. Bluecannon. He said people called him Hank, but Daddy said I should always use mister or miss or missus to show respect.

Mr. B's chair scraped on the floor, and I covered my ears with its shriek.

"Oh, sorry, kiddo. That is an awful sound, isn't it?"

I nodded.

"I need to add felt feet to these chairs."

Clack, clack, clack. For bony hands, Mr. B moved fast with his Legos.

"Dey need slippers for their feet. Dose are quiet. Why do you buy dese Legos already built into dings and take dem apart? Don't you play wif dem? Do you save dem for your grandkids to play wif? Are you saving dem to make an enormous castle or pirate ship?"

Maybe he *was* a secret pirate.

He didn't answer.

I focused on taking apart a trickier section of an already put-together spaceship. I liked the flat pieces. I used my nail to dig under the locked-in pieces to wiggle them out. Mr. B had big hands. He used little metal tools for the harder buildings.

"Sorting keeps my hands busy, and it passes the time. Keeps my mind sharp. It's good for the noggin." He tapped the side of his round head. He had big ears. He needed a beanie because he had so little hair. He must get cold! Nana could knit him one, too.

I'd be sad if nobody came here to play. Shawn and Liam could visit. Daddy said two chickens left on a trip, but the others were fun to talk to. I missed Ronnie's morning wake-up calls. Miss Josie didn't like me to get too close to their home.

She was quiet, like the librarian, and always seemed sad. Was she missing her mommy, too?

I wondered if Mr. B would want to meet Nana. He might marry Nana, have kids who play with Legos, and feel less lonely.

I explored the living room. Daddy said not to touch anything that could break. I kept my hands behind my back.

Mr. B had lots of pictures of Tillie. She was pretty. In one picture, she was holding a little boy.

Mr. B also had lots of books. And dust. Oh! And a bowl of ribbon candies. Mr. B always sucked on candy. Another yucky sound! But he was my friend, so I tried to ignore it. I stuck one candy in my pocket. I wouldn't hide it like the golden Legos. Those I would hide so Mommy couldn't sell them. Mr. B said they were special. They needed to be protected.

I wondered when Mommy would come back to get me from Daddy. My tummy felt sick. I wasn't sure if I wanted to go back to her anymore. Daddy was nicer.

My fingers fluttered on an enormous chest beside the couch—it looked like a pirate's chest. Mr. B crinkled one eye, like a pirate. He didn't have a parrot, though.

He let out an old-person groan. "Well, kiddo, let's call it a day, okay? Would you like to stay for dinner tonight?"

"I have to ask my daddy."

"Good idea. Do you like to cook?"

I nodded, although I never cooked a dinner. "I like to bake cakes wif Nana."

"What are your favorite foods?"

I shrugged, returning to the table to drink my chocolate milk.

"Perhaps we will find a rainbow in my fridge?"

"I love rainbows!"

He smiled at me again, the way Nana did. "I know."

He put his Lego tools in a bin. "Let's check the mail. I'm supposed to walk more. Time to make this hip move."

I followed him through the door. He took a long while to get down the steps with his walker. Then we walked to the mailboxes. We waved to Daddy, working on Miss Josie's porch. The walker's wheels got stuck a few times in the rocky driveway. Mr. B poked inside the mailbox, then winked at me. "Nothing yet. Do you like puzzles?"

I clapped my hands. "Yes!"

"I have a few you might enjoy."

I nodded and fiddled with the Lego pieces in my pocket as we made the long walk back up the driveway to Mr. B's cabin. "Can I use your bafroom—de real one inside?" What if the outside one had a snake in it?

He patted the top of my head. I liked it. "Sure, sure. I don't like the outside one much either."

14

HANK

Morgan would've said a missile had landed in my kitchen. Then he'd release a wry, sad laugh. Morgan Caldwell's smile concealed grief, and held wisdom born from war.

Inside and out.

He never hid his demons well. Now, Jo...oh, she hid them too well.

Tillie and I had done our darnedest to hold Morgan together all those years ago. Tillie helped him build his gardens, plant the apple orchard, and line the driveway with rhododendrons and azaleas. We dedicated the the bright orange azaleas and angel-white rhodies to our Theo, too. These efforts only covered wounds. They didn't heal the heartache. While Morgan let the sickness take him, Tillie and I forged a new way.

Reminded of my sweet wife, a sweet bird with an angel's face hummed beside me as she used the hand masher to wallop the potatoes. Lark's mash dance sent a tuber flying across the room.

"Oh, heckeroo!" she said.

"Great Caesar's ghost," I concurred. Squatting to pick it up was out of the question. Jo would need to help me later.

"Is dat anoder ghost?"

"Nah, kiddo. Just a saying."

"You sure like ghosts."

"Not spooky ones."

I stood nearby because cooking with the walker was a pain in my tush. What happened when we geezers wanted to use both hands? Stand on one foot? Adrienne never explained that to me.

She was going to scold me again tomorrow during her PT visit. She had a hard job putting up with old coots like me. The photocopied guide of fourteen exercises sat under a morning mug of tea. Exercises? Try torture. I completed them, but as soon as I finished ten reps, it was time for another round. I took today off.

Victor was a big drag with his brutish occupational therapy. He drank far too much caffeine. What occupation? False advertising, that's what. Nurse Needles was the worst of the trio. A sadist if I'd ever met one.

"Will Miss Josie be happy?" Lark asked, mashing.

Out of the mouths of babes, Tillie always said. *Would* Jo be pleased with our masterpiece of scrambled eggs and mashed potatoes? Yes. She coddled me, and for her to see me make a meal beyond spaghetti or hot dogs would please her. The kitchen had been Tillie's turf, not mine.

Would Jo get riled because I invited Everett and Lark? Yes. Did I care? No.

Would Jo ever find happiness?

If she followed in her uncle's footsteps, no.

We had sent in the Medicare forms last week. Now we waited for processing and reinstatement. Jo underestimated my ability to notice how this hip money mess had clearly triggered her past trauma. Being a bother or causing pain was the last thing I wanted. How had I allowed the coverage to lapse? I missed Tillie's organization.

I patted Lark's beanie-covered head. "She will love it. She loves eggs. Using fewer egg yolks means my cholesterol will be happy."

"What's cholesterol?"

"A measure of the good and bad fats in your body. Yolks—the yellow part—have more fat than whites. We'll save the yolks for Miss Jo. I'm sure she'll whip up something tasty using them. Maybe custard or eggnog."

Lark nodded, wiping a splatter off her forehead. "What's eggnog?"

I smacked my lips. "A rich holiday drink I have at Christmas."

A shadow crossed her chipper expression. I hoped none of her long hair found its way into the food. I brushed the lengths of it behind her shoulders. "Tillie used to wear her hair up in the kitchen. Do you have a hair tie? One of those, uh, scrunchie things? An elastic?"

She shook her head.

"Do you like Christmas?"

She gave a vague shrug.

This year called for a tree. My last official celebration of the holiday was my final Christmas with Tillie four years ago. Since then, I'd settled for drinking spiked eggnog by a fire, reading Dickens, listening to the *Swingin' Holiday Bazaar* record, and a having a light dinner with Morgan. Sometimes I'd visit a friend or two, but I hated to intrude on their family gatherings. Tillie and Theo had been my only family. My two sisters died years ago, and their kids never bothered with me.

Last Christmas, Morgan was in the hospital. He died after the New Year, then a lawyer contacted me, contacted Jo, and the settling of the estate began. She joined me in May. The loneliness from January until then had been unbearable.

With Jo, Everett, and Lark here, this year would be special. Our homestead needed sunshine.

Another potato cube shot out of the bowl and thudded against the backsplash tiles.

"How's it going, Muscles?"

A sweet grin stretched round cheeks. "Great! Aunt Penny lets me mash, too. I miss her."

"I'm sure you'll see her again soon."

"She's having a baby. Dey kicked us out." A frown cloaked the smile.

I eyed my kitchen. Bowls, spoons, eggshells, potato peels, sudsy water in the sink. How did we create this mess with just a few ingredients?

Tillie laughed at me in my head. Her sultry laugh. Shivers prickled my spine.

"You're always welcome here." I inspected the dry-looking white chunks in the bowl. "How do we make them creamy? Milk?"

Lark nodded. "Aunt Penny uses salt, pepper—a little because it makes me sneeze—milk, and butter."

"Splashes of each?"

I was asking a five-year-old how to make mashed potatoes. Tillie laughed again. Heat filled my cheeks.

This was better than spending my days alone in the basement sorting Legos.

After rinsing, then crushing the milk carton, I lobbed it into the recycling bin. I added butter to the mashed potatoes. I saved the eggshells for the gardens and the potato peels for the compost since the chickens couldn't have them.

With a chin flick to the counter, I said, "Why don't you set the table? Do you know how?"

She was on the move. Of course, she knew how. Is this how kids were these days? Independent at five? Or was it because of Lark's absent mother?

She grabbed one item at a time, first the forks. Set them, came back. Then the napkins. Set, came back. Plates and onward, dancing her way with twinkle toes around the puzzle pieces scattered on the floor. Though we started the puzzle on the trunk coffee table so I could sit in my uncomfortable hardback chair—no couch for me, Adrienne warned sternly—Lark preferred assembling on the floor. A floor that needed a good sweep. With my brain and body tired from skipping PT today, I had sipped tea and watched Lark assemble the puzzle instead. She had an eye for puzzles.

The twang of remorse hit me harder than expected as I looked at the mushy potatoes resembling baby food. It made me think of Theodore. Tillie had made all his food from scratch. Now, Theodore shared a grave with Tillie in Silent Creek Cemetery.

A knock sounded on the front door. "Bet that's your daddy. Want to grab it?" I covered the potatoes with a dishcloth to keep them warm. Tillie's trick. The eggs stayed warm under a low heat in the oven. *This old geezer remembers some things, my love.*

"Hi, Hank," Everett said from the door.

He popped into the kitchen when I didn't respond.

My joints were going to hurt tomorrow. I should've taken the pain medicine, but it was missing. I swore it was in my bathroom cabinet, but it wasn't there when I last looked. Like everything else, the pill bottle would turn up. Sometimes brain fog rolled in like the mountain mist, so who knows? Maybe I misplaced it.

The chap began grabbing bowls and utensils and dropping them in the sink. He lifted the dish soap and a sponge. "Let me help. Least I can do."

I waved him away. "No, no, I've got it."

"Really. I like cleaning. I'm so sorry to have—"

"I enjoy her company." A croak lodged in my throat. She was like Theo. Did that explain my heightened sense of aliveness, awareness? Not from the back and hip pain and torturous exercises with Adrienne, but from Lark's presence? My memory had been soggy like mashed potatoes until recently.

Theo had been six. Just off to school when...

I grabbed my handkerchief and blew my nose. "How's the porch coming along?"

"Almost done."

Lark said from the doorway, "Daddy loves cleaning!"

I quirked a brow. "Does he?"

Everett smiled. "I don't *love* it. I like to do my part. Any way I can."

"Carolyn gives him a better grade when he keeps de house clean."

"Clean houses are happy houses, Tillie would say." I patted his back. Who was Carolyn? Lark's mom? Everett was too old to get grades. He wore no ring. Never spoke about a wife, ex-wife, or girlfriend. Just Penny, his sister-in-law. "Thank you. I may sit for a few minutes."

He nodded. "Birdie, let's make Mr. Buchanan hot tea."

"It's Hank. No need for the mister. Tea would be lovely. Thanks."

"Okay," she said, a bee buzzing through the kitchen. Delight sugared her voice, a summer day to my gray clouds.

The energy I felt being around Lark evaporated. The couch beckoned me...

"Birdie, see if Mr. Buchanan needs a glass of water while this kettle heats?"

She already skipped her way to the counter. Heavens, the girl was desperate for activities and approval.

I shifted my old bones to the couch, and eased into it, allowing the cushy comfort to relax joints and muscles. Bodies had too many parts, and mine were getting creaky.

A few moments later, Lark shook me awake, a cup of tea in front of me on the coffee table. "Josie's here. Dinnertime!"

I rose, my body revolting from sitting on something other than the permitted ninety-degree-angle hard chair. Eh, so Adrienne was right. I stood, rolled my wheels, and grabbed a doggy treat from the jar before heading to the door.

"Hi, Miss Josie!" Lark said. "We made dinner."

Jo looked vexed. She was a saltine some days! But saltines were best when you were feeling unwell. Jo had a good heart. She needed more life in her life. I was determined to convince her of this. And the answer rested with our dinner companions.

15

— · —

JOSIE

Dinners on Sunday were sacred.

Me, Hank, and a place setting for Tillie's spirit.

Hank invited our new neighbors. Again. Sneaky man. Will this become a thing? The more annoying question—did I want it?

Plans, schmans, Hank would say.

Nothing lately had been in my plan.

Lark was adorable. Everett was kind. But he was my tenant and employee. So why this chumminess? Hank's involvement in Everett's hiring was enough, but now this was too much. Meddle was Hank's middle name.

While carrying the baked ziti to the kitchen, my gaze caught the decorated table. My next thought was if this meal was kid friendly. Kids were particular with tastes, smells, and textures. Layered artichokes and zucchini didn't have kid appeal. I'd already picked up on some of Lark's quirks, her speech issues included.

"Right in the middle, Jo. I left a spot for your tasty work." Hank gestured to the lavender trivets, which he must have pulled out of the Conestoga cupboard.

Chip licked his chops behind me, awaiting his treat.

Mismatched covered bowls sat on the dining room table set for four. Where was Tillie's setting?

"Smells delicious, Josie." Everett took the casserole dish from my hands, placing it on the trivet.

"Smorgasbord!" Lark said.

"What a great word, Birdie," he said.

"Mr. B taught me it, Daddy."

A smile from the depths muscled its way to my lips. "Did you help make this wonderful meal?"

She brimmed with satisfaction. "I did!"

"Then it will be yummy. What's on the menu?"

"We have a full rainbow now wif your spaghetti, Miss Josie." She pointed to the ziti. "Yellow and white eggs and potatoes, the purple beets and green pickles we found in Mr. B's fridge, blueberry jelly and brown bread my daddy brought over, red and orange tomatoes and more green dings in the spaghetti..."

And now Hank would have a week's worth of leftovers. This wasn't too bad, even though I wanted a quiet night with just Hank.

We sat to eat.

The mashed potatoes had chunks floating in a pool of gritty milk, the eggs weren't half bad, and my ziti hit the spot. In solidarity, I even put a pickle and beet on my plate.

Throughout dinner, Everett conversed with Hank about his current projects. But he kept glancing at me. I shifted my focus to Lark. This felt weird...and good.

Kids I was better at. After my ruined marriage and abandonment by friends, my students had been my saving grace. Then I lost my job and all hope.

Lark played with her fork in the mashed potatoes, drawing lines and crisscrosses. She scooped small bites of egg into her mouth, chewed at a snail's pace, and followed with a chaser of chocolate milk after each bite. The ziti sat untouched on her plate, as did the pickles and beets, and her food remained segregated. She nibbled on buttered bread.

With perfect timing, Hank brought up the greenhouse. "A tight timeline until the ground freezes, right?" He looked at me.

"Everett would know." I forked a bite of ziti into my mouth. He was flying through tasks.

A glint of excitement danced in Everett's eyes. "Digging will be minimal, and depending on weather, I can dig into November or even December."

"Where will you put it?" Hank inquired.

"The meadow, where it's flat and away from trees and buildings' shadows," Everett said.

I added, "We want to capture as much sunlight per day as possible, at least six hours daily, and to make sure the wind shear is minimal." Growing veggies in winter brought hope. Everett's enthusiasm was contagious, and my confidence in being prepared for the cold months had bloomed in his presence. He'd even offered to tutor me on planting, transplanting, and maintenance. I wished I could hold on to that enthusiasm and stop being so cranky.

Everett paused in his eating, contemplating my wind scenarios. His good manners meant he hadn't even blinked at the soggy potatoes and eggs. He must have a steel stomach. He said, "I was thinking about the design more. Alternatively, we could build a greenhouse attached to your cabin. South-facing is ideal, so it gets the sun, but your front porch faces south. We could face it southeast, on a side wall. The drawback is that we need to pour a concrete floor. But with vents, solar heat from the addition will warm your house, too."

Concrete?

He must have seen my face because he backpedaled. "But a freestanding unit won't need much for a floor. How is the wind in winter?"

I shrugged while Hank said, "Blustery."

Everett dragged his fork through the potatoes, scraping. Was he designing in the mash? Oh, yes, he was.

"You decided on dimensions, so that's set. We'll anchor the greenhouse into the ground with steel plates or concrete tube footings." He drew those in with a tine. Catching my stare, he flashed a smile.

Hank glowed. Lark adored. I...I found myself grinning.

Everett looked at me.

I sipped water. "Adding heat to the cabin is tempting, but my southeast-facing side may not be suitable for work. Gilda's pen is there, along with a big tree that gives her shade." The tire swing on the tree had long been tossed, but memories remained.

"Good points. We'll stick with the original plan." He continued, tapping his finger for each task or item. "To finalize it, we need to consider the topography of the land, the frame material—wood, aluminum, or PVC—ventilation, climate control, electricity requirements for heating, though there are more natural options like compost piles."

"Anything you need, I'm game." I took another bite of ziti.

"I would love to hire a guy to help with some of it. My friend Anthony, from my vo-tech days. Is that okay?"

I blinked through fatigue, internalizing a sigh. Another person on my property. Why not? Fighting this battle was futile. "That's fine."

"Should we walk the property more this week, too?" he asked. "I can tackle the fence repairs."

"Sure. Midweek?" I yawned through a nod.

"You look tired, Josie. We can clean this up if you need to rest," Hank said, yawning himself. Lark must have given him a run for his money today.

"I'll clean up." Everett was already grabbing plates. "I'll re-heat the teakettle, too."

I didn't argue and slipped on my jacket. "I'll be by tomorrow morning to get you for your four-week post-op appointment, Hank."

Lark giggled while assisting with clean-up.

For the first time since Hank's fall, I skipped my evening routine of reading a book or watching an old movie on Morgan's boxy television and VCR.

I kicked off my boots, slung off my jeans—nearly stepping on a meowing Holly—and slid into pajamas...then under the thick duvet. I set the alarm since Ronnie was no longer my rise-and-shine clock.

And I let the quiet of the cabin lull me to sleep.

16

HANK

When Theo was three, I took him to the summer fair in Silent Creek. After our ride on the merry-go-round, I thought I'd lose my caramel corn, and according to Tillie my face was the color of celery. That's how this medical nonsense felt. A carousel of people who thought they knew better than this old geezer.

At the end of the post-op meeting, I took out my handkerchief to blot a sweaty brow as I sat in the ugly gray office. Bright light streamed in behind the physician at the desk. I licked dry lips, thirsty after his thorough examination of the incisions and evaluation of my mobility, strength, and gait. What was this, a military entrance exam?

He had a carrot-top mop—far less becoming than the lovely red waves Jo inherited—black-rimmed glasses, and an all-knowing appearance. He fiddled with a folder on his desk. I had spices in my cabinet older than him.

Hip is healing nicely, he said. Keep up the good work, he said. I could drive in a few weeks, after the PT, OT, and Nurse Needles were done, he said.

He clicked his fancy pen, not looking up from the opened folder. "How's the pain?"

I swatted the air.

"From one to ten, Mr. Buchanan?"

"Three," I lied. It was closer to five on the worst days, but I wasn't taking any pills. Those pills had gone AWOL.

He jotted notes, skimmed the chart. "Do you need any prescription refills? The oxycodone?"

"No."

He wrote more. At least he wasn't tapping fingers on a keyboard the way Dr. Beaver did at my annual physicals. Dr. Beaver was in his mid-sixties, old-fashioned and conservative in his treatments, but even he couldn't escape technology—which I was beginning to dislike as much as Jo. This year he'd made me take a memory test on a computer. I suspected it was more of a test for my agility by clicking the mouse.

Jo spoke up from beside me. "You sure?"

My nostrils flared. The pills hadn't turned up yet. They should have been where I put them. Maybe mice ran off with them or they rolled under my bed. I didn't know. "I don't need them anymore," I said, surprised at the heat tingling my ears. Saying that I didn't need them was easier than admitting I lost the pills.

Dr. Patronizing paused in his rapt chart-reading. "I'll submit a refill for the warfarin. You let me know if any pain returns and I can refill the oxycodone. You're on a good track, Mr. Buchanan." He turned to Jo, not me. "How are the therapies?"

"Good," she said for me.

"Good," he echoed. "He has two more weeks of occupational therapy and nurse visits. I'd like his physical therapy to continue through the end of October. We can follow up then."

Great, more of Accountable Adrienne, Vivacious Victor, and Nurse Needles. It helped to give them nicknames, my trick from the dawn of time to put names with faces. Though I blanked on this doc's name. Dr. Smug?

Jo nodded.

"You're ready for full weight bearing with the walker," the doctor said, turning to me. "How do you feel about that?"

"Like a spring chicken."

"I want to get you onto a cane. It depends on how your body responds to recovery."

Great. An old man's cane next. I sighed. I was a sour lemon today. At least Jo complied with my request not to chuck me into Lupine Meadows. Last summer, Stewie moved in there. He died a month later. People moved to retirement communities to die. Not me. I would die on my own terms. God and I forged an agreement on that long, long ago. Besides, I'd never be able to afford to survive there long term. I unfolded a handkerchief and blew my nose.

The doctor scrawled notes on a checklist. "We're a month out. How far can you walk on excursions?"

Did my slow, arduous journeys to the mailbox count? "Adrienne has me perfecting my technique." I rubbed my jaw. "A block, but with rests. I haven't come to town much."

Jo leaned forward from her chair. "What about a ramp?"

This woman and her persistence! *Let the ramp go, kiddo. You're getting a greenhouse.*

The doctor turned to her. "Unnecessary. He may appreciate it later, but if he's progressing with the stairs, he should be okay, especially once he moves on to the cane. You live near Clemens Ridge?"

She nodded.

"He can do flat nature trails, but I prefer him to walk on sidewalks or other paved surfaces."

We lived on the slope of a mountain—and looking over Dr. Smug's shoulder, a clear autumn day showed off the beautiful peaks in the distance.

Josie shook her head and tightened the scarf around her neck. Even she seemed tired of Boy Wonder in front of us.

"Grocery trips count. Or a few laps in the mall?" he offered. "The town of Silent Creek is in a notch. Some flat trails there? Or walk up and down Main Street?"

Jo paled. The mall and Jo? The two didn't mix. Wasn't she from the mall rat generation? Or was she too young for that? Everett could take me out once a week for a walk. Like a dog. *Want to go for a stroll? Good boy.*

"We need to do a follow-up X-ray and run blood work and we'll get you fitted with a cane. You can schedule it with reception."

Jo's shoulders fell. X-rays and blood work meant more money and driving out and about. I'd sent in the Medicare forms, hadn't I? I scratched my nose. Yes. We printed and photocopied my entire life at the library the other week when we went grocery shopping. She said she would mail them for me, since we couldn't do all of it on the computer.

Jo tapped my forearm, giving me her "it'll be fine" face. I returned it with a squeeze of her hand. Her infinite patience brought Tillie to mind. Is this what Theo would do? Take his old man to the doctor? Play Scrabble with me? God had given me a second chance when He brought Jo to my property this year.

We both left the doctor's office in Plymouth, silent in our own thoughts.

Not until we turned onto Main Street in Silent Creek did I realize Jo was talking.

"...grab your groceries? I have your list with me."

"That's a Sunday thing."

"I know it's Monday, Hank, but we're here and we didn't have time to come yesterday. Kill two birds with one stone."

That was an awful saying. Tillie loved birds. We used to have a half dozen birdhouses and feeders. She would paint or draw our feathered visitors on special paper or canvas at her easel. Chickadees, blue jays, robins, goldfinches. Oh! That's what I would do—pull the feeders and houses out of the shed and set them up with Lark. Yes, I loved that idea. "I don't want to walk around the aisles."

"The doctor said you need to walk on flat surfaces, Hank."

The turn signal clicked through my pouting.

I hated shopping without Tillie. No more stops in the floral department to pick up a spray of daisies for my darling wife. No stops at the bakery to ask Eugene—now replaced by an unapproachable pip-squeak—what today's special was and grab croissants. Sundays now included attending church, a quick visit to the Jolly Jellies, a quicker grocery trip, then a drive home.

"Why don't you visit your Jolly Jellies today while I shop instead? One of them can join you on a walk along Main Street," she suggested, turning toward the donut shop. "The weather is lovely today."

We didn't meet on Mondays. "Yes. Drop me there."

She'd probably load me up with too many bran flakes again, but I would take that risk if it meant escaping the stark fluorescent lights and loneliness of the grocery store.

She parked, grabbed the walker, and opened my door. My car was wheezing its last breaths. The sedan in the barn had vines growing on it, while Jo's truck made questionable sounds, too. She mentioned buying a new vehicle, but then I had my fall, and with it, her aspirations fell, too. I was such a burden.

"I got it. Just put it in front of me." I adjusted my sweater and brown Fedora.

"I won't be too long. Half an hour?" She hesitated. The town clock tower chimed two.

"I'll be fine, Jo." *I'm eighty, not eight.*

She turned the ignition, and a belt screeched.

"Don't forget peanut butter," I said. Lark liked the sandwiches I made her with Jo's raspberry jam. Delicious. Her baking needed some finesse, but her cooking and canning were going well.

Now her angled brows lifted over Emerald Isle eyes. "Peanut butter?"

I hadn't eaten peanut butter since my time with Tillie. My darling lathered it on her rye toast every morning, her smile still as white as the day I met her. Now peanut butter got stuck in my expensive dental work.

I pulled out the cash from my wallet and shoved it into her hand. "Yes, please." She hesitated to accept the money. "Jo, you know how it is. I have a budget for groceries. Stop footing my bills. We got the Medicare squared away. I've got Social Security, too. We'll chip away at it, and you scheduled that financial advisor for me?"

She nodded.

"Don't you worry."

Tillie's illness had taken some of our retirement funds, but I'm sure I still had some, and it was time we used that to foot more bills. Morgan made wise investment choices. However, Jo had fifty years remaining, and if she kept refusing to work or socialize, how long would the money last for her? My injury alone took a sizeable chunk of the inheritance. I'd seen the numbers in her fancy notebook when she wasn't looking. My good friend was generous to leave money for my care, but I wished he hadn't. Not if it took from Jo. From what she told me about her ex-husband, she had come here with nothing else in her account besides Morgan's money. Tillie knew what to do in such situations.

Oh, Tillie, I miss you so much. Some days I'm blessed if I remember to match my shoes.

I pretended to make my way into The Daily Donut, but once Jo was out of view, I continued oh so slowly—curse this walker—down Main Street.

In front of the hardware store, I passed Everett's truck, the bed overflowing with equipment for the greenhouse and fence repairs and the hundred other things Jo had him doing. Good. It was a suitable arrangement for all.

Working the land had never been my strength. I was useless around the homestead now. I often wondered if Jo would do better with me gone and living in town, and a hired hand living on the property instead. Everett would be a great replacement for this old man. I saw how he looked at her, too. He was a man smitten and trying to hide it.

He was a solid guy. I found it peculiar he didn't leave for work much, but judging by the time he spent in his cabin, I suspected he worked from home. I wondered how he convinced Jo to allow him to set up the internet. I admit, I snooped. Well, I asked Lark. She liked to talk. The man had a computer and all those snazzy things for it.

I paused at the hardware store's entrance. Opening doors with a walker was tricky. Just as I was about to give up, Sharon Roberts, the town busybody, appeared. "Oh, Hank! Good to see you. Heard about your fall. What an awful thing!" She held the door open for me as she exited.

I waddled in. "Thanks, Shar. Doing well. Say hi to Jim for me."

She adjusted her giant handbag. A whiff of strong perfume tickled my nose. "Will do. We miss you at church coffee hour. See you again soon?" Blinking dark brown eyes gave me a once-over.

Was my zipper down? Booger hanging out of my nose? Why did I feel like she was watching me? I had no juicy gossip for her mill. "Yes, yes. See you soon."

She paused for a moment, probably wondering what else she could ask me. "Be well, Hank."

"Mm-hmm. You, too."

She carried on her way and my nose thanked her.

I turned toward the front of the store. Everett stood at the register, checking out. That boy needed a decent haircut and shave. I paused halfway up to the counter to catch my breath.

"O'Reagan, you've got some balls coming back here," a gruff voice said from beside Everett.

He stiffened, not looking at the instigator. "I'm not bothering anyone here, Sheriff. Like I've said before."

Brian Dumont, dressed in his pressed uniform down to stiff hat and gun in holster, poked Everett's shoulder. "You and your brother should've stayed away. The town is better for it. What a disgrace to your legacy. Your parents were smart to leave while they still had their reputations intact."

I thought the sheriff had moved out of Silent Creek after his election two years ago. Guess he hung around. With his wife having run off with a younger man, and his son, Connor, getting himself in trouble all the time, wouldn't the chap be wise to leave this quiet town behind? He had a whole county to bother. Why was he pestering Everett?

I rolled in what I called my hipster hustle toward them.

A glint of disgust flickered in Brian's pebbly eyes as they followed Everett's hand, which was filling out a form on a clipboard.

Why was this Brian's business?

I'd told Jo to set up some accounts here, but she refused because she hated technology, auto payments, and anything that put her "out there." That woman made me sigh so hard someday I might bust a kidney. According to Lark, though, Everett was a whiz with computers. He could set Jo back up in the technological world and show her it's not so scary. If Jo continued as she was, she'd soon live in Morgan's gloomy bus in the woods.

"Sheriff Dumont, good day. How's the campaign going?" I removed my Fedora and dabbed at my damp brow with a fresh handkerchief. I always carried two. Before we moved into the cabin, Tillie was a nurse and she taught me the importance of carrying two. One for sweat, one for nose.

His demeanor shifted from night to daytime in a heartbeat. Good politicians had that knack. "Ah, good, Hank. How's everything at the cabin?" He looked toward the door. "Josie with you?"

"She's getting my groceries." I turned to my friend at the counter. "How's business, George? How are the Jolly Jellies?"

"We are short one. When will you be back?"

"Soon. Norm called this week. Alan, too. Guess you all miss my sunshine!"

"Of course we do. I've got something for you. Hang on a moment." George's smile creased his chubby face. He coughed and cleared his throat. Those cigars would kill him.

Everett handed over the paperwork.

"I'll get this set up for you right away," George said. "Be sure to show me photos of the greenhouse when it's all done."

Everett nodded with a quiet thanks.

George turned to Brian. "Need anything else other than that box of nails, Sheriff?"

"No. just these." He placed them on the counter, casting Everett an irritated look. If he were a cartoon character, he'd have smoke coming from his ears. He was like a bear with a sore head. I laughed inside. Guess he didn't like me interrupting his little bullying moment here.

As George checked him out, Brian's phone rang. "Uh, hey, Wagner. What is it?" He stepped back toward the fertilizer display, mumbled a few yeses, and rubbed a thick hand over a tired face. "Keep him there. I'll be over in ten." He shoved the phone back into a pocket.

He picked up the nail box, and it rattled in his hand as he pointed at Everett. "I've got an eye on you, O'Reagan."

The bell at the door chimed with his departure.

Ahhh, it made sense now.

Everett must be related to the former county sheriff, the honorable Grady O'Reagan. How had I not realized that sooner? Probably because Everett was older, like late-thirty-something, and Nora O'Reagan had her children at a young age, too. I gave Everett my first real, hard look. Same sandy-brown hair, brown eyes, and broad build as his grandfather. It all made sense now. My marbles might roll around, but I hadn't lost them yet.

Despite Everett's even-keeled composure, I could see that Brian had riled him. What had he and his brother done to deserve such scorn?

George scanned Everett's paperwork. "So you're all set? No need for a concrete mixer or gas-powered hole digger?"

Everett shook his head. "Penny's lending them to me."

George nodded, typing information into the computer. "Okay. You're all set."

I puckered a smile at George, who lifted a large basket from behind the counter. "Any chance you have a bag of birdseed?"

George eyed me. "Sure thing. This is for you, my friend." He tapped the wrapped basket of delicious sweets on the counter. "A few of your favorites. We planned to visit you today, actually."

I peeked beneath the wrapping. Sugar-sprinkled jelly, Boston cream, glazed. Yum. I would share them with Lark, Everett, and Jo.

George disappeared, then reappeared with a five-pound bag of birdseed.

"I'll carry those for you, Hank," Everett offered, taking both the donuts and seed. "Is Josie parked outside?"

"Aw, thanks. Just bring them out to the bench. She's getting groceries, but she'll be back soon."

We made our way outside, where Brian was leaning against his truck, puffing away on a cigarette. He spotted us, tossed the butt, ground it out, and hopped in his truck. He did a U-turn and laid down rubber in the direction of the grocery store.

17

—·—

EVERETT

"He's a wingnut. Don't let him get under your skin, kid," Hank said.

"No biggie." Dumont sure had a hair across his ass for me. I grabbed a bag of gumdrops from the front seat of my truck and pointed to the bench. Hank inched his walker over, his stride more confident.

"It *is* a big deal. He's got an election to win, and he will use, abuse, or flatter anyone he can to keep himself in office."

"He's lost this voter," I said. Could ex-cons vote?

Hank coughed with a hefty phlegm-loosening. "This is the thing about Brian...during his last campaign, while he was police chief of Silent Creek, he won accolades for his grandiose and heroic capture of an escaped felon. During his first term as sheriff, he's worked hard on public safety and outreach programs. People like him. Not his ways, but he gets things done to keep our community safe..." Hank hesitated, as if he forgot what to say or he wanted to deliver the blow softly. "He looks for the next big fish to fry to get him on the front page." He readjusted his sweater with a shaking hand and lowered his voice, though nobody was around. "Rumor has it that Brian has done things, uh, what do you say…grimy, no, uh, sus?" He tapped my shoulder. "Is that the word?"

I raised my eyebrows. "Uh, morally gray?"

Hank nodded. "Yes, yes. That. Watch your back, kid. Don't want you to be his next patsy." He stared off at the storefronts across the street.

Hank's drift was loud and clear. Peachy. I was glad he didn't ask me about what I'd done to be Dumont's punching bag.

I offered the gumdrops and Hank reached into the bag. "Love these. Can only suck on them, or else they get stuck in the pearlies I paid a mortgage for. Same with my butterscotch candies." He scratched the side of his nose, working the gumdrop in his mouth. "Brian's got an eye for Jo, too. That could be the reason he's razzing you. Word travels fast in Silent Creek. I'm sure he knows you're living at our place now."

I swallowed, not allowing the heat to rise in my chest at feeling like an outcast in my hometown. "When is Josie coming?"

"Whenever she's done getting my groceries. Hope she doesn't sneak in any of that hippie grass or seaweed. They bind me up."

I snorted.

"Tillie made sure I ate my greens, but I draw the line at fad diets," he said as he popped a licorice gumdrop into his mouth.

"My grandmother loves that flavor."

Fading gray eyebrows shot up into his much-receded hairline. He nosed around in the bag for two more black gumdrops. "My Tillie was friends with Nora, but I haven't seen her in years."

"Yeah, she lives at Lupine Meadows." If Hank knew Gram, did he know my history, too? If he did, he never let on. I should have assumed everyone here knew everyone. *Duh, O'Reagan.* Dumont must've read my rap sheet, despite records being sealed...because law enforcement was an exception to the rule. My tapping foot stilled, and I nibbled on a nail. Hank wouldn't tell Jo, would he?

He nodded. "People go there to die."

I reached in, took a red gumdrop. "Gram's doing well. We visit her a lot. She has a wonderful group of friends. The place is a bit...hippie," I said with a smirk, using his word.

Hank chuckled.

"We're going this afternoon. Want to come? Do you know anyone else there?"

He shook his head. "Not anymore. It's a germ factory."

Gram was a spry eighty-three. Never a sniffle. Played cards, took over the communal kitchen like a badass, assisted in the flower gardens, took Zumba classes, went bird watching, walked the paths, baked with Lark. I bet she and Hank would get on well and he'd change his opinion about the Meadows.

I glanced at my phone. I needed to pick Lark up from Penny's, but I felt uncomfortable leaving Hank here alone. I promised Penny I'd watch Shawn and Liam when she went to see Jake again next week. Despite his incarceration in Massachusetts, she made the effort to visit him whenever she could.

We watched passersby, cars, school buses, dog-walkers. We sat in silence, embracing the cool, sunny day while eating gumdrops. My phone's weather app showed clear skies and temperatures in the fifties to sixties all week. Perfect weather to build a greenhouse. I did my best to dislodge the thoughts of the sheriff from my mind until

I could speak with Gram. With the ASS out to get me, I had to work even harder to keep my reputation from being tarnished further.

Things were coming along. Using my modified internet at night, I completed the ProspNet project and turned it in today. The payment transferred to my bank account soon thereafter. The job fired up my fingers and neurons. To do what I was good at—testing firewalls, writing code, and breaking into networks to determine security vulnerabilities—had me riding an adrenaline rush of excitement. They contracted me to do more work. The gray and black hat options didn't even enter my mind anymore. Legit only, from here on out. I couldn't believe I even considered that *other* opportunity. I had yet to delete that other email account though.

I couldn't wait to dig into the greenhouse work. We decided upon wood-framed with polycarbonate panels. I wanted to finish it before winter. For Josie. But also for myself. It was time to prove who Everett O'Reagan was.

My phone rang almost divinely. "Hey, Anthony."

"Hey, Ev. Just checking in. When should I show up?"

I loved Anthony's conscientiousness. He'd come a long way since slacking off through our classes in vo-tech. He was now Silent Creek's best electrician, and he did part-time contracting work. I suspected marrying his hard-as-nails high school sweetheart kept him on the straight and narrow. Anthony was one of the lucky ones. He also never gave me a hard time about my tainted past.

"Eight tomorrow is good if it still works for your schedule." Handling the foundation was a multi-person job: digging, leveling, and pouring the concrete footings, assembling the stringers, and capping the frame. Footings needed three or four days to settle before proceeding. It gave me time to assemble the rafters and framework.

"I'll be there with a couple of Angie's famous nut rolls."

I smiled. "My stomach can't wait. See you then. Thanks, buddy."

A noisy belt screeching announced Josie's arrival in Hank's car. Her features scrunched with concern. She loosened a light scarf, the pink flush on her cheeks a stark contrast to her pale skin. "Hank! I thought you were at The Daily Donut. I couldn't find you."

"You found me. Did my steps as requested, Your Honor," he said, rising with his walker. "And I found a friend."

She hopped out of the car, wrangled her scarf, huffed, and gave up, tossing it inside. "Here, Hank." She assisted him into the front seat, then nestled the basket of donuts behind her seat on the driver's side.

I passed her the bag.

"Birdseed?" She raised her eyebrows.

Without thinking, I grabbed her shoulder. The forwardness of the touch made me drop my hand in an instant. "Hey, Jo-Josie. I..."

Her eyes flashed in irritation as she blinked.

Say something. Anything. Her hair was loose today. Most days, she wore it up in a ponytail or messy bun. It was a luxurious wavy cascade, thick, and with golden highlights that belonged to cartoon princesses, according to Lark. "Uh..." Where had my words gone? Sometimes our conversations came easy, other times it was like getting a root canal. But I persisted. The project. Yes, the project. I would need her help with raising the walls in a few days.

"The cold food needs to be put in the fridge. We'll see you back there." She glanced into the bed of my truck, filled with supplies. "Got everything you need?"

"Yes. Sure." *Uh, that went well.*

She hopped into the driver's seat.

Hank rolled his window down, offering me the bag of gumdrops back.

"No, you can keep them."

The belt rattled again as Josie shifted into drive. "Hey." I leaned into Hank's window. "I can help you fix that. I just replaced my timing belt. Want me to look under your hood?"

Oh, that was a new expression. Heat flooded my insides as her pale pink lips made an O.

"She'd love that," Hank said. "Thanks, Everett. You're so helpful. Glad to have you around. Tell Birdie I have a surprise for her when she comes back. And say hi to Nora for me." With soft blue-gray eyes glinting, he tapped the dashboard. "Come on, you old beast. Take us away."

"Will do."

Josie drove off, leaving a wake of fumes. One minute she was receptive, the next she was as ruffled as a rooster. Ugh, poor Ronnie. Bad analogy.

Why was I trying so hard with her?

As I strode down the sidewalk to my truck, I paused by the spot Dumont vacated. Curiosity led me to crouch and check out the cigarette butt on the curb. Nope, not the same brand as the one I'd seen by Josie's shed. Was that good...or bad? I picked it up and tossed it in the nearest trash bin.

After picking up Lark at Penny's house and a quick trip to the auto shop, I drove to Lupine Meadows.

"We're visiting Nana?" Lark squeaked.

"You betcha." I had an ulterior motive today. I wanted to ask her about asshat Dumont.

As we drove to the retirement community, my chest tightened with the ominous feeling that life was waiting to serve the next punch. I mentally prepared myself for my chat with Gram. I needed answers. Turning past the expanded flower beds that lined the community center building—my first landscape project I assisted with this spring—I located the numbered guest spot for Gram's unit.

Lark froze mid-unbuckle. "We don't have a gift for Nana!"

Her panic snapped me out of my own haze. "I gave my gumdrops to Hank." I dug around in the glove box. "Breath mints?"

Lark's face was thunderstruck. Horrified, even. "Daddy..."

I nodded. "Of course not."

Where was my head? I always brought Gram something sweet. Pulling up Lupine Meadows' website on my phone, I skimmed the calendar of events. "Today's Sorbet Day. Think Nana would like that?"

Lark pondered, chewing her lower lip and balling her hands. "Dink so."

I corrected her, "Th. *Think* so, Birdie."

"*Th-th-THink* so."

"Good."

Scouring my car once more, just in case, yielded nothing but receipts, crayons, and smashed crackers. "What flavor do you think she'd like?"

Lark released her knotted hands. "Raspberry!"

I slammed the door with a thud. "Let's go."

We made our way along the maze of stone walkways connecting the brick buildings. We passed residents strolling about, sitting on benches, or walking dogs. Enormous pots of mums greeted us at Grand Central, as Gram called it. The sprawling one-story community center was home to themed daily activities and the fitness room, a cafe, administrative offices, nursing staff and medical facilities, and other gathering spaces. Outcrops of row-house-like residential buildings flanked it. This place cost big bucks. Besides the multitude of activities, residents owned their homes, paid fees, and had more independence than they would in a hospital setting. A bus even chauffeured them to town.

The well-lubricated automatic doors whooshed shut behind me as we entered the main building. Upbeat Caribbean music played from the nearby cafe. Fresh fruit exploded from a display surrounding iced treats in a portable freezer table.

The staff knew me by now. Correction, they knew Lark. I was the chump who walked around with her. I got a few nods and hellos as we scooped raspberry sorbet for Gram. Lark chose the rainbow sherbet, a content gleam in her eyes. She found rainbows everywhere.

We walked to Gram's first-floor condo, which like the others, had a small parcel of green lawn in front.

I paused at the entrance gate. "Should we call her first? She could be out."

"Let's surprise her!"

If she wasn't home, we'd leave the treat in her freezer with a note. I had her spare key. Though Lark spent long days here, she wasn't permitted to sleep over. The Meadows had strict rules about overnight guests...as in, none allowed. Especially the ones under four feet tall. Gram want-

ed to visit our cabin herself, but Josie's eight-hun-
dred-page rental agreement discouraged visitors outside "normal business hours"—whatever the hell those
were—and didn't permit overnight visitors either. I had
never considered inviting a woman over or going on a
date. Though I wouldn't have minded cozying up with
Josie.

Uh, what?

Where had that thought come from?

Overnight guest rules. Right. I snorted under my
breath. Hank wasn't completely wrong about this place.
I understood how so many regulations would cramp his
lifestyle and freedom.

Gram deserved a nice last home. She'd supported
Granddad's career as a naval officer, county deputy, then
high sheriff. In the wake of his passing, she'd sold their
home and moved here.

Gram opened her door after the second ring. "Oh, my
sweeties! What a surprise." She waved us inside, pulling
her cardigan close around her. "How is my favorite bird?"
She kissed Lark's beanie-covered head.

A blue and orange mustache encircled Lark's mouth.
"Chirp!"

"I see you found the cafe." She pulled out a tissue
and bent to dab at Lark's sherbet ring, then turned to
me with an expectant look. I wiped my feet on the mat
before stepping inside.

"We did." I gave her the sorbet. "Hope it's okay. We
didn't call first."

"Always okay, sweetie pie. I was getting ready to bake
cookies." Gram asked Lark, "Want to help?"

She jumped up and down. "Yesss!"

"Birdie, could you check on Nana's bird feeders first?"

Lark did as asked, without a fuss. My heart squeezed, a tightness of both admiration and regret. I knew why she was this way.

Gram situated herself on the seafoam-blue couch and released a sigh.

The condo's nautical theme paid homage to Granddad's naval time. His medals, awards, and honors sat displayed on the gas fireplace mantel. With its framed lighthouses, anchor switch plates, and buoys in the tiny flower garden, the condo still felt alien to me compared to her old Victorian. I never talked about Granddad Grady or his time as sheriff. But there he was, framed in his glory, on the wall behind Gram. He stared at me over her shoulder in disapproval.

"Out with it," she said, scooping a spoonful of her sorbet.

I dragged my hands through my hair and heaved a strident sigh. I was tired of "keeping it together" in Lark's presence. Life was shit sometimes.

"You'll go bald if you keep doing that. And such lovely hair, Ev dear. Just like your father's."

Lark's singing danced inside on a breeze through the screen door.

"How's the new place?" she asked.

"Good." I had limited time before Lark grew bored with the birds. I pushed out, "Do you know the sheriff?"

She puckered her lips, now stained dark pink.

"Did he say something to you, Ev?" Gram placed her cardboard sorbet cup on the glass coffee table, undoing my resolve with a glare.

I gave a noncommittal shrug as my knee began a restless bounce.

She heaved a sigh. "He's more bark than bite."

"Are we talking Chihuahua or Doberman?"

"Depends on who you are. He held a special coat drive here last week, buttering up voters. Good turnout. I'm voting for the other guy, though."

I swallowed. "Why does he have a bone to pick with me?"

She glanced out the rear door at a distracted Lark. "His wife left him a few years ago. I am unsure if she left him for someone else, got tired of the dream life in Silent Creek, or something else. My friend Loretta told me he's bitter. And his son gets into trouble a lot. With the law. The sheriff's always bailing him out. It's not a good image for a person running for office, I suppose."

"He's looking to distract the public with somebody else. Me. Hank said the same thing, though Hank doesn't know my past. Apparently, Dumont does."

"Oh, how is Hank? It's been years. Ever since Tillie passed..." she said, ruefully.

"He's good. Told me to say hi."

She fussed with her sweater and necklace, hiding a smile. "Does he hang with those greasers at The Daily Donut?"

"Greasers, huh? Been watching too much *West Side Story*, Gram." I nodded. "Yes, the donut group is his street posse."

She let her smile loosen. I did, too.

"Hank had a sweet wife. Before her illness took her away from the sewing circle, I knew her."

"He says this place is a death mill."

She chuckled. "He would say that. A few of his friends who moved here died, but they were already sick. Still got that spunk in him?"

"He does." I settled my restless knee but couldn't fight the parental guilt rising in me. "He hangs with Lark a lot."

"I'm sure she loves it. He still has that Lego collection?"

I guess Gram knew Hank better than I thought. "Yup. I wonder if, due to his hip injury and recovery, he may long for more outings. Me dumping my kid on him—"

She flung her palm up. "Stop that. You're resourceful, finding positive places for Lark to be while you work to provide a home for her." Offering me her sincere smile, she added, "As for Hank, he's a good man. You're wondering if he knows about you?"

I went to drag my hand through my hair but stopped. "Well, if he knows you, he knows our family."

"No worries, sweetie. Hank might be loose lipped, but he's not one to spread information like that around. Either way, I'll call him. There's a big band concert coming up in a few weeks. I'll invite him over. We can catch up. It's been far too long. And I bet he'll change his tune once he truly experiences the Meadows. His new landlady is not looking to kick him out, is she?"

"Oh, no, not at all. Please, don't grill him with questions. If he knows about me, so be it."

"Got it. I'll work my magic. Catching up with him will be good, regardless."

I glanced at Lark as she headed toward the door. "Hank said Dumont won the last election by catching an escaped convict or something."

"Let that one rest. You've got nothing to worry about. Just steer clear of him. I can spill some tea with the ladies if you really want more details."

I held up my hand. "No. Don't be spreading rumors or nonsense, okay? He's my problem, not yours."

"Everett Grady O'Reagan, he shouldn't *be* your problem. You made a poor choice. You served your time. If the sheriff and others can't see that, then they can stuff it."

I laughed. Had to love it when Gram got testy and protective.

Lark came barreling in, the screen door smacking against the frame. Gram lowered her voice, keeping eyes on me. "You have different priorities now. Don't let a wet rag like him bother you." She turned to Lark. "Hands!"

Lark screeched to a halt, her shoes squeaking on the kitchen tile. She hurried to the sink to wash her hands, which were covered in birdseed. Dirt, too.

Gram rose, nimbly walked to me, and gave me a side squeeze as I stood. Her head came to my shoulder. She whispered, "God gives second chances, Ev."

I followed her gaze to Lark.

She lifted an eyebrow. "Now, do tell me. How is everything with you? How is your new landlady, Josie?"

18

JOSIE

Serenity came over me as I drove Hank home from the hardware store. Aside from the weasel horror, life was going well since Everett's arrival. He was tackling the property tasks like it was nobody's business. Hank thrived with his therapies and received the green light for the next step in his treatment. Lark kept Hank company sorting Legos and playing, and I took much needed time to rest. Finances were looking okay-ish, too.

When Hank's car thumped and pulled hard to the right, I knew my luck had expired.

"Dammit!"

I removed my foot from the accelerator, attempting to maintain the car's alignment, and then let the Buick come to a halt on the roadside. "Son of a...argh!" I said, my pulse soaring.

"Jesus, Mary, Joseph, and the wee donkey!" Hank concurred. "That was an event!" He took out a handkerchief and dabbed his brow.

I checked the tire, my mind on the perishable groceries in the back seat. Busted. I leaned against the hood, crossed my arms, and counted with my breaths.

Seconds later, blue lights appeared behind us. The microsecond of relief I felt dissipated when I saw who it was. "You've got to be kidding me." We had just seen Brian Dumont at the grocery store, his truck parked beside Hank's Buick. Now here? I swear to God the man was following me. Shivers pricked at my scalp.

Hank rolled down his window. "The cavalry is here!"

I wiped hands on my jeans trying to adopt Hank's optimism. Without cell phones, we were stranded on a back road, halfway to home.

Brian approached, his shoulders set back, his footfall heavy on the shoulder's gravel. "Got a flat, have you?"

A pinball of panic bounced around my rib cage. I had just been thinking things were improving. Silly me. I planted on a gracious smile and buttoned my peacoat against the chill. "I must've run over something."

A nail? Glass?

A flat tire was just that. A flat tire. The weasel had been a freak occurrence. The suspicious holes in my perimeter fencing were from wear and tear. My missing gloves and shed lock and other items that grew legs and walked away would show up. This was all just bad luck. Nothing more. Coincidence.

"That's a shame. Do you have a spare?"

Hank volunteered out the window, "Never needed one."

"I'll call in for a tow truck. Will you need a ride?" Brian rubbed his nose, his dark eyes watching me and hardly glancing at Hank.

We could call Everett with Brian's cell. I didn't have his number memorized, and it was written down at home. Living with no technology had sounded amazing at first, but as life threw me platters of lemons, I realized some connection to the outside world wasn't too bad. Carrying a burner phone at least was warranted from here on out. "Yes, thank you. We don't want to bother you, though."

He dialed. "Not a bother."

As we waited for the tow truck, Brian helped me load Hank's groceries into the back of his truck. Getting Hank into the high seat of the extended cab proved challenging, but we managed. The tow-truck driver was nice. I would ask Everett for a ride this week to pick up Hank's car. I ticked my nails on my teeth as I slid into Brian's passenger seat.

He made small talk as I stared out the window. "How's the place holding up for you?"

"Good." I fidgeted with my coat buttons, wiggling as close as possible toward the door.

"Heard you have new roomies."

I sighed. Silent Creek wasn't so silent in the gossip department. I wondered what else people were saying about me. His phone rang, and he took the call for the rest of our drive, allowing me the freedom to be quiet.

As he put the truck in park in front of my house, he said, "Let me help you carry the bags in."

I waved his offer away. "No need."

Please just go. His phone rang again, and irritation furrowed his brow.

I helped Hank into his cabin and then unloaded groceries faster than a NASCAR driver.

On the last trip, a can toppled out of one of my canvas bags and Brian scooped it up after sliding his phone into his pocket.

"Thank you again for your help, Sheriff."

His hand paused on mine for a moment as he handed me the can. Then, he held my look for longer than comfortable with a weird rub of my shoulder. "Always a pleasure, Josie.

You be safe here, now." He tipped a finger to his hat. "Don't be a stranger. And it's Brian, remember?"

I nodded and returned to the cabin, my fingers cold, my heart thrumming.

An hour later, the uncertain spin of tires on gravel and Chip's single bark alerted me to a stranger. Son of a biscuit. This was getting out of hand.

I rounded the cabin, carrying a pail of Gilda's second milking. I was so tired of milking her. The chickens clucked as I passed them, excited to eat a bowl of oatmeal. They were such spoiled monsters. After an afternoon of managing animals, I now needed to handle more people. Who now?

The car struggled at the final steep slope before the gravel loop in front of my cabin. I eyed the driver: a woman in business attire. Chip barked again. *Yeah, buddy, I see it's a stranger. Thanks.* Gosh, I was salty today. I deposited the pail on the porch with a thud.

The woman parked, emerged, and as she approached, her heels snagging on dirt and stones—not a wise choice for a country visit—she offered me a weary smile. "Good day," she said. "I'm looking for Mr. O'Reagan."

Glasses too large for her face dropped low on her nose. She pushed them up and adjusted her purple scarf, hugging a portfolio to her chest with her other arm.

"He should be back soon."

"And you are?"

Shouldn't I be asking her the same? I raised my chin. "Josie Sawyer, Everett's landlady. I own this property."

"I'm Carolyn Abrams—" She thrust out a hand in greeting, but the sound of Everett's no-nonsense turn up the driveway cut her words off. His truck wasn't quiet. At least his didn't wheeze and thunder like Hank's Buick or Morgan's truck. Speaking of...where was Don with DMV locations for me? And my Everett intel, now that I thought of it. The credit report I'd run had come up with zero red flags at least, but something nagged me. I wanted more info on my boarder.

A bit late for that, Josie.

Crickets from the Smythe base camp didn't mean bad news. Don was thorough in his investigations. If he'd found something awful, he would have already called me.

Everett jumped out of his truck. He dashed to greet us in record time. Lark popped out, strolled over to Chip, and scratched him behind an ear. Everett skidded to a stop beside the woman.

Thank goodness. He could take care of his visitor. A client?

He brushed his hands on his jeans and shook the woman's hand. "Oh, Ms. Abrams. Nice to see you. You're early for our appointment."

"You haven't updated me with your new address. I spoke to Penny—" she began.

With an arm around her shoulders, he escorted her to his cabin. "Oh? You didn't get my message. Glad she could help you. My place is this way. We can have our meeting there."

"Oh, I wouldn't mind chatting with—"

"I'm sure Ms. Sawyer is busy," he said.

Ms. Sawyer? What was Everett up to? Why would his client want to speak with me? As a reference?

"We need to discuss your work, Mr. O'Reagan..." she said, wrestling her heel free from a pothole.

"Yes, yes. The business plan... Got the website design set up already."

She followed him into the cabin. Everett hollered over his shoulder, "Lark, come inside, okay?"

Lark danced up the steps, counting as she went. "I'll be back later, gator!" she said to Chip.

His tail wagged.

Gosh, what a client. The woman seemed irritated the moment she set foot on the property.

The strange interaction explained Everett's computer and Wi-Fi setup. Hank told me about it. I wasn't pleased, but Everett had broken none of the rental agreement terms, either. Although I never forbade Wi-Fi access or work from home, I had specified that no in-person business should be conducted on the property. If meeting clients here for his—web design or landscape work?—was necessary, he'd have to find office space in town.

Except honestly, it didn't irk me as much as I thought it would.

Resigning myself to talk to him later, I made for my cabin. "Come, Chip. Let's finish dinner. Tonight calls for R and R." I'd purchased a nice lavender bubble bath from a boutique in town and intended on a long soak and pedicure. "First a quick call."

After pulling out a burner phone, I dialed, determined to get through to Don. There had been no answer, not even a voicemail last time. Wasn't four weeks long enough?

Like a child who'd scalded their hand on the stove, I was cautious. Especially with Everett O'Reagan. But, as much as I hated to admit it, I *liked* his and Lark's presence here. I hungered for connection more than I expected after moving here.

I needed to know if it was safe to sate that hunger.

When Don picked up, I didn't wait for a greeting. "It's Hyacinth."

"Oh, hey, Hyacinth. Weather cooperating for you in Seattle?" His voice was grainy.

The subterfuge weighed me down. I pinched my fore-head and said, deadpan, "The coffee sure makes up for the rain."

"I love a Peruvian brew in a French press."

I rolled my eyes and released an audible sigh. "I haven't heard from you."

"We had...uh, a flood."

"A flood?"

I heard movement, shuffling, and Libby in the back-ground nattering about power cords. "Yeah, the big coastal storm that came through the Northeast a few weeks ago? Turns out my place is not so flood proof. Then a pipe burst. It's a mess. So much equipment, files, ruined. This has waylaid me, but I haven't forgotten."

I waited, fidgeting with the zipper on my fleece.

"No, Libs. Put that in the box over there. Yeah." He blew his breath out. "We're in the middle of moving. I'll continue to work once we settle into the new location. How is the electrician coming? Did you get my contact info?"

Electrician? I blanked. Oh. Driver's license. "Not yet. Been waylaid here, too. Did you text it to this phone number?"

"Yes." He cursed under his breath.

"Never got it."

"Hmm. Okay, well, are you ready for it? Got a pen?"

I grabbed one. "Yes."

"Don't laugh."

"Never."

"His name is Jesús Christian. He's got magical skills." Don laughed at his own joke.

"Does he turn water into wine?"

"No, but he'll work magic at the DMV. You need to make appointments online, but if you call and ask to speak to JC, he'll arrange a good time for you. You'll go through the usual steps for the license, but he can handle your insurance and registration in your corporation's name with less hassle. All legal. Some employees can be hard-asses with putting the corporation's name. Do you have a car to purchase?"

"Not yet." I wrote JC's name and the direct phone number on a piece of paper.

I heard papers shuffling.

"Okay, so, O'Reagan...nothing stands out as a red flag yet. Clean as a whistle. I found a questionable gap in his employment record, though, of three years."

I picked at the dog fur on my fleece. "What could that mean?"

"Could be nothing. Unemployed, took time off, searched for work, stayed home with kids, lived abroad—no military background—maybe moved or did informal jobs."

"He has a young daughter. Maybe he was home with her? He does contract work, landscaping. And IT, I think. Web design."

"That might be it. He'd need to report that to the IRS, regardless. I'll check other sources. His record shows he's bounced around between Massachusetts and New Hampshire over the past ten years."

I never asked Don what his "other sources" were. The less I knew, the better. "And?"

"A gap could be various things. I was checking on a few options when the flood happened. He's clean. Almost too clean." He exhaled. "Not gonna get you upset over ifs, so let me dot my i's and cross my t's first before you panic."

"Why would I panic?" Okay, I was panicking. When people say don't panic, you panic, right? With an icy hand, I pushed the phone closer to my ear, afraid I heard him wrong.

He paused.

"Don..."

"A gap means either he is legit clean, or he has a sealed record."

Sealed record? Don left out the important adjective—*criminal*.

"Look, don't freak out, I'm checking off boxes. I do this for everyone. Don't send yourself over a cliff. However, there is something else not related to O'Reagan..."

The blood left my face. What else? My shoulders tightened, and I blinked blurry eyes. "Tell me."

"They released Tate from prison three weeks ago. I tried to get a message to you, but apparently, your phone doesn't pick up texts or the messages are blocked. Check on that."

I rubbed my temple. *Stupid burners.* "Tate is out?" I curled into myself, knees to my chest, pressing the phone to my ear. Early. Of course. *This* was why I covered my trails, why I hid. I had known this was inevitable.

Would this be my new normal...forever?

He was quick to say, "I've been tracking his location. He's still in the state. Got an apartment in Chelsea and he's working. I don't think he's looking for you. I'll monitor him. You guys settled everything before he got sent away."

Yeah, but Tate held grudges. Tate blamed me for *his* deceit.

I squeezed my eyes shut and nodded, though Don couldn't see. Chelsea made sense; his parents lived there.

"You okay?"

"Mm-hmm." No, no I was not.

Tate never resorted to violence. Tate never hurt me physically, but the damage he'd done to my psyche felt irreparable some days. He had stolen my identity, spent my life savings, and was a narcissist to his core, even throughout the prosecution, conviction, and divorce. What if he got wind of Morgan's inheritance? Money was his drug of choice.

My heartbeat quickened with the race car in my brain. It had pissed him off when I pressed criminal charges. How could I not, after he ruined me? I'd been gullible, but not stupid. I wondered if prison offered Narcissists Anonymous. Nobody would show. It wasn't part of their MO.

I wiped sweaty palms on my jeans.

Was Tate a changed man?

My gut said no.

Would Tate beg forgiveness and attempt to lure me in with his charms, just to screw me over again?

Yes.

"Don, am I safe?"

"Yes," he said. "You have the dog, the pepper spray, the wild-goose-chase paper trail, tracks covered..."

I thought about Morgan's gun, that was in a case in the basement. No. I wouldn't need it. It was rusty and in an even rustier case. I didn't even know how to use it! "Could he possibly discover my location?

"Nothing is ever a hundred percent. You're staying under the radar. He might've been a whiz with the identity theft stuff because he had access to you and your passwords and accounts, but Tate is an addict, not a computer genius or a gumshoe. He can't find you, and he can't touch your money—that came to you after the divorce."

Not convinced, I said, "Okay, thanks. Check in when you can with updates. Call this number. Leave a message. I'll set up the voicemail right now. I'll make sure the texts are working, too. Send me a test one in an hour."

"Will do. Be safe, Hyacinth."

19

EVERETT

Shit. Shhhhhit.

Did Carolyn tell Josie who she was? And why she was here?

"Are you dirsty, Miss Carolyn?" Lark asked on her way to the kitchen. She dropped her backpack, filled with a few toys from Penny's house, a portable DVD player, and a handful of movies. She plopped her coat on the floor beside it.

"Hang it, please, Lark," I said, my mind going a mile a minute.

Carolyn's gaze slid around, taking in the dusted surfaces, organized counter, ironed curtains, Lark's drawings taped on the fridge, and a framed picture of us.

"Tea or coffee?" I offered, waving a hand at the clean couch. She couldn't bitch about any messes here. No Shawn or Liam to destroy stuff. Not like the pigsty Lark lived in with Fran. I liked tidy, minimal.

"Tea, please." She opened that goddamned red notebook and clicked a pen.

Peachy. Let the interrogation begin.

I located the basket of teas included in Josie's welcome package. "Lark, why don't you bring your backpack into your room and let Miss Carolyn and I talk for a few?" She nodded and scurried off, a cookie in her hand. I needed to make dinner soon. I'd bought real chicken...a step up from nuggets. I wanted to invite Josie for dinner sometime.

Carolyn smacked her lips. "Where to start?"

I filled the kettle and rested it on the stove. Flipped the burner on. "What does that mean?" I located the mugs and spoons, too tired to filter my responses. What a day. First Dumont, and now Carolyn. *Easy, O'Reagan. Come up with your spiel.* I had seriously lost my finesse. Lying got old. Embellished truth was the only way.

"Well, first, you told me you were following up on a rental and gave me this address, yet you didn't officially file it with the office."

"Sorry." *Just don't ask to talk to Josie,* I prayed. I didn't think Carolyn needed to speak with my landlady so long as I had a binding residential lease. I pulled that paper out of a folder, and placed it on the coffee table in front of her. Josie was my employer, too—albeit under the table. I'd need to push the conversation to the ProspNet work, since they had 1099s and a legal paper trail. Carolyn could follow up with them.

She scribbled a few notes. "I thought you were being employed by Ms. Sawyer, for work on the property. But you mentioned website design. A business plan? Is this for your landscaping business?"

I pretended to look for sugar in the cabinet. "Yes, the uh business plan and website is for the landscaping work. Ms. Sawyer's work is progressing well. I just got supplies to build a greenhouse. She has enough work to keep me busy until spring." I took a breath. "While I get my landscaping business up and running, my primary income is currently from a few contract jobs. Some…" *Don't say ethical hacking.* Carolyn was obtuse about it. "…website assessments, web design. One company, ProspNet, hired me for more work. I can show you the paystub and I'll get a 1099 in January."

Alright, the work was technically cybersecurity. But Carolyn only needed to see evidence of paid work at a legitimate employer. Nothing prohibited me from doing computer science jobs.

She jotted down notes. "Sounds promising. How steady is this contract work?"

"I have contracts for a few other projects with different companies." I waved to my computer setup on half of the dining room table. "You can call their HR offices."

She sucked her teeth. "It's not my place to judge your *choice* of vocation, but be careful where you tread, Mr. O'Reagan."

You made your judgment clear since day one, lady. This job was reminiscent of a bank robber returning to the scene, now employed as a bank teller. I got it, I did. But I was different now.

She sighed. "Please provide your employers' information. Just email me. Does Ms. Sawyer have documentation for your hire here?"

I clenched my teeth. "Carolyn, Lark is my priority *here*. You know this. Legit all the way. I'm trying."

"I know." She adjusted her glasses. "So, Ms. Sawyer?"

I couldn't lie. She'd check. "She's given me a reduction in rent in exchange for property maintenance. It's a trial run. Then in the spring, we'll work on the formal paperwork." Was that a lie or truth? *Steer her away from Josie.* "Like I said, I'm also applying for my contractor licensure, registering my business, and setting up liability insurance so I can start my own landscaping company."

"This is the business plan and website you mentioned?" She quirked an eyebrow.

I nodded.

"Please submit paperwork to the office and keep us informed of the business. Do you plan to operate out of the home?"

No reprimand today? Had she come around to this idea? I swallowed. "Yes."

She put her pen down on the notebook and crossed her legs. "Three jobs are a lot for anyone under normal circumstances. You'll be able to balance these three jobs—the work for Ms. Sawyer, your computer contract work, and the landscaping business? That's a lot for a single parent. A lot of hats to wear."

Did she comprehend the humor in that pun-filled statement? *At least not the black hat type, lady!* "Yes."

She flipped a page in the notebook. "How is Lark?"

"Good. I got the health and dental set up. I can send in that information."

She held my gaze. "Thank you."

The kettle whistled, and I turned my back to her, relieved for a moment to avoid her stare.

"How is living here?"

"Lark likes it. Loves the trails, the chickens, and our neighbor, Mr. Buchanan, who has a million Legos." I poured too quickly, and hot water splashed my counter and hand. I hissed. "This is a far step up from the conditions Fran had her living in."

"I'm not here to judge Lark's mother. I'm here to deem *your—*"

I raised my voice, turning to face her. "—home adequate and safe. You make that abundantly clear each time you visit." She opened her mouth to respond, but I pressed on.

"This place is fine. The homestead is eco-friendly, off the grid. And I've got honest-to-goodness work. We are good."

"Look, Everett..."

Ice formed in my veins. Time to sit. I handed her a cup, then settled into the armchair beside the couch, pretending to be busy stirring my tea.

"You're making good progress with the living situation, the insurance for Lark, and your jobs...but the program doesn't work if you don't show up." She dunked the tea bag into her mug and placed it on the coffee table. A splatter of liquid hit the wood. I grabbed a napkin to swipe it clean. Bribe her with a cookie, too?

The program.

Bloody f—

The damn program! *Solidarity in Sobriety.* I forgot to go last week. *Oh, shit.* And Sherlock here did her due diligence and checked in with our recovery group secretary to make sure I attended. Our group was very low-key, but in my case, DCYF required a check-in to confirm I attended.

I tittered, fighting every urge to clench my hands or run them through my hair. "I'm allowed one strike, right?"

"This isn't a game."

No shit, Sherlock. I sipped my tea. "I honestly forgot, Carolyn. I've been swamped with setting up my consulting work with the IT firms, creating the landscape business plan, and managing the work here. Moving in here took time, too. I got distracted."

"Do you think you're taking on too much?"

How could I not? These tasks were all required of me by DCYF. This was for Lark. This was our life. "No."

I expected a sardonic retort from an overworked, underpaid, and sleep-deprived social worker.

Instead, Carolyn uncrossed her legs, set her red note-book down, and knotted her hands together. "Missing one recovery meeting isn't the worst thing, especially with all you've been doing. I see you working hard to get your life together. You've been an active participant in the group. Please don't miss another."

My jaw dropped. Was Carolyn giving me a warning, a slap on the wrist?

The notebook returned to her lap, and she readjusted her glasses. "Now, one more thing before I visit with Lark and tour your home."

The random piss test you ordered two weeks ago wasn't enough? I chewed the inside of my cheek and double-hand-ed my mug, allowing the warmth to calm my mind.

Breathe in, out. Cinnamon and clove wafted up from the mug. Inner peace.

I had to get a grip.

"Mr. and Mrs. Rossi requested a visit."

"Not here," I said so fast it surprised me. I stilled a bounc-ing knee.

"They're permitted visitations."

I would not allow them here, ever. Not to my home. "What if I meet them in town? At a park? They can play with Lark." I swallowed a gulp of tea and burned my tongue. *Play, my ass.* They would scrutinize us. Pecking like vultures with a fresh kill, talons out.

She blew on her tea before sipping. "I don't see why not. But if I hear that you've been uncooperative with them..."

"Yes, another strike." *In your Red Book of Sin.*

"You have their phone number?"

"Yes."

"Good. Arrange it, soon." She snapped the book shut and shoved it into her bag. She leaned back on the couch, her mug in hand, and said, "Tell me about this property. There are chickens?"

I quirked a smile. "And a goat."

20

— · —

LARK

Today was chicken day! I met them on my first day here, but Daddy told me to give them space. They were sad and missing their friends. How could I ignore them when they squawked and wanted to play with me? A lot of sounds bothered my ears, but bird sounds didn't. Even when Ronnie used to be here, I didn't mind his morning *cock-o-doodle-do!*

Daddy said that Ronnie and two of the hens went on an adventure. I searched for them in the woods once, but Daddy called me back. He didn't like me to wander. Instead, I played in the treehouse—where I kept my special things.

I thought Miss Josie missed the chickens, too. She was quiet and liked to save her words. She liked to protect her stuff and put locks on everything. I didn't like people taking my things either. Mommy used to take my stuff and say she'd return it, but she never did. Mommy took a lot of naps, too. And when I napped, I would wake up and my stuff would be gone. My nice shoes and jacket and pink dress Grandma got me. Mommy said they were at the cleaners, but she never got them back. They lost them. Then once, some men with a big truck came and took my bed. Maybe it was so when I rolled out of bed, I wouldn't hit the floor so hard. Mommy moved the mattress on top of the faded spot where my old rainbow rug used to be.

I missed her. Daddy said she left for a little while. How long is a little while?

At least he explained things to me and didn't yell. Sometimes he thumped the table with his fist, but he never got mad at me. Nana said he had a "patient soul."

I ate my cereal and banana, my legs wiggling. My legs got as excited as my fingers. Chicken day!

I asked Miss Josie again last night, after dinner, when Daddy explained the rest of his plan for the vegetable house, if I could visit the chickens. This time she said yes. Adults said yes if you asked enough times.

I lifted my bowl of sugary milk and slurped. Mr. B knocked on our door right when I was finishing.

Daddy answered. "Oh, hey, Hank. You walked over here?"

Mr. B waggled his furry eyebrows. "Yes, sir. Anything to hide from Adrienne. She may look like a softie, but she's a bulldog."

Daddy muffled a laugh.

Mr. B's voice always sounded sleepy. He said, "The steps are getting easier. Adrienne has me doing laps to the mailbox, and on the steps. I'm supposed to graduate from the baby walker to a cane soon. Might need a few trips in town, though, to walk on flatter terrain. If you need to go to town, would you mind taking me? Jo...she's..."

"No problem, Hank," Daddy said. "I'll be happy to take you to town. I'd love to repay you for the time you spend with Lark."

"No repayment necessary. Time with her is gift enough."

Mr. B thought I was a gift? My heart felt fuzzy.

I skipped over to his side. "A cane? Like de kind wizards have?"

Mr. B's gray eyes shone like river rocks in the sun and I loved his floppy ears and big smile. He said, "I imagine a cane could serve as a magic wand. Will it transform me into a wizard?"

I clapped my hands. "Yes! Or the cane is..."

As if he read my mind, he said, "A pirate's peg leg?"

My jaw dropped. He *was* a pirate!

Daddy stepped closer, drying his hands on a dishtowel. "Do you need anything, Hank? Lark and I are going to visit Josie's chickens."

His eyes grew brighter. "She's letting you visit the birds? Birdie's birds!"

I covered my giggling mouth. "Yes!"

"Speaking of birds, I have a project for you. If that's okay with your dad?"

I tugged on Daddy's hand, and my legs began their happy dance again. Tappity tap tap!

"Of course. I'll be working on the greenhouse today."

On our walk to Miss Josie's, Chocolate Chip came outside and danced around to the thumps in my chest. He was a friendly dog.

I wanted to be a bird for Halloween. One with rainbow feathers! Daddy said I could sleep over at Aunt Penny's house. I'd never gone trick-or-treating before, but through our window I used to see the kids outside on the street in their funny costumes. I had to make my first time the best!

The chickens clucked hello when I got to the—

"What's der home called?" I asked Miss Josie, who was filling their water.

"Oh, this is a coop."

"I'll be over at the greenhouse, and then later, let's check those fence spots you mentioned," Daddy said to her.

She nodded.

Daddy looked at me. "After visiting the chickens, please go straight to Mr. Buchanan's, okay, Birdie?"

"Yes, Daddy."

"Thanks," Miss Josie said to him. "And I'll make sure she gets there."

"It's not far," I said, but nobody heard me.

She turned to me, a smile making her look pretty. She made me think of *The Grouchy Cow*, my favorite book. She didn't look like Grouchy Cow, obviously. More like the princess in my other book. But she acted like Grouchy Cow. Grouchy Cow pretended she didn't like other cows because she was afraid. They left for the Pretty Pasture without her. She was lonely. The story ended with Grouchy Cow being happy as her new friends returned to eat with her in the tiny pasture at her farm.

Did Miss Josie have no friends? Is that why she was sad? Daddy said she was salty.

Could people be salty or peppery?

Which was I?

I didn't like salt or pepper. I liked rainbow sprinkles!

Miss Josie pretended she didn't like people, so they would leave her alone. I think she liked her animals the most. Animals wouldn't leave you, or take your things, like people did. Ronnie and the hens would surely return with exciting tales!

Today, Holly sat behind the screen in the window and watched us. "Hi, Holly!" I waved. She meowed. She was a furry mix of colors: brown, white, and orange. Mr. B got Holly at Christmas and so he named her Holly! What a fun name.

The chickens pecked the ground.

"Why is deir house called a coop? Because dis is where dey poop?"

Josie laughed. "I don't think that's why, but it would make sense. Their home has two parts." She pointed to the pen. "This entire enclosure is a coop. The house part is their henhouse, with nesting boxes for the hens to lay their eggs and a couple of roosting bars for them to perch on at night. I lay fresh bedding daily to keep it clean along with a special garden powder to help it not smell." She pointed to the outside area. "This is the run. Wire and special walls that go into the ground surround everything. Your daddy helped install them to keep predators out. Do you know what a predator is?"

"Like foxes or big animals dat eat dem?"

"Right. Predators desire chicken for breakfast. Or they steal their eggs. I let them run around during the day, but at night they're snug and safe inside. I close the door." She tapped a lock hanging off the latch. "This lock is very important."

We poured a bag of grainy stuff into the outside feeder. Then she lifted a pail. "I have yummy food for them today."

I peeked in the pail. It looked like the scraps from dinner Daddy put in the compost bin in our kitchen. "Dey eat dat, Miss Josie?"

"Lark, you can call me Josie. Don't need the miss, unless you prefer it." She handed me a piece of watermelon. "Here, they love melon, apples, sweet potatoes, blueberries, red cabbage, and spinach."

"Dey like rainbow foods?"

She looked at the pail of scraps. "I guess *they* do. *They* eat a bunch of foods. Even pie."

Why was Miss Josie saying *they* louder? I scratched my head. Ohhh. Like what Daddy did with my words.

"Pie? Dey. I mean...*th-they* like dessert, too?"

"Yes. Certain foods are off-limits for them. I keep a list on my fridge of the no-no foods."

"Mr. B said he has no-no foods, too." I dropped food on the ground for the chickens. After one discovered the watermelon, they took turns pecking at it until it was gone. I giggled.

Josie laughed under her breath. "They are funny things. I treat them to warmed oatmeal on colder days."

"Why do dey look so funny? Did dey lose deir feathers?"

"They're molting now. Their feathers will grow in. Kind of like how we lose our teeth, but they molt every year. They look funny, huh?"

"Do dey lay eggs?"

"Do they lay eggs?" she corrected.

I pinched my brow. I didn't enjoy having my words corrected, but Daddy said I had to learn to say them better before kindergarten. I nodded. I walked around the group of chickens eating and scratching the dirt.

"They usually lay one a day. Hank tells me they stop for a few weeks in winter, which will be soon. They need lots of sunshine for laying. I read a book from the library when I moved here so I could learn more about chickens. I was about to collect the eggs. Want to see?"

We poked into the henhouse. One chicken was sitting in there. Her feathers were brown and white. All the chickens looked different, like people. Light brown, red, white, and brown mixed with white.

Josie pointed to the red one. "See her lovely feathers? She molted earlier and now has her new feathers in. That one inside with brown and white feathers. She's broody, that one. She will sit and sit on the egg. She collects the eggs of the others and sits on those, too."

"Oh! Because dey are special to her, and she doesn't want anyone to find dem? I mean, *them.*"

"Or she believes they need extra care."

She was a smart chicken to hide her special things.

"Dey don't have names?"

Josie cleared her throat. "Not yet. I feel kind of silly naming them, especially since they've lived here a few years with Hank."

"Everybody needs a name."

Josie was quiet. Was she thinking about names? Was she sad and missing the chickens that went on an adventure?

She handed spinach to the chicken in front of her, then crouched and gathered the eggs from the nesting box.

I said quietly, "I don't want Daddy to leave again."

Josie moved the basket aside and stopped poking around for the hen's hidden egg. She looked at me. Her eyes were pretty. Green. Like princess jewels. "He left?"

"Like Ronnie. He went away. But he came back." I fidgeted with the hem of my long sweater and brushed my hair back out of my face. Daddy said I'd get a haircut soon when he had time. Daddy didn't have the special spray Aunt Penny used to detangle it. He brushed my hair after bath time and the comb always got stuck and I cried. He tried to tell me it was okay, but we agreed we'll go to the hair place. He was a good daddy. I hoped he didn't leave again.

I chewed my lip, turning away from her gemstone eyes. "He's back now."

HANK

After getting Josie's professional opinion, I laid out supplies for my playdate with Lark. Pipe cleaners, string, Cheerios, peanut butter, old paper towel rolls, birdseed, and a few of Tillie's birdhouses and feeders. They needed a fresh coat of paint. I found a bag of unopened chocolate chip cookies. Then I paced—in my walker—to add steps. *Must get the mileage in,* Adrienne said. Fine, then. Even though I was ready to shove the walker into the wood stove and watch the tennis balls melt in the raging heat. Ha! My arms were less shaky and movements more confident now that I could put full weight on both legs. I was getting the swing of things. Oh, swing... Today called for the big band records, though I wasn't sure Lark would appreciate the tunes. Too loud for her sensitive ears. I walked over to the record player and picked a slower selection, my buddy Frank, then turned the volume down.

I even cleaned the house today. Well, the parts I could reach. Added steps made me feel less useless. Tillie was better at chores. In the short time between Morgan's hospitalization and Josie's arrival, the homestead had fallen into disrepair. At least I'd collected the eggs, fed the little creatures, and kept the coop moderately clean. I paid some fella to plow the driveway.

Since Josie's arrival, I found my thoughts falling upon Morgan and Theo more. Theo would have been ten years older than Josie now. Despite his flaws, Morgan had been there for me and Tillie, with a listening ear, when my sweet Theo went home to heaven.

Morgan was a good friend, but he had been drafted in 1969 and never was the same after.

Out of the blue, he called me fifteen years ago at my home outside of Portsmouth.

"When can you come visit again?" he had asked.

I paused in my rocking of the porch swing, as I licked the last of the frosting off my fork from my leftover birthday cake. Nothing beat cake for breakfast. Tillie had outdone herself with a four-layer chocolate cake with raspberry mousse and a ganache.

Butterflies fluttered around her expansive garden of early blooming bee balm and irises. A black-capped chickadee perched on the bird feeder hanging from a branch on the old oak tree. It was a pleasant day. I said, "I'm not sure."

"I've got Parkinson's and cancer."

I laid the plate down beside me. "Oh, Morgan! That's horrible! Dammit. I'm so sorry. What can I do?" I shifted in the swing, trying to persuade spring's warmth to ease my arthritis and the ache I felt for my friend.

"Come live here," he urged.

I hesitated. Morgan never asked for people's help. I tapped a worried hand on my brow. "Tillie and I were thinking of moving to Florida to be near her sister."

As though sensing my mention of her, Tillie danced by, humming, a glass of iced tea in one hand and a gardening trowel in the other, her movements as light as a bird's.

She handed me the glass. Her face fell when she saw my frown. "Is that Morgan? What is it, Hank?" she whispered with a squeeze of my shoulder. I forced a smile. I'd tell her later.

She returned to the garden. Yesterday, she shipped Morgan a box of cookies. I had just retired. Florida held an appeal. My joints couldn't handle New England winters anymore.

"Florida's for hippies." I heard the clink of a glass bottle.

"What about VA benefits?" I suggested.

"Bloody bastards did this to me. Not letting those kooks touch me, not with their smarmy doctors or shitty benefits. They'll inject me with more poison!"

This side of Morgan scared me.

I sipped, composing my thoughts. "But you need care, Morgan."

"I'm still flush from the lawsuit in eighty-four. Have more than enough to hold me over in stocks, too. I've hidden a lot of the money," he added in a devious whisper. "The spooks won't find it. It's not in the bunker. Somewhere better."

Was this another one of his hallucinations? Then again, Morgan had proven me wrong on more than one occasion with his ravings. The bus, for one. Though I couldn't for the life of me remember where it was located, I had seen it once while we hiked along the back of his property. If the man had the audacity to stash an old school bus in the woods, what was stopping him from hiding a box of money?

"I mean medical care, Morgan." I remembered a quote about "convincing a man against his will but him being of the same opinion still." Who had said that? Somebody famous.

Morgan persisted. Once an idea entered his mind, he became unyielding. "I fixed up the other two cabins. My sister and her kids stopped visiting, so now I have all this space. She claimed it was because the kids were getting too old, busy with sports and stuff. She said I needed 'help.'" Another cough.

Sister? Kids? Throughout the years, he never mentioned having a sister with children. He lived the bachelor life, too, afraid of the Agent Orange birth defects his buddies experienced with their children. He now suffered from both disease and cancer. My poor friend.

"Would love to have you, Hank."

After the phone call, Tillie and I considered the decision for a week.

And that was that. We went to the mountains. After moving in, Morgan's mind and body declined, making it the right choice. His rants became intolerable. Delirious with pain and paranoia, he kept telling me to finish his bus bunker and to re-hide the mysterious treasure. I forced him to at least get medical care. His cancer had gone into remission.

Then three years ago, after Tillie's passing, Morgan and I visited a lawyer in Silent Creek, drew up his will and trust, and he mentioned Jo by name for the first time. He had no family beyond his sister, Deborah, her husband, Joseph Sawyer, and their three kids, Josephine, Kyle, and Phoebe. At that moment, he revealed that he had left everything to Jo—aside from the provision for my well-being which I didn't know about. I would have told him to not do such a thing.

The patter of little feet in little shoes sounded on the front porch, pulling me to the present. Sometimes I got so lost in memories that I forgot where I was. Surprisingly, my hearing improved enough to bring me back.

"Mr. B..." Lark said. "Are you in dere dancing? Don't you hear me?"

Dancing in memory, kiddo. A sad one, though.

Lark being here was like Theo's spirit had returned. I saw Theo in everything now. In Jo. In Lark. In the flowers we planted for him. In the wind rustling the trees.

"I'm here, Birdie. Old bones. Come on in."

Everett said it was okay I called her Birdie.

She ran inside, the screen door banging behind her. She eyed the table, and I would be damned if I wasn't knotting my hands together, eager to impress her.

"Oh, Mr. B! Is it craft time? I love craft time! Daddy sometimes lets me stay for bof craft hours at de library because he is busy on his 'puter doing work. I can't wait for school. I'll get to do crafts all de time!"

Whew. I hit the nail on the head. Sorting Legos bored the sweet girl.

My heart skipped, and I sipped a cup of lemonade. Josie received a bunch of lemons from Mitch this month, so she'd brought a pitcher of cucumber lemonade. She had grown bolder—and better—with her food and drink experimentation. Living out here seemed to spark extra activity in her brain—as it had done for me.

Or in Morgan's case, it led a man to a point of no return.

I couldn't allow that to happen to me or Josie. But now we had Everett and his daughter. Life had returned to the property.

Lark bounced in her seat. Her dark eyes widened. "What are we making?"

I cleared the phlegm in my throat, and she grimaced. "Oh, sorry, kiddo. Bad habits are hard to break. You love birds. I love birds. My lovely Tillie, she loved birds."

"Miss Josie loves her birds. Chickens are birds. She's afraid to name dem." Lark twiddled one of the pipe cleaners.

After I explained my idea to Jo earlier, she stopped back at the store to grab the pipe cleaners. She also bought Cheerios for me, knowing I liked a bowl every morning. Heart health and all that.

"Why's that?" I poured Lark a glass of lemonade and brought it in with a plate of cookies.

She shrugged, already absorbed in the craft supplies. She fiddled with a pink pipe cleaner. "I dink she is afraid dey may leave like de other chickens."

"Hmm, well then, we should help her name them."

21

——·——

Josie

Everett ate an apple while lounging on the grass next to a million working parts for the greenhouse. Last week, his friend came to assist with the foundation, and today they finished framing. Lots of noise, work, grunts, and male chumminess. Envious, I had watched them interact. I missed Hannah's companionship. Sometimes I missed my sister, too. I wasn't sure how our good bond broke. More like drifted. After Mom's death five years ago, Phoebe moved to Australia, Kyle went to Texas, and then the situation with Tate escalated and lasted for over a year before he was convicted. Then Kyle's death on the job. Dad's increased distance. And Morgan's out-of-the blue inheritance. Life had been a roller coaster. Was my plateau of peacefulness coming?

I would go batty if I kept musing about days gone by or missed opportunities. Keeping busy settled my mind, at least.

I unloaded pumpkins from the bed of the truck and placed them on the porch. Hank had given me a pillow last week that Tillie had sewn with the words *Home Is Where*

You Rest Your Head, and I positioned it on the Adirondack chair.

"Thanks again for your help," Everett said, walking Anthony to his truck.

"Anything for you. Now that you're back, bring Lark over for dinner at our place. Angie insists. We were just talking about that one time in programming class. Remember Mr. Springer?"

Everett laughed, hooking his thumbs into his belt loops. "Well, he had that coming."

Anthony placed his toolbox in the bed of his truck. "I'll call you next week."

With a few more inside jokes, Everett saw his friend off.

The greenhouse had three walls and a roof. Everett was still framing the last side, which included the doorway and windows. He'd need my help with the polycarbonate panels.

Seedlings sat on the kitchen counter, nearest the big window for sun, waiting to be re-homed in the greenhouse. They were growing well as long as I kept them away from Holly. I couldn't wait for the winter veggies. Or rather, veggies that would grow. I snorted at my ineptitude, but with Everett's promise of help, I was optimistic.

I paused on the repaired porch. *Ahh...* No more squeaks. Sturdy workmanship. Everything had a pleasant rhythm. Still, my nagging thoughts persisted.

Except for losing things, a voice said. How was I misplacing all these things? Gloves, spare car keys, the locks on both the shed and *now* the coop... What next? Was I losing my mind? Did I do more harm than good with lists and routines? Was I becoming like my uncle?

I blinked the thoughts away and went inside.

The scent of simmering apples and cinnamon wafted through my cabin. I stirred the two large pots, monitoring the timer. The double batch of applesauce would last until spring, and Hank appreciated it. Mason jars, rings, and lids sat washed and lined up on the counter beside the immersion blender. Water boiled in a gigantic pot on the wood stove for sterilization. And a pile of peels—I kept half the peels on the apples for the sauce—sat in a bowl nearby for the chickens. Hank said they liked carrots, too. The carrot harvest was decent. It surprised me. Hey, I could grow a few things.

I poured two iced teas and made my way out to where Everett sat with Lark, who was recounting her latest escapade.

"...an' frough de woods de bird princess made her way to de upside-down big yellow castle, hidden beneaf..."

Everett interrupted, "I sure hope the bird princess was not traveling alone. And why was the castle upside down?"

Lark played with the bright red dress she wore over blue striped leggings. Wavy hair fell across her shoulders and got stuck in her mouth as she spoke. Everett pulled the strands away and tucked them behind her ear.

My insides quivered with the adorable gesture.

Lark said, "No, she had her dragon, Brownie."

"Why was the castle hidden? How did she find it?" He finished the rest of his sandwich in a few bites. Sunlight caught on the light brown hairs above his lip. His cheeks were pink from exertion.

"It's a secret castle. Only she and Brownie could find it. She followed de secret trail in de magical forest."

Lark's speech impediment nagged the SLP within me more and more. In fact, I'd written out a few exercises and games I could do with her. Now to broach the subject with

Everett. The sooner she worked on her issues, the better. Not being a physician, I couldn't officially diagnose, but I had to speak up.

"Do the trees talk, too?" he asked.

With a pointer finger held up, she said in a loud whisper, "Only to de princess."

He laughed at the ending of her story, pure paternal love dancing in his brown eyes.

"Tea?" I said, a frog in my throat. *Get your act together, Josie.* No, my ovaries were not quaking, too.

He took the glass, his fingers brushing mine. "Thanks, Josie."

He practically purred my name. Goodness. Was I reading too many Regencies? Yes. Yes, I was. They were far better than the psychological suspense novels I used to read a hundred years ago before I lived a real-life version of one. I stood nearby, trying to not shift from foot to foot, as Lark finished her sandwich while talking about a show she'd watched at her aunt's house.

"I could use a helper today with my applesauce." I smiled at Everett, but then slid a subtle look to Lark. "I have the pots boiling, but I need a jar helper."

"Me! Me!" Lark hopped up from her spot.

Everett winked at me. My insides did another somersault.

"Sounds like you found a helper, Josie. You sure?"

I gave him a genuine smile. "I wouldn't ask if I didn't mean it."

"Yippie!" Lark made for the cabin.

"I'll be right there," I hollered after her. "Don't touch the stove, okay?" I chewed on the inside of my lip. "Hey, Everett...I had a question..."

How much was I willing to share about myself to help Lark? Though Don's uncertain intel pecked at me, I reminded myself not to assume the worst about Everett. Trusting others was crucial for my success in the new world. This past month proved life always finds you, despite your hiding.

"What's up?" He moved around greenhouse parts on the ground and picked up a hammer.

I inhaled a steeling breath. *Keep it simple. Share only essential information.* "I used to be a speech and language pathologist." There, I said something. "I..."

"I suspected you had a teaching background. All that organizing, laminating, and you're patient with Lark."

I nodded.

"Her *th* sounds and stuff, right?" He swiped dangling hair from his brow. "I was hoping she'd outgrow it, but it's getting worse."

God bless him for making this easy on me. "It's pretty common. Often, kids will substitute a *v*, *d*, or *f* for *th* sounds, which are the last ones kids acquire. I don't think she has apraxia or a severe phonological disorder, more likely an articulation delay or disorder."

He motioned a hand over his head with a swooshing jet sound.

I laughed. "Sorry, I fell right back into my SLP-speak. Anyway, it's what I do, uh, did. Worked with kids with a range of speech and language issues. I'd be happy to work with her, and then when she goes to kindergarten, they can evaluate her and create a speech therapy plan at her school." I didn't mention my thoughts on Lark's hearing sensitivities or her other sensory triggers. I noticed her playing with food, her limited food choices, rainbow clothing preference, and how she responded to sounds. Everett had mentioned her

nightmares, too, and I wondered if she had generalized anxiety, generalized sensory processing disorder,
or more specifically misophonia. Or something else had
triggered these behaviors.

Reel it in, Josie. I wasn't a neuropsychologist, so I had
to keep my comments to my field, to what I knew best.

"What would it involve?"

"One-to-one time. I have this game called Zap! which
uses popsicle sticks. We would work on her voiceless
and voiced *th* sounds through games and conversation.
I bet Hank has some games in his basement we can use.
Classic ones."

He shuffled his feet and stared at the cabin. "I...can't
ask that of you."

"It's nothing to ask. I enjoy her company. You're going
the extra mile in your job here. I may need to pay you
soon," I teased.

One tough topic at a time.

He stretched his arms overhead with a soft groan, his
t-shirt lifting and exposing his abdomen. The movement
stretched my imagination.

"You sure?" he asked.

"Absolutely."

He stepped closer. "Thanks, Josie."

Chip barked from his spot on the porch. Our gazes
skidded down the driveway. A black truck idled at the
bottom, obscured by the overgrown rhododendrons
near the mailbox.

"Is that—?" My stomach twisted with the familiarity of
the vehicle. I didn't need binoculars.

He squinted. "Dumont?"

The driver sped up and left just as quickly as he arrived.

"I swear he has a bone to pick with everyone. What is he doing here?" Everett scowled.

I crossed my arms. "He gave me and Hank a lift home a few weeks ago. We had a flat tire. The mechanic pulled out a few nails. Maybe he was coming back to check on us...?" Even I didn't believe my explanation.

"Nails?"

I shrugged. I hadn't exactly driven through a construction site or anything recently.

"Why didn't he come up, then?"

I swayed, my vision caught on the now empty road. "Is he bugging you, too?"

He turned to his work. "Not really. He was just being a cocky ass the other day. His mind was elsewhere, and I was the punching bag, you know? Wrong place, wrong time."

"Ah." I was not sure I believed him, but I clapped hands on my thighs. "I'll be inside with Lark if you need me."

"Thanks."

"Hey, can we walk again tomorrow? Some animal is clearly enjoying itself with the fencing. A few more holes popped up. It would be nice to repair it before winter."

"Sure thing," he said, searching for a tool.

Slower steps brought me to the cabin. Everett had already repaired a few spots in the fence. Now more areas were pulled back. Did I have a bear making this parcel of land its home?

Or was it something or *someone* else?

The missing items. The nails in the tire. The fence. Sketchy Brian Dumont.

Chip brushed against me, sensing my unease. I glanced at the forest's edge.

This is not personal, Jo, Tate's voice reminded me.

Shut up, Tate. Shut up! Dammit, it is personal when your own husband screws you over!

"Hi, Josie!" a sunshiny voice said upon my entrance.

I blinked away fear, quieted the paranoia, and released the negative energy. "Ready to make sauce?"

"Yes!"

A few hours later, we lined up sealed jars.

"So many!" Lark beamed.

"The apple trees were fruity, weren't they?"

"Dey were." She dropped onto a chair at the table.

The lids popped as suction took hold. She giggled with awe and propped her chin upon her hands. "What next?"

Oh, how I loved, and had forgotten how much I missed, the enthusiasm of kids. "Have you heard of the game Zap!?"

22

Everett

The next morning, waiting for the world's slowest coffeemaker to brew, I reviewed the schematic on my laptop for the greenhouse. I stretched my lower back and shoulders, willing the ache away. A few ibuprofen tablets chased by orange juice were in order. Manual labor fought me on every turn. I could see the shoreline of forty, but sometimes, I felt older.

At least the hardest part of the construction was done. I thanked the weather gods for the warm streak. Anthony had been a tremendous help. We also painted the wood white to minimize heat absorption in summer. Once completed, Josie and I would customize the inside with shelving, benches, and tables. I had a few metal-framed benches ordered and sketches to show Josie.

I hoped she liked it. To see her green eyes sparkle with delight, those pink lips turn upward with a rare smile...

Uh. Needed to nip those thoughts. I could not be crushing on my landlady and boss.

The coffeemaker gurgled and hissed and gave up its battle with a beep. I poured coffee into a thermos with a splash of milk, then walked Lark over to Hank's. He insisted they had an ongoing "project."

"Birdie, come back when Mr. Buchanan's therapist comes today, okay?"

She nodded.

I added, "And no wandering." Whenever his therapists came over, I made sure she was in my cabin or the tree-house or playing in the meadow nearby. She was fast, and if I wasn't watching, she'd wander off into the woods. For the most part, she listened. But she was five, after all, and her mother's daughter.

To my surprise, Josie was waiting for me by the green-house, two jars in her hands.

"Applesauce as a thank-you." A rosy blush filled her pale cheeks and a puff of condensation formed before her lips in the crisp morning air. Even her edgy eyebrows seemed softer today.

I took the applesauce and smiled. "Thanks. And thank you for working with Lark."

"She's a joy."

A crackle of silence passed through us as a bird cawed. Gilda bleated from her pen. Chip's tail wagged as he brushed against me for a rub. I stooped over to scratch his ear. The cat meowed from inside the front windowsill.

"Are we able to look at the fence today?" She admired the greenhouse, hands on her hips. "This is looking great."

"Let's try. I would love to check out the wind turbines this time, too. They should send somebody out in the next week for the servicing appointment." We had everything else here—the heating, electricity, and plumbing—all under control.

After years of changing schedules, my current tempo felt right. Wake, work, talk to Josie, dinner with Lark. Hank insisted on watching her during the day. The two made an interesting pair. She had DVDs for evening entertainment, and with the makeshift Wi-Fi, we could stream shows.

I'd completed a second project for ProspNet, got the employment paperwork for Carolyn, and set up consulting gigs with two other firms—word-of-mouth advertising was going well, and the companies were willing to give an ex-con a chance once they saw my good work record. Plus, I had the ball rolling on the contractor licensure. I'd dug deep into my savings for the liability insurance.

Penny was being especially nice, too. She offered to create Lark's peacock Halloween costume.

Life was okay.

My phone buzzed. I fished it out of my pocket. Josie pretended to not notice, instead absorbed with walking the length of the greenhouse. I explained, "Might be Penny. She's on bedrest now. Her sister is here."

I swiped. It was just the reminder for the recovery meeting tonight. Yeah. That. I shot off a message to Penny, letting her know I'd be by at seven with Lark. Whether texts got to her was a crapshoot with the limited coverage here, but the cell phone booster helped when I was closer to my cabin.

Meeting nights were late for Lark, but she'd snooze in the truck on the way home.

Two texts from Fran's parents popped up. I froze, holding on to the one bar of reception I had in this spot.

Ugh. Fine. I'd call later to set up our "playdate." Even seeing their name on the screen made the bile rise. I pushed it down with a sip of mediocre coffee and looked at Josie. "Ready?"

A hesitant smile poked its way from the depths. I liked her smile. Pink lips, straight teeth, and a softening of strong cheekbones covered with strawberry freckles.

She said, "My hands are yours."

And with that, we set to work.

"Hold that flush while I secure this, okay?" I maneuvered around Josie, working on the flashing, my chest brushing her back while she held the panel in place against the rafter. "No falling on my watch."

She snorted. "I'll try not to."

After the first panel, we got the hang of it. Josie took to it like a pro and followed directions well. Move this, lift that, shift over here, carry this here, hold this.

She balanced on the lower wall beam and me on a ladder beside her while we attached the panels along the rafters and roof first. I hoped I didn't smell. The water in my cabin heated at a snail's pace this morning and I had overslept because Lark kept me up half the night, so I took the world's fastest shower. "Good. Now only a hundred and one more to go."

She laughed.

I tingled.

On we worked, moving around each other, finding a rhythm. Flashing, foam supports, panels. There was no avoiding our proximity, and I much preferred hers over Anthony's.

By midday, the temps perked up, and I stripped down to my t-shirt.

She slipped on the beam, and I caught her by the waist from my position on the ground, preventing her tumble onto the nearby table saw.

"Argh!" She gasped and locked eyes with me. Wide, unblinking.

Damn, her eyes were intense. That's all I could say. Late afternoon sun caught the golden highlights in her red hair. I felt her heartbeat pounding through her back and into my spread fingers. If I was a dancing guy, I'd call this position a dip. And this moment was one of those cheesy ones from the movies Penny watched.

Josie blew out her breath.

"You good?" I released her, reluctantly.

She swiped at invisible sawdust on her hair, shirt, legs. Her cheeks were more flushed.

It was sexy.

"Good. Slippery shoes, I guess. Tread's wearing out."

"You walk a lot of miles."

"You don't know the half of it."

A few bruises and cuts, a banged thumb, a lunch break with Lark, and hours later, we stood back to admire our work. We'd even finished the door and windows in front.

"Wow," she said.

"We do fine work."

"You did. I only helped hold things."

"Couldn't have done it without you, Josie."

Before us stood a nearly complete greenhouse with a sturdy foundation, gambrel roof, and four sides with corrugated aluminum on the lower half. It looked sweet.

Sweat beaded on Josie's forehead. She pulled out her ponytail, threaded fingers through the waves, then fixed her hair into a messy, loose bun. Frizzy wisps framed her face. A look at her watch told us it was—

"Yikes! Four o'clock!" she said. "Gotta take Chip on his walk, then milk Gilda, and check on Hank." She wiped her hands on her thighs, preparing to leave. Chip padded around the meadow, chasing birds. With a holler, the dog came running, a bullet of brown and mahogany.

I grabbed her hand, then released it. "Can't you skip one walk? How about an early dinner? So, we can sit here and bathe in the glory of our work?" I offered a grin, not wanting our time today to end.

"I'll eat later." She hurried to the cabin to retrieve the pail for milking.

The sun moved behind a cluster of gray clouds, predicting an evening shower. I pulled the flannel on with a shiver. "How about you milk the goat, and I check on Lark and make us sandwiches? Have one while we check the fencing and walk Chip. We can make it a working dinner."

"I'll eat later tonight." She tented her hands over her eyes and squinted toward the sun.

"We worked hard today. Bodies need fuel."

She pursed her lips. "Okay."

I made turkey and cheese sandwiches for me, Josie, and Hank and a PB & J for Lark, then checked in on the Lego Duo. Hank was alone at his table, prying apart two bricks. "Where's Lark?"

He scratched his head. "I was napping, and she must have stepped out. Thought she was with you."

Suddenly, she reappeared through the door. My pulse settled. "Lark!"

She flinched.

I exhaled. *Keep it cool.* "What did I say about wandering?"

"I was near you and Josie, Daddy. In de—*the* treehouse. You were busy."

Had I become so distracted with the greenhouse, and frankly, by Josie, that I missed seeing my daughter outside? I needed to do a better job of monitoring her. I'd seen a few larger tracks that looked like a coyote.

Hank assured me they would be good for another hour, so after a kiss on Lark's forehead and depositing sandwiches, I returned to Josie. She stepped onto her porch, zipping up a light jacket.

"Turkey and cheese? I used a tomato you gave us. Your tomatoes are plump." Words that could have been misconstrued caused my cheeks to heat up. I overcompensated for the slip. "Uh, you claim your gardens haven't been productive, but I beg to differ. This last batch of tomatoes is good. You'll be a pro with all your winter gardening and then ready to take on the summer next year."

"I wish I had your confidence." Her stomach growled.

I laughed. "A stomach never lies. Time to eat and walk."

My phone pinged with the two-hour reminder to get on the road. "I need to go to Penny's tonight, but I have an hour."

Her eyebrows squeezed together. "I walk fast."

"So do I."

"We'll do a three-mile perimeter loop. Takes me under an hour."

I stepped back, letting her and Chip take the lead. We ate our sandwiches in silence. As she finished hers, offering the crust to Chip, she said, "That was delicious. Thank you. I tend to forget about lunch."

"I've noticed."

The uphill trail brought us along the western side of the property, and we reached an open meadow. I heard the whoosh and saw the blades of the first wind turbine before we emerged from the forest. I shielded a hand over my eyes, looking up, my jaw slack. Wow, it had to be—

"Eighty feet high," Josie said. "That thing intimidates the hell out of me. Thank you for scheduling the tune-up."

"Glad I did. No way am I shimmying up there!"

"Me neither." She laughed.

Her candor floored me. It only took a month, but was Josie Sawyer letting down her guard?

"Are you okay with me spending more time walking these trails and doing fall clean-up?"

"Sure. That would be great. I haven't ventured too far into the interior. I mostly stick to the periphery."

"I'll begin with that and proceed inward. Might not be until spring. Lots of ground to cover."

"Not a rush."

The evening's waning light cast shimmers across her cheeks, and there was no mistaking her smile. She looked surreal in the setting sun as highlights accentuated her angled features.

I swiped hands through my hair. *Stop that, O'Reagan. That's your tell.*

We crisscrossed the meadow via a trail of pressed-down grasses. Good. I hated ticks. It only took one minor incident with Lark to put the fear of God in me. "Your uncle installed the turbines?"

"I presume so. This place was all woods when he moved here. He did a lot for the property. I used to come as a girl."

We passed the second turbine. Josie paused, checking the fence at the edge of the property. Some spots had broken or bent links, but nothing disconcerting. Why was she so concerned about this? By the age of the fence, broken links were a given. I already fixed a few spots where animals had pulled it back.

"There used to be walls here." She pointed to piles of broken stones on the other side of the ugly six-foot fence.

I imagined the labor of pulling down the old boundary walls with an ache in my heart. "Were animals causing trouble? Hunters?" I loved stone walls. Many served as property boundaries. The chain-link felt forbidding and reminded me too much of a time not so long ago.

An angry shiver rippled down my spine.

"I don't know why he changed it," she said. "Only the western and northern edges have the chain link. It's newer. The rock wall on the northeastern and eastern borders is more intact."

I nodded.

She walked on. I followed, trying to not watch how the curve of her jeans molded to her bottom in all the right places. She crouched at one spot. The dirt under the fence was loose, as if dug by paws. Chip sniffed around the spot and then took a leak beside a nearby tree stump.

"An animal was determined to get in here."

"Perhaps." Her voice trembled as she ran fingers over the bent links at the ground. She pulled pliers out of her pocket to force the links back.

Clearly an animal did this, not a person.

Whoa.

Hold up.

Was Josie running not from something but from some-one?

That theory explained an awful lot. I tried not to label people, but she was a tad neurotic and always on edge. My belly knotted when I thought about the cigarette by the shed. None of Hank's therapists smoked. And Dumont didn't smoke that brand. Now, the sheriff was a menacing one, but he wasn't the reason for her edginess. He was a meathead who sought a woman to protect and voters to secure his re-election. *And he needs a fall guy, someone to be a freakin' mascot at his celebratory parade.*

After Hank's and Gram's warnings about Dumont, I cleared out any email, and all contacts connected with my gray hat associates. Delete, delete, delete. New me. I was done with old me.

Josie jotted something in a palm-sized journal, and we carried on.

Trying to be chill, I said, "What brought you here? To Silent Creek?"

I expected a dismissive wave. Instead, she didn't pause for a beat, too focused on the trail zigzagging through maples, beeches, and dense hemlocks. She walked as if she hadn't heard me, but oh, she had.

Boots crunched on fallen leaves speckled brown, yellow, and orange.

Finally, she said, "What makes you think I wasn't born here?"

I pushed aside a branch before it made work of my face. Damn, she was fast. "Well, your accent has a hint of Massachusetts."

She stopped, and I collided with her backside. My hands almost fell into an inappropriate position. Thankfully, all I grabbed was air.

"Never thought I had one. I—" She cut herself off, shaking her head. "Never mind."

Having ruffled our rhythm, my jaw clicked. "I was wondering because I grew up around here, like I said. My grandmother lives in town. I moved to Massachusetts in my twenties, then came back here this year. Anyhow, I thought

I knew most people who grew up here. And you said you visited your uncle here, from somewhere else?"

The path turned eastward, and Josie kept her steady pace like an undeterred commuter train. Chip trotted ahead, smelling things or marking his territory.

"Silent Creek High is a small school," I continued, digging deeper into my interrogation. Curiosity clawed. "You're a few years younger, but I would remember you, even though I went to the vo-tech school." How could I not remember her?

"I'm not someone people remember."

Dang, Josie.

She added, "No. I didn't grow up here. But my family visited over my summer breaks."

Josie was a book of secrets. One I longed to read. A little brittle, with hundred-year-old paper, Josie's pages needed to be turned with care. I was unsure if my inner hacker craved another challenge or if the man in me yearned to truly understand her.

We walked in silence until I blurted, "Sorry for the questions."

"It's okay. Sometimes..." She waved a hand and gave up on her statement.

"Sometimes what?" I caught up beside her on the wider part of the path as we looped around the eastern edge of the estate. I was winded. How did she do this daily?

"Never mind."

The quietest babble of water whispered through the trees, and I craned an ear to pinpoint its location. Were we getting close to the lake? Josie pulled loose branches away from her path. I made a mental note of what required clearing, but the trail was good.

The fence ran out, replaced by another stone wall cleaved by the creek.

"Is this...?" I paused. The moving water whirled around mossy-covered rocks, sighing happily, if creeks could sigh. Chip stopped to lap up a drink.

"Silent Creek? Yes."

"Same one I cross over twice on the way to town and flows behind my cabin?"

"The same one. It gets wider and faster with the waterfall at the end of Silent Lake. There are a few watering holes where teens gather. Here, it's a trickle."

"I knew the creek cut through the mountains, but didn't realize it started this far north."

With a deft step, Josie hopped over a few larger rocks in the eight-foot-wide creek to meet the continuing path. I did the same.

"It begins a few miles that way." She pointed north, beyond the rock wall toward the rising peaks of the White Mountains around us. I glimpsed a distant granite peak through the trees. Their beauty never got old, not from this viewpoint, by the cabins, or in town.

"Ever been to the swimming holes?"

She smirked. "Once, as a kid. Ice cold! Even in summer."

Along an outcrop, the trail made a sharp turn and descended toward the homestead. I could eat a second sandwich. At least the recovery meeting had coffee and donuts. "Oh, wow." The lake seemed immense and the distant mountains were formidable in their grayness. Dark blue waves rippled the water. I squinted to see the small dock. I could see the cabins from here, too.

She breathed out a sigh beside me. "This never gets old."

"Do you fish?"

"Yes, and you're welcome to fish, too."

I worried hands through my too-long hair. "What brought you here, Jo? I mean, really?" Damn, I was a pest. I was persistent. "I mean, it's a beautiful spot. A great place to find solace."

I expected another redirection in the conversation. Her response surprised me.

"Circumstance." Not holding my eye, she bit her lower lip as the wind played with the loose hair escaping her bun. She shoved her hands into her jacket pockets, staring off into the distance.

I'd struck a nerve. More like a root.

"What brought *you* here, Everett?"

"I have family here, like I said."

She narrowed her eyes. "But you moved away. Something brought you back...and took you away."

I dug sweaty palms into my jeans pockets and chewed her words over. "Circumstance," I said.

We turned to head down, and my shoelace snagged on a root. I crouched to tie it and froze. "Uh, Josie, do kids ever come up here? Cliff jump or anything?"

"Not that I know of. No easy access to this point without passing the cabins. Why?"

I nosed my boot tip at another cigarette butt.

23

—·—

EVERETT

Wednesdays were penance nights. Sobbing, clapping, and a weird vibe filled the basement room of the First Congregational Church in Silent Creek each week at the recovery meeting. I never got used to it. I always left more depressed, the guilt of what I'd done no lighter. Tonight, a unique feeling ran through my veins, one that I couldn't put a name to.

Time with Josie made me realize someone had really wronged her. A deep fear had been instilled in her. This afternoon, I saw it as clear as an awakening, with the holes in the fence, her meticulous searching, the cigarette on the cliff. Everything added up. Seeing the color drain from her face at the outcrop made me realize she was running from someone who smoked. The brands of the two found on the property didn't match Dumont's. Most smokers were creatures of habit, sticking to the same brand. If not the sheriff, then who?

Either way, someone had hurt her. Badly. It got my wheel of shame turning. Or maybe it was the next step for my healing road. A weight had been lifted when I deleted my other email account.

When you're a hacker, you don't see the flesh and blood beyond the screen, beyond the thrill. Was someone suffering because of my actions? The hacking had always been at a higher level, affecting corporations. What about the individuals connected to those businesses? Families with kids, little old ladies and their retirement accounts, spouses of the partners in the firms my hacking programs attacked. Moving beyond alcohol—or in my case, hacking—was only the first step to the people here. The rest of the journey was about the person. Me. In fact, so little of the group's guidebook revolved around alcohol. Ditching it was only step one. My step one had been deleting that other email account. Stat.

It was time to let it out. Attendees at these meetings were extremely secretive. None of the information shared within these four walls left the group. It was as safe as safe could get. Tom, the current secretary, reported my attendance to Carolyn. That's all.

Skirting my way slowly around the people gathered outside in a cloud of smoke, I went inside to the refreshments table.

Sipping the burned coffee, I regretted it. Ugh. Who made it today?

The wonky ceiling fan that would never be fixed hummed above my head, as the nearby radiator hissed and sputtered. The faint scent of mold always sent me away with a bigger headache than upon my arrival. Fun times in the church's basement. Fun times.

Joan bumped my shoulder. Some of the cat hair clinging to her thick jacket brushed off onto my black t-shirt. "Oh, sssorry," she slurred, reaching for the sugars. She dumped four packets in her coffee.

She was usually more composed. Guess it was an off month for her, the poor woman. "No problem. How is Sissy?" Joan loved to talk about her cat.

She just responded with a sad smile. Guess not today.

Despite my reluctance to share, I came to like these people in the motley group. One guy I spoke to last month renamed our group *Drunks R Us*. He never returned after the one meeting, but the name stuck in my brain like bubblegum on a shoe.

I felt bad for them. Whether self-inflicted or caused by others, we all endured a kick to Shitsville, but we got ourselves into these messes. We chose to give something else, in my case, hacking, our power. I admitted my part in this shipwreck, but my time in prison was over. I came out, ready for change. Or maybe I *hadn't* been ready yet. One bad drink, one bad push, and a fast-tracked purgatory courtesy of the Rossi family, and here I sat.

I wished for a special place in hell for Spencer and Ann-Marie. Then, I glanced upwards, apologizing to God for my non-Christian thought. I didn't apologize for *having* the thought, just for thinking about it here.

It was time I stopped blaming them. I had my own sins to own up to.

The bitter coffee commiserated with the acid in my stomach. Why was I still drinking it, then? I covered a yawn, which answered my question. Lark had another sleepless night. Claimed she heard a monster whistling and scratching outside her window. Said she saw it breathing smoke like a dragon. I even walked around the cabin at two a.m. Saw nothing.

My gaze panned the room. There was no guest speaker tonight.

"Let's gather." Old-timer Robert volunteered to chair this meeting, and he brandished a hand in the air, then launched into his usual spiel after we moved our chairs into the kumbaya circle. "Welcome to *Solidarity in Sobriety*. We are a fellowship of people who share their experience, strength, and hope on the journey of recovery..."

While contemplating how I was going to share my story today, I nibbled on a stale donut. Usually, they at least tasted good because most people got them from the donut shop Hank loved. I had planned to bring back a jelly donut for him, but these were bargain bin donuts, not from The Daily Donut. At least I was on coffee and snack detail next time.

Robert continued, keeping his tone light, offering smiles to those around the room. "We self-support and are not allied with any political or religious institution... Our only membership requirement is a desire to change..."

Sandra, who was the group's treasurer, passed around a basket for donations. The money went toward the organization and church.

I cracked my knuckles.

Robert asked if there were newcomers. We celebrated anniversaries of sobriety. In his cool voice, he reminded us that no cross-talk or interruption was allowed while a person shared.

I gave up on the sludgy coffee, laid my donut on the plate, and put both on the floor beside my chair. Robert opened up with a reading from our daily reflection guidebook. Then he said, "We share whatever is in our hearts here."

After Eric, a soft-spoken guy I chatted with about landscaping, shared his story, everyone looked at me.

I always passed on my turn or shared the very watered-down version of why I was here. "I'm Everett. I'm here to be a good father for my daughter."

"Welcome, Everett," they all said.

"Tonight, I want to tell you more." A deep, cleansing breath. I technically didn't have to share. Tonight called for more participation on my part, though. Over the past six months, I'd come to know these people and their pasts. We were all on the struggle bus. They got me. I got them. Pride had kept me from sharing.

So, I let it rip. "I am *not* an alcoholic. Never have been, never will be. I was released from prison this spring for a crime I did commit however. I served my time. I have felt, for a long time, like a person given an incorrect diagnosis, I come here each week, getting the wrong treatment. But, even though alcohol is not my vice, I am on the same road of recovery as you all. I was a hacker. I did shitty things to others because of the thrill."

Joan burped, her watery eyes glossing over.

Eric's brow furrowed, confused.

"A hacker who got busted for cybercrimes," I clarified.

A middle-aged woman, Margot, dressed in designer everything, fidgeted with her emerald pendant, avoiding eye contact with me. This group wasn't unfamiliar with being arrested. Some had DUIs, including Margot, a former kindergarten teacher. Nobody appeared shocked by my admission.

Eric asked, "What are cybercrimes? Like robbing a bank online?"

Robert waved a hand. "No cross-talking, Eric."

"I'm a hacker. Or, I *was* a hacker. Hacking. Computers. Like breaking into organizations and stealing information. I wrote codes and programs for dodgy people. Not great stuff, I know. I did what I did. Before I realized it was too late, I got in over my head. I served my sentence. Got out in early spring, like I said." I swallowed, expecting judgment from their expressions, but I found sympathetic eyes upon me. They could relate. Not with hacking, but with screwing up. None of us here were perfect.

I went on, "The mastermind behind the fraud job got twenty years in prison. They slapped me with a laundry list of offenses—phishing and fraud, using a computer to steal sensitive information, using encryption to commit a crime, and modifying a computer program, to name a few. My lawyer, paid for by my grandmother, landed me the bargain deal of three years. Even got my records sealed early." I paused for a beat. Did that make me sound smug?

"Nine hundred and twelve days. In prison, even a short stay makes you realize your mistakes. You count every day. Upon leaving, my sole determination was to create a better life for my daughter."

I had their full attention.

"Unsure of my emotions, I visited a bar upon my release. Had a beer. One. I am not an alcoholic. I hardly drank before I was in, a beer while watching a football game with my brother or something. That's it. I don't touch the stuff now. But, I had another addiction. I got my jollies from the keyboard. Digits. Codes," I emphasized. "Here's the thing. I was set up. I was furious when a stranger provoked me for no reason. We fought. Cops were called. I split. Police arrived at my home the following day due to an anonymous tip. Empty booze bottles had been planted in my trash. I spent one more night in jail and got released because, lo and behold...the punk didn't press charges."

Even with sealed records, law enforcement could look up my night in jail during spring. I bet my last dollar Dumont had extended his iron fist to do that.

I pushed on through the silence filling the room. "Somebody paid a guy to get beaten up. How screwed up is that? And I was so angry and buzzing from one drink, that I let him irk me enough to throw some fists. I did that. Me."

Terry, the old guy who reminded me of Hank, shook his head, thin-lipped.

"My daughter's grandparents have deep pockets. They're trying to get her from me. I know they were behind it, but I can't prove it. However, as much as they have done me wrong, I have done myself wrong, too. I have to stop blaming them. I must take ownership of my own actions and take care of my side of the street. I admit, I screwed up, too. I beat the crap out of the guy at the bar. If I hadn't been so revved up, I wouldn't have engaged with the guy." I exhaled. Was I still making excuses? "I served my time for my crimes. I'm here so I can keep my daughter. If I have to come to these meetings and share, so be it. She's worth it. I submit to random drug tests and steer clear of any drugs or booze." I lifted the cup and sipped it. "Please, someone else make the coffee. It's terrible." My humor didn't hit the mark.

An empathetic air hung in the room like the static cling from the dryer. I felt zapped.

Margot dabbed at her eyes. I grabbed the tissue box on the small folding table in the center of our circle and handed it to her.

I blinked at actual tears. It could have been the scent of Joan's perfume, or the room's mold eating away at my corneas, or I was tired.

Something, though, lifted from my chest. Instead of a tightness in my lungs, they expanded with air. I added, "My daughter's parents are prime examples of what not to be. Dad, a felon down to his last dimes, trying to make his kid's life better. A mom who..." I shook my head. I wouldn't go there. This meeting wasn't about Fran. This meeting wasn't about the Rossis. It was about me. It was a place for me to own up to *my* mistakes. I inhaled, reining in the memories. Crap, more tears. Margot handed the box back. I didn't cry. Like, ever. "If I'd paid better attention to my daughter's mom, she would still be around. If I hadn't been so selfish, so caught up in the thrill..." What-ifs tumbled through my head. Oh, Fran. Poor Fran. I'd been so angry with her.

Wow. Damn. That felt good.

Margot fixed her makeup. Joan patted my arm. Eric blew his nose into a tissue.

Robert leaned back in his seat, hands clasped, nodding.

Other attendees shared their stories, and instead of tuning them out as I'd done previously, I listened more.

As we closed with prayer, I listened to the words, felt the meaning of them in my bones.

Just. Wow.

Wow.

I may have been put in here for other reasons, but now that I let it all out, I realized this was the *exact* place I needed to be right now.

I was at a turning point. No more blaming the Rossis or Fran or the guy in the bar. This was about my own forgiveness and healing. It felt good to be honest with myself. I had acted powerless up until now, giving half-measured effort. It was time to go all in. Deleting my gray hat contacts and emails had been the first step, like the alcoholic pouring the booze down the drain. The physical temptation was gone. This was step two.

Afterwards, while we cleaned up the refreshments, Eric and I chatted about a big deck project he wanted done on his property. I told him I could stop by and assess the area, give him a good estimate. Told him I was starting my own landscaping business. We swapped numbers.

On my way out, I texted Penny, who was watching Lark. Told her I'd like to talk to her. I hadn't physically put the computer in my brother's lap, but I sure had a hand in it. I had many steps to go to offer myself forgiveness and make amends with others. I'd start first with my sister-in-law.

24

HANK

I was flat on my back on a thick blue yoga mat on the living room floor, staring up at the timber-lined ceiling. Cobwebs. Too many. I'd need to ask Josie to help me with them again. Tillie used to stand on a chair and dust them away.

"Home stretch. You can do this," Adrienne urged me with her usual gusto, always a positive cheerleader. How she had the energy to tolerate my crabbiness was beyond me.

Why were these moves still so hard? Because I was an old man. I moaned. These took forever. "You sure you weren't a drill sergeant before you did this?"

She tsked. "You're not the first to ask."

I yawned. I didn't need the misplaced medicine, but I had a hankering for a sleeping pill. Sleeping on my right side and back made me want to blow a gasket. "When can I sleep on my left side?"

"Soon."

"You always say soon."

"You're showing significant progress. You'll be done with me by the end of the week and flying solo."

I heaved through the heel slide. "You're a good babysitter."

She readjusted my leg, monitoring form. "Nah. I work as a quality control expert."

Seven.

Eight.

Two more to go.

Was that a spider? Yes, a big, furry brown one. The creature crawled around the corner joints where its massive web had doubled in size since my last time lying on the floor. Lying on one's floor, one sees a whole new world. The gross world I was lax on cleaning.

Switching to the other leg, I shifted focus to the knots in the wood. Morgan had done a good job building the cabins. Sometimes my electricity went on the fritz, but I blamed the weird wind cycle we had, or the fancy-schmancy solar panels.

On cue, the lights flickered.

Maybe mice were eating the wires just like they ran off with my pills.

"You like watching my chicken arms and drumsticks?"

She guffawed, deep and throaty. "The only drumsticks I like are the battered and fried ones at Mason's Roadhouse."

We moved on to quad and glute sets.

I liked Adrienne's sass. Between Everett and sweet Lark, Anthony, the fella who helped with the greenhouse foundation, and my clown circus, the homestead was hopping with people. My blood pumped with a familiar sensation, something I missed. The energy was inspiring, addictive. Everett made sure I got to town a few times a week, too. Without Tillie, I'd never feel whole again. But for now, this place was a temporary fix until my soul returned to God.

Out of the blue, Nora O'Reagan had called me this week, too. I suspected Everett had put her up to it. Either way, I'd taken her up on the offer to see Tony Wonder and the

Wild Swinging Rabbit, a local jazz ensemble that played the classics. We'd had tea afterwards and I could tell she was trying to sell me on Lupine Meadows. The place was actually not as bad as I thought.

Adrienne and I moved through the rest of the exercises: abductions, adductions, seated maneuvers, knee flexes, extensions. She kept the pressure of her guiding hands light, but steady.

"I'm going to miss you. Who will pretend to laugh at my jokes?" I said.

Her smile reached both cheeks, revealing the gap between her two front teeth. She had a hundred black freckles over dark brown skin. Today she wore her short hair under a wrap that matched her purple scrubs and funky tie-dyed clogs.

"Lark would love those."

She lifted a shoe up, showing it off. "Oh, Hank. That little girl is a doll. Give her a squeeze from me. She's adorbs."

"She is."

Once we finished, I donned my coat and grabbed my cane. Then we made our way down the long driveway.

Adrienne's outstretched arm hovered behind me in case I needed it. "You've got a talent for this, Hank. Just don't become too dependent on the cane. Ditch it once you feel ready."

Around the bend in the driveway, I looked up from my concentration on coordinating the cane with my steps, especially near the ruts.

And froze.

The bushes.

"What in tarnation?"

Someone had hacked them to bits!

"Need to slow down?" Adrienne asked.

"No!" I quickened my gait.

"Easy, Hank. Easy—"

My knee gave out, and I collapsed, taking the cane with me.

"But the bushes!" A sob worked its way up my chest and lodged in my throat. "Tillie's flowers. They've been decimated!"

"Which?" Adrienne followed my gaze to the rhododen-drons. They were—had been—glorious. Gigantic wonders. In the spring they were a gift of stunning, white flowers interspersed with blazing orange azaleas. Morgan had taken extra special care of them, our memorial to Theo. My son had loved the color orange.

Now? Scattered leaves and broken branches all over the ground. Like someone bulldozed them. This wasn't from pruning unless Everett had taken a chainsaw to it and went mad... No. I saw him the other day. He'd been hand-shearing them just a little to give them a nice shape and said he would do a more thorough prune in the spring after they bloomed. Had somebody run over the bushes in their car? Or truck?

"Oh, Hank, I feel stupid because I noticed they were, uh, trimmed when I arrived," Adrienne whispered. "Sorry to not have mentioned it."

"Trimmed? They were massacred!"

She sat next to me on the gravel, as I was unable to stand.

"I thought you wanted a better view between the cabins and the road. They were becoming quite the hedge hiding the property. Now someone can see straight up here."

"Theo's bushes..." The sob broke through. "My boy's bushes. He's gone. Tillie's gone. And now the flowers are gone."

"Oh," she said softly. "Oh, Hank. Need me to find Jo for you?"

Who did this? When? It must have happened at night—but Chip would have barked. Yesterday when we were all out? Jo and I returned after dark. I didn't remember noticing the damage then. Honestly, I had been half asleep on the ride home. Guess Jo didn't notice either.

Theo had been so young when he died, but our sweet boy loved to work in the garden at our first house in Portsmouth with his mom. The flowers were...they were...

I held my head in my hands, pain shooting up my side with each sob.

Adrienne rose and offered her hands. "Let me get you back up to your cabin, okay? Let's talk to Jo."

25

— · —

Everett

On the outskirts of Silent Creek, I sat on a dilapidated cedar bench at the playground. Merely seeing the equipment gave me tetanus. The primary structure where Lark played was plastic and metal and circa 1980s.

I shifted, avoiding the uneven plank jutting into my ass. Graffiti covered the arms and back of the bench. Like the library and the older sections of Main Street, this rickety playground was overdue for an upgrade.

I needed to start somewhere with my new biz. I could put in some bids.

My imagination wandered. Pressure-treated pine or cedar, hang a tire swing, install a sandbox...

Imagining what I could create was better than contemplating hacking and deceiving. Those thoughts became fewer and fewer. This road of redemption felt different. Each completed project on the homestead was small rush of accomplishment.

A luxury engine's purr revealed the arrival of the Rossis. They parked a few spaces away from my truck.

The paper cup of warm coffee in my hands couldn't abate the chill, much less thaw the dread in my gut. All it did was burn my tongue.

They stepped out of their shiny fifty-thousand-dollar sedan. Of course, it was black.

Matched their intent.

Deep breath, O'Reagan. You've got this. You can do this for Lark.

Another sip, another burn. I sucked my teeth.

Spencer approached first, Ann-Marie always a step or two behind, her purse clutched to her chest, eyes darting around. *No, you will not get mugged here. Nobody wants your pearls or five-hundred-dollar pumps.* I forgot how much she resembled Fran. Ann-Marie was the refined version of her daughter, complete in designer sweater and black slacks. Lark had inherited the wavy, dark hair, but when I looked into Ann-Marie's gaze, all I saw was ice in the brown, nearly black, irises.

Lark's eyes held life, joy, innocence.

I wore casual khaki slacks, an ironed navy dress shirt with the top two buttons open, and boat shoes. Hell, I shaved! My hair, well, needed a cut. My mind associated short hair with iron bars, so I didn't mind it a little wild. I also liked the way I caught Josie staring at me when I brushed my hands through it. Now I fought the urge to do just that as I met Ann-Marie's stony glare.

"Everett," she said. "You're looking…" She paused as if it pained her. "Clean."

Long ago, they liked me. I had won them over in the beginning, during my whirlwind romance with Fran, before our tornado split. But really, the guise had been part of their superficial niceness. I would never be good enough. Not for their daughter.

Spencer—dressed to impress, matching Ann-Marie's attire and frosty air—blew right past me to greet Lark. "How is our favorite granddaughter?" He squatted to her level.

Try your only granddaughter.

Lark giggled. "Great!"

I tossed the coffee in the trash, then shoved my hands in my pockets, while they chatted with Lark for a few minutes, starting with sugar-sweetness, but then morphing into backhanded comments.

"Everett, do you own a brush?" Ann-Marie raked bright pink manicured nails through Lark's long locks. "Sweetie, I could buy you a better hat than this one."

"It's a beanie, Grandma. Keeps me warm and makes my heart smile."

"Is she in preschool yet?" Spencer asked me.

Ann-Marie took out a tissue from her beaded purse. "Sweetie, let me see your hands. Were you in the dirt?" She wiped at them.

They unleashed a few more passive-aggressive remarks before I had enough. "Lark, why don't you play so Grandma and Grandpa"—I swallowed bile at such undeserved monikers—"and I can catch up."

Lark slouched and played with her zipper. Before Ann-Marie could chide her about little girls having proper posture, I added, "Can you show them that thing you do on the bars? The flip?"

Ann-Marie gasped. "A flip? She's in a skirt!"

A skirt with leggings. *Loosen your Spanx, Ann-Marie.*

Glee returned to Lark's eyes, and she rushed to the monkey bars. "Watch, 'k?"

"We will." Spencer rubbed his chin. As a burst of wind blew past, it disturbed not a strand of his thick gray coif. *Use much gel?* His hair was hardened like a Ken doll's.

Ann-Marie gagged and covered her mouth as a few mulch chips flew into her face, but then she started right in. "There's a lovely preparatory preschool in Connecticut. We think she should attend it and come live with us. We have connections with the headmaster at Brighton Heights. We can get her in without any cost to you."

"No."

"We're her family," Spencer said in what I assumed was his boardroom voice.

"I'm her father, and we have family here."

"You can't mean your brother? He's still in prison," he said.

I eased the clench of my teeth. "She has her aunt Penny, her cousins, and my grandmother, and Lark adores her—"

Ann-Marie threw a hand to her chest. "I'm her grandmother. Yet you won't let us see her!" She laced her tone with hurt. Fake hurt.

"You're wasting your visit to argue with me." Did she even know Lark's birthday? Favorite color? The names of her dolls? Favorite books? What kept her up at night? Her nightmares about being left alone and hiding in a closet? About the weird clicking and hissing and whistling she insisted she heard outside her bedroom window? About the monster she insisted lived in our woods? I told her old cabins and the forest made interesting sounds.

Spencer stepped in. "Look, Everett. We only want what's best for her. She needs a stable home, not a shack in the woods! Do you even have a job? How are you providing for her? You're not doing that hacking nonsense, are you? Is she interacting with her peers?"

Ann-Marie touched my arm. I struggled to not recoil. "She needs a safe home, Everett. She shouldn't worry about her father's jail time or his excessive drinking."

Oh, she did *not* just say that.

She blinked tears. "If she saw what you did to her mother."

What the actual hell? I never laid a hand on Fran. I loved her. Though I wouldn't mind if someone forcefully shoved the fancy pearls down her mother's throat. Something in my neck twitched. I tried to take the high road. "Lark needs to be with a parent. She's happy here. I was gone. But I am here now and will always be here for her." I softened my voice. "Fran is gone, Ann-Marie."

Ann-Marie pushed her chin out. "She left because of your—"

I jerked my hand up. "Don't finish that sentence."

She flinched.

"Your daughter was the addict. She left. Left!" The wind caught my words as they echoed in the open playground. A mother sitting at a nearby picnic table took her son away to the swings. "She wants nothing to do with me or her daughter."

Rage erased Ann-Marie's façade. "Now you listen. Lark had a pleasant home with Francesca. She had—"

"Did you know Fran hocked Lark's stuff? Her furniture, even? Sold it, to pay rent, or more often for drug money? When I returned, your granddaughter had only her clothes. She was sleeping on a mattress on the floor."

"And whose fault was that?" Ann-Marie scoffed.

If I had eaten breakfast, it would be on my shoes right now.

Spencer slung an arm around Ann-Marie's shoulder as she shook with racking sobs. Heat filled his voice. "Where were you all this time? Huh? In prison! If you hadn't screwed up, Francesca could have...would have..."

"Don't you dare shift the blame to me, Spence." I blamed myself enough.

Ann-Marie sniffled, adjusting her sweater. "Francesca loves Lark."

"Where is she, then?" My pulse shot through the roof. "If she loved her daughter, she'd be here!"

"That's because you—" She amped up her weeping to an embarrassing level.

Did this woman think I did something to Fran? Was she believing her own warped lies?

"Daddy?"

Shit.

Lark was at my side. "Nobody was watching me," she said in the smallest voice.

How much had she heard of the conversation? My hands shook. I leaned down and scooped her up. "That's because we need a closer view to see your form. Show us again?"

She nodded, mute.

I carried her to the play set and stood beside the monkey bars. "I'll spot you, okay?"

Another nod. A sniffle.

I didn't turn around once, despite feeling the death daggers on my back. A few minutes later, I heard the whirr of the engine starting and the car leaving the parking lot.

JOSIE

I packed up the freshly baked dinner of perch that Everett and I caught together, along with broccoli and mac and cheese casserole. With Chip by my side, I walked to

Hank's cabin. He hadn't been himself since his collapse over the bushes, but we had resumed our Sunday Scrabble games.

I arrived with a forced, hearty hello to his somber shrug.

Dinner passed quietly. Glassy, sad eyes held mine. He swallowed the last drops of his Old Fashioned. "Everett said they'll grow back," he relented. His voice grew softer. "Some things start afresh with an even greater beauty. Like Tillie's hair after the chemo. She was more stunning."

I reached across the table and squeezed his hand. We shared a look filled with loss, with hope. "Everett and I are working on installing a security system."

Hank's heartbreak and my reemerging worry intertwined. Who would have run over the rhododendrons and azaleas? And why? It wasn't a freak accident. No burned-out rubber or broken glass around that tricky bend in Clemens Road. And someone had run the shrubs *over*. Repeatedly. Deliberately. Then they decimated the tops with a chainsaw or hacksaw or something. The attack occurred while we were absent, concealed by the night until morning. I kicked myself over not seeing it sooner. Had they known we weren't here? That shot a sickening wave through my gut.

My mind tumbled to all the pieces of this ridiculous puzzle.

The sheriff driving by.

The cigarette on the cliff.

The nails in the car tire.

My missing things.

The fencing.

The weasel. Alright, *that* had been an animal. I saw it.

Sweat moistened my armpits. *No. Paranoia, you do not have a hold on me anymore!* Coincidences. Random, weird, discombobulating things, my rational brain told me.

We cleared the dishes together. "Do you want to talk about...him?"

"What's there to say? Theo's gone. Tillie's gone."

Hank's verve post-recovery had been so encouraging to see. *Please don't let this set him back.*

"If you tell me more about him, like you do with Tillie, perhaps it won't hurt as much? I would love to hear about him...when you're ready." I reached for the soap and sponge and began scrubbing the dishes.

"Why don't *you* talk about your family? Your parents, your brother and sister, your ex-husband, your former job. Any of it. You've locked that away, Jo. You're as silent as the creek running through this property. People are not meant to be alone, but you insist on isolating yourself."

A sharp pang in my chest made breathing a sudden challenge. I focused on scrubbing and rinsing. Hank dried. "They're still thorns in my heart. Like your Theo." I inhaled. "Okay, let's talk. What do you want to know?"

"Only the bits and pieces you choose to share." He squeezed my shoulder.

So, I did. As we cleaned, brewed tea, and set up Scrabble, I shared the abbreviated version of my family's highs and lows. I told him more about the Tate ordeal, from the deceit to prosecution and conviction, the betrayal, my job.

Tate is out of prison.

Shut up, inner voice.

"Phoebe married a guy in Sydney. No call, no announcement. I had to hear it through the grapevine. She didn't want to bother anyone with it, I guess, considering Kyle's death and all my mess."

"Maybe you should reach out to her? I know you came here to hide, but hiding isn't the answer. Everyone has their troubles, even Phoebe. Ask her. People must be worried about you. You're smart and kind, and you won't admit it, but you like the company here, too." He sat in his armchair, flipping over Scrabble pieces.

I batted tears from my eyes. "Long ago, all I did was..." I shrugged and sipped my tea, a blend of chamomile and lavender. "I sought validation in my job, my peers, even the parents of the kids I taught. I tried to please..."

"...everyone but yourself," he finished for me.

"When I stopped trying, I realized that the street never ran two ways. It's why I don't make a big fuss over my birthday. Nobody ever remembered. I never got cards or even a message. Even Tate forgot during our last years together. Despite being surrounded by coworkers and kids I could call family, I've felt...alone...orphaned most of my adult life. Then Morgan..." My voice broke. "He remembered me."

"I'd never forget you, Jo. I love you, kiddo."

I sniffled. "I love you, too, Hank."

"Morgan knew we'd make a good pair."

I nodded and rubbed my nose.

"I like Everett and Lark, too," he said.

"Me, too." They would make this Scrabble game far less dreary.

Hank drew his letters, and I drew mine. "What about finding a job in town? One that will use your skills, your education as a speech therapist. Whatever makes your ticker beat with contentment. Adrienne said they hire speech pathologists at nursing homes and in healthcare, too, not just in schools or clinics. Or try a whole new vocation."

"That's an idea." I scrubbed a hand across my forehead. "I pushed everyone away. I've got no family or friends left." Blinking watery eyes, I looked at his sincere expression. "Except you, that is. What would I do without you, Hank?"

"My old bones are more of a burden than helpful."

"Baloney."

"You'd survive. It's what you do. Besides, I'm not going anywhere. You're stuck with me, my dear."

We both laughed.

"Those weren't your people, Jo. Or they were, and they served their purpose. Some people stay for a moment, some for a phase, and others for a lifetime. God opens and closes doors. You can create a new family. You're here to start afresh. But nobody said you must start alone." He moved letters around and put down his word—FLORA. He released a soft chuckle, pleased with himself.

I reorganized tiles, deliberating upon a word. When I'd gone to town today for errands, I parked near the community park. I people-watched. A pesky ache had wrapped its claws around my heart.

I saw Everett and Lark playing. I considered saying hello, but an older couple joined them. Family. Everyone had family. Was I imagining it when I felt like Everett and Lark could be my family, somehow? I adored Lark, and time with Everett...whether cleaning machinery, planning a schematic, or walking or fishing together...sent my pulse soaring. In a good way.

The interaction on the playground seemed cordial at first, Lark dominating the conversation, her gestures animated. Then, as she dashed to the slide, the exchange between Everett and the couple grew downright tense.

Raised voices. The wind blowing in the opposite direction meant I could only read body cues. He was pissed.

Before becoming a certified snoop, I drove home.

Families came with drama. I saw Everett's discomfort when he interacted with the man and woman, even from afar. Perhaps they were his parents? Out of habit, I read his body language around here, too. I wasn't watching his every move around the property, but I wasn't *not* watching him either.

Now, as I sat with my lovely Hank, my companion and surrogate father, I built on the F he'd laid down.

Then I stared at the word I'd created:

FAMILY.

26

EVERETT

Lark was a maniac, loopy on candy, high on life.

Oh, to have her energy. I scrubbed my chin with a gaping yawn. The clock read three p.m. Trick-or-treating hadn't even started.

She punched me playfully in the gut. "No yawns, Daddy! It's de—I mean *the*—best night of the year!"

I tickled her ribs in return. She squirmed and laughed, the Velcro tail feathers falling off.

My heart warmed. I vowed to make her Christmas better, too.

Josie had stopped by with a small candy bag for her. Chocolate bars, fruity gummies, crunchy this and nutty that, even a chocolate peacock lollipop. Sweet. Considerate. If Josie only knew how much her gestures meant to Lark...and to me. My daughter had convinced Josie to name the remaining chickens. I cracked up when I heard about Frittata, Noodle, Snowball, and Clementine.

"Maybe we'll get chicks in de spring!" she had said.

"Slow down, Birdie. Let's fix this." I followed her to the bedroom with the foam feathers in my hands. Penny had gone all out on Lark's costume. The spray of the tail was royal blue and emerald with gold lattice, matching the intricate top and layered tulle skirt.

"Sleepover tonight!"

Penny's baby was due any day, and with her sister, Claire, staying with her, the house was orderly and clean. Claire was a bit too controlling but amen to her for keeping Penny's devil children in line. They asked Lark to sleep over tonight to give me a night off.

Stream macho guy flicks without disturbing my over-sensitive non-sleeper? Hells, yeah. Unless Penny went into labor, and in that case, I was on kid-duty while Claire joined her for the delivery.

First, trick-or-treating. Well, trunk-or-treating at the town center where local businesses or townsfolk gathered their cars together, trunks out and open, each ornately decorated with outlandish themes, and gave out candy. Safe lighting, lots of candy with less walking, and even police supervision. It was a win all around.

I tossed her overnight bag into the truck. Getting a squawking bird buckled in the booster seat with all the fluff of the skirt proved challenging.

"Almost got it," I said, surprised at working up a sweat. She secured the top clip.

"Ready?"

"Ready!" She smiled through chocolate-covered lips. I reached over the front seat and grabbed a package of wipes. Penny had drilled parenting advice into me from day one. "Always have wipes, water bottles, snacks, and spare clothes in the truck, even for girls."

I balked at the advice. "Even for a four-year-old?"

"*Especially* for a four-year-old." Still applied to five-year-old Lark.

The crunch of gravel and the pitter-patter of paws alerted me to Josie and Chip. I turned around. "Hey."

"Hey," she said in our now customary greeting. She pushed a headband into my hand. Craft store mini peacock feathers, a bit of ribbon. "This is for Lark...if she wants. Thought she may like to add it to her already outstanding costume." She looked over my shoulder at a smiling Lark.

"Ohhh! Dank—*thank* you, Miss Josie."

I smiled. "Thanks. She's wired already."

"It's my pleasure to spoil a child with sugar, then return them to their parent." Josie's eyes sparkled.

I paused, grasping for an excuse to hang out with her tonight. We could talk about the property's needs more. We already finished the greenhouse with shelving, and she gathered her pots for the winter crops. I'd been secretly working on a fire pit for her. Bought the materials, drew the schematic. Would it be an early Christmas gift? A thank-you?

Win a woman over with your workmanship, O'Reagan? How classy. I hungered to spend time with her, but not be talking about the property.

My inner voice echoed the words of those who belittled me. My dad, the corrections officers, the Rossis, Carolyn, Sheriff Dumont.

I shuffled into the truck while oh-so-casually asking, "Do you like pizza?"

"Who doesn't?"

"How about I bring one back and we hang out? Watch a movie or something?"

She crinkled her brow. "What about Lark?"

"She's having a sleepover at Penny's."

"Ah..." She untwisted her hands, then lodged them into her vest pockets. The search for an excuse played in wrinkles across her forehead.

I rolled the window down. "Just pizza, Josie. Chillax with a movie. Plus, you can review a few of the speech-language pointers with me. Lark's been enjoying her time with you."

From the back seat, Lark perked up. "Zap! is fun. And other games, too."

I asked, "What's your favorite topping?"

She patted her thigh for Chip to follow as she turned away, but not before answering, "Pepperoni. I'll see you in a few hours."

I started the truck. Two turns and it was on. *Come on, baby, make it through winter, please.* That's what I got for a deal from the local used car place.

I drove to Penny's to pick up Claire and the boys.

The children running around the town common were like ants scavenging. I must have passed a hundred cute young goobers. Local businesses took part, designing their trunks to be spooky, cute, or downright over-the-top elaborate. The hardware store made their trunk into a creepy haunted house, the library had a cute reading fairy handing out candy in front of a cardboard bookshelf, and Deanna's Cafe had a jungle with dangling strands of coffee beans. Even the local dentist gave out treats—small trinkets and free toothbrushes. All the warm fuzzy feelings hit me in the right spots. Perhaps what melted my insides most was seeing Lark enjoying it.

"How's that tooth?" the dentist asked with an orthodontic-straight smile.

"Good!" Lark rummaged through the bowl of trinkets.

"Thriller" played from a local DJ van. Food trucks served apple cider and cocoa and greasy foods that made my stomach grumble, and adults got into the spirit by dressing up. Claire, Lark, Shawn, Liam, and I walked up and down the rows of cars until my feet ached.

"We done yet, Birdie?" I squeezed her hand.

She said through a yawn, "One more, Daddy."

"You said that three trunks ago. Come on, Twinkle Toes. Let's head back and count your bounty."

"I'm not a pirate. I'm a peacock!"

I laughed. "Your, uh...birdseed?"

She scrunched her face. "Ew."

We reached the last of the trunks in the massive main circle, and my feet slid on the wet grass. I had been trying to avoid the public safety area all night. Unlike the other vehicles with decorated trunks, here, an ambulance, fire engine, police car, and the sheriff's truck all sat side by side, each with attached purple and orange balloons, and they were allowing kids to sit behind the steering wheels for photos. At least they didn't embellish their corner like a prison. *Kids, this is what happens when you break the law.*

"What a beautiful bird! A peacock?" I eyed the woman's name on her brown deputy sheriff's uniform—Wagner. She blinked bright eyes and had a big smile, along with gold hoop earrings and cropped black hair. She seemed harmless enough. Now to get my breathing under control.

Memories knocked on the door in my brain, and I double-bolted the lock. Not now. I was here. Now. Not then.

Lark leaned in. "Oh, you have a star on your shirt. Are you a..." She scratched her chin in contemplation. "Policeman?"

I corrected, "Police officer, Birdie."

The woman chuckled, handing Lark a lollipop that was, interestingly, wrapped in gold foil and star shaped. "Close. I'm a deputy sheriff." She turned to Liam and Shawn, offering them candy, too. Liam was dressed as a masked villain from a movie, complete with light-up mask and freaky-looking gloves with scales and long claws. Shawn was a gunslinger from the old West, a Nerf gun in his holster.

"Do you capture bad guys?" Lark asked.

"She has a gun!" Shawn mimicked shooting. Claire swatted at him, looking mortified.

Deputy Wagner said, "You're partially correct. I currently work in law enforcement, previously as a police officer, and before that, I attended college. What I do differs from the state or local police officers. I make sure people arrive in court when they're supposed to, and I help police officers find missing people, and I do lots and lots of paperwork." She tittered, her smile brightening.

Ever since Dumont pegged me as his easy prey, I wondered who else in his department knew about me. Damn small towns. Her posture and expression gave zero hint at whether she knew who I was. Smiles hid the truth.

"Do you have a gun?" Lark asked.

"Okay, Birdie. We took enough of the deputy's time." I gently took Lark's shoulders to move her along. She didn't budge.

Wagner knelt to Lark's level. "Want to know my best weapon?"

I lost my ability to move, to think, to act. If my kid blurted out that her dad was an ex-con, so help me...

I'm sure Lark understood what my "missing time" meant—we skirted the topic, kept it vague, but one time she asked me about prison. Either Fran or the Rossis must have informed her. It was time for us to discuss where Daddy was for three years. Soon. Soon.

Regardless, it was time to vacate the premises.

Lark leaned in, clasping the pumpkin bag of candy to her chest.

Wagner said softly, but firmly, "My voice."

Lark asked, "Does it shoot laser beams or someding?"

The woman stood and released a deep laugh, her heavier bosom bouncing. She tapped my forearm. "You've got a sweet girl here, mister." She wiped a tear at the corner of her eye. "No. But my voice is powerful. Remember yours is, too. Speak up when you notice something wrong. A firm voice can have a significant impact."

Liam snorted with his hands on his hips. "I'd rather have a gun."

Claire moaned. "Let's go to the truck, both of you." She turned an awkward smile to me and pushed the boys away.

A gruff throat clearing nearby snapped me from my stupor. Son of a gun. Did Dumont have a sixth sense? Knowing my luck, he'd been casing me the entire night.

I thanked Wagner and ushered Lark away, feeling Dumont's eyes on my back.

A short while later, after dropping off Lark, she gave my legs a bear hug.

"Love you, Daddy! See you in de morning!"

Before I could reciprocate, she went to play with the boys.

I ordered a pizza so I could pick it up on my way home. Movie and dinner with Josie, then a peaceful night's sleep. No night waking to deal with, or monsters under the bed, or weird clawing creatures that Lark insisted were outside. Again, twice this week she vowed she heard footsteps and saw shadows, and I had thrown my boots on, walked the perimeter of our cabin. Nothing. This was getting old, fast.

Though, my daughter had super ears.

I inhaled.

Focus, O'Reagan.

I couldn't get to the pizzeria and home fast enough.

27

Josie

I paced the floors thin while waiting. Chip's tail wagged and ears perked as he absorbed my restless energy. He shadowed me, his nails clacking on the wood with each step. I wore cozy socks over painted toenails. Lark had convinced me to go with red. I wore my most comfortable leggings and a tunic sweater.

A crisp night meant I had the wood stove going. With three cabins consuming energy, I worried about a drain on the grid.

The glass carafe of homemade apple cider in the fridge called my name. I waited to heat it. The task would give me a distraction while Everett was here. Or was I going to his place?

This was not a date. We were just hanging out.

Two barks announced Everett's return before I even heard tires on gravel.

I'd wait. Let him make the call. My fleece-lined boots sat at the door, ready to be slipped on.

I accepted Everett's invitation in order to break down my self-imposed barriers. He and Lark checked all the boxes on the safe and nice list, even with Don's precautionary warning. I remained prudent but open to the idea of...

Of what?

Friendship. Trust.

You can do this, Josie.

I heard the familiar footfall of Everett's boots meeting my steps and porch.

A knock.

Long inhale, exhale.

You can do this, Josie.

As I opened the door, a gust of cool air knocked into me, followed by the yeasty aroma of oregano-laced heaven. "Hey."

Everett's smile reached his amber brown eyes, allowing Dimple One and Dimple Two to emerge. "Hey. I've got pizza."

"That you do." *Okay, stop the awkward stuff.*

Chip's tail tapped the floor beside me. "Want to come in? I have apple cider and the wood stove going."

"Thanks."

After wiping his boots on the doormat, he strode to the counter to put the pizza box down.

I shimmied around him to grab the necessaries—dishes, napkins, cups. I pulled the salad I prepared earlier from the fridge.

"You've got a roaring fire there."

"The dampness has been getting to me. I wonder how it will be here this winter." I held up the bottle of cider. "Warm or cold?"

"Warmed, if it's easy?"

"I'll put it on the stove."

While the cider heated in a pot, we helped ourselves to pizza and salad.

"How was trick-or-treating?"

Everett maneuvered around me with the slightest graze of his hand across my lower back. "It was great for her first time."

My stomach squeezed. Many children would visit my previous home. I had gone over the top. Tate said spending so much was silly. Not to me. "First time?"

He shrugged. "She's always been with her mom."

Don's gap in Everett's record. He was away. Where? With the love I witnessed between him and his daughter, I found it strange he would voluntarily go away for so long.

He was so close now. I inhaled. Wood smoke, pizza, and *Everett*. I couldn't pinpoint it. Some days he smelled like sweat and labor. Other days, the linen scent of laundry. Yesterday he held a whiff of pine. The pepperoni masked it, but I detected a hint of grapefruit. His aftershave? I liked the clean look on him, but was glad he hadn't trimmed his hair.

He hovered, waiting for me to go first into the living room. I pointed to the sitting area. I took the armchair; he settled on the sofa. I bit into the pizza and quieted a moan.

"Lark must miss her mom." I thought of my mom. Unlike Dad, she and I had been close. Then her death plummeted Dad over the edge. I was lucky to get a call from him once a year. My heart hurt for Lark's loss. The pain of losing a parent too young was immeasurable. I'd been almost thirty, and Mom's death from cancer still crushed me, but I held on to our good memories. Sometimes that's all you have.

"I think she does, but she never mentions it."

Where *was* her mom? Divorced? Purposely absent? Dead?

Holly meowed from the kitchen counter near the open pizza box. "Holly, down!" I tapped the chair, and she hopped off with an emphasized trill, came over to her scratching pad, scratched the heck out of it, and then finally nestled next to my hip after a silent leap.

"I notice you don't leave the property much," Everett said. "Work doesn't take you to town?" He cast a look around the interior. "No home office setup?"

I got up to ladle the cider into mugs. "No. Why do you ask?"

"Just wondering. You're so good with Lark. Do you miss the kids?"

Obviously, it looked off, me young and healthy, and not working. I knew these questions were going to come, eventually. And eventually was now.

I handed him a mug. "I do. I haven't sought employment yet since moving here in May." Keyword: yet. *Was* I willing to look for a job? "I have enough savings to hold me over for a bit." It was a stretch of truth, but a vague enough answer. Placing my mug on a coaster, I returned to my seat, then nibbled on the pizza crust, buying myself a moment. Then a bite of salad with the last of the fall tomatoes. "How's the new job going? The website design for your new landscaping business? Your client seemed, uh, miffed."

"Good, good. She's satisfied with the update on the project. I hope my internet setup is okay. The majority of consulting work is done on the computer, so going to town for internet use was quite a hassle."

"That's fine." I actually was okay with it. The man had to work.

"Won't be able to kick off really until spring. Lots of moving parts."

"You sound busy."

"Never too busy to build a greenhouse." The craters he called dimples returned.

"I love it." I blew over the rim of my hot mug.

"Glad to hear that."

I sipped spiced cider. Oh, this was good. Another superb Tillie recipe. Her books got the most use out of anything in my kitchen.

He regarded the room. "You don't have a computer or television. What do you do at night?"

Wallow alone, I wanted to say. "I have an old television in my bedroom with a VCR."

"VCR? They still exist?"

I laughed. "They do. My uncle was old school. I can get VHS tapes at the library, but the selection is limited. Time for a DVD player."

"What about streaming?"

I gave a dismissive shrug to mask my shudder. That required credit cards. Big fat nope.

He slid his hand over his shaven chin. "Must get lonely."

The movement drew my attention to his opened shirt, defined collarbone, and the spot on his neck where wild hair met corded muscle. I admitted, "Sometimes."

"Want to come over and watch a movie after dinner? The connection is slow, but it works. I own a few movies on DVD, too. Though most are about princesses, superheroes, and animals."

I laughed.

We cleaned the dishes, working in a comfortable rhythm, Everett washing as I dried. This was new to me. Tate had never washed a dish in his life, always asking me why we didn't use paper plates.

I had to stop thinking about Tate.

Everett topped off the ciders. "Why don't we bring these mugs with us?"

I wiped slick palms on my thighs. "Okay."

We left Chip behind. The evening's chill bit my stove-warmed cheeks as we walked to Everett's cabin.

He slid his shoes off at the door and I did the same, glad for fuzzy socks tonight. I wondered if he'd have found my toes cute. Silly thought.

"Might need a fire here, too. Puts less strain on the heat pump." He took the cider and put the mugs on the coffee table, right in front of the sofa. Oh, he was smooth.

Like I suspected, Everett kept his place clean, though not spotless. Crayons and paper lay scattered on the carpet, and he grabbed a pair of tights from the couch and threw them into a laundry basket outside the bedroom doorway. "She couldn't find the right color to match her costume," he explained.

"She looked adorable."

"Hope she sleeps tonight. Candy and Lark do not mix well." He covered his yawn with a fist. "In fact, sleep and Lark are opposites."

He'd mentioned this before. "Does she get anxious?" I stacked kindling into the stove.

"Yeah. Every little sound bothers her. She says she can hear me out here, sipping or eating. Hell unleashes if I eat something crunchy or must blow my nose. I think her superpower is super hearing. Plus, everything seems to be too hot, too cold, too scratchy. She complains about the night sounds outside, too. She's got a wicked imagination. I did some googling, and she wasn't on board with kid-sized noise-cancellation headphones. Not for sleep at least. I don't blame her. And she refuses to try earplugs. They don't fit, anyway."

"I could suggest a few things to try. Some of my speech kids had anxiety and sensory challenges, too."

"I'd love that, thanks. You make impressive lists." He pointed to the laminated pages above the trash and recycling bins with a grin, both dimples in full glory.

While he took over starting the fire, I sat on the couch. A blue checkered quilt, not one provided in my quick cabin decorating, lay over the back. "This is nice."

"My grandmother. She's punchy. I think she gets on well with Hank. She mentioned taking him to a concert the other week."

That made my heart smile. Who didn't love Hank? "So...what are my animal-superhero-princess movie options?" I teased, pointing at the computer setup. A docking station, keyboard, pile of books and papers, pens, sticky notes, mouse, and laptop with speakers made up Everett's work alcove.

I fought a swell of anxiety. This felt too comfortable, too fast. I dragged the quilt over my lap, a shield.

He grabbed the laptop and set it down in front of us, then popped it open. "I figured with no cable or fiber-optic setup, no point in a big television." He typed in a passcode, opened a streaming app, and turned the computer toward me. "You pick."

I balled clammy hands beneath the blanket. It was just a computer. And not mine. Not linked to accounts or identity. So what if it resembled the same model I'd destroyed with Drano, a hammer, and the freezer?

Come on, Josie. Get a grip.

The screen laughed at me as I swallowed. The acid of the cider stung. An internal pressure in my chest told me I'd forgotten how to breathe. No. No, I could breathe.

One in, one out, my brain ordered.

I did.

One in.

One out.

"You okay?"

"How about a game instead? I think I'm, uh, televisioned out." I retreated into the quilt, lifting my knees to chest and putting distance between me and the laptop. It's not like I hadn't used a computer since moving here. I went to the library when necessary. Why was this one triggering me?

"Game it is." Everett's steady voice penetrated the fog. He reached forward, closed the laptop lid, and then pulled over a deck of colorful cards. "UNO?"

"Okay."

I focused on the rainbow-colored cards. Lark's favorite, I'd bet.

After dealing, he rose to check on the fire, then cleaned the mugs. It was his way of giving me breathing room. I probably looked like a space cadet.

Trembling, ice-cold fingers lifted my pile of cards. UNO. I could do UNO.

We played without talking. Each time I attempted to speak, the words dried up mid-sentence. This was more awkward than my first date at sixteen.

"Glad to see you've returned," Everett said after a few moments.

I laid down a red five. "I'm sorry I—"

He put down a green five.

Wild card, me. "Blue."

We played a few more cards. Ever so slowly, Everett asked, "What was it, Josie?"

"What was what?" Okay, there. A complete sentence.

Gorgeous, kind eyes pulled me from the depths. "Something made you move here. To unplug, disconnect, and get away. You had a moment there with the computer."

I shrugged. "I'm a Luddite."

He lifted an eyebrow, not buying my reason.

I pinched my eyes closed again for a moment, then played my card. "It wasn't just one thing."

"It usually isn't." With a voice so tender I nearly melted, he said, "Everyone's got their breaking point. You had a different life before you moved here?"

I needed him to pull the words from me, to be a lifeline. What pushed me to move? Kyle dying? Friends leaving? Getting fired? Sure, they all contributed to my decision. The criminal charges and prosecution, the divorce, everything. Tate. He was the main reason I fled. "My life got complicated, and it called for me to be in a quiet place."

"Quiet is nice. I was missing the energy of the city, but here...I see the stars, I hear the wind. It's peaceful."

He rambled on about Lark and his grandmother and learning new things. How could I tell him what weighed on my heart like a two-ton brick? As the stove warmed me, a rising internal heat grew, grief transforming to anger. "People suck. They disappoint you. They screw you over."

He played a card. "They do."

"Ex-husbands suck."

He grunted, compassion softening his gaze more. "Ex-wives, too."

We assessed each other. *There, that was incredible sharing, Josie.*

I slapped a card down, allowing anger to embolden me. "And what is with Sheriff Dumont? He gives me the creeps."

"I could not agree more. He oversteps. Takes his anger out on others. Not our fault his wife left, and his kid gets into trouble."

I'd heard about the wife from Hank. Interesting. That explained why he was protective around me. Did he know I was a runner, too? He was a sheriff. Of course, he did his research on me. Was he trying to help me or was he fulfilling some missed opportunity? He couldn't "save" his wife from herself, but he could save me? Nuts. Shivers went down my spine. "He acts worried about me being alone. I'm not alone. Hank is with me. And you two." My body tensed. "And if he's so worried about me, he sure shows it in a screwed-up way. The destroyed bushes. How do we bring that rat bastard to justice?"

"We don't know if it was him for sure. Neither of us saw him do it. And if he wants to protect you, why would he do that?"

A tsunami roared within me. If not Brian, then who?

I swallowed a bitter taste.

Tate?

I had one card in my hand but didn't say UNO.

Everett remained chill, playing the Skip card, then a yellow three. How did he hold himself together so well? "I gotta tell you something, Josie."

Holding his gaze, I trembled.

"On the night when the weasel attacked..." He paused.

"You mean attacked and *stacked*? That was so messed up, Ev. Weasels do that?" I dropped my card and hugged my arms to my chest. What if it had been a person?

"You saw the weasel."

"Yeah."

"Anyway, that night, I found a cigarette by your shed."

Another cigarette? By the shed...which was damn close to my cabin! He was just telling me this now?

"I figured it was nothing. One of the therapists."

"None of them smoke."

"Right. Then we found the one on the cliff path. Dumont smokes." He shook his head, baffled. "He drove by here that one time. Then your flat tire. I saw him buy nails that day."

"You did?" My mouth was dry.

"I checked Dumont's brand after he tossed a cigarette outside the hardware store. Not the same brand. Smokers are creatures of habit. So my theory went out the window."

We both sat silently, me gazing across the room, Everett nibbling on his thumbnail. The wood stove popped and crackled.

I finally said, "The fence, too."

"That could be animals."

My mouth went from dry to cottony.

"Josie, I don't think all this is Dumont. Some of it...like the nails in your tire. Yes. And we know he shows up here randomly. He doesn't have it in him to destroy the rhodies and azaleas, though. What is the point of that? Like you said. He wants to protect you, not hurt you."

A primeval chill prickled skin.

Everett said in his always calm voice, "Josie, please tell me."

"My ex smoked, too. Same brand we saw on the path. But it's a common brand..."

Everett shifted forward, closer to me. He took my hand and squeezed. "Do you have reason to think it's him?"

I shrugged and rubbed my nose. "He doesn't know I'm here." I paused. "There's so much more. I can't...not right now..."

He pulled me into a hug that went deep into my weary soul. He smelled like Everett. Like home.

He didn't tell me it would be okay. Everett was a practical realist. He survived.

"There seems to be theft happening here, too," I shared.

He held me tighter, his hand stroking the back of my head. "Like what?"

"My gardening gloves. Twice. I thought I was being forgetful. I bought a new pair! Hank mentioned misplacing his medicine. My shed and coop locks. I know I didn't lose them. A favorite coffee mug. And...it's stupid, but I had money hidden in a tea canister in the kitchen. My crazy uncle, he has money all over in random places. I don't know why. I emptied the canister so it could hold the speech game I made, and later I couldn't find the cash. I swore I put it in a drawer. Holly loves to scurry off with things, but uh, not a stack of twenties. Some days...I—I think I'm losing my mind like my uncle."

Stolen money propelled me back to Tate's deceptions. He told me I was being paranoid—again—when I couldn't reconcile the charges on the bank account, when cash I'd left around disappeared. The missing fundraiser money.

Bastard.

I pulled back from Everett's embrace, struck by self-doubt.

He grabbed my hand. "Don't go. It's okay. I'll listen."

"My ex, he said I was disorganized. I just misplaced things or forgot."

"Josie, you're the most organized person I know. You didn't lose or forget those things," Everett said. "We'll get to the bottom of this. There's always an explanation."

Chip barked.

Once.

We flew to our feet and reached the door simultaneously.

"Wait, Josie. Wait!" Everett threw his boots on, neglecting to tie them.

Tires squealed as a vehicle peeled out of the driveway.

28

EVERETT

I wanted to punch something. Or someone.

Violence got me here.

Instead, I offered what I could. "I can walk around and look—"

Josie waved my idea away. "No point. They—he—whoever he is, is gone."

The vehicle had sounded like a truck engine, but everything echoed differently on the property. "Let's check on Hank, then," I said.

She nodded, hugging herself. She hadn't brought her jacket, and it was getting late and cold.

As we approached Hank's cabin, his outdoor light flickered. "I'll change the bulb tomorrow. It's been flickering a lot. Has he mentioned any other issues?"

She knocked softly. "Just the stove, but you fixed that."

No sounds of a television or record player. His curtains were drawn, no light shining. "He's asleep."

She chewed her lip and wiggled his knob. "Locked. He keeps it unlocked during the day even when he's away, but locked at night. He's fine. We can check again tomorrow morning. I don't want to rouse him."

"You sure?"

"No, but Chip hasn't barked. He alerted me to Hank's fall two months ago. He would've sensed it." She gave a soft snort. "He seems more therapy dog than home protection dog."

"Let me walk you to your cabin."

She didn't need walking to her place. She was an independent woman. She let me, nonetheless.

We went through the silent routine of checking the chickens and goat. I stood in the right spot, waved a hand, and triggered the newly installed motion-sensing light shining on the pen and coop. The animals were fine. Chip gave two subdued barks from inside.

She walked around her cabin, flicking on every light. Chip barked twice more from his bed and wagged his tail happily. Danger was gone.

And what about those damn monsters at Lark's window? I shivered. Real or not real? Chip never barked those nights. Could he have sensed someone from the distance of Josie's cabin? My cabin was farther from Josie's. Hank's was closer. Those cigarettes and this whole bullshit situation screamed trouble. Had Lark *seen* someone real? She had an overactive imagination, but Lark didn't lie. Some fibs, but that was it. My mind was muddled with doubt. If that had been a real person, wouldn't Chip have barked?

"Good boy. Good boy." Josie dug into a treat jar and gave him one.

I poked my head around the corner to her bedroom.

"Nobody's here. Chip would have raised hell," she said.

She adjusted the damper on the wood stove. The cabin was toasty. In her kitchen, she chewed on her thoughts, hands cupping the edge of the countertop behind her.

I approached. "Do you want me to hang? I can stay on the couch. I'm a night owl. I can read the last few books from your OTG library there."

"Feel free to take them all. I'm so wired I doubt I'll sleep."

"We can stay up. Play a few more games?" I pointed to a puzzle. Being with her beat a full night's sleep any time. I'd sleep when I was fifty.

"Too many brain cells needed for that." Her gaze lingered on mine. Dark evergreen eyes guarded what had to be the turmoil bubbling inside of her. "Sorry I freaked out earlier about the computer and...stuff. Tech and I...we just don't meld well."

"No sorry is ever needed."

Her lower teeth tugged on her upper lip. "We can try our original plan. Do you like old movies?"

"I've watched a few with my grandmother. She loves Cary Grant, Jimmy Stewart, Grace Kelley, Ingrid Bergman."

Josie brushed past me—hmm, how had I gotten so close?

"She has good taste. Did you sneak a look at the movies I have there?" She pointed to the coffee table.

"No." I'd been too focused on drinking the cider and watching Josie's mouth move while she ate her pizza earlier.

"I decided on a whim to check out Hitchcock classics in honor of Halloween. *Rear Window*, *Vertigo*, and *Notorious*."

"Oh, *Rear Window*. That's an excellent one. More suspenseful than scary. Saw that with Gram."

She poured two glasses of water. She then rummaged in a cabinet to pull out oil, popcorn, and salt. "Don't laugh, but the television is old. I wasn't lying earlier. It's boxy. On wheels. I guess we could drag it out from the bedroom to here? No cable cords. I just use it for movies. But I have a comfy chair in there, too."

"Nah, the chair works." My pulse tried to not gallop. Movie, comfort, popcorn, Josie's bedroom. *She's your boss. She's your ticket to freedom from the claws of DCYF.*

Josie prepared popcorn on the stovetop while my pulse hovered on the edge of pandemonium. Butter and salt infused the air.

As we entered the bedroom, she clicked on each light. I lightly brushed my finger over the back of the armchair.

"I refinished that when I moved here. It was my first project. Forget everything else...I wanted a comfy reading chair." She laughed. "Everything here was old, neglected. I love to curl in an armchair with a good book."

I tapped the arm. "You did a fine job."

Once she sat on the bed and I on the chair with popcorn, Chip entered. She patted the duvet cover. "We've set ground rules about not going on furniture, but he knows when I'm anxious and he likes to snuggle, so we make exceptions. His trainer would not approve." He curled up beside her.

I never wanted to be a dog more than in this moment.

She grabbed something from her nightstand and tossed it at me. "Tonight calls for chocolate."

I looked at the Oh Henry! bar. "Never heard of these."

"You're missing out." She tore one open and bit into it with a moan.

The opening credits came on. I could see why Gram loved this movie. It was great, and flew by with little commentary from us, but I kept sneaking looks at Josie.

Chip yawned, stretched, and moved off the bed halfway through. He nosed my knee. "No popcorn, Chippy." He reluctantly plopped on the floor, leaning half his body against my calves.

During the credits, Josie released a cat-like stretch and yawn. "That was a good one." She glanced at Chip. He indicated his need to be let out. "He usually makes it until morning, but since we're up so late, so is his bladder."

I stood, my knees creaking. Comfy chair, but tired legs. "I'll do it. Do I need the leash?"

"Nah."

"I'll let him out and then go home." The rest of my words involuntarily got caught in my throat. I didn't want to leave. *Should I stay?*

"Okay." She rose to clean up the popcorn, and I followed Chip to the door. The wood stove was down to hot embers. Josie's lamps sent a glowing beacon out of the front doorway. I leaned against the jamb while Chip went about his business outside. The sky and woods held the piercing dark that came with mid-autumn. Quiet. Eerie.

Josie came up behind me, her steps soft creaks upon the floor. She flicked on the amber-yellow porch light.

Her voice was hoarse, barely a whisper, answering my unspoken question. "I'll be okay. It's fine. I've dealt with creeps before."

"You deserve better."

She stepped closer and stood at my side. My look followed every subtle movement: the smooth swallow of her throat as her gaze clung to Chip's movements across the meadow, the tapping of her fingers against her lips, the subtle expansion of her chest with a deep inhalation.

I turned my full body to face her, my heart sprinting beneath my ribs. As if it were already second nature, she turned toward me. I approached as she stepped back, pinning herself to the doorframe.

She lifted her chin as I rested a hand on her hip. Unblinking eyes captured mine, inviting, waiting. Leaning down, I kissed her. It felt right.

Our kiss was electricity. We could harness it and charge the power grid for a month. And damn, did she charge me. Lips upon lips, hot, seeking. I slid one hand behind her neck, and she abandoned the doorframe to lean into me.

She tasted like salt and chocolate. I ran my fingers through the hair that drove me absolutely crazy. God, it felt as smooth as I imagined. My thighs pressed against her hips. Pleasure lit parts of my body I forgot existed.

I pulled back an inch or two, tracing a hand along her cheek to her chin, then feathering my fingers through her glorious waves again. Tingles of delight rushed to my chest. I was glad she couldn't see my arousal in the dark.

After another kiss, this one softer, deeper, as I drank in the glory of Josie and lost myself to the dizziness, I leaned my forehead against hers, both of us heaving. "I shouldn't have—"

"You should've," she said.

I rocked back on my heels and held those dark eyes with my gaze. The soft porch light cast shadows across her high cheekbones and strong brows. Our hands had interlocked. I forgot how good it felt to hold a woman's hand. I didn't want to let go.

My lips hummed from the intensity of that kiss.

I wanted her mouth on mine again. I wanted to taste all of her. Bring her back to the bedroom.

Cold seeped in as Chip scrambled past us and into the living room.

"Go get some rest, Ev. I'll see you tomorrow," she said, squeezing my hand before letting go.

Damn.

I nodded, wordless, remembering the feel of her soft skin against my face. With my pulse beating in my ears, I walked a little off-kilter.

She left the porch light on until I reached my place. When I looked back, she was still standing in the doorway, leaning against the doorframe.

I swallowed. That kiss threw a wrench into everything. My hand fumbled with the doorknob, and I went inside with one last glance.

I thought I saw a smile, but perhaps it was just my imagination.

I allowed myself to imagine it.

We both closed our doors, and she put out the porch light.

LARK

My tummy still hurt from Halloween, but the candy was worth it. I saved a few candy bars to hide. It was colder today, so I wore my new jacket. It was a soft hug. And rainbow colored.

I was glad Daddy didn't hate rainbows like Mommy did.

He said she loved me, and sometimes unhappy people didn't realize when they hurt you. Mommy lied, though. She took my things, and it made me sad. He kept telling me it was different here and nobody would take my stuff. I wasn't sure I believed him yet.

I waved to Daddy as I skipped to the treehouse.

I carefully climbed the ladder, then gave Daddy another wave to show him I was here. It would please Josie, Daddy, and Mr. B to see what I did for them.

Chip barked hello from his cabin porch. "Hi, Chip," I hollered out the window once I was inside the treehouse. Dogs had super ears, too. They could hear whispers. I wondered if Chip heard the scratching and whispers outside my bedroom. But he never barked. So maybe he didn't? Or he knew the monster. Or the monster was extra sneaky.

The treehouse was the perfect place to hide the special things I didn't want to be sold or stolen. I reached the little trapdoor on the floor. It creaked open, but it didn't scare me. The chest of treasures was where I'd left it. Whew. I pulled the box out.

It was stinky inside the treehouse. Like dirt and old wood. Daddy fixed it up. He made sure no nails were sticking out and replaced some of the wood planks.

My tummy grumbled. I had to hurry. Lunch was soon.

I smiled as I took the stuff out of my bag. They would be so happy I had this here for safekeeping!

I added the candy bars, matches, shiny spoons, Mr. B's watch, batteries, and a few small baggies of goat food and chicken food to the box of treasures. I carefully took the two eggs out of my pockets. Josie said they were special and needed to be protected.

So many special things! I was proud of myself. Josie's extra car keys, gloves, the shed lock and the lock for the chickens' house, Mr. B's pills, a flashlight, Josie's mug and the money she left out, and Mr. B's golden Legos. I put money from Daddy's wallet here. Money was important to adults, and I didn't want them to lose it. I added paper and crayons. I couldn't keep my rainbow beanie here because I needed it, and if I wore it on my head, nobody could steal it unless they took it while I slept. I wanted to put the pirate's treasure here, but the box was stuck in the wall of Mr. B's basement and it was too heavy. Plus, I didn't know how to open the box to see what was inside. Perhaps there were skulls inside it! I hoped not. Gold coins?

I gave Kitty a kiss—she lay on the floor beside me. She would go in last.

Creaks on the ladder made my heartbeat flutter like a butterfly. I returned the treasures to the chest, but Kitty's dress got caught on a nail Daddy missed.

"Hey, Birdie...I've come up to check out the treehouse..."

No, no, no!

Daddy couldn't see the treasures! They had to stay hidden! What if he took them? I whimpered. *Come on, Kitty!* Her dress tore as I ripped her away from that naughty nail. I slammed the treasure chest shut just in time.

"Hey... What's the commotion?" Daddy's head poked through the door. The treehouse wasn't big enough for an adult to sit inside with me, but even with his wide shoulders, he could wiggle sideways and lean in. He looked at me.

"A squirrel got inside," I lied. Lies were bad. Mommy smacked my bottom when I lied. Daddy never did. I looked away. My knee bumped something on the floor.

Mr. B's pills rolled toward the doorway...and came to a stop at Daddy's hand.

29

— · —

Josie

With a loaded basket of sleeping remedies for Lark, I headed out my door for Everett's place. Ever since that kiss, I was finding both reasons to speak with him, and excuses to avoid him. It was silly. I was an adult. He was an adult. A few kisses didn't have to put a wedge in our friendship. We could...

I didn't know what to do, but not talking to him wouldn't solve my problem.

Chip gave me an expectant look from his spot on the front porch. "Yes, we're going to see Lark. Come, buddy."

He fell into step beside me. A refreshing fall day with a cornflower-blue sky just fed my already buoyant mood. The weather and I aligned our tempers often. Sunshine fueled my inner optimist; the dreary days fed the pessimist. I was a seesaw. Today, I practically floated to Everett's front porch.

I adjusted the basket filled with lavender bath salts, melatonin and magnesium gummies, homemade weighted blanket, white noise machine, and Himalayan salt lamp to my hip so I could knock.

Chip whined beside me. "What's up, bud? Missing Lark?" His ears perked, but he didn't issue a bark.

Muffled voices, one deep and one high-pitched, paused in their conversation with my knock. I heard the scamper of feet, a loud sob, then a door slam. Uh-oh. Unhappy five-year-old?

Everett opened the door a moment later. "Hey, Josie."

Chip whined again beside me. What was up with him?

"I—I..." Apparently, I'd lost my words. I pushed the basket into Everett's hands.

"What's this?" A somber brown gaze held mine. My insides fluttered. That whole butterflies thing? Yeah, a menagerie of wings moved about in my stomach. But this time it was concern rather than infatuation. The dimples weren't out to say hello, and that wasn't a smile in his eyes.

I swallowed, calling on my inner SLP. "A few more sleep suggestions for Lark." I tapped the laminated list in the basket. "There are instructions. Thought she may...that you may want to try a few?" I lifted my eyebrows. *You know, after our talk the other night?* He did remember the other night, right?

Gratitude softened the surprise that had been carving a frown on his forehead. "Thank you."

A squeaking hinge in the cabin caught my attention. Lark poked her head out of her bedroom. Wide eyes captured mine. She whimpered, then slammed her door.

"Sorry, I can come back another time." I retreated from the porch. Poor girl. Something was upsetting her. Did she have another bad night's sleep?

Everett laid the basket down on the floor inside the front door. He grabbed my hand. "Don't go...I..."

Louder sobs came from Lark's bedroom. My gut twisted. I hated to see crying kids. I always wanted to fix it.

I squeezed his hand. "It's okay. See you later."

Everett pressed his lips together with a nod. He squeezed my hand back before letting it go and disappearing into his cabin.

On the way back from taking Hank to vote, while I was contemplating dinner and avoiding thoughts of Everett and our kiss, red and blue lights flashed in my rearview mirror. I slowed and pulled over, assuming the police car needed to pass, but it stayed behind me and followed us onto the shoulder. I released a flavorful word.

"Jo! Cussing like a sailor now, are you?" Hank looked into the side-view mirror. "At least it's not that cad Sheriff Dumont. He needs to do something else with his free time other than pester you and Everett."

The vehicle behind us was a brown sedan and with sheriff's office decals, not Brian's truck.

Clammy hands scrabbled for the copy of the registration—Morgan's old one—in the glove box. Why bother? The expired tag on my license plate was enough to condemn me. I fished in my purse for my Massachusetts ID. A warm flush beginning in my neck spread faster than a bush fire up to my cheeks. I was supposed to have met with JC and get this car crap resolved.

Be nice, Josie. Law enforcement officers are your friends. They're here to protect you. Those were my brother's words. I missed him so much.

I opened the window, a gust of cold air blasting my hot cheeks. Blinking watery eyes, I turned the car off and put the keys on the dash. To let them see my face, I loosened my scarf and removed my hat. *Be respectful. Tell the truth.* And stop the tears. I wiped the blurry vision away.

"Good day, ma'am. Do you know why I pulled you over?" a firm but calm voice said at my side.

"I was driving the speed limit, Officer." I shot a look at her. Dressed in a crisp brown uniform, she evaluated me with almond-shaped eyes beneath a broad-brimmed light brown hat. "Uh, Deputy, I mean." They did patrols, too?

"That you were. License and registration, please."

I handed them over, numbly.

"Oh, Shanae! How are you?" Hank said, leaning over me to smile at her. "I picked up jelly donuts today. Want one?" He shook the bakery box in his lap.

She tried to mask a smile. "Ma'am, is this your vehicle?"

Obviously, she knew the answer. "My uncle's. He passed away. I've been meaning to get the registration transferred over."

"Are you living in the state or visiting?"

I swallowed. "I moved here in May."

"You need a new license, too, if your residence is New Hampshire." She flicked up a dark eyebrow above brown eyes that said she would not put up with people's bullshit.

I nodded. "I understand."

The hat made her infinitely tall and foreboding, and I felt like a microbe under a scope. She shot a look at the windshield. "Same with the inspection. I'll be right back."

As she returned to her vehicle in what felt like slow motion, I listened to my rapid breathing, blinking unfocused eyes. Inspection, insurance, registration, license. *Dumb, Josie. Dumb.*

Hank tapped on one of my shaking knees. "Shanae's a good one, Jo. She'll give you a free pass. She must've just come from one of her shifts. She usually handles criminals and courthouse things, not tickets. That's the local police. But sometimes on these rural roads, the deputies run shifts to fill in scheduling gaps. It's been harder to recruit officers in recent years. Don't worry, Jo."

I clenched and unclenched my hands, urging icicle fingers to warm up. "Hope so. Ugh, Hank. I can't believe I procrastinated with this."

"It's okay."

An eternity later, my hands no less icy, my heartbeat no slower, she returned and said in a matter-of-fact voice, "This vehicle is registered to Morgan Caldwell." She handed my license back.

"Correct. My uncle." Hadn't I established this?

"Do you know the location of the DMV?"

"Yes."

Hank leaned over me again. "Shanae—"

"Hank, on duty it's Deputy Wagner."

God bless him, he smiled the Hank smile that disarmed friend and foe alike. With sass, he said, "Deputy Wagner, she's been dealing with this old fuddy duddy." He brandished his cane. "I broke my hip and had surgery two months ago. She just inherited the cabin and property from Morgan this May. The property's been a, uh, a quagmire! She's been busy." He laughed at himself and whispered, "Daily crossword comes in handy sometimes." He said louder, "Anyway, busy, like I said."

"I see."

Leaning into the seat back, I nodded, tears returning. "Yes." I wiped my nose to hide a drip.

"Ms. Sawyer, I'll give you a warning, but please take care of your license, registration, inspection, and insurance as soon as possible, okay?"

"Okay, yes. Thank you." I let out a breath.

"And welcome to Silent Creek," she added.

Just then, the sheriff's black truck passed us, stopped, and pulled in front of us. Really, Universe?

"I met Morgan once. My father knew him in Vietnam," Shanae added.

I pushed out a meek smile, trying to transition from panicking to making small talk. "I came here as a girl."

Enlightenment widened her eyes. "My sister used to visit Morgan's property to swim in the lake. Trish. She was friends with your sister...uh..." She tapped a red nail on her chin. "Patty?"

"Phoebe."

She cleared her throat as Dumont approached in his slow swagger. "Right." She shifted back to business. "Okay, Ms. Sawyer, please take care of this."

"Yes, Deputy."

Hesitation played across her soft features—or was it concern? She reached into her pocket and pulled out a slip of paper and a pen. She scribbled on it and handed it to me. In a whisper, she said, "If you ever need anything, call me. Even after hours. I don't live too far from your place. I know it can get isolating up there."

I took the slip, blinking. What?

Concern wrinkled her brow.

"Thank you. I—I—I've got Hank."

She stepped back. "That you do."

"Something wrong here, Deputy Wagner?" Brian said on his approach.

"Nothing, Sheriff." She nodded to him in respect. "Was going to give her a warning. Expired registration and inspection. She was on her way to the DMV."

I appreciated her stretching of the truth.

He dismissed Shanae with a gesture. She nodded and returned to her vehicle.

He snatched a look at my truck's extended cab. What was so special about it? The groceries sat on the floor in canvas bags.

"How are you today, Josie?" He neglected a greeting to Hank.

"Good, good. Just brought Hank to vote while on our errands. Heading to the DMV now."

Never mind that he didn't vote for you.

I glanced at my rearview mirror. Shanae sat in her car for a long minute before doing a U-turn and heading back toward town.

"Am I free to go, Sheriff?" I licked dry lips and offered him a smile.

His tall frame blocked the minimal sun out today, casting a shadow into my truck. "It's Brian, remember? How are the new tenants doing on your property?"

"Very well, thanks." He knew *everything* about me, so I would not play games. I wanted to get home, eat melting ice cream, cuddle with my dog.

Fear released its hold on me. I was fed up with Brian Dumont. I hoped he lost the election. Kudos for his public service, but he was sketchy, and I wouldn't rule him out yet as the person causing havoc on my property.

"I'm surprised, given your history, that you let someone like Everett O'Reagan rent one of your cabins."

"Excuse me?"

He must've seen my mile-high eyebrows, because he added, "Please be careful around him, Josie. Wouldn't want to see anything happen to you, like with his ex-wife. She's been missing. No need to worry. I've had an eye on O'Reagan ever since he got out."

What the hell was he talking about? Missing ex-wife? And got out of what?

Everett's three-year gap.

All I saw was my reflection in Brian's dark shades. I needed to get home before my thoughts gave me mental whiplash. I cleared my throat. "Is there anything else?"

"No. You're all set." He scratched the graying beard on his round chin.

"Thank you."

He turned on his heel, but paused. "And next time, Josie, please don't lie to my deputy."

My cheeks burned. I didn't feign ignorance.

He pointed in the direction from which I'd come. "The nearest DMV is that way."

30

—·—

Everett

"But, Daddy, I can't. She'll hate me!" Lark pleaded, her eyes puffy from crying all night. Again. I refused to chase her around the cabin as she progressed through meltdown number gazillion. She finally stopped tossing things and flopped into her seat across from me at the table.

"Five things you can see, Birdie." I sipped coffee, though it wasn't cutting through my rupturing headache. I slid an egg onto her plate, knowing she'd pick at it. I'd tried scrambled, fried, fluffy egg whites, and even "green eggs" with her food coloring drops, to no avail. She'd only eat the peanut butter toast and whatever fruit I served. Sometimes dry cereal. I'd been a picky child, too, but when you're an adult with limited means or limited choices, you learn to eat what you're given.

"Lumpy eggs."

I lifted an eyebrow and trained my eyes on her.

She plopped her elbows onto the table and cradled her cheeks in her palms. "A white mug. Orange juice. Scruffy hairs under your nose."

Lord, even her huffing was like Fran. Sometimes I wondered what she inherited from me. All I saw these days was Fran.

Lark's eyes stared at something above my head. "A spider!"

I jumped from my chair, saw the offender, and then grabbed it in a napkin to let it outside. Could spiders survive the cold? Lark didn't let me kill them, so the cold it was. "Four things you can feel."

She moaned.

"Birdie..."

She took her strawberry lip balm from her pocket and lathered it on. "Creamy ChapStick."

I continued sipping the gingerbread-flavored coffee and eating eggs while Lark named her four things she could feel, three sounds, two scents. She ended with her one taste. "Salty eggs."

I tapped my fork on the table, contemplating how we were going to bring up Lark's stealing with Josie today. That was the reason for my daughter's fits last night and this morning, after all. She had to apologize, there was no doubt. Lark gave me a grimace, and I stopped tapping. She dragged herself over to the couch. I was going to suggest coloring in her mandala book, but Lark beat me to it. These mindfulness practices were helping. As she calmed down, I pondered over the Josie situation. Between Lark's stealing and my enlightening night with Josie, my brain was in overdrive.

What I knew about Josie:

One, the ex-husband—he was sus. Was he violent? Was he looking for her? She was afraid of him. Whatever he had done, it had left its scars.

Two, she hated technology and anything putting her on the digital or real-world grid. She preferred to stay as anonymous as possible. She was wary of strangers, the town, and sharing. That supported number one.

Three, she left her former life and was slow to start a new one here.

Four, she did all transactions in cash, avoiding credit and accounts.

I slumped over my breakfast. My bet was this guy had been a hacker, addict, or abuser. She never flinched at my or another's proximity. It was a known fact that people close to you orchestrated many cyber and identity thefts. But your own spouse? Was that it? Had her husband ruined her finances and reputation? Was he looking for her, or was the guy in jail? It was a jump, but my hunches were usually correct.

Eggs and oatmeal lost their appeal. I chugged water to dilute the caffeine hitting my bloodstream from the nicer coffee I splurged on from Deanna's cafe. My chances with Josie were slim. Not with my checkered past. How could she be with a guy like me, given what happened to her?

I'd gotten my thrills the wrong ways. I had wanted to push that past under the rug ever since getting out, but here it was, punching me brutally in the face. Living for Lark drove me now.

Oh, Lark.

My darling daughter was taking and hiding things. She wanted to protect what seemed most precious to us. I got it, but that didn't make it right.

The truth of the matter was my daughter stole things. Just like her dad. Different ways, different things, different reasons.

"Come back to the table, Birdie."

Having already gotten bored with coloring, she was prone on the couch. She rolled over and pressed her face into a pillow. Her voice came out muffled. "No."

"Come to the table now."

She sat up and plodded to the table, her face not meeting mine. She pulled out the chair, eased herself into the seat, and finally looked up at me.

"Do you understand why stealing is wrong even if you think your reason is right?"

She nodded.

I wasn't sure she fully got it, but we talked about it a lot last night. I mean, she was five. Kids understood more than what we gave them credit for.

I swallowed. "Remember when Daddy was away?" She'd need to know, eventually. Now was as good a time as any.

"Mommy said you did some bad dings, and you weren't coming back."

I shifted my chair so that I was positioned beside her. Squeezing her hand, I said, "I was always coming back. But I did do some bad things. I stole things."

Her face turned ashen. "Like Mommy?"

"Not exactly." Now was not the time to explain or rationalize Fran's mistakes.

She looked down, her voice small. "Like me?"

"I stole other things—stuff from a computer—that were important to some big business people. I made poor choices. I broke the law. Laws are like rules, right?"

She nodded.

After a swallow, I said, "I went to prison."

"Like dose bad guys in cartoons wif de funny striped clothes?"

I brushed a hand across my chin. "Yeah, sort of. I spent a lot of time thinking about what I did wrong. I'm making better choices now. I don't do those bad things anymore. Do you have questions for me?"

"Am I going to prison?"

I pulled her into my lap. "No, Birdie. However, you will need to apologize."

"Mr. B first?"

Easier of the two, yeah, I get you, kid. Josie scares the crap out of me, too.

"Josie first."

JOSIE

The green-and-blue area rug wasn't thick to begin with, but it must have been growing thinner from all my pacing lately. Everett was a criminal. Just like Tate. Or worse? What did he do? Did he murder his wife? Was I allowing a murderer on my property?

I clenched my fist. This was unbelievable. And Everett was *not* a murderer.

During the entire ride home yesterday with Hank, my buddy had tried to talk me off the ledge.

"No," he'd assured, "you're not a chump. Everett is a good guy. There must be an explanation."

Well, then I wanted one, dammit!

I remembered Everett's sweet words and sweet actions and sweeter kisses...

No.

Charmers were good at charming. Everett didn't seem like a narcissist though. Had Everett been fooling me all along so he could move in and...and...I don't know...get to Morgan's money? The fence, cigarettes, truck—was that him, or a friend helping him in some sort of long con? He was with me when most of these things happened—a perfect alibi. Win me over by "helping" me? Just like Brian Dumont?

Did he know about Tate and use that to his gain?

My throat was dry. No, no, no. Paranoia lied. Everett didn't do that. He had a questionable past, that's all. But what was it? What had he done?

Of course, I'd called Don right upon my return home yesterday. No answer. So now, for the past day, I stewed.

There was a knock on my door.

I blinked away the tears, then flung the door open.

I opened my mouth to let him have it, but there stood Lark beside him. She wiped a gloved hand on a snotty nose. Her eyes were pink. Why was she upset?

I couldn't confront him in front of her. But if I waited too long, the fire would dim in me, and I would forgive him.

Empathy pricked my resolve when I looked at his face. The uncertainty etching a deep canyon in his forehead, the repentant chestnut eyes, the lips I kissed. He gently squeezed Lark's shoulders as he moved her in front of him. Those hands had caressed my spine, rustled my hair, and traced the nape of my neck.

Poof! Resolve completely gone. Gosh, I was weak. I had softened too much since they moved in.

"You know," he said somberly.

"Yes," was all I could manage.

Lark began to sob. "Please don't kick us out!" She wrapped her arms around my legs.

Reflex had me returning the hug. "Oh, Lark. I won't do that." How could I? She lacked a mother. She needed a home. Somewhere safe. Was this place safe? Was she part of the con?

How could I even think such a thing?

I knelt to Lark's level, hoping to settle my raging thoughts by comforting her. I brushed her hair back from her forehead. "Everything will be okay." Why was she upset again? What happened to that bright-eyed sweet girl I'd come to know?

Everett finally spoke again. "Lark, please do as we talked about."

Her eyes, wider and darker than his, held mine. "I'm sorry, Miss Josie. I'm sorry I took dose—those things."

What things? I blinked, dumbfounded. What was going on?

Everett held up a bag.

"You're not losing your mind," he said.

"Huh?" I squeezed Lark's shoulder, then stood. "What are you talking about?"

"I thought you said you knew. All the missing items around here. Lark was...uh, keeping them safe."

"You can say it, Daddy. I stoled dem—them!" Her cheeks turned pink, matching the blotches on her forehead.

"Good correction on the *th*, Lark." I was a loony woman here, focusing on such a trivial thing. "But what is this about stealing?"

Everett handed me the bag. "It's all in here. Even Hank's things. I took back mine. She was hiding them in the treehouse."

What? Why?

Lark stared up, waiting for me to acknowledge her apology.

"I forgive you, Lark. I'm sure you had your reasons for keeping the items safe. Your daddy explained why this was not the best choice, I assume."

She nodded. "Mm-hmm."

Everett squeezed her hand. "Mr. B next, Birdie. Give me a moment here with Josie."

Lark nodded again and made her way to Hank's cabin. Everett and I watched her drag her feet in the gravel, then eventually plop onto the front porch. Chip gave two happy barks from inside my living room.

"Go ahead."

My pup ran to join her, picking up a twig along the path and bringing it to play fetch.

I turned back to Everett. In the sunlight, his hair glowed shades of brown and honey, but his expression slackened. He looked five years older and dreadfully tired in the span of seconds.

He said, "Her mom...Fran, Lark's mom...she's missing."

"Why are you telling me this?"

"Because..."

"What happened, Ev?" I steeled myself for what he was going to say.

"She did drugs, and I was *away*, not there for her." Shame and pain punctuated his words. "When I returned, she was too far gone. When I came to pick up Lark from her place..." He paused, scraping fingers through his hair as if trying to brush away a bad memory. "She left Lark as if her daughter was some...some...afterthought. I'm all she has now."

Away. I'd originally thought the time gap meant a military deployment—but Don had no record of it—or a traveling adventure. No. He had been in prison. For what, though? *Ev, tell me.*

Before me stood a hurting man. An ex-con.

I reached for his arm. "Oh, Everett. I'm so sorry. Poor Lark."

Pain darkened in his eyes. "Fran had left our four-year-old kid alone, hiding in a closet, and empty needles on the counter beside a Post-it note."

Shame about my own hasty departure from my former life, the note left for my friend, stole my words. My breathing hitched. I pressed a palm over my lips to restrain the cry. He removed it and stroked the back of my hand with a thumb.

His breath mingled with mine. "I'm sorry I didn't tell you sooner. It's why Lark hid things. Fran would sell her stuff."

"I'm so sorry, Ev," I whispered.

We locked eyes for a long moment, then he said, "What is it you said you knew—"

"Daddy!" Lark hollered from Hank's porch.

Everett turned to me. "Talk later?"

I nodded, too spellbound to say more.

31

— · —

EVERETT

Josie closed herself off after Lark's apology. We never did get that talk in. A talk that I knew was about me. I just knew. Somehow, she figured me out. This wasn't about Fran or Lark. Josie wasn't the type to shy away from that. This was all about me and my past.

My reason for dodging her every chance I got, too? I was a big coward. Chickenshit.

Thanksgiving rolled in quietly.

Lark and I spent the holiday at Penny's. Claire was staying through Christmas, so her husband was in town, too. He talked about football and his restaurant. I indulged him, though neither topic interested me. He offered me a beer, and I politely declined.

Gram poked me in the ribs. "You're somewhere else, Ev. What is it?"

I shook her question away as I scooped out pie to take home. "Tired."

She squeezed my hand. "Parenting will do that."

I didn't correct her. Lark had been sleeping better over the past few weeks. The stuff Josie had given us in her basket of magic was working. On her laminated sheet were other ideas to try, including more mindfulness exercises. One being a rice sensory bin. I literally had two ten-pound bags of rice in my truck and a clear bin, both waiting to be combined when I got back to the cabin.

I set up an evaluation with a neuropsychologist for Lark in the spring. Waiting lists sucked, but I was told getting into a specialist within six months was fast-tracking it.

My daughter's little Zen zone helped with the anger constantly brewing in me, too. A text message from Spencer had hit a nerve this week. They wanted to see Lark over the holidays. I texted back nicely, arranging a time. My visit with Carolyn in November had gone well. She thought by the New Year, my case could be closed.

So close. The finish line teased me.

Penny's baby girl, Emily, let out a shrill newborn wail as I slid a piece of pecan pie onto a takeaway plate. Something was missing today. Jake was missing, and my parents were checked out, but there was something else. Someone else. Well, two someones.

I slid two pieces of pumpkin pie onto the plate, for Josie and Hank.

"Good idea. Bring extra home," Gram said, stowing away leftovers in Penny's fridge.

I yawned, tired from too much turkey and too much togetherness. "Ready to go?"

Lark and I departed Penny's house around five, with Gram in tow. She sat in the passenger seat, holding the covered plate. A mixed aroma of pumpkin, apple, and roasted pecans livened up the cold cab of my truck.

"Nana, what are you doing dis—this—weekend?" Lark said from the back seat.

"Oh, my usual. Cards with the ladies, sewing circle, walks around the park. Coffee again with Hank. Want to visit?"

"Yes!"

As she exited the cab, I offered to walk her to her door. She blew me off with a wave. "Tell Hank one o'clock sharp on Saturday."

"Will do." I liked that Hank and Nana were hanging out. It was good for both of them.

En route home, Lark asked, "Will Josie and Mr. B like our pies?"

"I hope so."

Lark helped me make the pumpkin, which turned out surprisingly good.

My slow steps trudged behind Lark's eager ones up the porch at Hank's house as a cool rain began to hit the ground.

Time to test the waters again. Though I'd been avoiding Josie as much as she was avoiding me, I was still visiting Hank when he needed something fixed or looked at. Lark came over to play a few times.

Chip barked twice from inside, so I didn't even need to knock.

"Hey, kiddos. Just in time for Scrabble," Hank said when he opened the door.

Lark smiled and clapped her hands. "I love games."

He patted her beanie-covered head. "A fun game to learn your letters."

"I can read a few words now." She stuck out her chin.

"Then you'll ace this and be a great partner. Come, come. It's chilly tonight." He shepherded us in without resistance.

"We brought you pie." My gaze locked on Josie's.

She took the plate with a soft, "Thank you."

Lark added, "Daddy and I made de—the pumpkin! His first pie, Josie, and I give it an A plus!"

My cheeks warmed.

I followed Josie to the kitchen. "Want me to get plates? Or did you already eat dessert? Smells wonderful in here."

"I've got it. We haven't eaten dessert yet. I made a pineapple upside down cake."

"Not your usual Thanksgiving dessert."

"Tillie's tradition, I was told." Josie fluttered a hand to Tillie's picture. "I wanted to make the holidays special for Hank."

"He's blessed to have you." I squeezed her shoulder. A current of energy shot to my belly. "Look, Josie...I..."

Removing plastic wrap, she heaved a sigh. "It...us... We're landlady and tenant. It was a mistake, Ev. And whatever...with you...before..." She tapped a finger on the counter. "No need to explain."

"If that's what you want," I said, thunderstruck.

I mean, what did I expect? Was this about the kiss or about my past? Josie operated like me. If you pushed away first, it hurt less. At least she wasn't kicking us out. But how could I keep living here with an iceberg between us?

I blinked back remorse. We shuffled through the motion of plating thin slices of each dessert. "My favorite way to eat dessert. A bit of everything."

"That's the only way, right?" Her light words didn't match the exhaustion she gave off. She was not okay. And I so badly wanted to fix it.

We gathered around the table. For Scrabble, I teamed up with Lark, and Hank and Josie played on their own.

What began as awkward gaiety morphed into something real as the game progressed. Josie loosened up, and I felt her genuine enjoyment. This, the four of us, felt right. If I could just mend my relationship with Josie. I'd hurt her while trying to protect myself.

Dammit.

As Lark played none other than the word BIRD, the lights flickered. Freezing sleet beat against the windows.

"Blustery out there," Hank said, trading in a few tiles.

Through light conversation and pie, we carried on with our game for another half hour until the lights went out. "We just changed those bulbs last week." I scratched my chin. Shit, this was something beyond my scope. I got up and checked a few appliances, the thermostat. No electricity at all. "Could the batteries need cleaning again, like what happened in September?"

"Not sure," Josie said.

"I'll grab candles." Hank made his way to the kitchen drawer.

"Does this happen frequently?" Josie eyed the well-used candles with suspicion.

He lit several and laid them on the table beside the game board. "Here and there," he said.

I tsked. "Hank, you've got to tell me these things. I thought it was only bulbs burning out. Your power keeps going out, too?"

Josie pulled back the curtains. "Lights are out at your place, too, Ev."

"I left them off." I was already pulling on my boots and jacket. So was she.

Josie paused at the door. "Be back soon, Hank. Will you two be okay?"

Lark was eating more pie.

"Gotta eat it so it won't spoil," Hank suggested. Lark nodded, a whipped cream mustache above her small lips.

We grabbed two flashlights and checked my cabin first. Power *was* out. "So, it's both of us. Same issue as before?"

Josie's porch light glowed, puncturing the dark, wet night.

She pulled a hood over her hair. "I've had no troubles. What about you? Besides today and that one time."

"None."

She sighed. "Battery shed."

We trudged through the pebbly sleet, our boots crunching a path to the shed.

Batteries, inverter, and controller all passed the test. We cleaned the connections again, to no avail.

"Towers next?" I asked. I was getting better at the off-the-grid workings, but the electrical still baffled me a bit. I'd been slacking on my nighttime reading, opting for sleep.

"Guess so. We've ruled everything else out. No need to check the solar since the system already switched to wind."

I scratched my head. "The towers were serviced in October, though. They should be fine."

She shrugged as we passed Hank's. "Come, Chip." She motioned to him to join her from his position on the porch.

He yawned and stretched and was at our side in no time.

I followed her toward the forest's edge. "There's nothing we can see from the ground. We'd need to dig up the wire or scale the towers. Neither we can do tonight. It's best to call a professional to come look at it again."

"I'll check on my own, then." She made for the trail, her flashlight beam leading the way.

Hank poked his head out and hollered up to us, "It's back on!" He pointed toward my cabin and his.

Josie ignored him.

"Where are you going? Anything else to check can wait until the morning," I said after her.

"I didn't ask you to come. Go back. I'm fine."

Chip scampered ahead toward the trails he knew so well.

I hurried up the ridge behind her, shaking my head. Dammit, she was stubborn. She shined her light along the ground, where I presumed the wire ran—underground. I didn't have X-ray vision. This was pointless.

We reached the fence before she spoke again.

"I'm so tired of troubleshooting, of fixing things." The flashlight shook in her hand. "Living here was a stupid idea! I miss my family, my friends."

"Whoa, Josie. Take a breath. And I'm here to help."

Her outburst was far better than the cold shoulder. Thanksgiving must have triggered something.

She stopped walking and turned on me. "I never should have moved here."

"You had your reasons to get away and come here."

"And you would know, wouldn't you?" she fired back. "You're just like *him*."

My heart plummeted to my feet. Crap, was she comparing me to her ex-husband?

. She hugged her arms to her chest, shining the light up. I shoved my small flashlight into a deep coat pocket, then pulled her into my arms. "Tell me, Josie. Tell me."

The distant glow on the cabin porch backlit her. I tried to see her face. Her flashlight, pinned between our chests, dug into me. She trembled in my tight embrace. I slid softer, pleading hands down to her hips. "My God, Josie, please...just tell me." My voice broke. My everything broke.

"Identity theft." She dug out the words. "Tate, my ex. He did it. He drained our accounts. My retirement money. He stole from my school fundraiser. He used my identity to support his gambling addiction. He raked me over the coals. And the worst part? He made me feel paranoid. Like I was making things up! Nobody but my brother believed me and he's not alive anymore to help me. It cost me every-thing."

I forced out the words, "Not everything. You're here. You're whole. You have a new life."

"He lied to me, Ev. Just like you! And now I'm off searching the woods at night like a lunatic, looking for some reason why the power's not working, something other than ran-dom glitches in the grid. To find out who is tormenting me! I will be damned if I'm told I am crazy again. I can't help but think it's him doing all this shit on my property. That *you're* doing it. That even Brian Dumont is behind it."

I didn't break the connection of my hands with her hips as I tried to take away her pain with a touch. Pain I had contributed to. "I am here to help. Please believe me. I'm as confused as you."

"I can't trust anyone. I question everything," she said in a desperate whisper. "Even with Lark's confession about stealing stuff, it doesn't explain everything else. This is not all coincidence. It can't be all in my head, Ev. It can't!" She sniffled and punched my chest lightly. "And you lied to me, Ev. Why didn't you tell me?"

Shame blurred my vision.

After a long stillness, I cut the silence engulfing us. "I'm sorry that happened to you. You're not crazy. I believe you. And I swear to God, I am not the one doing all this effed-up stuff here."

Say it. Say it now.

With a clear voice, I said, "I was in prison, Josie. For three years. That's why I was absent from Lark's life. I..." My throat thickened. "Cybercrimes. Hacking. Not identity theft. Nobody I knew. It was—" I sighed so freaking loud it bounced around off trees. Cybercrimes fell under a broad umbrella—one both Tate and I stood beneath. All I had was an explanation. "I did the wrong job for the wrong people. Wrote the code to break into a company, high-level fraud...nothing like what Tate did to you. It wasn't...it was..." I shook my head. "I won't excuse my behavior. I did what I did. I served my time. But all this around here"—I waved to the woods—"is not me. I should have told you about my past."

I stepped back and shoved stiff fingers into my pockets.

The sleeting picked up. The sound of it hitting leaves and branches crackled eerily.

She spoke through chattering teeth and ragged breaths. "You're trying to make things right for Lark. But, Ev...if you're...if you're hacking again...here on my property..."

"God, no! My work now is a hundred percent legit. Consulting and contract work for real companies. Look them up with the BBB. I'll get 1099s and all the tax documents."

"So not web design and consulting for your landscaping business?"

Shit, okay, I had lied a bit. "Not exactly. No. But I am also setting up my landscape work. I need something stable for Lark. The consulting is just money to tide me over." I had to tell her all of it. "I have a DCYF case on me, Josie. That's why that woman came to visit. She's my caseworker."

She gasped and recoiled.

Afraid to approach her, I blinked wet lashes and wiped the sleet moistening my hair and forehead. "It's hard to explain." I said, empathically, "I've *never* harmed Lark. I had a beer at a bar one night. Got in a fight. One stupid mistake shortly after I was released. I don't ever drink. Ever. Now I gotta jump through these hoops to prove I'm clean and on a solid track. Home, job, safety for my kid." I didn't say that Spencer and Ann-Marie had set me up. What was the point?

"Let's go back," she suggested.

I shared too much. My skin prickled, but I steadied my ragged breathing. "No. Let's check the turbines. I believe you, Josie. Something's fishy here."

"The fence issue was likely an animal." She released a defeated sigh.

"What if it was some*body*? That prick Dumont or your ex... Where is he now?"

"He was released from prison two months ago."

My stomach dropped. "Let's go look."

"Okay."

We traversed the path side by side. Chip took the lead, sniffing everything that needed sniffing. I chewed on my thumbnail, my mind aching so much from our shared confessions.

After ruling out the turbine, we returned to the perimeter. I'd repaired most of the fencing holes. Expecting to hit another pile of branches I put aside earlier in the fall, I pivoted to maneuver around it, but the branches were gone.

I targeted the beam of light around the log I'd left the branches near. Fresh, large footprints in the old snow from the storm earlier in the week. "Have you been up here this week?"

She shook her head.

"Those aren't my footprints. Somebody was here. Someone moved a pile of branches I had set aside."

"Maybe you're mistaken where you put it?"

"No."

The beam from her flashlight shuddered. "And Lark...she didn't come up here?"

"No. These prints are too large. Lark goes to the tree-house and back, that's all, and I watch her like a hawk now.

Never goes on the trails. Take a breath, Josie. You're holding it." I grabbed her hand. Ice met ice. I whispered, "Should we come back in the morning? Call the police? I don't have a weapon. I don't even have a pocketknife."

She whispered back, "Morgan's gun is in my basement, but I've never used it."

We looked at each other.

She swapped her large flashlight for my smaller one. "Use that. I'm too shaky to hit anything with it."

I aimed the beam toward the woods. "Let's see where these footprints go. Stay behind me."

"Okay." Chip remained by her side. He hadn't barked yet. Good sign so far. I still wondered how far away he could sense people.

More footprints. All over, back and forth. Sweat dripped down my spine despite the frigid night. We kept walking, shoving errant branches aside.

"Holy crap," I whispered, my light falling on yellow metal between patches of rust. "The bus."

"Wow, I guess there is a bus, and somebody has been here," she whispered, pointing to the footprints in front of it.

How the hell had they gotten the bus up here in the middle of the woods? It looked decades old and was surrounded by newer growth. I couldn't see anything through the filthy windows. "Chip isn't barking. Good, right? Nobody's inside, or he knows them?" I shined my light through a broken window. Nobody appeared inside...unless they were hiding.

"He's met the sheriff, but not Tate."

I crouched beside a dead fire, my hand hovering. "Cold."

I opened the bus door.

The hinges creaked loudly. I held the flashlight up as a weapon. Violence would get me into deeper trouble with DCYF. Dammit, I didn't care. Whoever was on the property was trespassing.

I said in my deepest, most menacing voice, "Come on out, you asshole. We know you're here."

Nothing. Nobody. No movement or shuffle.

Josie's fingers were a death grip on the shirt tail sticking out from beneath my short jacket.

The overwhelming smell of funk and metal and time twisted my stomach. It smelled like madness. Her uncle's madness.

The bus wasn't even buried or anything, so I wasn't sure what kind of bunker Morgan had expected to make here. Vines snaked all over the exterior, and even through some broken windows.

My flashlight beam jumped from one thing to the next as we clambered to the rear door. The seats of the bus were all gone. Cabinets, bins, glassware, boxes, and tables filled it to the brim. Chip sniffed everything. Not a bark. All we found was dirt and decomposition and junk.

I tripped on a rolled-up sleeping mat and blanket that looked newer. My gaze froze on the table nearby. Cigarettes. Not the sheriff's brand. These were the same as the ones by the shed and on the cliff.

Josie squeezed her eyes shut. One word came out in a horrified, sobbing whisper. "Tate."

32

Lark

"Mr. B, I need to use de bafroom." I frowned. "The bath-room."

"You know where it is, kiddo." He was cleaning up the game board and pieces.

After using the toilet, and while washing my hands, I heard that sound again.

A clicking. The hissing. It came from outside the window.

Sometimes I heard it at night in bed. Daddy never heard the sounds. But I smelled something, too, when my window was cracked open. That gross smell. Like Mommy. Stinky.

Then came the whistling. Was it the wind through the trees? Or the monster again?

Mr. B would believe me.

"Mr. B..." I walked into the living room. "Dere's a monster outside."

"Is that so?" He paused in his cleaning and held my look with his happy eyes.

"Should we call 911?" I said in a whisper. "Do dey have a monster squad?"

"I'll take a looksie outside," Mr. B said.

I grabbed his arm. "No! He's scary! Smoke comes out of his eyes and mouth! I've seen him. First de clicks. Den de smells. I saw him peeking around and whistling. I dink he's looking for de pirate treasure."

"What do you know about the monster?"

"He has two legs and two arms. I thought it was a giant snake because of the hissing. But snakes don't have legs."

Mr. B smacked his lips. "Let me look outside. We'll tiptoe."

First, he locked the front door. Then he turned down the lights in the big room and peeked out the window. "Great Caesar's ghost!"

I yelped and brought my fists to my chin. A ghost? I wished I had Kitty here for protection. I hurried and hid under the table. "Come on, Mr. B!"

"She always has that journal of hers. Where is it?" He rustled around.

"Mr. B, we need to hide, not write stories."

"There it is." He pulled out a slip of paper, then walked over to his telephone and dialed.

I had to find my happy thoughts. Rainbows and cats and chickens and the fun games with Josie. Ugh, Mr. B needed to hide!

"Good evening, Shanae. This is Hank. Sorry to bother you tonight. Yeah. Uh, we've got a lurker here on our property. Might be the devil that ran over my bushes." He listened. "Thanks. Yes. We're inside, but Jo and Everett are out in the woods looking for..." He scratched his head and paused, listening. "I don't know. No, no weapons."

He hung up. "Let's sit, kiddo."

"I'm okay under here," I said, but I didn't believe myself. "Don't you want to hide?"

Mr. B took out his handkerchief and dabbed his brow. "Would you feel safer if we hide in the bedroom? I have a television. We can put on a movie."

"No. No. I want the monster to leave!"

"Kiddo, I can't lean down there. Please, come up here. I won't let anyone hurt you. The police are on their way. We'll lock the bedroom door if it makes you feel better."

"And move a chair against it?"

He nodded.

I sniffled and came out. We went back to the bedroom to hide.

JOSIE

We returned to the clearing wet, cold, and bewildered. Chip's solitary bark sounded in the night.

Everett and I both froze as Chip barreled down the hillside to the beat of my quickening heart. I tried to call him back, to no avail. He was hot on a scent. A specific scent. He'd gone crazy sniffing around the bus. Had he located the prey—or person—associated with the smell there?

A whistle carried on the wind. An uncontrollable shudder swept through my body. My brain denied it, even as I saw the dark figure sitting on Hank's porch, a cloud of cigarette smoke in front of his face.

I cupped a hand over my mouth. "Oh my God, Ev. It's Tate. Where are Lark and Hank?"

Everett pointed to the back window of the cabin. The lights flickered on and off in rapid succession. "Is that Hank?"

"That's the back bathroom."

"I think he's signaling us," he whispered. "Let's call the police." He took out his phone.

Too late. Tate began the walk up the gravel driveway toward us.

Chip released several singular barks, punctuated by growls. "Heel, Chip," I ordered, though I preferred to let him tear Tate to shreds. My dog obeyed, but he showed his teeth beside me. Rafe and I were just beginning the attack commands. A well-trained dog only bit and restrained, according to Rafe. We'd never tested the commands together.

"Think the flashlight will work?" Everett shook it.

The joke missed its mark.

"Is he violent?" he asked as we stood frozen to our spots.

Holding on to Chip's collar, I said, "Never."

"What do we do, then? I can—"

"We buy time. Hank has a phone in his bedroom. He'll call the police."

"Silent Creek is a half hour away."

My heart drummed. "We talk to him, then." Tate loved to listen to himself talk.

We stopped in front of Tate, keeping a cushion of six feet. "Hi, Tate." My tone betrayed me. I couldn't pretend to be okay with his casual appearance here. I shoved shaking fingers into my jacket. Where was that pepper spray when I needed it? At some point, I had stopped carrying it. So much for feeling safe again.

"Hey, Jo." He snuffed out the cigarette beneath his shoe.

"This is private property," Everett said.

By the minimal light from the porches and half-moon, Tate looked dreadful. The dissolution of our marriage had stolen the luster from his hazel eyes and prison took the rest of him. He was rail-thin, his hair shaggy and no longer shiny. Not so long ago, he had prided himself on his good looks. He tapped a leg—a nervous gesture I remembered. Perhaps prison had also snatched his smug confidence as well.

I forced myself to keep eye contact.

Tate inched closer, lit up another cigarette, and took a long drag as if it were the best thing he'd had in a long time. He blew smoke in Everett's direction. "Is this the sort you hang out with now? You open your legs for white-trash felons?"

Sickness twisted my gut. This was not the Tate I'd married. Not the man I'd loved. I stuck my chin out, but I didn't defend Everett. I was still hurt. So hurt. "Why are you here?"

"Can't I come see my wife?"

"Ex-wife. The one whose life you destroyed."

His smile turned callous, and his words turned heated and dark. "Destroyed?" He gestured to the property. "You've got a good deal here, sweetheart. You want to talk about destroyed? What about my time in prison? What happened to *until death do us part*? We could have fixed us. We could have figured it all out, if you just trusted me."

Trusted him? I had! And he stole everything from me. I bit the inside of my cheek. He was still throwing the blame at me after all this time.

He took another long drag as if doing so would alleviate all his pain, all his sins. "I'm here because you needed to be taught a small lesson. Now you can see what it's like to be haunted by the person you love most."

What? What in God's name was he going on about? So, Tate *had* been behind the fence, the bushes...all to exact revenge upon me for responding to his thefts? Twisted. I knew he'd had an ego, but...

Deep down, that's why I had disappeared after all. I was afraid of his retribution.

"I've heard you've come into money," Tate said. "Also heard the old coot hid it on the property somewhere."

Of course, the other reason he was here. That would explain him lurking around the property. How did he know about the money? Had I screwed up? I'd done everything Don suggested.

As if reading my bewildered mind, he added, "Don't act surprised. You can quit the Pollyanna act. People inside talk, sweetheart. This guy's brother is still serving his time."

Blindsided, I turned to Everett.

"I didn't say anything to my brother. I haven't seen Jake since the spring. Penny...maybe she...Christ," he muttered. "He's serving time in Massachusetts, and she visited him a few times this fall. I didn't know... Maybe she told him about my move here and about you."

What the actual hell? Tate, Everett, *and* his brother were all felons? Really, Universe?

Everett answered my baffled expression. "Long story, Josie. Yeah, my brother is serving a second sentence. He got sent away earlier this year. He'll be home in a few months."

"Look, sweetheart," Tate began, looking straight at me, "you owe me. A little money and I'll be on my way. This hick and you can finish playing house after I leave." He pulled another cigarette out of his pocket but didn't light it up, instead twirling it in his hand. "You sure like his kisses."

My legs went liquid, and Everett caught me before I lost my footing. Tate had seen us kissing. He'd been watching us that night.

Something clicked in Everett. He stepped forward, clenching one fist at his side and wrapping the other tighter around the flashlight. Sensing his desire to strike Tate, I moved, too, and pushed a hand to Everett's chest. "No. He's not worth it. Think of Lark."

Tate darted toward me and grabbed my wrist. "Come on, sweetheart. Let's go. I want the money."

Go where?

A rumble of a growl rose in Chip's throat.

"Let me go, Tate."

A siren wailed from the main road. Then blue and red lights illuminated the clearing as two police cars rolled up the driveway.

Tate dropped my wrist, sucker punched Everett in the jaw, and bolted toward the forest.

I stumbled from the jolt of Tate releasing me. Recovering, I yelled at Chip, "Attack!"

Righting myself, I grabbed Everett by the elbow. He was hunched over, stunned.

Blood dripped from his lips and down his chin. "I'm okay." He wiped the blood away and sprinted toward Tate.

My heart racing, I ran, too, then tripped on a mound of underbrush in the meadow. "Chip!" I hollered as I found my feet. I gasped, remembering the second command in the attack sequence. "Hold 'im!"

Chip caught up to Tate and nipped at his pant leg, bringing him down, then clamped his jaw around his thigh.

"Gah!"

I reached them. Chip's eyes were wide with obedient intent.

Tate cursed and screamed and whacked at Chip with his fists. Everett stood over them, flashlight poised to strike. He breathed hard, and the flashlight shook in unsteady fingers.

"Out!" I ordered Chip, and he immediately released his hold. "Good dog. Good, Chip," I panted, patting his head once he came back to me. Go me, for remembering the commands!

Officers ran up the hill to join us and restrain Tate, not that he was going anywhere. Knowing they had it under control, Everett and I hurried to Hank's cabin. My mind whirled with dizziness, thinking of all the things that could have happened, but didn't.

"The cavalry is here!" Hank said as he and Lark emerged from inside and stared in bafflement at the goings-on. The tension in my chest released. Thank God they were okay and the interaction with Tate hadn't escalated.

Deputy Shanae Wagner strolled toward me. "Hank, Josie," she said. "Happy Thanksgiving."

I didn't bother to look to see if Brian was here. He'd lost the election. I wasn't sure if he continued acting as high sheriff until the new sheriff was sworn in, but either way, I was relieved for Shanae's presence.

"We've got this under control, Josie. Why don't you sit inside? Somebody will be with you soon." She was already ushering me into Hank's house.

I nodded. "Okay."

Everett rubbed his jaw and winced.

The cops hauled Tate past us in handcuffs. He exaggerated a limp. "Your dog better not give me rabies, or I'll sue you! I know where you live now, sweetheart."

The glare he gave me could cut through the darkness shrouding the clearing. At least the sleet had ceased.

"Keep up the threats, Mr. Sullivan," Shanae said as he was brought to the nearest police car. "We'll add them to your current charges. Skipping court hearings are a big no-no, especially for past offenders."

Apology played in her dark eyes as she turned back to me. "I'm sorry I couldn't say more when I saw you a few weeks ago, Josie."

I balled my hands together, not grasping everything that had transpired. "I knew he had been released, but I thought he was in Chelsea, in Massachusetts." What I wanted to say was: I thought I had done a better job hiding.

"Yes, he was. But he went back to his old games, I guess. This time in New Hampshire. We suspected he may seek you out."

I nodded, still reeling. She said "we." We, as in the sheriff's office, as in Brian Dumont, who was nowhere to be found. Now I realized why he'd been so protective of me. He knew about Tate. I wouldn't make excuses for his behavior, but it explained his bullying toward Everett. Regardless of his compulsion to protect me...if he had been the one to toss the nails in the road to "save" me...that was really screwed up.

A short while later, we gave our statements, and one by one, the cars departed.

After saying goodbye to Shanae, I lumbered to Hank's freezer to get ice. I wrapped the ice in a towel and brought it to Everett, who sat at the dining room table with Lark curled in his lap, her head against his chest.

He gave me a fat-lipped half-smile. "Thanks," he whispered.

I sat on the overstuffed couch, and Hank shoved a steaming mug of hot cocoa into my hand. He looked at our haggard expressions. "More pie?"

33

HANK

The *Swingin' Holiday Bazaar* collection doo-wopped throughout the cabin. Christmas called for something jolly. We all could sure use some jolly. I six-stepped my way around the room, happy to be past the PT and OT and needles, to move with the beat, a trusty cane as a dance partner.

I cherished what I could in the days I had left here at the cabin. This morning, I'd scooped a card off the porch. A homemade one from Lark with a polar bear in a rainbow hat and a long red scarf on the front. It read: "*Mr. B, your hugs are like a beer. Wishing you Christmas cheer. Love, Lark.*" I laughed, assuming she meant "bear" not "beer." Everett probably helped her. I hadn't heard the knock. She'd left snowy footprints in her wake. I got a few others—from Shanae Wagner, a few of my friends, Nora, and even Adrienne.

My phone rang, and I six-stepped over to the receiver. "Hank here."

"Hi, Hank," a sweet voice said.

I reached the record player and turned the volume down. "Evening, Nora. Getting ready for the holiday bells choir at church?"

"Last chance to come with me."

"Perhaps I'll join you for the Christmas pageant on Sunday? Need to talk to Jo tonight."

Nora released a soft *ah*. "Think she will handle it okay?"

"Not sure. She's had a rough go of it lately." I swallowed. How was I going to break the news to Jo that I was moving to Lupine Meadows? I glanced around the cabin that had been my home for the past two decades. Christmas made me think of Tillie, of Theo, of Morgan. Everett was kind to take a few of my favorite photos of Tillie and Theo and digitize them for safekeeping. He put a virtual album together on his computer and sent it off to get printed. What a sweet kid, but all I really needed were two photos, one from our wedding day, me in a crisp navy suit, Tillie in a calf-length lace dress and with roses pinned in her hair. I still slept with the photo in my pajama top pocket. The other was Theo's baby picture, also tucked in my pocket. This way, they both stayed close to my heart.

"Let's have breakfast on Saturday," Nora suggested.

"I'll see you at nine. Enjoy the bells." I stirred Baileys and eggnog in the holly-embellished glass carafe. Jo's homemade eggnog was lip-smacking good.

"Night, Hank."

I wondered what my Tillie would think of me spending time with Nora. I cast a look up, but all I saw were more cobwebs. *You'll always be my true love, Tillie. You, and Theo.*

With a sigh, I turned the volume back up on the record player and sat on the couch, waiting for Jo. I had gifts under the tree for everyone. For Lark, a Lego birds kit. Lego had a kit for everything, it seemed. For Everett, I bought a gift card for the hardware store. Boring, but practical.

As for Jo...

She strictly said no more farm animals.

Her gift couldn't be wrapped with a ribbon and bow. It was time for me to move out. The best gift I could give her was to stop being a drag on her resources and time. My heart squeezed. Sometimes the toughest course of action hurt the most. Everett and Lark were still here, so Jo wouldn't be alone. The problem was that nobody was talking.

I shrugged. Those kids would work it out. I'd given up meddling. It did me no good, did them no good. They had their own paths to navigate.

It would be difficult to tell her the news.

I blew out my breath, steeling myself. I was old. Forgetful. Tired. I needed to settle somewhere with reliable resources, access to medical care, and, frankly, more companionship with people my age. A few visits to Nora over the past month cemented my decision. That woman could talk the shoes off a salesman! She was a hoot.

How would Jo take it? She was like a daughter to me. I wasn't moving across the country, though. Plus, me moving to town might get her *out* more.

This past month, I reviewed my accounts with the fancy financial advisor, and I passed his assessments. Medicare was up and running again. With the advisor's help, I settled all the remaining medical bills. If I had just taken better care of my finances earlier, Jo wouldn't have been put into this muddy situation, even if Morgan had purposely left money aside for my healthcare. The advisor determined I had enough money to live at Lupine Meadows for five to seven years if I remained frugal in one of their lower-priced studio units. And after that...well, we'd cross that bridge later.

I tried to focus on the positives. If I hadn't broken my hip, we wouldn't have met Everett and Lark, now would we?

Like I've always said, God works in mysterious ways.

As much as I had warned Jo, I found that I, too, had become a lonely hermit like Morgan. There was nothing wrong with living off the land, but shutting out the world wasn't healthy. I couldn't bring Tillie or Theo back. I still had time to live. Jo, Lark, and Everett all showed me this. They'd brought life to my days.

Lark's card for Jo sat beside mine on the table. The wee bird was too scared to give it to her. Poor thing. I thought Thanksgiving's Scrabble game had brought peace among us, but then Everett came clean with Jo, and then her goon ex showed up. What a circus! Even after Tate's arrest, the tension was a heavy cloud swallowing us. It was time for that cloud to evaporate.

Jo's knock sounded at the door.

"Coming..."

Chip barked twice. I put a dog treat in my pocket.

"Hi, Hank." She stamped her feet, then knocked off her boots. "It's flurrying again." She shook out her hair, snowflakes falling from it. She evoked the image of a fairy—beautiful, evasive, mysterious. Tough but tender.

Jo headed for the kitchen to set down the covered pot.

I waited until halfway through our dinner of chicken corn chowder to broach the unavoidable subject. "It would be nice to have more friends over for Christmas. I could bring out Tillie's fancy dishes." I spread butter on a piece of homemade bread, then slid Lark's card across the table to Jo. She wilted. "Kiddo, she was too scared to deliver it to you."

I still couldn't believe that Lark had heard and seen Tate out her window all this time. Poor kiddo was still shellshocked from all that had gone down.

Jo rubbed her chest, admiring the picture Lark had drawn on the inside. Four chickens, a goat, a cat, and a dog. Snow. Trees. It was the homestead. It was lovely.

"Company would be nice, wouldn't it?" she said.

I sensed more sadness than excitement in her reply.

She folded the card and set it aside, then lifted a shaky hand as if it hurt to do such a simple task. Unusually dull green eyes locked on my face, her stare full of so many thoughts. "Am I being stupid?"

"You're hurt. It's hard to accept what he did...what Tate did, too...but they're two different men. One is trying to atone, and one is back in the clink."

"I know."

I bit into the bread. Crusty outside, warm and soft inside, the way I liked it. Jo spoiled me. I'd miss her cooking. Nora was a talented baker, though. I sighed. The tug-of-war in me was a beast. "So why are you avoiding Everett?"

She shrugged.

"Listen, kiddo. His path in life has been topsy-turvy. He's a decent fella who screwed up long ago. He is working to pave a better path for his daughter. And he is good for you."

Her lips trembled as she stared at the Christmas tree. We'd chopped it down together, me hobbling, her sawing, dragging, and then situating it in the stand. I dug out the old ornaments—red and silver balls, and white lights, with a homemade angel atop. Theo's special ornament, a *baby's first Christmas* teddy bear, hung front and center. Tillie's favorites, too—her birds—were a nesting flock upon the branches.

That reminded me—I needed to water the tree. The Douglas fir was getting brittle. Bending low remained a challenge. Squatting was out of the question. When Lark visited, I asked her, but her last visit was a week ago. She and Everett were spending more time in town visiting his family and less time with us.

After cleaning up dinner, we sat at the couch. "Should we light the candles?" It wasn't Sunday, but that was okay.

Jo retrieved my Advent wreath from the sideboard.

With the lighting of each candle, we read a passage from the Bible. I closed my eyes, sending a prayer heavenward to Tillie and Theo. I knew they were listening. Hope, peace, joy, love. Oh, my loves.

I shifted to adjust my posture, finally permitted to sit on my own worn-out and comfortable couch.

Jo stared into her glass of eggnog.

"What is it?"

She drew out a folded red envelope from her back pocket. "I got this today. In the mailbox here." Jo never got mail in that box.

I lifted a brow. "A Christmas card? That's great." Why in heavens had she folded it and shoved it in her pocket? Tillie used to hang them around a doorframe. I hung mine on the fridge with magnets because I couldn't find my tape.

"No, it's not great." She showed it to me. The postmark was from Sydney, Australia.

"Lots of stamps. A world traveler!" I teased. The spiked eggnog was getting to me. I'd have a headache in the morning.

She swiped at a tear, her gesture a chisel breaking my heart. She was going to be sad when I left. She and Everett needed to kiss and make up. If they did, then I'd have less guilt. "Who's it from?"

"You know who. My sister, Phoebe."

My ears heated. "Now you listen. I'm a pest. That's why I'm leaving. I'm tired of pushing you, kiddo. But I know a chance missed. Your mother and brother are both gone. Your father is a fool. He may be a lost cause, but you still have Phoebe. She's your sister, your blood. Yes, I reached out to her, a few months ago after I found her address in your journal. Now I'm done meddling."

She gaped, thunderstruck. "Wait, you're leaving?"

I shifted, wishing I'd put a pillow behind my back. "What did Phoebe say?"

She handed me the card. "It was nice."

I squinted at the handwritten note inside the card. Joy filled my heart. "This is great, Jo. She wants to reconnect. She had a baby."

Her body buckled like she had food poisoning. "I don't know, Hank."

I shifted closer and took her hand, my knobby, liver-spotted one in her calloused, youthful one. "Help me understand. What don't you know? You chose to come here and hide away from Tate and your past. But, well, Tate is back in prison. Why do you still want to hide?"

"I thought I'd—" She waved an aimless hand at the door with a pucker of her lips.

"Live alone here, disconnected from the world? Hide like Morgan?" My voice rose. I was tired of this. "The poison made him crazy, Jo. Despite his illnesses, loneliness truly did him in. Do you want to live and die alone?"

She fidgeted with the scarf around her neck. "What poison?"

"Vietnam. Agent Orange. That was part of the reason he never had kids of his own. You, Phoebe, and Kyle were the closest thing he had to children."

"What happened to him, Hank? You never told me. I thought he suffered from mental illness and his war time exacerbated it."

No more sheltering her from the truth about Morgan. This conversation was long overdue. I told her everything...about our work together, the war, our time apart, the madness that consumed his mind and body, his disease, and his last days. I dabbed at my sweaty brow, exhausted from releasing the words, from so much talking.

I said, "That bus was the final nail in the coffin. Morgan slipped into a dark night from which he never returned, Jo." A bitter laugh bubbled up. "Did you find his buried treasure in there, too?"

She shook her head. "Just rust and trash." She got up to make tea.

Upon her return, I said, "Your visits, your family's visits, when you were young, brought life to his days."

She said sadly, "Then we stopped coming." She placed the mug of steaming tea in front of me, a lemon floating in it. Jo loved a dash of cream, like Tillie.

I cleared my throat. "That was your parents' doing, not yours. Don't hold any blame for it. He had me and Tillie as companions. But we weren't enough to save him from the silent pain inside. Some people can't be brought back from their dark spirals."

She sipped her tea. "Why did he leave it all to *me*? I've never understood this. What did he expect me to do with this home, this land?"

I shrugged. "He saw your potential."

"For what?"

"Not sure, kiddo." I tapped her hand. "The answer is simply that he knew I needed you and you needed me."

She stared off across the room, lost in her thoughts. "Is it sad that I remember so little about him?"

"You were young. More good awaits you in this world, if you let it in, Jo."

She swept a pointed look over me. "So...you're leaving?" She hunched over and traced the holly pattern on Tillie's special holiday mug.

I coughed a few times, my lungs tired. Too much wood smoke. Lately, I couldn't get warm. "We'll talk details later. But yes. My Christmas gift to you. I'm moving to Lupine Meadows."

She began to cry. Jo didn't cry a lot. Now tears dribbled down along the side of her nose, and she wiped at them with her thumbs. I leaned in and gave her the biggest hug.

"Believe me, I surprised myself, too. Nora has really talked it up and shown me it's not a death sentence. I need to be around people my age, kiddo. I miss them. Don't get me wrong. You're the best thing that has happened to me in a very long time. But you need your space, too."

She pulled back and blew her nose into a tissue. "I have six hundred acres of space."

"Space from me and responsibility, doll. It's time you live your life. Call your sister. Find a job that makes you happy. Buy a better car. Dip back into technology. You've got a super tech geek neighbor who can help you. That wonderful fella waiting for you to call on him."

"It's not too late for that?" Hope bloomed in her eyes.

"Never. Do you forgive him?" Though Everett did nothing to Jo except leave some holes in his history, I understood why she felt betrayed. People see what they wanted to see. She saw her Tate situation all over again.

"Yeah, I guess so." She wiped at her eyes.

I looked heavenward. *Oh, Tillie. Help me here?* My sweet love never responded, but I closed my eyes for quite a while, relishing the kiss of a memory. I squeezed Jo's hand. "I've met many people. Do I trust him? Yes. My gut says yes. He's apologized, Jo. He's served his time and has reformed himself. We all make mistakes. For a long time, I atoned for Theo. Back then, I didn't trust my intuition."

I took a deep breath and continued.

"Theo and I had been on a walk, us two, getting fresh air...that day my world collapsed. Our boy loved to be outside. He was an overall healthy kid, but on our walk, he got very dizzy, his breathing became irregular and fast, and he lost his coordination. We had been worried about his bed-wetting, appetite, mood changes, weight loss, and tiredness. He was constantly thirsty, too. So, we had already addressed bed-wetting with his pediatrician, but in hindsight, we didn't mention the other symptoms, and the doctor reassured us that the nighttime bladder issues were normal for a boy his age."

Her green eyes were rapt on mine, big, gleaming with sadness.

I swallowed. "So that day, after he fell on the walk, we took action. By the time we got him to the hospital, it was too late. His blood sugar was sky high, and he slipped into a coma. Doctors told us he had undiagnosed type-one diabetes which led to diabetic ketoacidosis and cerebral edema." I snorted. "Big words, I know. But a parent who loses a child will never forget them."

"You did all you could, Hank."

"Did I? Would my boy still be with us if I acted on what I saw? Would I be a grandpa? What could I have done differently?" I rubbed a hand over my face. "Tillie was never the same after his death. We had our trials. She volunteered with an organization that raised awareness for childhood diabetes. We supported important causes. None of it would bring our Theo back. We tried for another child, but it wasn't in the stars. We became content. Then, when her cancer came, I got her to the doctors early. I would not make the same mistake again! Thought we had it beat. But her body gave up its fight after a few years. And Morgan...nobody could save him."

More tears flowed from Jo's eyes.

"I've felt like a helpless fool for so long. I couldn't save any of them, Jo. Not Theo, not Tillie, not Morgan." My voice cracked. "That's why I meddle, why I pay attention. I want to help." I waved away the memories and pain. "Everett is good. Let's not be too late on this, okay?"

She pursed her lips and nodded. "Okay."

After more hugs and tears, Jo let herself out, promising to check on me again first thing in the morning.

I blew out the Advent candles. Bending over would be the death of me, so I left the tree lights plugged in. I adjusted the wood stove, put our mugs in the sink, and trudged to bed. Under the covers with my favorite pajamas on, I gave Tillie her evening kiss and tucked the photo in my pocket. I brushed a finger over my son's face, and tucked his photo into the pocket, too. I slept hard.

In the bleakness of night or dawn, I couldn't tell, I awoke to Chip's barks near my bedroom window.

Woof, woof, woof.

Over and over.

Then a high-pitched screech. A car alarm?

Three more urgent barks.

I shouldn't have had the second spiked eggnog. My ears rang. I shook my head and regretted the movement as vertigo erupted in my skull.

The screeching grew louder.

Had the dog heard an animal nosing through the compost bins outside again? Coyote? Bear? Skunk? Deer? Wind? Chip wouldn't bark for no reason.

I coughed, blinking. The wood smoke lingered. No light from the alarm clock pierced the darkness. The power must have flickered off again.

Three more barks, closer.

Alarm. The high-pitched shriek wasn't a car.

The fire alarm. In my cabin.

After wrestling myself out of bed and catching a toe on the thick rug, I found my cane. The pungent smoke became an acrid burn in my nostrils.

I stumbled. My eyes stung. And my head. Ohhhh... It—

Glass smashed nearby. I tripped and fell.

34

Josie

Everett dragged an unconscious Hank through the side window while flames snapped and snarled. Wordless, I watched.

Forget fight or flight. Was freeze an option?

I couldn't freeze. I ran to assist Everett.

Chip panted and barked, racing in a circle. He'd never been this agitated, even when he wanted to tear off Tate's leg. As he got underfoot, I located my words through a smoke-filled cough. "Back, Chip. Back!"

He backed away but circled around the driveway in a nervous reddish-brown blur. This wasn't a job for him. *Chip, you're not a search and rescue dog! You're a protection dog. And you've won your gold medal twice over now.*

The flames skipped across the roof. We guided Hank away from his cabin and settled him on a bench that sat under a maple tree. Bird feeders hung from the lower branches, each swinging with the wind.

"Chip, porch." I pointed. "Lark."

He hurried to Everett's front porch and sat beside Lark, resting his front paws and head on her thigh to comfort her. She was a mess of tears.

I whacked my forehead on a bird feeder as I held my burner phone up, trying to get a bar of reception.

"Josie, my house. Use the landline." Everett bent over, coughing. Hank was coughing. Everyone was coughing.

I ran to his cabin. Every second counted. How far away was the fire station? At least twenty to thirty minutes, unless they had a smaller branch station or something. Hank's home would be ashes by then. And the wind could carry it to nearby trees and our cabins.

Lark heaved sobs through a snotty nose, clutching her Kitty doll to her chest. At least everyone was accounted for. "In, in, honey. Inside."

She and Chip followed me. "Lark, sit, okay? Chip, stay." I pointed to the couch, where Lark sat, staring, her shoulders shaking. Chip nestled closer to her fidgeting feet.

I leapt to the phone and called the dispatch, answered questions, gave information. "Please hurry!"

I ran back outside, my skull roaring from the thwack of my head meeting the bird feeder. I knotted my fingers. What could I do? The rain barrels weren't completely frozen yet, but I didn't have a motor for a hose. I'd shut the irrigation lines off for winter. Buckets at the lake? No. Not without an army. A water tender truck could reach the lake with a hose. If they got here in time.

Flames shot out of windows and slithered up the roof of Hank's cabin. Things inside the home cracked and broke as they succumbed to the fire. I was nauseated and shaking. None of the trees had caught fire—yet. Would the blaze reach them? Would the fire trucks get here in time to prevent my entire property from being engulfed? Neither of our cabins were close enough to catch fire, unless the trees surrounding them caught first... If so, the flames would hopscotch across limbs and bring the fire to the entire clearing.

Chip came outside. I tapped my hip. "Come." He bolted across the driveway and nosed Hank's leg, sniffing.

"I'm okay, buddy," Hank said with a wheeze.

Lark ran to him with a cup of water to drink, spilling half of it on her way.

"Why didn't I unplug the tree? Dampen the wood stove more? Did we blow out the Advent candles?" Hank rambled on, his voice hoarse, his words almost lost on the wind.

We waited.

Dawn slid up the horizon, but even the sun couldn't cast light into Hank's clouded eyes as we watched the bright flames.

Tears and sweat mingled on my cheeks. I swiped at my wet brow, wiping away a mix of ash and snowflakes.

Everett suggested we get everyone to his porch, across the driveway and away from the fire. After we moved again, I sat beside Hank and held him in a bear hug, the wool blanket around his shoulders scratching my chin. Helpless to do more, we watched the blaze lick and devour the front half of the house. A loud crash sounded in the clearing as part of the roof collapsed. I sent a prayer of thanks out into the universe that the fire hadn't reached Hank's room while he slept.

Finally, sirens and lights from the bottom of Clemens Road alerted us of help on its way. Half a dozen vehicles—police cars, fire trucks, an ambulance—crammed into the driveway. We sat in a daze on Everett's porch as the firefighters acted.

They scrambled to the lake with a drafting apparatus and hoses to get more water to supplement the tender truck. Fast streams hit the flames, releasing an eerie hiss. Wood cracked and crackled. Everett covered Lark's ears while she sat in his lap. All we could do was watch. Countless people crisscrossed the property while doing a million tasks.

"Oh, Tillie's things…" Hank cried. He clasped a hand to the pocket at his chest.

The fire took his and Tillie's last home.

The red and orange flames subsided, replaced by gray plumes against the dawn. Sooty tears dripped down our cheeks.

A paramedic fussed over me after she was done with Hank, while a pair of them checked on Everett and Lark. "I'm fine. I wasn't inside." I had a scraped cheek, a torn pajama pant leg, bruised forehead, and a skinned knee. She dabbed at the welt forming on my head, then checked my vision. I shivered, realizing I was only wearing boots and pajamas. She wrapped a warming blanket around me. I yearned for the comfort of Everett's heat. An odd thought now of all times, but my brain was a whirlpool these days.

Lark closed her eyes and drifted to sleep, and Everett carried her to her bedroom. On returning, he sat closer to me, and I lifted the blanket for him to share. I wanted his nearness. He draped his arm around my shoulder, and I leaned on him. He smelled of smoke. So much smoke.

At one point, somebody handed me a card. "A few officers will be back to collect samples and conduct interviews later today. Don't go near the scene before we return."

Scene?

Scene of what?

The man—a blur of uniform, black? Blue? Brown? I didn't know or care—continued, "The Bureau of Investigations will be working jointly with the State Fire Marshal's Office to investigate the cause of the fire."

I nodded.

Cause?

The faceless man walked away.

The fire was an accident. There was nothing deliberate here. Tate was behind bars and Brian Dumont had slid off the face of the earth.

Everett spoke the words aloud for me. "This was an accident, Josie."

I laid my hand over his bandaged one.

"Those flickers in Hank's cabin...were they faulty wires? A moody stove? The dry tree, a candle, the wood stove? Could we have prevented this if I—"

"Don't think like that. Hank is safe. We're all safe."

Lark cried out for Everett. He gave my hand one last squeeze and held my look as he stood to go. Morning fought its way through the haze, and a pale-yellow light bathed a face fatigued by the battle. Tenderness softened his chestnut eyes.

I fussed over Hank as we returned to my cabin, supporting him as he walked. "How about a shower and a cup of cocoa?"

EVERETT

Four days later, and only two days before Christmas, a vehicle turned up the driveway. Weren't we done with the interviews?

The investigative team had come and gone to collect evidence from what remained of Hank's home and interview us. Lark had been terrified during our interview, hanging on me the entire time. The authorities had to rule everyone out, even her. When the fire started, she'd been in her room. I was tucking her back in after another unsettling nightmare about the whistling stranger. As if guilt didn't already rack my insides for not seeing *that* clue! All this time, I thought it was her imagination and anxiety, but she'd been hearing—and oh my God, *seeing*—Tate outside her window.

It still *felt* like the morning after. My three middle fingers were bandaged, one of them splinted from the jarring I got while dragging Hank through the window. My lungs still felt heavy. My spirit heavier. I stepped outside as the vehicle struggled up the driveway.

Across from my solid, intact cabin stood the charred remnants of an old man's life. All his and his beloved wife's fine things—cookware, sentimental knickknacks, memory books, records, and pictures—years of memories, gone. My heart squeezed. After the investigative team left, Josie salvaged what she could. Thank God I'd digitized a bunch of the photos for Hank.

The unmarked car stopped at my door. A light sat on the dash. Detectives? Dread punched me another one because I just *knew*. This had nothing to do with the fire.

A man and woman dressed in street clothes emerged from the sedan and made their way toward me. A coil tightened in my stomach.

The man walked with an almost forced ease. Clothes that looked like he didn't care, but he did: airy, collared shirt, top two buttons undone—despite the bitter temperature—paired with jeans, belt, and a brown corduroy blazer. He had a British TV detective vibe. The woman was his counterpart, dressed in a sleek suit, with hair pulled into a high, tight bun.

Josie had noticed them, too. She was on her porch, watching. I thought she and I were entering the post-fallout ground of "okay-ish." Would the aftereffects of everything—my truth, Hank's losses, Josie's sharing—make us or break us? The past couple of weeks had been challenging. But last night, when she came by to check on us, I saw something in her eyes. Something had changed. Hope returned.

I nodded a greeting to the detectives.

"Mr. Everett O'Reagan?" the man asked. They offered their badges. Not that I needed to see them.

"Yes."

Lark came up behind me, whimpered, then ran back inside.

The man continued, his voice kind. I didn't buy it. "I'm Detective Hunt, and this is Detective Bergeron. We've been trying to reach you. We apologize for showing up unannounced, but your number is disconnected."

"I lost my old phone in the spring. Got a new number this summer, but I've got a landline here, too." The people that mattered—Josie, Hank, DCYF, Penny, Gram, and my employers—had my new number. And I wasn't unlisted. Detectives could find me. These two *wanted* to show up. Why?

"Could you come to the station to answer a few questions?" Hunt asked.

Always cooperate. Keep hands visible. Use titles. Be transparent.

"Can you please tell me what this is about, Detective? I answered the questions from the fire investigative team already." I tucked quaking thumbs into my jeans pockets, urging the coil in my gut to loosen.

They looked at the remains of Hank's cabin, then drew their gazes back to me. "It's about your ex-wife, Francesca Rossi," Hunt said.

Thank goodness Lark had retreated inside.

"I haven't seen her since she disappeared over eight months ago," I said, the coil tightening. Pretending and hoping had only been bandages the past few months. Fran wasn't coming back. Something happened.

Bergeron took out a small notepad and wrote something. She had a discernible edge, and scrutinizing eyes that reminded me of a teacher I had in elementary school, Mrs. Stockson, who could get the truth out of you by staring alone. "We have a few more questions."

Couldn't they request information from DCYF? Or couldn't they just ask me here? I shot a glance behind me. Lark was long out of earshot. Probably in her room, under her covers. "Did she come back?" *Let her be okay. Let her be clean and ready to parent again.* Futile wishes, but I hoped anyway.

"Sir, it'd be better at the station." Hunt's thinned eyes judged me.

I took my hands out of my pockets. Rested my arms like dead limbs at my sides. "I will be happy to come. If this is about my daughter's mother, I would like to know where she is. She left. We haven't seen her in eight months, like I said. If something happened..."

"Who said something happened?" he asked, his tone changing to accusatory.

"Well, *you*, Detective, if you're here asking about her."

Bergeron said, "Mr. O'Reagan, Francesca Rossi is dead."

A cold rush of reality traveled up my arms and tore into my chest like a rip current. Oh, God. Fran. Oh, God, Lark. If I could swing the pendulum toward a better life, Fran could have...could have tried, for her daughter.

The finger was being pointed at me, wasn't it?

Dead. I rubbed my throat. "Do her parents know? Our daughter..." Again, I turned back to the door and pulled it closed, even though I shivered out here in just a t-shirt and loose flannel. These two were watching my reaction like hawks. "I'll come down. Answer all the questions you need. I need to make sure my daughter is taken care of first. I can drive behind you."

"We have people at the station who could watch her..." Bergeron started.

A social worker? No. Hell no. Under no circumstances was I going to the police station, likely to be interrogated as a person of interest, with my kid in tow. "No. That's okay. My friend, uh, landlady can watch her." I pointed up to Josie. Hank now perched beside her. If needed, Josie could bring Lark over to Penny's.

The detectives started for their car. "All right, Mr. O'Reagan. We'll see you there shortly."

35

Lark

I rolled over. Again. I slept in baby Emily's room, on the noisy air mattress that squeaked and squished with every wiggle. My legs couldn't get still. At least Emily's room was quieter than Liam and Shawn's. They made fart noises all night. Daddy, when he slept, sighed. A lot.

Josie forgot to pack my white noise machine when she brought me here to Aunt Penny's, but Emily had one in her room. The sound was water and reminded me of the stream behind our cabin. In September, I had heard the frogs and bugs at night. But then later in the fall, the scary monster's whistling and hissing and clicking started. I stopped leaving my window open. And I locked it. Would I be safe here at Aunt Penny's?

I couldn't sleep even after taking the sleepytime gummy Josie packed for me.

Daddy had to go answer questions, he said. He promised he would be back. Mommy used to promise that, too. *Daddy is in trouble.*

I waited. My eyes refused to stay shut.

Daddy told me to think of cheerful things, so I tried. Nana and baking. Mr. B's bird feeders and Legos. Playing with the chickens and goat. Chocolate Chip and Holly. Going to school next year. Christmas! Santa was coming in two days. I never got gifts from Santa before. Mommy used to say he must've forgotten. Daddy promised me Santa would come this year.

Mr. B's Christmas tree burned down his cabin. That's what Mr. B said.

Emily grunted and began her baby howl. Aunt Penny came in and took her away while I pretended to be asleep. After they left, I got up, clicked on the small light on the nightstand, and sat on the floor in front of my small travel-sized rice bin. I unsnapped the lid, and dug my hands in, searching for a few of the plastic farm animals I had hidden in the rice. After pulling each out, I dragged my fingers through the rice, the feel of the grains tickling my fingertips. Grabbing a handful, I cupped the rice, and let it fall like a waterfall, whooshing.

A little while later, I heard a car in the driveway. I knew that sound! Daddy. I crept to the door to listen.

EVERETT

I bought a container of rainbow sherbet at the quickie mart on my way back, although it was ten p.m. and I prayed Lark was asleep.

Francesca was dead.

My ex-wife, the mother of my daughter, the woman I cared about long ago, who cared about me and Lark, before she let drugs destroy her life...was dead. If it weren't for our incompatible union, my sweet bird wouldn't be here. I woke each day for Lark.

The bag with the sherbet hung limply from my hand as my footsteps dragged along the rear walkway I installed this summer. I was proud of this job. Sable blend Urban Cobble pavers, granite steps, base stone, brickstop edging with spikes, polysand...

I sighed, holding the back doorknob, but not turning it.

My mind whipped back to the questioning. More like interrogation. Fran died on the evening of the fire. She'd been found a hundred miles from here. My alibi was as clean as a whistle.

But being in a police station had prompted a thousand triggers.

I'd walked slowly through a waiting room, shabbily decorated with red and silver garlands, a wreath on the front door, and a jar of candy canes on the desk. A pile of old magazines and children's books cluttered a corner table. An older man filled out a report at the glass partition where officers chatted. Behind it, an updated map of Silent Creek and the county stood out on the wall. I overheard "fire," then was regarded with a once-over by the two officers. I'm sure they all knew who I was by now.

I shoved my hands into my pockets, wincing as I remembered my bandaged fingers.

How did they think I could have caused a fire and killed a woman a hundred miles away at the same time? I was guilty of neither!

Sweat gathered in my armpits, not only because of the heat blaring from an ancient radiator. Had they updated the station at all since my teen years? I remembered that radiator. It was like they tried to sweat you out or something.

They buzzed me in, then brought me past the partition and to interview room two. Phones rang, people shifted from one desk to another, doors buzzed open, keyboards clacked, and my heart raced. I kept my gaze straight ahead even with my senses on overdrive.

Claustrophobia kicked in when they left me for twenty minutes on a rigid plastic chair. Waiting. I tried to not bounce my leg.

This was not the gray stony hell. Regardless, remembered scents and sounds flared and flung me even farther back. Mildew, the greasy food of the mess hall, footsteps echoing along the walkways, mattresses squeaking, people coughing and cussing, the scratchy blanket on the bed, a too-chatty roommate also locked up for fraud...

No.

I flushed the memories with mental bleach. I wouldn't be sent back there ever again. No way. No how.

Fran had been my wife. They were only questioning me. Ruling me out and getting information. Was this a murder investigation or had she died by her own hand...drugs?

Hunt and Bergeron came in with two cups of stale-smelling coffee and placed one in front of me. Still in his Mr. Cool persona, Hunt asked, "When was the last time you saw Francesca Rossi?"

I sighed by habit. "I only saw her once after I got released from prison in the spring. It was around mid-March. All other correspondence was by text or phone call. We arranged for me to pick up Lark for a visit, but when I got to Fran's place, she was gone. My daughter was in a closet, hiding. The apartment was a mess. I reported this already. It's on file with the police department." And DCYF, but never mind that.

"And how soon did that occur—you picking up your daughter—following your arrest in the spring after a fight with a man in a bar?" Bergeron asked, looking at her notes. "A Mr. Sh—"

I cut her off. "I wasn't charged with anything."

Bergeron raised an unfeeling eyebrow. "But you did spend a night in jail."

I said, "A week later. I picked Lark up a week after that bar incident, and it had been about a week since I'd heard from Fran. I went to pick up my daughter at the agreed-upon date and time."

"Do you drink and get violent often?" Hunt asked.

I gritted my teeth so hard my head hurt. "No. I made one mistake with a punk in a bar." I saw where they were going with this. My record as a felon, the bar mistake, my DCYF case. It all made me out to be a drunk and abusive ex-con. They still hadn't told me *how* she died. Was she murdered? Why else would they ask me all this?

Hunt tapped a record in front of him. "Hmm."

"Where were you on the night of December nineteenth?" Bergeron shifted in her seat and sipped her coffee.

"I was in my cabin all night. With my daughter. We had dinner, I tucked her in, and she was up again with nightmares around ten. I heard the dog, Chip, barking around five or five thirty a.m., just before sunrise. I saw my neighbor's house on fire and got Hank out."

"And you were alone, just you and Lark?"

"Yes."

"You were up?"

"I was tossing and turning. My daughter's waking makes it hard for me to sleep restfully. She hears noises and stuff. Has anxiety."

"What kind of noises?"

I pinched my lips to dampen the nausea. "The kind a crazy stalker guy makes walking in our yard, lighting up a cigarette, and whistling."

Bergeron tapped a finger. "Does she always hear these noises?"

Yeah, she still did, but they only resided in her nightmares. "No. But I think she heard that man who trespassed on our property, Tate Sullivan, long before we knew of his presence." Asking me random questions about my kid was a diversion. But why? What was the point of this?

"So, she didn't hear him the night of the fire?" Hunt's stony gaze held mine.

"No. He was locked up. What the hell do my daughter's sleep habits or the fire or that asshole Tate have to do with Fran?"

They were just trying to poke holes in my story.

They didn't answer me. Hunt leaned forward, sucking his teeth. "Were you out at all during the day on December nineteenth?"

"I was Christmas shopping."

"Can someone vouch for that?"

I stared at the steam plume above the coffee in front of me. "Yes. My daughter was at her aunt's house, here in Silent Creek, and I was shopping with my grandmother, Nora O'Reagan." *Notable resident in this community,* I wanted to add. Former sheriff's wife. Steadfast churchgoer. The whole shebang. I'm sure they already knew my entire pedigree. Hell, they probably knew my blood type and what side of the bed I slept on.

Hunt tapped his notepad. "Time?"

"From about one to four p.m."

"Where were you shopping?" Bergeron asked.

"Here in town. There was a holiday bazaar by local vendors and crafters. We went to a few shops, got hot cocoa at the cafe."

Bergeron sipped. "And before one p.m.?"

They thought they were slick, working backwards to test my timeline recall. Guilty people memorized a timeline from beginning to end. Detectives tested by going forward, sideways, backward. My alibis were solid.

"I was visiting my sister-in-law, Penny, that morning from nine a.m. til lunch, and dropping off my daughter there, like I said. Penny can also corroborate that."

"And lunch was where?"

"At Penny's house." I clenched my jaw.

"What did you eat?"

They'd ask Penny, too. Were they going to ask me the last time I went to the bathroom next? I hid my clenched fist under the table. *Breathe.* "She made chicken nuggets for the kids. I had a chicken salad wrap."

"And you arrived home to Ten Clemens Road at—?" Hunt flipped his notebook page as if he was pretending to look it up.

"Four thirtyish, closer to five p.m. It takes thirty minutes to get home from here. I got gas at the Sip & Go on my way. I have the receipt in my bank app. I can send you a checking account statement." I placed my hand on my bobbing knee. If I didn't have a criminal record, I bet I would have already been dismissed by now.

They then proceeded to jump all over in the timeline. Day of, day before, morning of, evening before. Thankfully, I was a busy person this week and was with somebody at almost all times—working on Tillie and Theo's photos with Hank by my side, visiting the hardware store and talking shop with the clerk, George, picking up jelly donuts for Hank at The Daily Donut. Visiting Penny or Gram.

They asked me to write down names of people to corroborate my alibi at each place—Lupine Meadows, Penny's house, the hardware store, the cabin, the bazaar, the shops. They wanted to look at my gas charge. My alibis were solid. So why did I feel so pissed off?

They gave a little information of their own. Fran had been found dead somewhere in South Boston. Though they suspected overdose and were awaiting the tox report, she did have a few suspicious bruises that suggested foul play, and apparently a man she'd been acquainted with had a warrant out for his arrest. I was surprised they gave me that information. *Had* somebody killed her? Why weren't they looking for that guy?

Either way, they pointed the finger at the ex-con ex-husband. I'd never live my mistakes down, would I?

I'd always be guilty until proven innocent.

Fifteen minutes later, I was free to leave.

"Thank you for your time, Mr. O'Reagan. Here is my card, if you should think of anything else," Bergeron said.

On my way out, I ran into the Rossis. Ann-Marie had raccoon eyes, dry tears smudging her mascara, and Spencer's face was gray. They had been in town to visit me and Lark, and I assumed they were being brought in for questioning as well. I'd bet my last dollar they would shift the blame to me during their interviews.

My heart was in my feet. Poor Fran. Poor Lark. I tossed Bergeron's card in the trash, and didn't look back.

Now, I shivered outside Penny's back door, thinking of the future.

I'd go to the cabin tomorrow. I'd make sure I paid my rent up through the end of my lease, and we'd find a new place as soon as possible. I couldn't stay there anymore. Not after everything. It was a rash decision, but with everything that had transpired over the past month, leaving was the best plan.

I had enough money now. As much as Dumont had tried to tarnish my rep or play me for the next big bad guy he brought in, my consulting work was going well. I lined up a few jobs for people interested in landscaping work for the spring, too. Anthony had done a great job helping with the greenhouse and was on board. Having watched Penny in action this summer, I knew I had it in me to manage employees. Consulting would fill in the holes during the offseason.

I had a plan.

I let myself into Penny's house, toed off my boots, and made for the kitchen.

"Hey, Ev," came a voice from the living room.

"Hey, Pen." I put the sherbet into the freezer, then looked in the fridge. A few beers—Paul's—clinked as I opened the door. I grabbed a cola.

Penny was on the couch, nursing Emily.

"How's she doing?" I asked.

"Baby or Lark?"

"Both."

"This little lady is great. She sleeps amazing. She senses I need it." She laughed, but then shifted to a serious whisper. "Lark was harder to settle. You'll need to explain it to her. I did my best to distract her."

I fell into the armchair and popped open the can. Taking a hearty slurp, I let the acid eat away at the taste in my mouth, the bubbles tickle my throat, and sugar salve my bitterness. "It's fine," I said.

"It's not fine."

"I know. My two favorite people were at the station, too."
I quaked, wanting to crush the soda can.

She shifted Emily to a burp position over her shoulder
and rubbed the small bundle's back until the tiniest dribble
of a sound came out. "Really?"

"Guess they were brought in for questioning, too."

"What'd they say?"

I grimaced. "Nothing to me. They looked really upset."

"I'm sorry they've given you such a hard time. Maybe this
will be closure for them." She softened her voice as Emily,
finished with nursing, began snoozing in her arms.

My anger cooled. "This is all my fault."

"That's crazy talk. You screwed up, trusted the wrong
person, made poor decisions. You didn't put the drugs
in Fran's hands." She covered a yawn beneath tired eyes.
"The Everett O'Reagan I know doesn't talk down on himself. You're making a fresh path for yourself, and for Lark.
There's bound to be bumps along the way. You'll get
through this. I have faith in you."

Penny's haphazardly decorated Christmas tree twinkled
in the late hour. Lark had made a handprint ornament
with Gram. Adornments from her and the boys, along with
strung popcorn, snowmen, snowflakes, and gingerbread
men, made for a happy tree. I liked it. Penny was a great
mom. "Can we stay here for Christmas?"

"Of course. Claire and Paul are staying at a B and B this
week. The couch is yours, so long as Lark is okay on the air
mattress for a few days. Santa comes to everyone, so he'll
find Lark here," she said in that mommy way. "Everything
okay with Josie?"

"I wish it were." I sighed, not wanting to detour down that
road now. "What do I tell Lark about her mom?"

"The truth."

We sat in silence.

"How do I tell my daughter her mom is gone...forever?"

A small voice came from the hallway. "Mommy's gone?"

Lark staggered into the room, dragging her blanket with her as though it weighed a ton. It snagged on toys in the corner, and she dropped it. I tapped the couch beside me. "Hey, Birdie girl."

Big brown eyes widened, wet from crying. She was far too alert for this hour. Time for me to pull out the rainbow sherbet, though nothing would ease the heartache.

She threw herself onto my lap, tossing a bear hug around me. I stroked her head, careful not to snare my hand in her messy hair. I inhaled the scent of citrus shampoo as her tears fell on my t-shirt. Tears began to fall down my own cheeks.

"I love you, Birdie. I'm here. I will *always* be here."

36

— · —

Josie

I survived my first winter.

Alone.

So alone.

Just as I had imagined.

Get what you wish for much?

I gagged that nasty inner voice by March.

By my own aptitude, I didn't exist on pickles or beets or pickled beets from Morgan's stash. Go me! I cooked, shopped, grew thriving veggies in my greenhouse—even fresh herbs—and I conquered more of Tillie's baking recipes. Hank remained my test subject, as I brought him baked goodies each weekend. Tillie's cookbooks, personalized with handwritten notes and memories, had been in my cabin during the fire. I was grateful that Everett made digital copies of Hank's photos, too. Hank and I laughed and cried as we looked through the album that had been left on my doorstep wrapped in a dogs-in-Santa-hats gift paper. A few photos of my family and Morgan graced the pages, too. Ones I'd never seen before.

I cracked my toes and slid my feet into slippers. With a steaming cup of hot cocoa, I shuffled to the couch, past the framed photo of twelve-year-old me on the tire swing that once hung from the maple tree near the lake. Left to my own devices, happy recollections rose to the surface, not just of childhood but of memories with Everett and Lark. Though lonely, I wasn't going crazy anymore. This time alone was good for me.

I couldn't deny that a few remaining dark thoughts entered the periphery of my mind now and then. Though the fire was deemed an accident, I found myself wondering if there was an arsonist on the loose in these woods. Irrational thoughts, ones I pushed away quickly. Nonsense. All those electrical glitches had been a red flag I'd ignored. I still felt bad about it, but Hank assured me it was nothing to lose sleep over.

Trust your gut.

Kyle's words. Hank's words. I refused to doubt myself anymore.

The fence, destroyed rhododendrons and azaleas, cigarettes, and the weird night visits were all Tate's doing. The random drive-bys and nails in my tire—Brian Dumont, I was certain. The poor weasels and fire at Hank's were sadly unlucky coincidences.

A spring rain tapped at the kitchen window, and Holly begged me to open her favorite perch. "Soon, girl. Soon. Let's hope no more snow." Oh, so much snow this winter. I caved and paid a plow service after the big storms. Morgan's old snowblower worked well enough, but the driveway was dang long and I'd felt like Dorothy on an endless yellow-bricked road gone white.

Hank was at Lupine Meadows, living life to its fullest. He had a new swing partner in Nora O'Reagan, though he was slower in his dance moves. We continued our Sunday dinners at his home. Sometimes Nora joined us. I saw where Everett got his charisma.

Hank wasn't ready to visit the homestead again, and I respected that.

Everett and Lark moved out before the first of the year, insisting they wanted a place closer to school for the fall. I knew that wasn't why.

So here I was. Living off the grid completely and utterly alone just as I intended a year ago.

The bitter cold, stocking up on food, snowy drives, and repeated repairs on this and that were bearable. I anticipated life in the woods would be a struggle. Roughing it? Fine. Between what Everett taught me, what I'd outsourced, and what I read, I was okay.

What hurt the most was that I missed *them*. All of them. Their presence was everywhere. The treehouse Everett repaired, Hank's birdhouses and feeders I kept full with birdseed, the collection of games I created for Lark, the gorgeous greenhouse, repaired fences, security lights—just, everything—everything reminded me of them. Even in the hollowed-out remains of Hank's foundation, which would be demolished in late spring, I saw the life we had for the briefest of times.

Silence and solitude weren't as freeing as I envisioned. I owed Everett a big apology. He hadn't swindled, used, or betrayed me. He was nothing like Tate.

I sighed. Either way, we were now...nothing. Even with more frequent trips to town, I avoided him. I saw him once, walking into the library with Lark, and I ducked behind a bush like I was fifteen and he was my high school crush.

Before moving out, Everett had offered to help me choose a laptop, complete with good firewalls and anti-malware. I declined. Now, though, I kicked myself. A growing part of me wanted to try again. I took care of the car stuff, got a new driver's license, and got a credit card. Baby steps. Some acts still froze me where I stood, but I managed. Slowly. I learned what types of technology to live comfortably with and without.

The nights were long and quiet.

The faulty wires in Hank's cabin—the cause of the fire, according to the investigators—made me think of the damaged wiring in my brain. It was a jumbled mess in dire need of detangling. Slowly, my misfiring neurons righted themselves.

I wouldn't be like Morgan.

In February, an electrician trained in off-the-grid living had come out, inspected my property, and addressed the remaining concerns. He would return once the snow thawed to assess a few other components of the grid.

Last week, I interviewed at Lupine Meadows for a part-time speech-language pathologist position. This morning, they called and offered me the job. I accepted. They agreed to hire me part-time on the condition of my continuing education coursework being completed by next year.

Really, the world wasn't as scary as my former self made it out to be. I would be okay.

With a yawn and a cat-like stretch, I rested my feet on the coffee table. I took a long, sweet sip of cocoa and pulled the quilt to my chest. Mom made this quilt, a blue-and-white Log Cabin block pattern. It had survived the Great Purge before my move here, landing in one of the precious few boxes I brought. Memories, new and old, surrounded me.

I had moved the old television out to the living room. Tonight, I popped *Rear Window* into the new DVD player—I wasn't ready for streaming. Who knew what the librarian made of me borrowing it three times already? I should just buy it, but I wasn't ready for online shopping either. My credit card was waiting for its first use.

As the opening credits started, I tapped a pen on the cover of the journal in my lap. Morgan's library of endless blank pages needed words, so I provided them. I opened a fresh page.

"Why are you always doing something?" I had asked the day Uncle Morgan took me fishing on the lake when I was twelve.

"I like to keep busy," he said.

"Why?"

"Why? So I don't feel..." Morgan paused, crinkling his mossy-brown eyes as he gazed across the sun-dappled water. "Aimless." He cast his line, and the plastic bobber fell with a soft plop on the surface of the water. "Everyone needs a purpose, Jo."

As a kid, everybody seemed a hundred years old. Even I could tell, though, that Uncle Morgan looked far older than his age. A brow wrinkled from constant worry, a smoker's cough, and a chronic frown.

Now, twenty-five years later, had I found *my* purpose? The secret to life?

I jotted a few paragraphs in the nearly filled journal.

Phoebe's Christmas card sat on the coffee table. My family was a missed opportunity, but not lost. Shanae and I talked about Phoebe during our coffee dates. Yes, I was socializing again. Slowly. Shanae was an incredible, multi-faceted woman, deputy, and mom. She made my sides hurt with her humor. A few weeks ago, while we chatted over hot drinks and chocolate croissants, Brian Dumont had entered the cafe, lacking his usual arrogant swagger.

A subdued but friendly smile appeared on his face as he approached, wearing his new green-and-brown uniform as the conservation officer for New Hampshire Fish and Game. Apparently, he loved to stay in uniform and couldn't escape his law enforcement call. I hoped he used it for good and wouldn't veer off course. I offered him grace, my other new growing point. Less saltine, as Hank said, and more pecan sandy. I had my rough spots, was nutty, but still could be sweet.

"Good morning, Shanae. How's it going?" Brian said.

"Holding down the fort," she said, blowing on her steaming mug of chai.

"Say hi to everyone for me."

"Will do. How's Connor?"

Brian scratched his shorter beard and cast a silent look through the front window. "Better. Went to see his mom. He has a new job."

"Good to hear," Shanae said, her genuine disposition always shining through.

"Josie." He nodded to me.

"Have a good day, Brian." I offered a smile.

He carried on his way to the counter.

After he was out of earshot, I whispered to Shanae, "That was odd."

She shrugged as she pulled a piece off her croissant with enviable red nails. "He's lost his bite. He's better. His son is, too. Brian's not a bad bean. He's just..." She popped the croissant piece into her mouth and contemplated. "Complicated. He misses his wife. She left him. It hit him hard. That feeling was misdirected. He saw you...and he wanted to protect you."

"From myself or from Tate?" I asked.

She waved a hand. "Both? He thought he had to save you from making the same mistake. Then, when our department got wind of your ex being out and all that, he went into hyperdrive or something. I caught him following you more than once."

I nodded and sipped my macchiato. "Leaving my ex-husband was never a mistake." I added, softly, "Nor was coming here."

"Amen."

We clinked mugs.

I offered Brian another cordial smile as he walked past us with two to-go cups. He nodded again in return.

I had to wonder about a few of his "misguided" adventures. Trying to nail Everett for doing nothing, to help his campaign, was flat-out wrong. The darn flat tire still bugged me. It was too fishy to be coincidence, but I forgave Brian for his missteps.

And that was that with Brian Dumont.

Paranoia never *really* had a hold on me—not with Tate, Brian, the misfortunes on the property, and even with Everett's secrets. I had solid instincts I'd learned to trust. I didn't need to always expect the worst conclusion.

Now, while I sipped hot cocoa and listened to the rain hit the roof of my cabin, I pondered. Brian Dumont had corrected his compass. I could do the same. A quick calculation told me it would be lunchtime in Sydney.

I located the box of burner phones in the closet. I paused on one, then tossed it back in. This was stupid. Why was I sitting in a closet or in the bathroom to snag a few bars of reception? I came back to the kitchen with an international calling card—they were old school but still worked fine—and picked up the landline. This summer I would get a real cell phone again, along with better coverage with the internet connectivity here.

Phoebe had written her new address and phone number on the Christmas card.

With a clearer mind, I dialed.

Everett

Shortly after Jake's release in April, Penny and I sat with him, intervention-style. We had a hard talk. *The* hard talk. Lark, Liam, and Shawn spent time with Penny's parents for the day. Pen's mom was a gem. She loved Lark to pieces. It gave me hope that Gram wasn't the only grandparent who wasn't an asshat.

Jake wasn't a violent sort, but prison broke his spirit. He lashed out, swore, and threw things he could get his hands on.

"I'm not a lost cause," he said, grinding the words through his teeth. He lit a cigarette and Penny swiftly took it out of his hand and discarded it.

"We never said you were," she countered, laying a hand on his arm.

"Quite the opposite." I held his gaze, matching the O'Reagan stubbornness. He'd inherited Mom's deep-set blue eyes, but they were cloudy, almost milky. "You're creative, resourceful, and have skills. Let's not squander them. No more prison, Jake."

He sneered. "What makes you such a saint now?" He paced the living room, fingers flicking for something to puff, or twist, or hold. The pallor of his skin was shocking. His reddish-brown hair was now trimmed, no longer neck length, but he hadn't adopted the use of a razor yet. Coarse scruff traced his upper lip and chin.

Penny poured each of us a cup of coffee.

"I'm no saint, Jake. I'm a dad looking out for my girl."

"And I'm not?"

I held my ground. "Prison changed me. The thrill of hacking is nothing compared to parenting Lark. Lark is everything. Everything. And building a good solid business has helped me. You can do great things. Don't screw it up. Your kids need you. Pen needs you."

I laid out our plan to him, the one Penny and I created a month before he was released. His pacing made me dizzy, but we let him walk off the steam while I talked through it.

He turned to Penny after we explained. "This is what you want?"

"Duh, you big dummy." She squeezed him in a hug. He returned it. Their embrace became murmurs and kisses, so I made for the back patio to grab fresh air. My pulse was soaring. I didn't realize how screwed up Jake would be after this second time in. His recovery was just within grasp, but would he make the reach?

As the weeks passed, Jake and I worked on expanding P&J Landscaping. Though the computer consulting work was going well, we decided to transfer the landscaping company into my name and Jake's. Landscaping had always been more of his thing, and Penny found herself relieved to let go.

One afternoon, while helping her clean the kitchen, I asked her again if she was sure.

"You're the right person for it, Ev. I've got my bookkeeping," she said. "You two always work better when together. Just—" Seriousness flashed in her eyes. "Use it for good, okay?"

"Straight and narrow," Jake said as he walked into the room, cuddling Emily in the baby carrier on his chest. He kissed Penny on the cheek and reached for a cookie from the fresh batch Lark and I made. I believed him this time. No hacking. No dark dabbles.

And in true Penny form, she landed the perfect work-from-home job that gave her the freedom she wanted but placed her in the field matching her education. She was the most sought-after bookkeeper in Silent Creek.

By May, Jake looked healthier and was adapting to landscaping again. Nothing beat honest labor in the sun-soaked mountains.

I checked off my mental to-do list. Jake: squared away, Lark: registered for kindergarten, DCYF case: closed, and my jobs: secured.

Lark and I rented an apartment in town, but the cabin in the woods nagged at me.

My life was complete.

Except for one thing.

Summoning the courage, in mid-May I made my way to Josie's place, a freshly baked Irish apple pie in my hands, courtesy of Gram and Lark. The flower beds exploded with daffodils I'd planted last fall, and new growth appeared on the rhododendrons and azaleas. I saw a hint of white and orange flowers. I rolled down the truck window and breathed in the woody scent of spring. It was early, but I caught the green of lupine in Josie's meadow. The wind whistled through the trees, and chimes sang in the maple next to Hank's bird feeders, which were filled to the brim.

I was glad to see them. All that remained of the cabin was the foundational basement and scattered piles of debris. I supposed there'd be no rebuilding it.

Was my foundation with Josie fraught with cracks, or did solid potential remain? I had to try.

We hadn't talked about *it*. About Lark's mistake, about my past, Fran's death, about *anything*. I could imagine how upset Josie might have been to see me escorted by the police for questioning. Then, in January, I left.

Chip's barks echoed as he scampered down the hill toward me. He jumped up to my waist, slobbering on my jeans. "I missed you, too." Crouching to his level, I stroked his chin and scratched behind his ears. I let him give me a wet kiss on the cheeks. "Here, from Lark." I drew a doggie treat from my pocket.

While he downed the treat in one second flat, I stood up, leaned into the passenger side of the truck, and pulled out the wrapped pie dish. Chip's tail tapped the ground as if he expected me to give him that, too. "And where is the lovely lady of the property?" I asked him.

"Behind you."

I whirled around. God, how I'd missed her. She walked from the goat pen carrying a pail of milk. A part of me wanted to let the dog have the pie, run to Josie instead, and lean her against the cabin to kiss her senseless...to finish what we started.

I swallowed, admiring everything about her—sure, she had a sexy body, but it was the light in her face drawing the breath from me. A frizzle of red waves fought to be free from her ponytail.

"Hey." I needed to do better than that.

She surprised me with a tilt of her head toward the house. Chip followed. I did, too. Both of us hoped for a taste of something, I supposed—the dog had eyes on the pie, and me, I wanted reconciliation and Josie's sweet lips.

After she took care of the goat milk, I laid the apple pie on the counter and stood there, like a fool. The earthy pine and cedar of the cabin hit my senses in all the right ways. I wanted to be here. I wanted Josie in my life. "I brought a pie."

She half-smiled. "I see that."

"Gram and Lark made it. Irish apple. Family recipe."

She inhaled. "It smells delicious. Thank you."

Where to start? Drop on my knees and beg for mercy? Yes. Start there. Instead of complimenting her on the grounds, how nice the inside of the greenhouse had looked when I walked past, and other neutral topics, I got to the core of the issue. No more stalling. "I'm sorry, Josie. I should have told you up front. I...I really needed a place for me and Lark. I didn't want you to pass judgment on me because of my past." I scrubbed a hand over my face. "God, if I had known about you and Tate...I..." I blinked, stopping the blame. This was my fault. "No. I still should have been honest up front, regardless."

She knotted her fingers together, leaning against the far counter in her galley kitchen. I stood on the other side of the open counter that flanked the living area. She felt miles away.

"You...it..." She nibbled a lip. "You don't have to explain yourself."

"I do." I leaned forward, my palms on the counter. She leaned back, placing her hands behind her, bracing herself against her counter. I took a gigantic breath and then offered my explanation.

"You know about Fran and why Lark did what she did." I was grateful to not rehash that.

She nodded, her green eyes understanding.

"And why I was in prison. I was...it wasn't my first time doing wrong." I lifted my hunched posture and fought every urge to run my hands through my hair. My belly knotted as she held my gaze. Emotions whirled in her eyes. "I was a stupid, bored teen. Even vo-tech couldn't keep me busy. I spent time in juvie. Minor offenses. I won't make excuses for my reckless behavior. Jake and I, we got our thrills with hacks. It was low level at first, simple pre-texting and social engineering...talked our way into places, to see what we could do. Then I took computer courses and learned code and it was...addicting."

I swallowed, hoping I hadn't already gone too deep.

Her lips were pressed together, and she waited, wordless. She lifted a nearby dishtowel and wrung it in her hands.

"I got talked into doing this job. Black hat...illegal stuff. The code was simple enough to write. The payout even better. I wasn't the mastermind, just the fingers on the keys. I'd just had a baby. I wanted money for us. Anyway, yeah, prison. Three years. Fraud, cybercrimes, phishing...a long list. It was company-level." Did that make me any less of a crook than her ex? Even if there weren't specific faces for the victims, there *were* victims.

Prison. Like Tate. Cybercrimes. Like Tate.

Her hands twisted the towel more, but she maintained eye contact with me, urging me to continue with the smallest of nods.

"I got out last spring. Jake did, too, but then he screwed up and was thrown back in. Then...well, the stuff with Fran, like I told you." A lump formed in my throat. "I brought Lark here for a better life. A new start."

I allowed silence to swallow me for a moment. I licked dry lips, and my pulse roared in my temples.

"Oh, Ev. I..." She stopped herself. She dabbed at tears with the towel. Were they for Lark? For her own hurt? Tate had really effed with her head. And here I was, explaining myself. I was no better. God, why was I here?

I knew why. Because I *needed* her forgiveness. I needed a fresh start with her.

I exhaled another steeling breath. "Anyway, a few days after I was released, while I was waiting to see Lark, I went to a bar. Long story short, I had one beer. I have no proof, but I'm certain my ex-in-laws paid a guy to get a rise out of me. They paid this bastard to fight me. Punches were thrown. Another night in jail. And, well, they have deep pockets. If they couldn't have their daughter, they wanted Lark. As a result of the bar fight and some strategically planted empty liquor bottles, I got slapped with a DCYF case. I attended recovery classes this past year. The woman who came here. She is—*was*—my caseworker. That's all settled now." I had told her some of this already, but it felt cleansing to explain it all.

I itched to move around the counter, to hold her, console her. Tears fell down her cheeks. She stopped wiping them.

"That's about it."

"That's a lot."

"It is." My heart raced. "There's good stuff, too."

She sniffled and wiped her nose. "Oh? You should have started with that." A small smile.

My pulse slowed.

I explained the new business plan, my chest loosening after unloading all the heavy stuff. I told her about Jake's changes, and Lark being in therapy. She listened, her eyes riveted on me. When all was said and done and she smiled again, I knew...I just knew that we could have a future together.

JOSIE

Everett finally stopped talking.

"*Tabula rasa*," I said, wishing I could hug him. "Well, not exactly a blank slate, as the philosopher intended. But we get to *start* over. A clean slate."

I wanted, I needed him to kiss me. Hold me. "I'm sorry, too. I jumped the gun, made the wrong assumptions."

"No sorry needed." His brown eyes glowed with affection.

"How are you, Ev?" I uncrossed my arms.

"I just told you."

I nibbled my lip. "I mean, *how are you*? You just gave me your life story there. How are you feeling?"

He crinkled a brow. "Getting there. Not sure my slate will ever be wiped clean, but I'm doing my best to write a new story for myself. You? I mean, I did some shitty stuff, Josie. And what Tate did..."

I held my hand up. "No more talk of him. You are a different person. We all make mistakes. You've done so much to make a better life for yourself and for Lark."

He pointed to the stack of journals on the counter. "Been writing?"

"A little. Writing my story. I've stepped on the grid with this and that. Got a DVD player. The librarian must think I'm a nut, always checking out *Rear Window*." Breathy, I said, "I miss you."

My gaze locked upon his. I could swim in those eyes. Spend nights within those arms. He swallowed and maneuvered a step to the right, closer to the edge of the counter. Closer to me. One more step, and he was around the corner, nothing between us. I closed the distance.

"I'd like very much to be part of your story, Josie."

"I'd like that, too," I said as we met.

He rested solid, warm hands on my hips.

I threaded my fingers through his belt loops. My pulse rang in my ears at the memory of his body pressed against me, his lips tenderly kissing mine.

"I'm sorry, Josie."

"You don't need to keep apologizing. Your past is your past. So is mine. Your present is your present. So is mine. And your future is unknown, but your slate, Ev, is clean with me."

He ran a hand down my cheek, then cupped the back of my neck. The tenderness shot excitement through my bloodstream. He smelled like heaven, like home.

His breath was hot on my cheek.

He gently lowered his forehead to meet mine. A tear trickled down one of my cheeks. He wiped it with a thumb, then kissed the path of its fall.

He leaned hard into me, pressing me back against the counter that only a moment before was my life raft in the sea of uncertainty between us. He kissed me thoroughly, imprinting the moment in my mind on the first page of my future.

EPILOGUE

JOSIE

Black flies buzzed hungrily around my legs. I hissed at one that nipped my toe. Serves me right for wearing sandals and shorts. I almost never did, but I had to show off my fresh pedicure—Evening Fuchsia, a lovely shade of deep pink. Lark, Phoebe, and I had a fun at-home spa day yesterday.

The scent of burgers cooking on the grill stirred my empty stomach. I turned off the propane connection. Everett came up behind me and planted a soft kiss on my neck. He took over plating the burgers for serving. I swatted at the pests that wanted to eat my flesh, then darted into the cabin to snag more citronella candles. I grabbed a bowl of macaroni salad from the fridge on my way out.

With Memorial Day came four things—those annoying bugs, Hank's birthday, the anniversary of my arrival to Silent Creek, and a day to remember Morgan's sacrifice. Even if his body hadn't died on the battlefield, his former self did, and I wanted to honor the man.

Hank beamed like a child and rubbed his hands together as I laid covered dishes on the picnic table. "I love your Amish macaroni salad. It's even better than Tillie's! A hint of sweet, a dash of tanginess." He laughed to himself. "Like you."

I poked his shoulder. "Har, har."

Nora slid to my side. "Need help?"

"Oh, yes, please. Could you and Lark get the rest from the kitchen?"

"Come on, Birdie." They made a few trips, bringing out the bowls and platters of chips, watermelon, salad, corn on the cob, and lastly, the gorgeous red velvet cake the two of them made for Hank.

Lark ran past him, releasing her parrot imitation while Hank said "Argh!" in his best pirate voice.

She laughed, mimicking him. "Argh! The treasure! The treasure!"

Like buried treasure, I had begun to dig out neglected relationships. This month was all about making amends.

First with my sister, then Everett, and this week I mailed a letter to my friend Hannah—she'd been hard to locate, since she'd moved, too. Everett suggested I email her on the new computer in my bedroom. I had told him, "Baby steps." Some habits die hard. Hopefully, my letter would find her well and we'd reconnect soon.

We gathered at the picnic table and on scattered lawn chairs. All of us: Everett, Lark, Hank, Nora, Penny and Jake and their kids, and Phoebe and her daughter. Everyone piled their plates with food and dug in.

"Delicious burgers, Everett," Phoebe said from beside me, chomping down on a second one.

"Hey, I made those," I teased.

Sunshine had brightened Phoebe's pale complexion. Laughter danced in her eyes. "Nursing makes me ravenous. Besides, I enjoy a good barbie. We have them all the time back home. On the next visit, Stuart can come."

Home. Her new home was half a world away, but she was here for three weeks, and after the awkward reunion, we'd reminisced and reconnected, forging our new adult friendship. Fishing, going out on the lake in the old dinghy, walks, trips into town, visits to a local waterfall...it felt natural. I forgot how much we loved each other. How had we let this slip away?

With the last sip of homemade iced tea came the daring to ask: "Have you heard from him?" She knew I meant Dad.

"No. I sent him photos of Jasmine after she was born last year. It was hard to track down the right address. He moved again and didn't tell me. No response." She squeezed my hand. "I'm sorry, Jo. I know how much it sucks. It wasn't only you. Even before Kyle's accident, Dad was absent. That's why I left. I couldn't deal. You and I weren't the best of friends growing up, but I've loved my time here with you. I love this new you." She slurped her tea and let out a burp.

I rolled my eyes. "Pheebs, you're a trip."

She snorted. I belly laughed.

"Seriously, though, how are we going to keep in touch? You live half a world away," I said.

"Email? Text? Video chats?"

I inhaled. "Getting there."

She put down her empty plate. "Then letters and postcards. Old school. Phone calls. Stu's company has a field office in Boston. He comes a few times a year for business. Jaz and I will come with him now and then. And besides..." She pointed a finger in Everett's direction. "You have a hot IT guy at your fingertips. I'm sure he can make sure your walls are secured." She tittered.

The smile didn't need to struggle to reach my lips. In fact, my face hurt from smiling today.

I slanted a look to Everett, who was entertaining Lark, Shawn, and Liam in their search for the perfect stick to roast marshmallows.

Jasmine wobbled on her feet in front of us and then fell onto her blanket. She let out a soft grunt and cast blue-green eyes at us. Phoebe put down her plate and sat beside her daughter on the blanket. She made mommy cooing noises and funny faces.

As the evening waned, she stood, yawned, and retreated into my cabin for Jasmine's bedtime.

Everett zigzagged around the yard, gathering dishes and bringing them into the cabin to be cleaned. The man loved cleaning. Having the help around here was heaven. Having him here was...happiness.

I crossed my legs as I leaned back in the Adirondack chair, perusing a new book—101 *Places to See in the White Mountains*. Time to explore the beauty of my backyard. Piled inside at my new desk, another one of Everett's handy masterpieces—the man was a god with his woodworking tools—were books for my continuing education courses and New Hampshire certifications.

Everett returned, saw what I was reading, and laughed over my shoulder. He nudged my rib and kissed me on the cheek before sitting beside me. The fire in the stone pit crackled. He handed me a hot cup of decaf. "Where to first?"

"Just daydreaming. What do you think about Australia?"

Delight widened his eyes and revealed his dimples—both, oh my heaven, I never tired of seeing them—as he leaned in and kissed me. "World traveler, are you now?"

I shrugged. "It's an idea."

"I love the idea." He looked around the yard, now bursting with late spring life—the seedlings in the gardens, the burgeoning trees, and swinging bird feeders. "What should I build next?"

"You've got projects coming out your ears and you want to do more *here*?" In the last few weeks, he'd assembled the fire pit, refurbished the antique desk, and was knee-deep in his new business.

He smirked and slid his hand into mine. "You bet."

My heart somersaulted.

He drew me onto his lap. Insects chirped, and a light breeze rippled my loose tunic top. Everett nuzzled my neck, and the eternal stubble on his chin shot gooseflesh down my body. I curled my toes. "Think Lark might want to stay over at my place tonight with Pheebs? Sleepover with Jaz? And you and I can have a sleepover in your cabin..."

Soft lips tickled the thin skin behind my ear, and his touch traced my spine one slow inch at a time. "Likely."

"How's she doing?"

"Better. The therapist is helping. Being here, you...this...it helps, too. Penny's parents are kind to her."

"When's the next party, Jo?" Nora asked on her approach. She wore her light coat and looked ready to head back.

"Not sure."

"How about Independence Day? The daylilies will be at peak then," she said with a wave to the meadow.

"I'd love that."

She gave Everett a teasing smile, lines crinkling around her stunning blue eyes. "I expect to see both of you next Sunday for our swing dance lesson."

Wild shouts rang out from near Hank's old cabin's foundation, which was scheduled for final demolition and removal next week.

I jumped out of Everett's lap. "Good gravy," I muttered. Shawn and Liam sure lived up to their terrifying reputations today between almost falling out of the treehouse, whacking a wasps' nest, and jumping into the lake fully clothed, sneakers and all. "What now?"

A cacophony of excited voices danced in the clearing.

"Come quick, Ev!" Jake waved both arms frantically.

"The pirate booty!" Lark hollered as she wiped dirt off her knees.

Everett, Nora, and I scurried down the driveway to the crumbled foundation. He chided, "We told you not to go in here. It's not safe."

"Mr. B said it would be fine," Shawn said. Dirt traced his forehead.

"We were excavating," Hank said with gleeful disregard for the danger. He maneuvered over charcoaled wood as if he didn't even have a new hip. I grabbed his elbow to guide him. He turned to Jake. "Bring it out, chap."

"Okay, everyone out! There are nails and splinters and loose things in here," Nora said in a grandmotherly tone, and they scrambled out of the stone and wood mess.

My sentiments exactly, Nora.

Jake hauled a rusty metal box out.

"Treasure, my dears," Hank said.

Grinning, Jake handed me the old military ammo box. I laid the heavy thing down on the grass. The lid was stuck. Everett pried it open with his pocketknife, mindful of the rust on the hinges and sides.

Gasps leaped through our gathering. The children jumped up and down.

"Great Caesar's ghost!" Hank said, dabbing at his brow with a handkerchief. "I always wondered what was behind that small door in the basement. I thought a leprechaun lived there." He winked at Lark.

He thumbed through the contents. Multiple plastic bags filled with dollars—twenties and fifties, it looked like—filled the chest. "Morgan didn't lose his marbles," he said.

"How? What? This is the treasure that Morgan went on and on about? I thought..." Heat tingled in my face.

Hank shrugged. "Morgan claimed he got money from a lawsuit in 1984 and made smart investments, then buried it on the property. I used to think he put it in that rusted hidden bus. But when you kept finding caches of money in weird spots here and there, I thought he hid it elsewhere. When Lark mentioned the hidden treasure box she found in my basement, we did a bit of digging. I guess this was it."

We counted the money, and sure enough, it was a treasure. Enough to secure Hank's lease at Lupine Meadows for a long while, so he wouldn't have to deplete his retirement funds. And some cushion for me, too.

I could visit Phoebe. I could do more with Everett. Do something for the community.

After the evening wound down, and our guests went home, I got cozy with Everett at his cabin on the property. I loved having him here again. He didn't mind the commute. We discovered the school offered a bus route out this far, too, so Lark was all set for the fall.

Tonight, I had Everett all to myself.

As I sat on his lap on the couch, his fingers caressing my back and mine tangled in his hair, I leaned down and brushed his lips with a kiss. I loved every moment with Everett, and I adored Lark. I saw myself giving my heart to them both. I saw a future.

"I'm so glad I found you, Josie," he said, chasing his words with another kiss.

"Me, too."

His words made me wonder. When a person says they want to disappear, is that truly their motive? Do they really wish to fall off the edge and be swallowed up by the abyss? For a long while, every part of me had screamed yes. I thought I wanted to escape the hurt. I wanted to check out of my life.

Then I came here to my refuge in the woods. To my new home.

Instead of hiding from life and love, instead of disappearing, I was found.

ACKNOWLEDGEMENTS

Who would ever think that an email masked as a literary agent's response to my query, which then proceeded to hijack my computer and corrupt it with malware, would lead me down the path of a new story? I know, I know. Never open attachments! But this was legit looking and there was no info on the agency's website that they had been hacked. Live and learn. And write about it.

Some days, I wish I could escape to a mountain in the woods, away from the headaches and heartaches of our world. Since that's not a possibility (yet), I had Josie embark on this adventure instead. Many people can relate to Josie's mistrust of the world and her desire to leave it all behind...and her need for connection despite this self-imposed exile.

I have many people to thank who have guided me along the way with Josie, Everett, Hank, and Lark's stories. First, a thank you to my good friend Lorraine, who has been the first set of eyes on every manuscript I've written. Josie started off a bit salty, but with Lorraine's guidance (and her tough love!), I molded Josie into something special. Second, I want to thank the fellow authors in the #5amwritersclub, who have been a great support (any time of the day!) for many years now. A special shoutout goes to the group of authors who joined me for the Unforgettable Characters and Incredibles Journey retreat, where they helped me breathe life and hope back into a manuscript I wanted to toss into the flames! I almost gave up on this one. Thank you, Ralph, for organizing that amazing retreat and keeping the 5 a.m. writers connected. A heartfelt thanks also goes to my amazing editor Therese, whose insightful edits shaped this story. And another big thank you to my dedicated beta readers who have read so many of my manuscripts before they were fully polished: Barbara, Keri, and Jill, thank you!

Every book comes with loads of research (online and in books) and consulting friends and experts along the way. Sometimes we spend more time researching and editing than actual writing. These authenticity helpers read bits and pieces of the story...a scene, a chapter, a character, or an area I am not as familiar with, or sometimes I sit down and interview them. Thank you to Lisa, Marlene, Jaime, and Elizabeth, and to the members of the Facebook group Cops and Writers for your expertise and guidance on addiction recovery, occupational therapy, DCYF, speech and language pathology, and criminal investigations, respectively. I also now have way too many books on computer hacking, off-the-grid living, the art of disappearing, and dog training, so I am ready if the time comes when I decide to slip off the grid... It's a good thing I like to garden.

And how can I not thank, well, a wood stove? An inanimate object can be thanked, right? A few years ago, I gifted myself a solo writer's weekend away to a quaint (err, rustic but cute) off-the-grid, wooded, Quaker retreat in western Massachusetts...in the middle of February. I had power, but no running water, no Wi-Fi, an outhouse with a view (the door was off), and a wood stove for heat. Talk about throwing me into the deep end. Even though I am an outdoors person, I stumbled a bit. Okay, I panicked when trying to figure out the wood stove. But I prevailed and became a wood-stove wizard and got used to talking to the birds or squirrels while I used the outhouse. It was a great way to unplug on this little adventure, and a perfect time to work on Silent Creek.

—·—

ABOUT THE AUTHOR

Jean has a penchant for the misunderstood, be it sharks, microbes, or wounded characters. A scientist by training, she now spends her days as an author and champion for her children. She draws from her interest in history, science, the outdoors, and her family for inspiration. She serves on the local library board of trustees and is an advocate for community, inclusion, and diversity.

A nature enthusiast who adores the national parks, Jean also writes for family-oriented travel magazines and websites. When not writing, she enjoys gardening, tackling the biggest mountains in New England, and going on adventures with her husband and children, while taking snapshots of the world around her and daydreaming about the next story. If she were stuck on a deserted island, her three essentials (besides family, food, water, shelter) would be: coffee, lip balm, and endless pink sticky notes.

Find out more about her books by visiting her website: www.jeanmgrant.com